ECHO

ALSO BY THOMAS OLDE HEUVELT

HEX

THOMAS
OLDE HEUVELT

ECHO

TRANSLATED BY
MOSHE GILULA

A TOM DOHERTY ASSOCIATES BOOK
NEW YORK

This is a work of fiction. All of the characters, organizations, and events portrayed in this novel are either products of the author's imagination or are used fictitiously.

ECHO

Translation by Moshe Gilula

Originally published in Dutch as *Echo* in 2019 by Luitingh-Sijthoff in Amsterdam.

A Nightfire Book
Published by Tom Doherty Associates
120 Broadway
New York, NY 10271

tornightfire.com

Nightfire™ is a trademark of Macmillan Publishing Group, LLC.

Library of Congress Cataloging-in-Publication Data

Names: Olde Heuvelt, Thomas, 1983– author. | Gilula, Moshe, translator.
Title: Echo / Thomas Olde Heuvelt ; translated by Moshe Gilula.
Other titles: Echo. English
Description: First edition. | New York, NY : Nightfire, a Tom Doherty Associates Book, 2021. | Originally published as Echo in 2019 by Luitingh-Sijthoff in Amsterdam. |
Identifiers: LCCN 2021035762 (print) | LCCN 2021035763 (ebook) | ISBN 9781250759559 (hardcover) | ISBN 9781250759573 (ebook)
Subjects: LCGFT: Thrillers (Fiction). | Magic realist fiction. | Novels.
Classification: LCC PT5882.25.L38 E2413 2021 (print) | LCC PT5882.25.L38 (ebook) | DDC 839.313/7—dc23
LC record available at https://lccn.loc.gov/2021035762
LC ebook record available at https://lccn.loc.gov/2021035763

Our books may be purchased in bulk for promotional, educational, or business use. Please contact your local bookseller or the Macmillan Corporate and Premium Sales Department at 1-800-221-7945, extension 5442, or by email at MacmillanSpecialMarkets@macmillan.com.

First Edition: 2022

Printed in the United States of America

0 9 8 7 6 5 4 3 2 1

COPYRIGHT ACKNOWLEDGMENTS

For Pieter
Because of the mountains

And for David
Because of love

Battle not with monsters, lest ye become a monster, and if you gaze into the abyss, the abyss gazes also into you.

—Friedrich Nietzsche,
Beyond Good and Evil

PROLOGUE

SOMETHING WICKED THIS WAY COMES

WHAT HAPPENED TO JULIA AVERY

But three, now, Christ, three a.m.! . . . The soul is out. The blood moves slow. . . . Sleep is a patch of death, but three in the morn, full wide-eyed staring, is living death! You dream with your eyes open.

—Ray Bradbury

1

Julia sees the people in the stairwell when she gets up at night to pee.

They're standing there in the dark and staring up at her, frozen like a photograph, as if they've been waiting for her. Her left foot is already on the top stair and she's about to put her right foot on the next, but her fingers clamp the handrail convulsively, and she stops. Of course she stops, because it suddenly penetrates her drowsy brain: *there are people in the stairwell and they're staring at her.*

Just now, she has woken up with a start. The bedside lamp dispels the shadows in the chalet, but outside the wind is howling around the roof with such vigor that the shutters tremble and the rafters creak. The sound of the wind fills Julia with an instinctive sense of doom, a familiar sense of doom. It sends her back to Huckleberry Wall, and the night it burned down. That was fifteen years ago, in the Catskills, and this is now and thousands of miles from home, in the Swiss Alps, but when at night the snow clings to the windows and the wind kicks up, all cabins are the same.

Creepy as fuck and completely cut off from the rest of the world.

She reaches under her pillow for her iPhone. 1:15, no messages from Sam. Damn it. Her stomach turns.

Julia throws back the covers and her body warmth, held by the down, disperses in the draft. The night chill hangs in the attic. It's the draft, eddying through the chalet like an echo of the storm, that has kept her from lighting a fire earlier that evening. She pictures the draft blowing life into the embers as she sleeps, puffing glowing cinders onto the rug and setting the curtains on fire. Fifteen years ago, her big brother was there to wake her up before the smoke suffocated her—she was six, he was nine—but the last time Sam called tonight was sometime before 10:30, as he was stuck in a jam on the Bern bypass.

The snowplows are doing their best, he'd said over a breaking connection, *but traffic's stop-and-go and the worst part in the mountains is yet to come. That is, if the valley is still open.*

Maybe he's given up and taken an overnight room. That's what Julia hopes anyway, because Sam's been under way too much pressure lately, and she's worried as hell—that he'll skid off the road and plow into a snowbank, or worse, 300 feet of nothing. She hears more than just simple concern in his voice when he asks her to be on the lookout for Nick . . . and to be wary.

Except it's been almost three hours now, and Sam still hasn't called. No sign of Nick, either. By now, Julia is more than worried. She's scared.

Barefoot, she crosses the floorboards, which crack under her weight, around the supporting wall, out to the landing.

The stairwell plunges straight down into the dark.

There's a light switch, but before Julia can grope for it, she's at the top of the steps and sees the people at the bottom.

They're barely more than silhouettes, black against black, but she feels their gazes fixed on her, senses the *purpose* in their presence. Six, seven figures, pressed together in the stairwell, motionless.

It's immediately obvious that they can't be intruders; the chalet is too remote for that, the night too remorseless. She also knows, triggered by some primitive survival instinct, that she cannot turn on the light. In the light, the people in the stairwell will no longer be visible—and *not* seeing them, while knowing they're there, is worse than seeing them.

Much worse.

The chill that envelops Julia as she walks back to bed is more than a physical chill. It's a cold in her soul, so elementary she has to brace herself against the force with which it possesses her. A floorboard snaps under her foot like a gunshot and she flinches, jumps into bed, pulls the covers up to her chin. She stares wide-eyed at the afterimages in her eyes, too paralyzed to know what to do next.

She can't see the stairwell from here.

In the safety of her bed, the oh-so-obvious explanation gradually dawns on her: she dreamed up the whole thing. Of course. Julia welcomes this possibility with overly eager conviction; it is, however, irrefutably logical. She certainly did get out of bed—her cold feet are proof—but her half-asleep mind made her see things that weren't there. Shadows on the landing transformed into human shapes, a sleep-induced projection of her fears.

You were awake and rational enough to wonder where Sam is. Awake enough to be seriously scared.

She pushes the thought away. There's no one in the stairwell. She's alone in the chalet. She remembers bolting the doors before going upstairs. Because, yes, she had been on the lookout, as Sam had asked. With a blanket around her shoulders, as she tried getting acquainted with the cabin's unfamiliar sounds. It felt—still feels—like it's alive. The cuckoo clock ticks its heartbeat. The slanting roof groans under the snow's weight, occasional loads come sliding down.

The worst is the storm's wailing.

There's something irresistibly alluring about it. Time and again, Julia is compelled to exchange her warm corner on the couch for the chilly front door, peering out its window. She can barely make out the spruces through the snowstorm, not to mention the mountain ridges or the trail that leads back to the village along the brook. The chalet stands isolated at the end of a blind valley. Higher up, there's only the reservoir, and behind it the treacherous glacier. At a quarter past eleven, she concludes that it's impossible for Nick to be wandering out there, in this weather. She checks the locks, listens to the strange ticking sounds coming from the heaters now that she's turned them off, and then turns out the light. If Sam is still going to come home, he'll call and wake her up. Julia definitely wouldn't mind.

So there couldn't be anyone else in the house. She is alone with the wind. The downstairs is empty.

It's just that . . . the house doesn't feel empty.

Nonsense, of course.

All she needs to do to be sure is take a look.

Of course she doesn't need to be sure, and certainly not to prove herself to anyone. But, like it or not, she still needs to pee.

Armed with her iPhone, Julia gets out of bed and walks silently around the wall.

There's the stairwell. Like a pit in the wooden floor.

She has to walk all the way to the edge in order to look into it and, admittedly, she doesn't want to. She doesn't want the only way to the bathroom to be through that dark hole. So she stays put. Listens to the ticking of the cuckoo clock coming from downstairs.

She extends her neck but can't see further than the top stair.

You're being ridiculous.

Julia takes a deep breath and quickly steps forward. Only when she reaches the top of the stairwell does she see it—and when her gaze latches onto what's down there, cold air is sucked violently into her body, and with an enormous jolt, the world comes to a standstill. Her lungs swell up like balloons, ready for the scream growing inside her, but it's as if the air is trapped, because when she puts her hands to her mouth, all you can hear is a stifled squeak.

The people in the stairwell are still there.

They're closer now.

They've all raised their heads and are staring right at her. But most terrifying is that they're staring right into her. In their faces lurks the frozen silence of insanity. The one up front, a tall, gaunt woman dressed in black, with pale, almost translucent skin, is standing fixed on the third step. She is followed closely by a fat man in a grubby white shirt. The others behind them are phantoms.

Completely paralyzed, Julia stares back. It takes a long time before she's certain that the people in the stairwell are more than a still projection or a lifeless afterimage, but then she sees the woman's index finger trembling and the palpitating, purple-black skin under her eyelids. Her eyes are large, fierce and concentrated, full of hate. She has the face of a psychopath who's on the verge of screaming. If she does, her face will shatter and fall off.

Julia finally manages to breathe. The air squeezes out of her lungs in a string of short, gasping cries. Her eyes well up with tears. She feels heat behind her cheekbones and a crackling stab in her brain, like electricity. *My fuses are blowing*, she thinks soberly.

She runs back to bed on legs that no longer feel like legs. The springs groan as she leaps in. She sits upright, one cramped hand pulling the covers up to her waist, the other clawing her face till it hurts. Pain is good, it clears the head. When she lowers her hand, she can feel half-moons of blood on her cheek and nostril.

A stair creaks.

Her gaze is fixed on the area of the vestibule that is visible behind the supporting wall. It's empty, but she can't see the stairwell. She looks quickly over her shoulder, as if expecting to catch someone behind her. There is no one.

That woman. That face.

Why did she have to look at her with so much hate?

Julia unlocks her iPhone and with trembling fingers swipes to the top of the recent calls list, to Sam's number. If she hears Sam's voice, she won't have to feel scared anymore. Then her nightmare will dissipate; with Sam's voice in her ears there will be no people in the stairwell.

It takes ages before she gets a signal and the phone starts ringing. It's a bad connection. It's storming not only around the roof but also on the line.

Pick up. Come on, come on, come on . . .

Voicemail. She moans in dismay and tries again.

When another stair creaks, she lets out a silent scream.

He picks up after the third attempt.

"Julia!"

"Why didn't you pick up?"

"Sorry, it's a hairy situation here on the road. Hadda link to my Beats first. Any news?"

"I . . . no." Not the news he was waiting for. She feels stupid. What should she say? That she fell asleep on sentry duty? That she's afraid to be alone—that she's afraid now that she's not alone? She wants him to talk, for his voice to make everything all right. "Where are you?"

"On my way. You okay, sis? You sound weird."

She listens for sounds from the stairwell but hears only silence.

"Yes," she finally says. "It's just this storm is driving me crazy. How long will it take you to get here?"

"Um, beats me. Get this: I'm driving behind a snowplow! Only way to go up tonight. After Bern there were no more jams, but only cuz no one's crazy enough to go out there. There's a weather alert for the whole west and they raised the avalanche alarm in the mountains to four, probably five tonight. Unbelievable. Some areas you literally can't see your hand in front of your face. Somewhere before Montreux, I went into a skid. Lucky there was no one next to me, cuz I slid sideways across the road, all the way to the shoulder, before

I got it under control. After that it got a bit better cuz they're spreading salt, but they can salt till the cows come home, it's not gonna do any good. Totally awesome, all the gear these Switzers bring out to . . ."

With the phone clamped between her shoulder and ear, Julia stands up. She feels a sudden urgency to go look, while his soothing voice is yapping on and on, to make sure there's no one there, that it's okay to go to the bathroom. Maybe she's acting like a child, but with her brother's voice in her ear—

Oh, Jesus, fuck-fucking-fuckery-fuck!

The phone slips off her shoulder and clatters onto the floorboards.

The pale woman in black looms out of the stairwell, up to her waist. Once more, she's standing there motionless, but her head and shoulders are turned and she's staring right at Julia.

Without pausing for breath, Julia stumbles forward to pick up her phone. That means she has to crawl closer to the hole in the floor, and as she tries to not lose sight of the woman, she sees fingers clinging to the edge.

Stocky fingers; a *man's* fingers.

"Hello? Hello? Are you there?" Sam's voice sounds tinny when she puts her ear to the phone. "Julia?"

"Yeah, I'm here." Somehow, she manages to make her voice sound calm. Hollow, dead, but calm. Sam won't notice a thing.

She looks up and gets the greatest shock yet.

The woman with the bulging, staring eyes is now standing next to the stairwell, right in front of her. The fat man in the grubby shirt is standing at the top of the steps, looking at Julia, and a third, gaunt face has appeared behind him.

In the split second her glance had strayed to her iPhone screen, the people had moved, and she hadn't even noticed.

Now they're standing still again.

Two bleeps sound in her ear and Julia has to bite her tongue to keep from screaming. She falters backwards through the vestibule, not letting the people out of her sight.

"Julia? Jules!"

"Sorry, I . . . I dropped you. Keep talking. I'm here."

Yes, she's here, but then she understands the mistake she has made: she's back in bed and can't see the people in the stairwell anymore. That means they'll move again. That means they'll come closer. But nothing in this world can make her go back there. At this moment of utter desperation, Julia needs the warmth and safety of her bed, because that's where all bad dreams come to an end.

"Anyway, so when I finally got to the valley, what I was afraid of actually happened: the road to Grimentz was closed. All the way from the highway. I thought of risking it anyway, but you know how narrow that road is and how deep the drop. It would be total suicide to . . ."

Julia really needs to pee. She pulls up the covers and presses her thighs together. She doesn't know what to do, can't get her thoughts straight.

Why doesn't she say anything to Sam? But she knows the answer: if she tells Sam, it will be a confirmation. Then there will be no ignoring the fact that there really are people standing in the stairwell, and she can't deal with that reality.

Sam babbles on, but his words barely register: ". . . until the snowplow came. I hadda scream to be heard above the storm, but I managed to get across that I had to get to Grimentz. The driver said I was crazy, that I had to find a place to stay down there, and then I hadda think something up, so I said my girlfriend was up there and about to have her baby any minute. That the contractions had already started and everything. So the driver stares at me, and then he says it's actually convenient for someone to drive the salt into the road. But he said I had to go slow, real slow, or the little critter will be semi-orphaned before even being born." He chuckles. "I think the main reason he let me trail him was cuz I spoke French. Otherwise . . ."

Two more bleeps, and then it suddenly comes to her: her phone is almost empty. Julia looks at the screen. The battery is red and there's a notification saying: Less than 10% charged.

And that was some time ago.

Julia leans over to the bedside table and the socket underneath it and breaks out in a cold sweat. She had started to charge the iPhone tonight in the strip next to the couch, but when Sam called at 10:30, she unplugged it. She forgot to plug it back in.

Her phone is almost empty and the charger is downstairs.

When she sits up, she catches a glimpse of something that makes all her muscles melt.

In the vestibule's shadows. A black shadow, darker than the rest, just behind the wall. One hand. One eye. Peeking.

The eye is staring at her.

Julia feels her urine trailing down her thighs.

". . . so we go up at a snail's pace. Seriously, it's hellacious. I think the road behind us snowed up again right away. Some of the time I can't even see the plow's taillights through the windshield and I'm only ten yards behind him. I was really lucky. He wasn't supposed to go any further than Vissoie tonight, but—You still there, Jules?"

She, stock-still, in a warm, wet spot on the mattress.

The woman, stock-still, hiding behind the wall.

A staring contest. Don't look away, or you lose. But Julia is afraid of something much worse.

Something dawns on her. "Did you get to the valley yet?" There's a sharp edge to her voice that could be mistaken for surprise, but to the discerning listener it's obviously hysteria.

"Yeah. That's what I've been trying to tell you."

"Please get here quickly," she whispers, and she starts to cry. Her whole body jerks, but her whimpers are silent and Sam can't hear them.

"I'm doing the best I can, sis, but I can't go faster than the snowplow. Eight or nine miles to go, I think. Half an hour, forty minutes tops."

Oh god. She wipes the tears from her eyes. They've blurred her vision and to wipe them away she has to close her eyes. When she opens them, she sees the people have come closer.

The woman is in front, clear away from the wall now. Behind her, to the side, the fat man in the grubby shirt. His hands dangle motionlessly next to his flabby body. Behind him, three more men in grimy clothes.

Half an hour. Sam will never make it in time.

As if to confirm it, her iPhone bleeps again.

"I tried calling Nick," Sam says. His voice has become softer, and in the background she can hear the constant swishing of the windshield wipers. "His phone is still off." Silence. "I'm scared, Jules."

Don't cry.

Don't look away.

Without averting her gaze from the people for even a second, Julia pulls up her legs and, with a grimace, pushes down her soaking wet panties. At least she doesn't have to pee anymore. She slides to the other side of the bed, searches between the covers for Sam's much-too-large sweatpants, which she'd kicked off when she went to sleep, and pulls them back on.

There are more people now.

Many more.

They've spread out across the attic.

Julia starts hyperventilating. She can't get any air. Tears spring to her eyes, her vision becomes cloudy. Eleven, twelve dark monoliths, as motionless as salt pillars, fade out of view at the foot of her bed. When she can focus again and the figures solidify into recognizable shapes, they are even closer. With a silent, choked scream, Julia scrambles backwards, against the oaken headboard. It feels like her hair's being tugged, her eyes almost pop out.

They're all staring at her.

How much closer are you going to let them get? her mind screams. *How much closer before you know what to do?*

The pale woman in black is now standing at the foot of the bed. She is big and formless, wearing an old-fashioned dark skirt and an equally old-fashioned woolen cardigan, which give her the appearance of a schoolmistress from a hundred years ago. But that's not what scares Julia the most. It's what she sees in the woman's face. Julia is looking at a face that's completely detached from the landmarks in her existence. Inside it there are no memories, there is no contemplation.

Only anguish.

Anger.

Aberration.

Sam is saying something.

With halting, raspy spasms, she finally manages to suck in some air. "W-wh-what?"

"Julia, what's going on? Are you crying?"

"No, I'm . . ."

"You are crying! Sis, what is it?" His voice sounds suddenly sharp. "Did anything happen?"

"Please come, oh god . . ." she whispers. The whispering turns to sobs as she tries to not lose sight of the intruders. She doesn't dare to blink. Blinking could be her death sentence.

"I'm coming! I'm on my way, you know that, but I can't go any faster! What happened?"

She finally brings herself to say it. "There are people here."

"What?"

"There are people here."

Silence. The swishing of the wipers. Two bleeps.

The woman is still standing at the foot of the bed. Her taut fingers contract. The dead skin under her left eyelid trembles.

"Whaddya mean, 'people'?"

"In my bedroom."

"Whaddya mean there are people? From the village? The people from the village who came earlier?"

"No, not them. There are people here . . ." She can only repeat it. But then it bursts out of her. "The whole room is full of people and they're staring at me. Oh god, Sam, they're getting closer! Oh Jesus. They keep getting closer. Help me. Please come right away. There's a woman and she's staring at me, she's standing next to my bed and she keeps staring at me . . ."

"Julia! Oh god, do they have eyes? *Do these people have eyes?*"

Do they have eyes? Why would he ask that? Of course they—

She blinks. She can't help it.

Julia finally screams, her face a disjointed mask of mortification. The woman is sitting ramrod straight on the edge of her bed. It's true: she has no eyes. She has holes for eyes. Where her eyes should be, two deep tunnels disappear into her head. In those tunnels, pitch-black darkness abounds. The fat man is now standing where she had just stood, not a second before. He too has blind, black tunnels instead of eyes. The others crowd behind him. Blind. Gaping. And all of them about to scream.

Julia is out of her wits. The nightmare is complete. She feels like she's being strangled, that the veins in her body are bursting open. That her heart is starting to leak and will stop beating in an instant, because it can't endure so much terror.

"Julia, get the hell outta there!" Sam yells in the distance.

But how? She is completely petrified. She's a prisoner in her own body, a hostage in a cell. And those people—of course they have eyes. How could she think otherwise? Intense eyes, staring eyes, digging into her own eyes. Or . . .

They *don't* have eyes.

Wait . . . they do.

Their visages shimmer; it seems like she can see both.

Julia slaps her face with both hands to distract herself from the madness besetting her. She shouts to her brother, who is too far away to help her, but it's a voiceless shout. Her throat is so tight she can't produce a sound.

"Get out of there, now! Julia! Julia!"

The woman is leaning toward her. Right in front of her. The fat man's hands are on the edge of the bed.

Julia abruptly tugs the covers over her head and rolls up in a cocoon. Away, away, she wants to get away from here. It used to be safe under the covers. She remembers it clearly from when she was a child. That queasy feeling inside, when you would wake up and discover that there was still a long night ahead. When the storm would bash the roof up at Huckleberry Wall and the snow would pile up against the walls and you were too old to wake Grandpa and Grandma up but still young enough to think the unthinkable. If you rolled yourself up in a cocoon, you were safe and nothing bad could happen to you. Then you knew Sam was nearby, in the other bed, and he was always watching over you.

"Sam," Julia whispers into her iPhone. "Sam, I love you. I need you. Please come quickly. I don't want to be alone. I don't want . . ."

The silence is oppressive.

Julia looks at the screen and it's dark. When she presses the side button, only the empty battery icon appears.

Julia starts crying again, silently, uncontrollably, terrified, but this time it's a submission. She feels the end is near and consciously detaches herself from the world to avoid experiencing it.

Here, under the covers, she's alone.

Alone in her cocoon. Alone in the chalet. Outside is the storm, the world.

Her heaving chest finally settles. Her foot is shaking, but then stops. It's quiet.

Something presses down on the mattress.

The covers are pulled tight.

Someone is lying next to her. In her cocoon. Someone who is hugging her like a lover. Like a brother.

She feels an icy hand on her shoulder. Julia shuts her eyes and imagines it's Sam who's holding her.

2

From *de Volkskrant*, November 9, 2018

WOMAN JUMPS FROM AMC, POSSIBLE CONNECTION TO AUGUST TRAGEDY

By our correspondent Robert Feenstra

AMSTERDAM—A 44-year-old woman jumped to her death from the roof of the Academic Medical Center in Amsterdam-Zuidoost. Her motives are as yet unclear, but a police spokesman has confirmed that she was a hospital employee. The AMC is withholding comment until investigations have been completed.

According to reports, the suicide is neurosurgeon Emily Wan, who was on duty during the August 18 tragedy, when 32 AMC patients died due to as of yet undetermined causes. In early October, after excluding the possibility of bioterror, Minister of Justice and Security Ferdinand Grapperhuis confirmed that there are no suspicions of foul play. Last week, the Dutch Safety Board announced that the first report on the case will be published by the end of the year.

The police cannot confirm whether Wan had been questioned in connection with the case. The dead woman is the third AMC employee to commit suicide since August.

Two years a widow, the neurosurgeon lived in Amstelveen with her two young children.

THE INVISIBLE MAN

NOTES BY SAM AVERY

"You don't understand," he said, "who I am or what I am. I'll show you. By Heaven! I'll show you."

—H. G. Wells

1

When the Airbus started its descent into Geneva, Nick, or whatever was left of him, was still in a medically induced coma. And up here in the mountains it was booming thunder. Up here, a nightmare of jerks and jolts in unstable skies. The Airbus circled endlessly and blind-eyed, then suddenly torpedoed through a break in the clouds, and I realized we'd been flying lower than the surrounding ridges all along. The total lack of orientation instantaneously twisted into a razor of claustrophobia.

Not counting Manhattan skyscrapers, this was the first time in sixteen years I had been confronted with the mountains.

No doubt about it: I *hated* the mountains.

Always did, always will.

I hated the way they closed in on us. The way they were leaning over the plane. Tearing right through the storm, jagged like a predator's teeth.

The mountains had bitten Nick's face off.

I couldn't figure what the guy on the line meant when he kept trying to explain about Nick's face. The Police Cantonale rep, I mean. Said something was wrong with his face. The face I knew inside out. Sharp angles, but gentle features, a primitive symmetry that made him look like a creature straight out of nature. What I adored most about it was the total lack of shame. My mind jury was still out on whether Nick's cool collectedness was because he simply didn't notice other people's gazes and jaw drops or because he was so used to them that he just didn't give a shit.

And there it was, the phone going off and me still thinking it was him: the same face smirking at me from the screen. The pic I took ten days earlier, the evening before he set off. I wanted to see that pic every time he called. *#bebacksoon* I captioned it on Instagram. In the ensuing days, Nick had put up a few of his own; polarized glasses and ice axes and death drops that would give any sane person the heebie-jeebies. *#livingthelife* was how he'd captioned them.

The reason I saw that pic was because the Police Cantonale had used Nick's phone to call me.

The drive to the CHUV, the university hospital in Lausanne, took ages due to the rain, and Harald and Louise Grevers, neither of them liked driving abroad.

Meanwhile, my mind was running in circles. *Would you stay with me if I became paralyzed? If some gas tank blunder burnt my face off? Would you stay with me if my legs were gone? If I had to eat liquids through a tube? Would you stay with me if I became brain damaged and could no longer love you as I love you now? Will you stay with me when I'm old and invisible?*

I thought, *Accident or gravity—we all end up mutilated.* That was from a Chuck Palahniuk novel, if I remembered correctly. But this accident *was* gravity. Not the kind that sags your once-fit body, but the kind that splatters you in one fell swoop.

Will you stay with me when my face is gone?

In the backseat of Nick's folks' Hertz rental, the mountains took me prisoner. Lake Geneva is the gateway to the Alps. This landscape was giving me the evil eye, I could feel it all over. A palpable malevolence hung over the water like a force field. As if a door had opened to something intangible but extremely menacing, something that was going to trail me for a long time to come.

The thing was, I was twenty-four and he was twenty-seven.

The thing was, we didn't wanna be invisible yet.

Or compensate. We were too young to lower the bar. Rejoice that he was still alive. Thinking thoughts like that with Nick in a coma, did that make me a scumbag? Shallow? But it was my world. So please, I'll take shallowness.

We met curling EZ bars at the gym, no less. Biceps: check. Pecs: check. Abs: check. The gym is the crème de la crème of the human casing, the antithesis of the bowels of the internet, where credit card pervs and butcher fetishists go to drool over mutilation and stumps.

Will I stay with you, if I can't handle this?

The mountains loomed on both sides, higher and higher. A tangle of nausea settled in my stomach. I flashbacked to that first time in the gym: Nick lying on the bench, glistening with sweat, pumping iron, shirt soaked. But this time he had no face. Where it should have been was now a deep, dark cave, the agglomeration of gravity and bad dreams.

2

His life wasn't in danger, but he wasn't out of the woods.

Before they let us see him, two Police Cantonale detectives took us over to the dental surgeon's office. He did all the talking, bookended by the bored cops. Who knows what protocol stipulated their presence, but for spicing up the party, they got an F. After a while, it made me feel so awkward I started thinking maybe some social reintegration initiative now has the Swiss police employing deaf-mutes.

The long-winded powwow was the kind of quintessential linguistic extravaganza any one of my professors would cream their pants for: Nick's folks talked Dutch to each other and English to the oral surgeon, the oral surgeon talked English to Nick's mom and dad and French to the cops, the cops talked zilchese—all four of which I have mastered. I know that scene from *Inglourious Basterds* totally cracks Europeans up—you know, the one where Diane Kruger asks Brad Pitt, "I know this is a silly question before I ask it, but can you Americans speak any other language besides English?" Well, I do. I also speak Spanish, passable German, took a specialized course on Creole languages, and I read (or used to) Latin. I'm doing my master's in linguistics at the UvA, and thanks to Nick, after three years, I'm fluent in Dutch (although I'd like to think my accent is less thick than he says it is, and to that, I say I can't help that your language sounds like you all have a gerbil stuck in your throat and are trying to spit it out while you speak).

The dentist's name was Olivier Genet, and when he spoke, it wasn't to me. Maybe cuz I'm an American or maybe cuz he was a Jesus lover. He had one of those comb-overs gone wrong, with the last strands of hair swept from the sides of his skull over his bald pate like a diaphanous mesh. *Alopecia androgenetica*, I thought. When he addressed only Nick's parents for the umpteenth time, I revised my diagnosis: mofo MPB. There was an imprint on his coat that said *Propriété de Centre Hospitalier Universitaire Vaudois*, and I wondered whether that applied to the coat or to the man.

Jerks like him are always something's or someone's property.

Genet said Nick was lucky. He got hit by falling rocks but he was still alive. Until he was able to spill the beans, it would be impossible to determine exactly what had happened, but enough could be deduced by the circumstances in which the mountain rescue team had found him. Had found Nick, cuz all they found of his climbing buddy, Augustin, was an ice axe.

Augustin must have gone for help in bad weather and fallen into a crevasse on the way down. Whatever was left of *him* was now frozen solid in the ice; "He Died in a Crack While Pursuing His Passion" would be his epitaph. His family had been brought up to speed.

"Oh, how awful," Louise kept saying. "Awful, for his parents. Thank God our Nick is still alive."

Yeah, thank God. Cuz Nick, as Genet said, Nick was lucky.

Only half of Nick's face had been smashed off. The rock had split open his jaw, knocked two teeth out, and ripped off most of his cheeks. *#livingthelife*.

"He was lucky," Genet said for the third time, and spread his thumb and index finger. "That closer and the rock would have got his eyes. That closer, he could have died."

I didn't get how this was "luck." That close the other way and he would have come home in one piece. That close and we'd now be in a sunny hotel bed having hot and steamy sex to drown out the memory. I was already trying to come up with the French for "hot and steamy" but checked myself, remembering *il dottore* was probably still treating Nick.

Harald asked if the place where the accident happened was dangerous, and I was gonna say, *Yeah, mountains, hello.* If you're at the bottom of the slope, you're not technically dead yet, but let's just say the clock is ticking.

Genet said he didn't know the exact location. "In the Val d'Anniviers, in the Pennine Alps. But the Air-Glaciers report only mentioned that it was a remote and inaccessible area. Precarious terrain, seldom climbed." He mumbled something unintelligible to his deaf-mute subjects, then turned back to us: "We'll inquire for you on which mountain the accident happened."

I thought, *What's the diff?* A mountain is a mountain is a mountain. A pile of frozen rocks, sans coffee corners, club sodas, or mojito bars, you shouldn't touch with a ten-mile pole. I didn't give a hoot what a chunk of land ignored by evolution for millions of years was called. Drill a hole in it, fill it up with nukes, and *boom*, you're recycling.

There were police photos, shot before they sewed up Nick's face, but Genet held on to them so we couldn't see. Turned them upside down, frowning, turned them right side up. "It will be difficult enough once the bandages come off."

Louise covered her mouth with her hands.

"Your son's lucky he was preserved well. He lay unconscious in the ice for hours before coming to, which stanched the bleeding and prevented swelling. The frostbite caused loss of soft tissue, which we had to suture with grafts."

Grafts?

"From his arm." He spread his thumb and finger again, closer this time.

I saw Nick's face before me: a bloody, gaping hole.

I saw Nick's face before me: necrotic and black, growing an arm.

Harald asked the million-dollar question: "Is there any permanent damage?"

Genet looked pensively at the photos of my boyfriend's perfect, mutilated face and said, "Plastic surgeons call it a permanent smile, and not without reason. At a later stage, we can perform corrective surgery to reduce scarring, and it may be possible to make everything suppler with silicone dressings. But thinking we can make these kinds of nasty wounds completely invisible is an illusion. No one tells you, but after a face-lift people are covered in scars. It's just that we apply the scalpel wisely. An incision above the eyelid. An incision around the nostril. An incision behind the ear. The difference is that with your son's rectification, it's not up to us."

Yeah, that's the word he used.

Nick didn't even get a report in the newspaper, no "Mountain Bites Happy Horror Grin in Dutchman's Face," because the next day the press headlined pics proving actress and Miss Swiss Heidi Lötschentaler's nose job and there was no space for trivial items.

"It will take about six months before the jawbone heals and we can insert dental implants. In the meantime, he'll have to wear dentures. But that's just the start of it. It's uncertain whether he will fully recover facial expressivity. You have to be prepared for problems of functionality such as impaired opening of the mouth, irreparable damage to motor nerves resulting in a drooping mouth or partial facial paralysis . . ."

My head started to spin. Somewhere in the distance I heard Louise cry. I tried to focus on the zigzagging vein on Genet's balding temple, a bead of sweat trailing down it.

". . . loss of chewing functions, limited nasal inhalation, reduced sense of smell and taste, impaired speech . . ."

The vein, his baldness, they were scars, too: old age.

". . . PTSS, partial memory loss, anxiety disorder . . . Is your son insured?"

And my brain on overload: *Please end me now.*

Of course, at that point I still hadn't noticed something was wrong. I was in shock. And I still refused to notice it when I left the hotel that evening and, after rambling through a tangle of narrow, annoyingly steep alleys, eventually ended up at the hospital, where the night nurse, Cécile Métrailler, nervously handed me the folded note.

Don't believe them. It wasn't an accident.

Sure I shoulda believed him. Who wouldn't believe his boyfriend when he says something like that? But Nick was suffering from the aftereffects of severe trauma, and Dr. Genet had said that he didn't remember the accident. So I thought Nick was hallucinating.

And I also thought that it would be my biggest worry. But *that* surfaced only the next evening, after something had so scared the shit out of poor Cécile that she hightailed it out of the hospital in the middle of her shift and didn't dare to come back.

That *something* was Nick.

3

He was sort of conscious when we finally got to visit him that afternoon, and they'd given him a pen and pad to communicate with. But he wasn't exactly writing epic poetry, just basic info—*No, no pain* and *Water, please* and *Black magic*—so the Police Cantonale dicks had to bide their time, hanging further up the hall like a coupla monitors on mute.

Truth is, opening that door made me shit bricks. Louise sensed it and squeezed my hand, but then went ahead into the room to see her son. It was all I could do to keep myself from turning around and beating it. I was scared of what was waiting in there, but I was also pissed off, cuz I'd begged him so many times to cut it out with that dumbass hobby of his, and I also felt sorry for myself because, dammit, the best we could look forward to now was looking back at how it used to be. Unfair? Maybe. But true.

Then I straightened my back, walked in, and saw what was left of the pretty Dutch boy I fell for three years ago. I wish I could say it wasn't that bad. But if I start fibbing now, the rest I have to tell won't be worth diddly-squat.

I recognized him cuz the light blue sheet was pulled back to his waist and he had no shirt on. Biceps: check. Pecs: check. Mutilated mummy mug: check. His face was wrapped in miles of tightly stretched gauze holding compresses in place. Fastened hit-or-miss to keep the whole shebang from falling apart and treating us to the hideous sight of what was squished underneath with a lick of pappy and putrid antibiotic salve. The only gaps were the holes for his eyes, his left ear, and his nostrils—one for breathing and one housing a plastic tube. Give him glacier glasses and he's the Invisible Man on a glucose drip.

His eyes were dulled by the morphine but were still his, and, passing over his mom and dad, they searched mine.

"Hail, Tutankhamen," I said.

This made Harald, Louise, and the nurse who was taking his blood pressure burst out laughing. Even Dr. Genet chuckled a little. I was secretly relieved, cuz it gave me the chance to look away from his glance. Woulda been too much to bear. Didn't wanna start crying with everyone there.

4

That first visit was pretty useless. Nick was still too groggy with anesthetics, and we were all too shocked to make it memorable. When I returned later that evening, I knew he'd be asleep, but I wanted to see him. *Needed* to see him.

As it often does in the mountains—didn't know it then, but do now—the sky cleared just before sundown. After dinner, Louise and Harald went for a long stroll along the lake. Their grief had made them irritable, as had the news that it would probably be a week before their son could be flown to Holland—less danger of infection. They asked me to join, but I declined and went my own way, uphill, circling back to the CHUV, wondering what I'd do if they didn't let me into the ward.

The hospital was very quiet. All through the long corridor from the open lobby to IC, one endless stretch of piss, body lotion, and disinfectant fumes, I saw just one patient and a coupla nurses, who greeted me politely as I passed. I focused on my feet, a cursory upward glance only when strictly necessary, cuz the view out the panorama windows gave me the jitters. The mountains on the other side of the lake were dark shapes dissolving into the clouds like some weird atmospheric phenomenon, more menacing than ever before.

No trace of the Police Cantonale in Nick's ward. Later, I heard they'd asked Nick some questions that afternoon—standard mountaineering deaths procedure. They'd scribbled a concluding report and split. Nick played ball and confirmed the mountain rescue's conclusions.

on't ask me why I was being candid with someone who'd been in my life ime than it takes to chug a tequila, but Cécile made some neurons in my dance and I liked her right off the bat. Sometimes you just feel it. Other e, other time, maybe we woulda been friends.

t will be very difficult," she said plainly. She handed me the washcloth. re. You probably want to wash him."

sure as hell didn't, and Cécile sure as hell knew it, but she saw how far I away from the bed, saw me avoiding what I eventually had to face: this Nick now; get used to it. Our lives would be defined by the moment the dages came off and Nick's irrevocably disfigured face would be unveiled. eaded it like a root canal. I kept seeing Dr. Genet turning those photos ide down and around again.

But worried as I was about whether I could deal with the impending dis- y, I worried even more for Nick's sake. The curse of being a beefcake is that oes to your head. You become an addict. Gravity is your nemesis. Mirror, rror, on the wall—one look and Nick's a junkie in rehab.

I was terrified that my face would be the mirror and then that would be the d of our happily ever after.

So I relieved Cécile of the washcloth and washed him. Cleaned his body, ery nook and cranny, which I knew like the back of my hand, every curve ding its own memory. I'm pretty sure the act of cleaning cleansed some- ing in me, too. I created a space for his imperfections and future scars, got know them, tried to get acquainted, taking the edge off the horror waiting r us underneath the memory of his old face.

When I was done, Cécile finally trusted me enough to remove the folded ote from her uniform pocket. She looked past me, checking the door, and id in a hushed voice, "He said to give this to you. It's in Dutch, but I used oogle Translate and it says he loves you." She blushed. "Sorry. I was curious."

I unfolded the note and read Nick's claim that it wasn't an accident.

The hospital room seemed to go mute. I suddenly noticed my heartbeat unning rampant. When I looked up, I saw Cécile press her finger to her lips. was stupefied; what I'd thought was edginess was in fact fear.

I thought, *Dr. Genet.*

"Listen, I'm on the late shift," she said, currying a faux sense of comfort, but how about coffee tomorrow morning? I know a nice place by the lake."

5

Next day, Nick was awake early, so his parents and I took turns sitting with him. Later that morning, Harald and Louise were gonna go to the Val d'An- niviers with Nick's car keys to pick up his Focus, which the Police Cantonale had found where he and Augustin had left it before their fatal climb. As soon

Even in his state, Nick could figure out there'd be h
anything about what was really weighing on him.

Confusing memories, images of horrors, vague, like a c
(*Dum-dum-dum duuumm . . . Roll credits.*)

I slipped into his room undetected. There was my perfe
ked on the bed. The light blue sheets pulled back, a plast
of his miserable, flaccid phallus, a young nurse with a full
curly, leaning over him. My perfect mummified lover, mc
attractive credit card perv with a cystoscopy fetish. Can yo
off the head, stick the bod on a stanchion, and someone'd s
thou for it and call it *The Torso of Apollo.*

Then I saw the tub of water, the washcloth, and the t
into a urine bag between his legs, and then the nurse sav
with a start.

"*Bonsoir,*" I said.

Funny how people just don't know how to react.

I said, "I sure am happy I didn't catch Dr. Genet like th
French; same goes for everything else I'd say to Cécile, see
only speak a coupla words of English.

She seemed to relax a bit—just a tiddly tad—and looked
vous, clear eyes. "You must be Sam."

"You got it. How'd you know?"

She smiled, but avoided my eyes. "Nick told me about you. Cé

"Hello, Cécile." I walked to the bed and shook her latex-glo
my boyfriend's naked body. "A *man* with those kinds of gloves
other things on his mind."

They say humor is a coping mechanism, but as an attempt t
ease, it bombed. She gave a shy splutter, but quickly turned her l
stuck an electric gun in Nick's exposed ear.

Her edginess was rubbing off on me. Looking at that answ
the-count noggin got me all antsy, so I transferred my gaze to th
on the rest of his body. Biceps: check. Quads: check. Reps: unti
plug his face with a slab of arm, plug his arm with a slab of thig
gery is shifting the scar to wherever it doesn't matter. The huma
all-inclusive DIY kit.

Thing is, a body like Nick's had no wherever-it-doesn't-matter.

Thing is, without a face, a body like that is worth jack shit.

I tore my gaze away from the bed and asked, "How's he doing?"

"Sleeping like a baby. Temperature and blood pressure are stab
in pain." First time Cécile looked at me longer than a nanosecond
you doing?"

Shrug. Considered bullshitting. Said, "Bad."

as it became clear when Nick could be flown to the AMC, they'd drive the car back to Holland.

Nick's cloudy eyes drifted eerily between the strips of bandage. Still morphine-muddled but less out of it than yesterday, me babbling a mile a minute to distract him from the obvious. *Flash*: Fazila and Rob were on trial separation, text from Faz, nothing new under the sun. *Flash*: Ramses versus Chef, one ear got frazzled, has gone outdoors only in backyard since. *Flash*: Weleda introduced a new Skin Food Facial for dry skin, which is absorbed more easily than . . . Oh, fuck. Caught myself avoiding his masked face. In the mirror on the opposite wall (the nurses had rehung it where Nick couldn't see it), I saw my reflection look away from the bed, again and again, a never-ending reality loop, till Nick took hold of my hand, shutting me up instantly.

I'm a monster

he wrote on his pad.

Flash: Ohio mother eats baby and she was trending. *#onlyinohio*.

I won't blame you if you leave me.

"Don't be ridiculous."

Those eyes. I couldn't force myself to look at them.

"No one's leaving, got that? We got this, together."

I sincerely hoped so, but we both knew reality would catch up with us sooner or later. We'd been inseparable for three years. Nick was why I didn't go back to New York. Our dream was to go there together, eventually. I taught him how to dance and he taught me how to love. But this reality loop wasn't about me; I knew that. If I were to look into Nick's eyes, I'd see the ocean that lay between our old life and our new one, and I had no idea how we were supposed to bridge the gap.

Louise and Harald came in with coffee. Whew. Beat-around-the-bush conversation. Suited me fine. When they left for Wallis, half an hour later, I leaned toward Nick and whispered, "Whaddya mean it wasn't an accident?"

Looked like he wasn't gonna answer, but then he slowly shook his head.

"You don't remember what happened?"

He looked away. A small red spot, like a tear, appeared in the bandages on his cheek.

"Not unusual."

He was leaking.

"I mean . . . memory loss. After a coma."

Nick picked up his pad, and as he wrote, I looked at his broad, bronzed shoulders, where I'd so often rested my cheek. The hollows under his collarbones that I liked hooking my fingers in. The stubbly chin, my perfect idea of sexy. The gauze, hiding something horrific instead.

I don't know. Afraid to think about it. Help me, Sam. Scared I'm going crazy. Don't trust my own mind. You'd run away screaming if you

His pen hovered over the pad for a long time before he added a few words, tore out the sheet and gave it to me.

Maybe it's for the best.

I wish he hadn't done that. What his unfinished sentence suggested was bad enough, but this was worse. It was *my* decision, not his, whether I could deal with sticking by him or should split because of something as trivial as a mutilated face. I hated myself for thinking it, but if he'd take that away, the last thing that was mine, I might as well throw all my organs in a steaming heap and donate them. You could tick a box not to include your heart, but why bother?

His eyes were open, he was alive, but inside, Nick was frozen in the moment he'd looked up and seen those rocks coming at him. Part of me didn't want to doubt Nick's state of mind—I'd be letting him down. But I couldn't ignore Dr. Genet's diagnosis. How could I convince him that the cold wind blowing in his head was no more than the echo of a torn face, the struggle of a traumatized mind? He wasn't delusional; he was tripping.

PTSS/morphine—a potent cocktail.

And there I was: staring at what he wrote.

At a loss for words.

Those shoulders. That Amenhotep-style head. They unerringly laid bare my inability to deal with the situation and to whisper to him the words he needed to hear. New thing for me, being the strong one. I didn't cut it, not by a long shot, because I needed *his* shoulders for support. His face to hold in my hands. His lips to whisper to me that everything would be all right.

Break the dynamics between two people and you're both left alone, staring wide-eyed out into your own darkness.

Walking away from that bed was the hardest thing I ever did. On the move, I confettied the note and stuffed the shreds into my back pocket. I said *Get some sleep*, said *I'll be back soon*, who knows what else I said, and then I was at the door. Last thing I saw as it closed behind me was that shattered body on the hospital bed, his dull eyes and, worst of all, his lonesome understanding.

In the corridor, life hit me like a tsunami, so hard I had to brace up. Didn't budge for a long time, fighting my panic and, despite everything, relieved that I was out and scot-free. But there was nothing I could do, and anyway it was almost eleven. I had a date.

6

"I saw his wounds," Cécile Métrailler said. "I've treated rockfall victims before and I can assure you, Nick is not a rockfall case."

The summer was hot-pressing Lausanne as I got out of the Métro in Ouchy. Little boats crisscrossing the water, windsurfer silhouettes glittering on the coastline. The mountains in the distance a mirage, ignis fatuus; reach for them and they're gone. Maybe the blazing sun blunted the sharp edges off the peaks, but that did nothing to soothe me.

"If a rock hits your face, it'll break your nose or a cheekbone. I mean, the bones that jut out. Nick got hit in the most protected area." She opened her mouth and hollowed her cheeks.

Cécile didn't use the word *rockfall*, by the way; she said *éboulement*. Everything sounds softer in French.

Admit it, even *équarrissage* sounds appealing.

"He broke his jaw," I put forward.

"Yes, but it split only because two teeth were so forcefully knocked out of it. One with root and all. What you'd actually expect is random damage over the whole bone; open, bleeding wounds; and contusions under the skin. But he's got . . ." Cécile put her hands to her mouth. 'Course, she realized I hadn't seen it yet. "Sorry, you probably don't want to hear all this *en détail* . . ."

"Is it that bad? Tell me the truth."

She could see I was struggling, and she answered as tactfully as possible under the circumstances. "It will get better. But brace yourself. His face will never be the same."

I stirred my iced mochaccino and shoved the glass aside. I mean, me, passing up a mochaccino? Armageddon. Big boys don't cry, but good thing I had my shades on.

"Will it . . . affect his work?" Cécile asked gingerly.

I knew damn well what she was implying. I shrugged. "He's a web editor for Tripadvisor and does freelance writing for Lonely Planet. You don't need a face to travel. Or write."

I thought, *But I need a face.*

"But if it wasn't rockfall," I finally said, "what was it? His note. Nick said it wasn't an accident. I thought he was delirious."

"Want to know what I really think?"

Nope. Also didn't want to imagine any sidewalk double takes due to the walking freak show next to me. But this was my life now, so I said yeah. For now.

"It looks more like a stab wound."

I stared at her.

"Sorry, it sounds bad . . . but it looks like someone stabbed him in the cheek with a knife, so deep that it came out the other cheek. And then wrenched it forward with force."

A horrible image popped up in my head: Nick, not bleeding to death, but single-footedly staggering down a glacier to a spot where his phone got a signal so he could call a chopper, the icy wind whistling through the hole in his face. It gave me such a jolt I almost kicked over the table.

"But wouldn't Dr. Genet have noticed that?" I said with difficulty.

"I talked about it with Dr. Genet."

"So what did he say?"

"He said, at first glance, Nick's wounds don't tally with what the mountain rescue said happened to him, but they could. Rocks can be awfully sharp. Nick's head would have had to be turned sideways, and the rock would have had to be shaped more like a tent peg . . . but it's possible. Another scenario, according to him, is that Nick's ice axe could have done it when he fell. Also improbable, but not impossible." Cécile flushed and played with her cappuccino spoon. "I said he must be crazy if he believed that."

"Really? What did he say?"

She looked at me intently. "He said if I didn't want to lose my job, I should keep my mouth shut and not ask any questions."

I whistled. "Wow. Is he always such a jerk?"

"No, and that's what's strange. Dr. Genet is a really friendly, competent surgeon. And he has a point when he says that even if something is improbable, you shouldn't disregard it as a theory, as long as there aren't any better explanations. It was high up in the mountains and his friend really did fall into a crevasse. The rescue team found his axe next to the opening, and they weren't roped together, so he was probably alone then. Weather conditions were bad. As long as Nick doesn't claim otherwise, there's no reason to assume that what happened to him wasn't an accident. And that Augustin had wanted to get help."

"But Nick *has* claimed otherwise."

"Right. And that brings me back to the nature of his wounds. I know what a stab wound looks like, Sam."

I thought, *And I didn't buy his story.*

My admiration for Cécile Métrailler was growing. She'd risked her job by meeting me here. I thought she had the right to know what Nick's last note said, so I took the shreds out of my pocket, flattened them, and spread them out on the table. Torn, ripped like his face. Another SOS mosaic.

"*Je crains de devenir fou*" is French for "Scared I'm going crazy."

"*Fuir en hurlant*" is French for "Run away screaming."

"But why would he say that?" I asked. "If they got robbed or if someone meant to hurt them, why is he still so scared?"

And Cécile's face all awkward, like I was the last person in the world to understand.

"Because what you say doesn't make sense," she sighed. "They weren't robbed, Sam. Nick's passport and wallet were still in his backpack. These are the Swiss Alps, not the Caucasus. Go higher than 10,000 feet and you only come across other mountain climbers, not muggers. And according to Air-Glaciers, they were in a totally remote area where climbers usually don't go. They didn't report any sightings of other climbers in the area where they found Nick." Cécile had trouble looking at me, but she didn't give up now, took my hand. "Do you understand what I'm getting at? If there was violence, it had to have been between them."

Shit.

"The nurses are all whispering about it, but no one dares to say something out loud. I thought you should know."

Augustin did it. Something happened up there and it was Augustin who did it. Augustin had mutilated Nick.

It suddenly hit me. Cold like a handful of ice. Chilly like whispers from a crevasse.

It was Augustin . . . but Augustin was dead.

You'd run away screaming if you . . .

If you found out what I did.

So I sat there, sweating behind my shades, dripping next to an undrunk iced mochaccino in a country I didn't want to be in, a country that, unlike the rest of the world, had no real horizon—only rows of ragged teeth stretching out into infinity. My own Invisible Man in the hospital, plugged into an IV pole, yellow and red juices leaking in and out of him, and me, scared, conspiracy-theory scared, that he had something terrible to answer for.

I slid my chair back and said I had to go.

7

Faster than a speeding bullet to the CHUV, but when I stormed into Nick's room, he was asleep. I called the day nurse, insisted she check his vital signs. Charmed by my concern, she assured me he was perfectly stable. That did nothing to soothe me, but I realized the fever afflicting him was raging only in his conscience. I stayed by his bed way into late afternoon, channel-zapping on mute between Swiss infomercials for Ab Wonders, Flex Belts, and Thighmasters till I almost OD'd on oiled six-packs. Pretty faces, laughing faces, plastic faces, they look the same everywhere.

Zapping through a thousand possible scenarios in my head, always coming back to one: self-defense.

Will you stay with me if my face is gone? Will you stay with me if I murdered someone?

It had to have been self-defense. In-your-face evidence. Like, literally.

Whatever the reason, things got terribly out of hand up there—cabin fever, mountain madness, whatever—and Augustin must have gone at Nick with some outdoor knife. Why? Dunno. Didn't matter. Nick, seriously wounded, had shoved him off. They were somewhere high. Ice tower. Glacial basin. Whatever the hell it looked like up there. Augustin fell. A one-way express ticket to reincarnation.

Not the kind of copy you hand in to Lonely Planet about your latest adventure, not the review you write for Tripadvisor sharing your experiences of the Val d'Anniviers.

Not what you tell the Police Cantonale or even your boyfriend.

Body Xtremes, Total Gyms, and Power Crunchers—ever more perfect, laughing faces living in perfect bubbles. *Zap* and they burst; *zap* and they're replaced. *Zap*, and Nick's perfect face would never laugh again. Nick's perfect smile slashed away by the memory of what he'd done. How could I've been so stupid? Why hadn't I seen it right away? Why hadn't I conveyed to him that he didn't have to face this alone?

Rather than distancing me from him, knowing what he did brought on a renewed determination to stand by his side. Immoral? Maybe. But this was something I could live with. Anything's better than the futility of an accident. Hell, even if it was something worse than self-defense, how could I ever desert him? Nick, *my* Nick, scared shitless cuz he was responsible for someone's death. That's why he hadn't said anything. And he didn't need to, cuz the evidence was buried in a crevasse, deep-frozen for the next ten thousand years.

By the time anyone might discover the ice mummy, it wouldn't be forensic investigation, just an archeological curiosity.

Augustin: Ötzi the Iceman 2.0.

8

When Nick awoke, his parents had returned. He was upbeat and even made jokes. Careful conclusion: he was happy to see me, not upset that I split. He complained about a painful pressure to the back of his face, but the nurse said there was still an hour before the next hit of morphine. Last thing she wanted was a junkie on her hands.

I said, "I'll take a dose. I sure could use it."

But instead, there was Louise and Harald and a call from the AMC. The doctor they had talked to, like them, saw no reason to keep Nick in an overpriced Swiss clinic any longer. Under certain circumstances, it was even possible to overrule the local quack's decision. Since Nick's mountaineering insurance covered medevac, Dr. Genet was in for an unpleasant lunchtime surprise. Your patient X, your experiment, your faceless Frankenstein, well, he flew the Intensive Coop. Wild guess, but if you ask us, it was merely falling rocks.

We sat by the bed, all four of us feeling relieved, till early in the evening, when Nick's next morphine shot kicked in and he had trouble keeping his eyes open. Louise and Harald said good-bye and went to the nurses' station to bring the night shift up to speed about their son's imminent repatriation.

Gave me the chance to finally try to say it.

"Nick . . . I'm sorry I left this morning." I bowed over him, so close I could smell the antibiotic ointment under his bandages . . . and under them, unmistakable and sinister, the wound odor. I laid my hand on his shoulder. "I'm here for you, okay? Don't be afraid. Whatever happened, you got my support, you hear? *Whatever happened.*"

Nick fixed his open eyes on mine. The morphine made it hard to tell which emotion they were harboring, but he squeezed my hand softly.

"And when we get home, I want you to tell me everything, okay?"

Another squeeze. I wanted to stay, but Nick took the notepad lying on his chest and wrote,

Go get something to eat with those two. Cécile will be here soon, but I don't think I can stay awake till then.

So I did, and I wish I hadn't.

Next to the hotel, we ate the best cheese fondue ever: Gruyère/Vacherin/tons of garlic/white wine. In the southeast, in the direction of Wallis, sky heavy and dark, faraway rumbling echoing against the mountains. Halfway through dinner, Harald got a call confirming the medevac the next day. Louise clapped her hands in delight.

"Oh, I'm so happy," she said. She laughed, eyes glittering, leaned toward me. "Want to know something, Sam? That man, the dental surgeon, that Jeanette or whatever his name is, I'm sure he's good at what he does, but like I told Harald yesterday, I think he's an awful man."

I smiled. "So I wasn't the only one."

And that's why, for the second time that day, I ran through the CHUV's corridors and stormed into Nick's room. Not in shock this time but excited about sharing the good news.

"Cécile, he can go home!" I yelped—but then I saw that the woman bowing over Nick wasn't Cécile at all. It was a nurse who was much older, heavyset, and when she looked up with a start, I saw dark rings under her eyes.

And something else.

It was just a flash before the nurse blocked what she was doing with her body, a flash before she fastened the bandages with those metal clips. But in that flash I *saw* something, and I could still see it the next day, when I was jolted out of a nightmare somewhere above the Atlantic, halfway to New York.

It's the things you leave out that are the worst.

My knees buckled, I sank against the doorpost, only just managed not to fall to the floor. Sat there, sprawled, slumped, till the nurse was done and turned to me. Blood gone from my face.

"Where's Cécile?" I managed to get out.

I stared at her latex gloves, at the metal tray in her hand. Stared at the strips of used gauze and wads of bloodied cotton, yellow-brown, disinfectant-sticky. When I spoke, I could barely recognize my own voice.

"Don't ask me where she is. Fifteen minutes ago she ran out of the ward, screaming. The concierge saw her leave the building. Kid was absolutely terrified, he said."

"What happened?"

"She was with that friend of yours. Something must have scared her witless. She was changing the bandages and left everything all exposed. Exposed! And he slept through it all, can you believe it?"

She nodded at Nick, but I noticed she didn't look at him. She was actually already halfway to the door, as if she couldn't bear another second in this room with her patient.

"I called her at least ten times, but she won't pick up. She needs to come back. We're understaffed as it is, and everything's going haywire."

"But . . . what could have happened?" I tried again.

"No idea, but if the staff find out, and they will, it won't happen again. She'll get fired."

It hurt to hear it. "Can I go to Nick?"

She gazed at me, hesitated, then held up her hand. "I don't want to have anything to do with this. If anyone asks, I never saw you here, got it? I'm assuming you'll confirm it."

"You're an angel," I said.

But the angel had walked away, one latex hand in the air, grumbling to herself about Cécile, God, and the world.

I closed the door softly. It was true: all the commotion had gone unnoticed by Nick. He lay there under the sheet, still as a stiff, face buried under all those new bandages. Behind him, the large window, looking out on purple-black thunderclouds and the foothills in the dying light. That window, it shook lightly in its grooves every time the lightning made the contours of the peaks appear in the distance. Maybe it was my imagination. What I didn't imagine was my fingers, trembling so hard when I texted Cécile that I had to start over three times.

Cécile, WTF?

No reason to assume she'd contact me if the hospital couldn't reach her, but surprise surprise. I got one text; and that was the last I heard from her.

Sorry. He was right, he's a monster.

9

The UvA gym, the workout bench where Nick lay glistening with sweat, the soaked tank top—it wasn't only where we first met, it's where we first smooched. In the locker room. Yeah, okay, *after* showering.

Don't know how we got there, don't care, but he pushes me against the tiled wall, tongue in my mouth, six foot four of macho-boy twinkdom, Dior Fahrenheit and body wash bouquet, one hand on my neck, the other guiding mine under his shirt. Nick, perfect-pec babe magnet, likely will have a girlfriend next week, but I'll take my chances.

Wrong about the girlfriend; three years of exemplary fidelity instead. But when he pulls back and smiles at me, the corners of his mouth are split open to the ears and I see a row of bared, bloody teeth all the way to the back of his mouth. I touch my own lips and it's like we just made out with a mouthful of raw mincemeat.

"It wasn't an accident, Sam," Nick says, and I can see his tongue, I mean the *whole* thing, and I start screaming. "*Augustin is dead, and it wasn't an accident . . .*"

10

I woke up in a panic, not screaming, just a groan from deep in my throat. I'd dozed off in the hard plastic chair by the window. The clock above the door showed 11:30 and the ICU was dead silent. Adrenaline supply not yet depleted, I staggered to my feet.

Nick was still asleep. Still hadn't moved, but the motionless mound on the bed defined the hospital room. Hate saying it, but I could barely dare to look. All the getting used to the situation wiped out in one blow by what I saw when I entered the room at the wrong time. The dream was a horror show, okay, but this was real.

He was right; he's a monster.

At the outdoor cafe in Ouchy, I had confided Nick's harrowing words to Cécile. I couldn't imagine what could have brought her to echo them like this. Maybe she'd come to the same conclusions as I did and was burdened with moral qualms greater than mine, but that was no explanation for abandoning her patient to his fate, just like that. What could scare an experienced nurse so much that it made her run away screaming in the middle of changing the bandages?

Nick slept. Sheet motionless. Lightning in the distance.

On the TV, the flawless faces and perfect six-packs had been replaced by experts analyzing Heidi Lötschentaler's nose job, but I barely registered any of it. I walked to the window and looked out on Lausanne's quarters, terraced on the various slopes, a cascade of yellow and orange light. Our hotel was more to the right, in the old city center, but my gaze wandered deeper down, to that mirror, the endless black lake that reflected the lights of villages pasted high up on the opposing mountains.

What drove people to live up there? And what had possessed Nick to make him so want to tempt gravity, to chase the clouds that ventured the highest ridges with such deceptive ease? Was life down below so pointless that he had to reduce his world to a spot from which the only way forward was downhill?

Something had happened up there, and from then on, things had gone solely downhill for Nick. Definitively for Augustin.

I realized that I was scared, irrationally scared, like a gust of wind on a cold winter night can scare a kid. Sounds became muffled, my thumping heart louder. I looked at my arm, felt the hairs creeping, as if the hospital room's canned air was charged.

Jesus, what's wrong with me?

When the lightning flashed again, revealing the contours of the mountains on the other side of the lake, I realized what had unsettled me: there was something *conscious* about them, something that deliberately made you stray from our trail of happiness. And once you lose your way in the mountains, gravity's going to come and get you.

"There are holes in the ice," Nick said.

I spun around to the bed.

A soft rustling sound accompanied the words that I thought I'd heard. Nick hadn't budged, except that his head had slid sideways, as if he'd turned toward the window in his sleep.

It was a figment of your imagination; save that to your hard drive.

I'm sure I coulda convinced myself of that, but then I saw that Nick's eyes were open, dark and drifting between the bandages. Awake. Despite the morphine, awake.

"Nick, you all right?" I asked. I walked over to the bed and took hold of his hand. It felt chilly. Unnaturally chilly. He didn't seem to know I was there, stared right through me to the window, his eyes searching the mountains beyond it. I'd have expected them to be dulled by the morphine, but they were unusually fierce, exhibiting uncanny concentration and reflecting the distant lightning's every spark.

Night terror, I thought. A *sort of waking dream. He's asleep, but with open eyes. It happens. He can't talk; the muscles in his cheek were all slashed. Besides, he'd tear out all the stitches*.

But then he looked right at me and spoke. "They look just like eyes. The water inside freezes and thaws, freezes and thaws."

His voice was subdued by the gauzes, but the words were articulated and clear, and I will never forget them.

A broad, horrific smile broke through from behind the mummy mask.

"And *you* will also find out what it's like to fall. To fall . . . and to fall . . . and to fall . . . and to fall."

My blood froze in my veins. That smile, I could see it in his eyes, like a stranger was staring at me, as if deep inside him, a door had opened and something else was looking out of it. And now I could see that grin on his face, too. It stretched the bandage seams tight, patches of blood blossoming on them like hideous flowers, so dark you'd swear they were black.

"Nick! Dammit, Nick, you're freaking me out!"

I grabbed him by the shoulders and shook him. His body shook like a rag doll, head rolling on his neck. "Nick! Come on, dude, say something! Talk to me, please . . ."

Stop! What are you doing? You could cause irreparable damage.

I stared at the bed in bewilderment.

Nick was asleep, as peacefully as before.

But the blotches of blood on the mask were real; the bandages were soaked with it.

The door flew open and the nurse, the one who wasn't Cécile, stormed in, aghast. She stared at the bed. I stared at her.

She stared at me.

Déjà vu.

Then I ran past her out of the room.

11

Next morning, I bought a ticket to New York at the Swiss desk in Geneva. This Airbus was bigger and disengaged itself from the surrounding ridges PDQ, but it was long after the last snowcapped summits were lost to view behind us and we were cruising westward in the sun-splashed sheer-clear stratosphere that I could detach my claws from the armrests.

Even then I didn't feel free of the mountains' clutches. That would take an entire ocean.

Landed at JFK at three EST. Phone on: sixteen missed calls, five texts, all from Louise Grevers. Didn't read them, didn't listen to my voicemail, whipped the SIM card out of my iPhone, bought an AT&T prepaid to use instead, then took an Uber into the city, where I stayed for the next three weeks.

No matter how far you've gone, or how long you've been away, home is where the door is always open, even when you're on the lam.

It was America out there, but Europe was never far away.

Just had to close my eyes and I'd see that swaddled mask.

Then I'd see those dark bloodstains appear and hear him say, *There are holes in the ice. They look just like eyes.*

MISERY

MESSAGES FROM NICK GREVERS

The pain was like the end of the world. He thought: There comes a point when the very discussion of pain becomes redundant. No one knows there is pain the size of this in the world. No one. It is like being possessed by demons.

—Stephen King

1

WhatsApp message, August 18, 8:13 a.m.

Yes, I'm OK. No need to worry. AMC in total chaos. They think it's a terrorist attack. Spooky shit!

2

Subject: More spooky shit
From: nick_grevers91@gmail.com
To: samalloveryou@icloud.com
Date: 8-18-2018 2:10 p.m.

Dear Sam,

You must have been so scared. Unbelievable, they even had it on CNN. It's beyond imagination. The hospital staff here is walking around with the dazed expression that anyone present in the scene of a major disaster would have. Aside from that, this place is like the eye of the hurricane. It's all passing me by. The only information I have I get from my iPad or the TV above the bed. There's a marathon broadcast on all the networks and I keep rereading the headline on the blue strip at the bottom: "32 Dead in AMC, Possible Bioterrorism."

At one point I looked out the window and I saw Gerri Eickhof and the NOS news crew down in the parking lot outside the cordon. I saw my window on TV. Thought maybe I should wave. With my head, ha ha.

There are crowds in front of the hospital. Gawkers. Family members of the victims seeking information. Family members of other patients, wanting to get in. I think my parents are among them, but I texted them that they'd better go home. There already have been scuffles.

Anyway, I was completely oblivious as it happened. I slept through all of it. But the aftermath was no picnic.

They've been monitoring me all day in the ICU, Sam, because they say I showed "suspicious symptoms." Don't worry. If I had any, they're gone now, because I'm back in my room and have been left to my own devices. There are rumors that they're going to relocate everyone to other hospitals, but again—no info.

What's there to say? Nothin', because no one knows jack shit, as you would say. So let me just focus on what I actually wanted to write.

I have to admit your Facebook post from yesterday made me laugh. I knew right away that it was okay to message you. A selfie in the middle of the crosswalk on 5th Avenue . . . at the exact same spot where we made the selfie last year that's framed in the kitchen, only now you're not next to me but next to Julia! Same pose, leaning back a bit; same smirk, same shades; you even thought of the Starbucks cup in your right hand (because you did it on purpose, of course). The yellow cabs and the sea of crossing New Yorkers complete the resemblance. And then the tag: #livingthelife. An inimitable Sam Avery joke, way out of line when things are already fucked up, but I've known you long enough to know it must have been your only way of attempting reconciliation. There has to be an edge to everything you do, doesn't there?

That's one of the things I like best about you.

Man, does it seem like a long time ago, the two of us in New York. In love and inseparable, Julia always following our footsteps to your favorite clubs—your sister had missed you so much! That all came back to me when I saw your post. Life seemed so nice and simple back then. Weird how one photo can unlock a whole torrent of memories and emotions.

That's why I still haven't uploaded the photos from my GoPro to my iPad. The photos of that last ascent with Augustin . . . the pictures of that place, where things went wrong. I know I still can't remember part of what happened. Not as large a part as I'd like, to be honest, but enough for some relief. Sometimes life is inadvertently merciful by concealing the most terrible things from us, like a sheet spread over a body after a terrorist attack or a plane crash.

But the mind's curse is that it *wants* to remember . . . and I'm really afraid of what will happen to me when the sheet settles and the lines underneath become visible.

Or if it's pulled away.

Everything before August 8 seems so far away. It's like the memories are someone else's. And it was only ten days ago. Ten days! Can you believe it? It feels like an eternity, in which everything has been reduced to a sort of mental confusion, drugged and disoriented and not sure of anything except for that awful pressure behind my face. Not pain, there's too much shit in my body for that, but a *pressure*, constantly building, like there's a balloon expanding in there that's about to burst. It overpowers everything else, even the disgusting smell of the cream they smear under the bandages, or the drip-feed tube in my nose. (Of this I hallucinated—I kid you not—that it had fused into me, like a plastic umbilical cord to a fetus. Ahhh, the morphine!)

Anyway, I sleep most of the time and that wears me out. My sleep is fitful and full of bad dreams. Slowly but surely, it's dawning on me that I've woken up in a nightmare in which not only does my life before August 8 seem to be that of a stranger, but in which *I* have become a stranger.

All I have to do is bring my fingers to my face: I can't recognize the shapes I feel anymore. The shapes behind the mask. Can you imagine how terrifying that is?

The doctor says that the bandages can come off in a couple of days. Like it's a treat. I'm so dreading it, Sam. Just thinking about it scares the hell out of me. That face. I haven't seen any of it yet, and I don't want to. I've been talking with a psychotherapist (well, she talks, I type) to psych up to it, but I don't think it's possible to psych yourself up for something like that.

It doesn't even *feel* like my face anymore, because of the pressure. I imagine it getting heavier and heavier and that before long it will fall off. And that it will reveal something awful. Something that lies *beneath*. That's the real sheet that will soon be pulled away, Sam, and I'm not sure I can handle it.

I wanted to tell you I don't blame you for leaving. You asked on FB if I could remember anything from what we said to each other those first days in Lausanne—nothing in fact, sorry. (You didn't break up with me without me remembering it, did you? Ha ha.) I remember you were there and that you left on the day they flew me to the AMC.

Now that I think about it . . . I wrote you notes, didn't I? Of course, on that notepad. *So* Agatha Christie. I can tell you that with my iPad my world has become a whole lot bigger. Frankly, I was bored to death, before everyone around me started dropping dead and we became international news. All of us here in the facial freaks ward wanted to go out tomorrow night to Club AIR, but I guess that's out of the question now . . .

OK, I'll stop. I'm just talking shit now. You know I always do when things get too serious.

Truth is, the muscles in my cheeks were slashed and I can't talk anymore. Looks like even with speech therapy I'll probably sound messed-up for years. I'll look like a monster.

No, if I were you I don't know if I would have had the courage to stay.

We have asked each other that question so many times, like every couple newly in love. *Would you stay with me if I ended up in a wheelchair? Would you stay with me if I got mutilated for life?* Pretty dramatic, right? I know what the morally correct answer is. The *in-love* answer. But you're young. There's so much you still want to do. There's so much you still *can* do. And me? I know what the realistic answer is and I'm more afraid of *that* than of all the rest.

Because Sam, even if I understand it, I still hope you'll come back soon. I know you'll need time to think. But please come back. I need you. I know, because of what happened to *me* last night.

I went to sleep wearing my hospital gown, but when I woke up I was standing naked in the corner of the room, my hand gripping the IV stand, which I must have rolled along with me in my sleep. My face was burning. A flaming pain that reminded me of the feeling you get when the blood flows back into your fingers after they have been frozen. Just like before . . . only ten days ago, to be exact, when Augustin and I were forced to spend the night in that crevasse, high up on that mountain, while the storm was howling over the glacier and blowing drifts of snow over the ridges. Only it wasn't my fingers now but my whole face that felt like it was thawing. God, the *pain*. And I was *cold*, Sam. So cold that my brain got misty and my body numb.

The IV stand was rattling and the solution bag swung back and forth and I only realized later that it was because I was shivering so badly.

I stood there endlessly, apathetic, cold all over. When the pain finally ebbed away and I could think clearly again I realized that strands of bandage were dangling from my face, stinking of disinfectants. I can't remember doing it, but the only logical explanation is that it was me who'd pulled them loose.

And I realized something else. In my right hand I held a small but razor-sharp piece of rock. Gneiss by the looks of it, but pointy and unusually dark. I recognized it immediately.

How did it get in my hand? Now by daylight, I still can't explain it.

The last time I saw the stone, I had put it in the inner pocket of my North Face jacket and my parents took it home with all my other stuff. I'd picked it up on the Maudit's summit, as a keepsake. Of course, the summit! We'd reached the top; I only remembered that then. We'd reached the top and then everything went wrong. No . . . by then everything had *already* gone wrong. And now I was standing here, 450 miles away and I had that summit literally in the palm of my hand. There was a terrible heaviness to it. I almost dropped it.

That was the worst. It was quarter to four in the morning and I staggered back to bed through that dark, mirrorless room, shivering uncontrollably with those bandages hanging like strips of skin off that unfamiliar, pressing face. I've never felt so miserable and alone. And scared, Sam.

Back in bed I put the stone in the nightstand and pulled the sheets up to try to get warm. Only then did I hear the muffled chatter coming from the intercom in the hall. In my ward, where patients recuperate from surgery or receive long-term care, they don't have intercoms in the rooms (to not disturb the patients, they told me later). At that time the only thing that seemed strange about it was that the noise just kept going on and on.

I called the night nurse and it took her ages to come. That was strange, too. But she changed the bandages. I told her I must have tossed and turned them off in my sleep. She gave me some more covers and a temazepam, but then she felt how cold my skin was and then I saw the worry in her eyes. And after she took my temperature it wasn't just worry anymore, it was total panic. She called, but no one came, so she went out to the hallway and started to shout.

Before long, a battalion of doctors rolled me to the ICU. After that my mind is a blank. I only remember lying there, plugged into monitors and shivering in the same bed I've been in for over a week, and as the sedative started to take effect, I thought I could hear that same storm howling in the distance, full of hollow menace.

The cold, Sam, it wasn't a normal cold. It was the same cold I felt up there. Up on the Maudit. And the cold brought back all kinds of things. Things that happened up there.

Augustin is dead, and it's that place, that *mountain*, that's to blame.

And I'm afraid that . . .

Six times I've tried completing that sentence and six times I pressed backspace to delete the whole thing. I can't write it down, not like this. I want to be able to look you in the eyes when I tell you what I think I remember. I want to see that you believe me. Because even though I may be a wreck physically, I don't want you to start doubting my mental health. Not you. That's all I got left and it isn't much. If what I think I remember is true, my own doubts are more than enough.

You want to hear something really freaky? There are rumors here that some of the other patients—the *victims*—froze to death. I mean, how could that even happen?

Come home, Sam.

I love you.

I need you. Now more than ever.

Yours,

Nick

P.S. This morning two detectives came who asked the same two questions in about fifty different ways: what did you hear or see (nothing) and how do you feel (my face is gone, how do you think I feel). I didn't say anything about the cold because it didn't occur to me that it might be important.

Maybe it isn't.

3

Subject: Re: More spooky shit
From: nick_grevers91@gmail.com
To: samalloveryou@icloud.com
Date: 8-18-2018 5:59 p.m.

Yes, I wrote that email myself and no, it wasn't recounted by a priest during an exorcism. Not by the Cloverfield monster either. Thanks for the colorful imagery. But fair enough. It's not cool of me to scare the living daylights out of you, and not tell you what actually happened.

N.

4

Subject: Re: 'My dearest Mina,-
From: nick_grevers91@gmail.com
To: samalloveryou@icloud.com
Date: 8-22-2018 12:51 a.m.

Dear Sam,

Really had to laugh at your subject line. You're such a creep. You'd come up with something to shock everyone even at my funeral.

But there is something romantic about it, don't you think? Writing each other these really long emails after a disaster like that. Like we're playing a role in our own gothic romance.

Okay, so here it is. My story. I didn't think I could piece it together so clearly because I remembered so little of it at first. But once I started writing, it all came back to me. It ended up pretty long. I'm not saying this is the whole thing, but it's most. The important bits.

But it didn't serve me well, Sam. There are things, *places*, which are better kept concealed and that mountain is one of them. But you asked me to, so I told the truth, as far as I can recall. I can only hope it doesn't make you lose faith in me.

Honestly, I'm not well at all. I feel weak, like I've been put through the wringer, and I'm terribly scared. They're taking the bandages off tomorrow. I don't want them to. Everything is going to be different. But who am I kidding? Everything already *is* different.

And there's more. I have a bad feeling that refuses to go away. It doesn't have anything to do with what's been going on here in Amsterdam. Maybe if you're like me, someone who willingly and repetitively treads on dangerous grounds, you develop a sixth sense for it, because in the mountains, you have to be constantly alert. But that sense rarely fails me. All the symptoms are there. The slight tanginess in my mouth, a subtle aroma in the air, like the smell of ozone before a thunderstorm. The tense atmosphere, the silence, the day-to-day things that for some reason suddenly seem strange—I can feel it in every corner of the hospital room. I've learned to take premonitions like this seriously, Sam. I don't know what's in store for me but I'm dreading it.

And I think it has to do with what happened up there.

I wish you were here.

Come home.
Yours,
Nick

AT THE MOUNTAINS OF MADNESS

NICK GREVERS'S MANUSCRIPT (PART 1)

I could not help feeling that they were evil things—mountains of madness whose farther slopes looked out over some accursed ultimate abyss.

—**H. P. Lovecraft**

I am responsible for the death of Augustin Laber.

Not in absolute terms, because, in a way, dying—the very last breath, when the heart stops beating—is the one thing in life that a man does utterly alone. And not even directly; there was nothing I could have done to prevent it from happening when his time came. He simply slid away from life with dizzying speed, into darkness. But I was the one who had discovered that mountain, Le Maudit, and I was the one who had suggested embarking on that fatal expedition. So I am responsible. The longer I think about it, the more I know it is true.

The moment I seal Augustin's fate comes when we finally leave the rocky section of the ridge behind us and reach the Zinalrothorn's north shoulder. I am quite shaky after what happened higher up on the crest. Besides, it is a long way down. We are still at 13,000 feet and the descent into the valley leads down a razor-sharp, steep snowy ridge above the gaping amphitheater of the north face. Much lower, it follows a long, crevassed glacier tongue, crosses endless boulder fields, and finally brings you to a trail entering the Val d'Anniviers.

Augustin eats his Amecx Fast Bar in silence, a preoccupied expression on his face. "Don't worry about it, man," I say, as laconically as possible. "It'll have been a killer tour, when we make it down."

But, like me, I'm sure he can hear that the euphoria about our successful ascent has dissipated from my voice. The temptation of danger, usually a titillating dance with an enigmatic, veiled mistress, has suddenly rebounded hard into our faces, because of his stupid mistake. Right now, he's probably thinking, *Mistakes can be fatal up here.* Or actually, *Fehler können hier oben tödlich sein*, since Augustin is German, of course.

The Zinalrothorn is a splendid peak, a tremendous monolith that, like the ruins of an ancient castle wall, towers above the surrounding glacial basins and proudly adorns the crest between the Zermatt and Zinal valleys. There is no easy route to the summit. What's more, we have decided on a solitary alternative, starting from the imposing north side, in search of the mountain's essence, which is concealed under the mysterious landscape's inviolability. It is a compelling landscape, one that gives you the illusion of being in a place where no man has ever set foot before. If you, the climber, hear the mountain's call, it will bewitch you, it will intoxicate you, and you will realize that you could fathom her only if you succumb to it—if you go *up*.

Up till this point the climb has gone well, but progress has been slow; this morning we discovered that the entire north ridge was coated with a treacherous layer of rime. The last days' brief depression in the midst of an otherwise hot stretch of summer has even resulted in a thin layer of fresh snow.

When we look up toward the ridge during approach, eagerly anticipating what lies ahead, we see banners of ice crystals swirling in the first gleaming rays of sunlight between needles and notches, which makes the mountain, crowned with a halo of frozen, silvery mist, appear to be undulating with life.

The pinnacles guarding the ridge have names that speak to the imagination. I know every single one of them from legend alone: Le Rasoir, Le Bosse, Le Sphinx. Razors, hunchbacks, and lions of Ancient Egypt that must be conquered via dark, slippery slabs and ledges and over deep precipices. We are forced to wear crampons the whole time, and instead of the route's prescribed two and a half hours from shoulder to peak, it takes us almost four. But weather is perfect—sunny and clear skies—so today, this won't pose any problems. We're the only climbers for miles around. A guide-with-client who left the hut this morning just after us had opted to retreat lower down due to the tricky conditions. The silence is immense and is broken only by the scraping of my crampons against grooves and cracks, the tinkling of carabiners, and my breathing in the thin air. We know where we are, we have only ourselves to answer for, and we're doing what makes us whole. The sense of belonging we get when we reach the summit is overwhelming.

You've often asked me why I climb mountains. You've also often asked me (I wouldn't say begged, though it's not far off the mark) to stop. Our worst argument was about this, and it was the only time I was really afraid that I would lose you. I've never been able to fully explain it to you. I wonder if it's at all possible to fully explain to someone who isn't a climber. There's an apparently unbridgeable gap between the thought that I risk my life doing something as trifling as climbing a cold lump of rock and ice . . . and the notion of traveling through a floating landscape, progressing with utmost concentration while having absolute control of the essential balance that keeps me alive and that, therefore, *lets* me live. Conquering that gap is possibly the most difficult climb in the life of any alpinist who is in a relationship. Of any *person* in a relationship, coming to think of it.

[*And what can I say? That you were right? Augustin is gone. You saw the state I'm in. How will I ever be able to face you again? We gambled and we lost; of course it seems indefensible. But I can't accept it just like that, because what happened to Augustin and me on the Maudit wasn't simply a futile mountaineering accident.*

I still can't believe that he's gone, Sam. I keep thinking about his parents. The authorities couldn't give them a body, but they also don't have a story, and that makes it all the more tragic. I'm the only one who can give them that. But isn't it better not to tell them? If you think differently after reading this, tell me, okay?]

Augustin was a young gun. It was only the second time we went to the mountains together, so you could never really know what to expect. I was still pretty bummed out about Pieter lacking the time to go anymore due to his kids, because he was always my go-to climbing buddy. I never told you much about Augustin, did I? He was six years younger than me and overambitious with youthful enthusiasm, but we clicked. He was studying political science and was active in the Grünen's youth wing. I came across him by sheer coincidence while I was searching for online photos of a remote, difficult route in the Swiss Alps which has barely been documented. But apparently Augustin had climbed it with his father a year before. We started chatting on Facebook, him with his amusing corrupted English, capitalized nouns; and the Rest is History.

Augustin was a much better climber than me. He lived in the Schwarzwald, elevation 4,000, near Feldberg village, so his lungs had a born advantage on me as far as acclimatization is concerned. But it's the felsic outcrops that jut out of the hills out there, and which he had climbed since he was a kid, that led to the inevitable difference between our characters and ambitions. Whereas I always approach the mountains with respect and an almost solemn reserve, Augustin submitted himself to them with abandon. The reservations I feel before every climb were completely foreign to him. He seemed to hold power over the mountains and he entered their arena as a lion tamer; he subdued them, subjected them to his will. Next to my insecurity, his confidence bordered on the fatalistic.

But of course that's an illusion. Mountains are untamable. What Augustin held power over was himself. It enabled him to climb the most impossible, sheer mountain faces. And he was *good*, Sam. When you saw him move in the vertical, it was with such agility, it seemed like the laws of gravity didn't apply to him. His calm self-assurance surpassed bravado. He scorned the impossible, got high on defying the fall.

Those kinds of big walls are not my cup of tea. Dangling in a harness all day and having to perform daredevil feats above a gaping abyss scares me stiff. I distrust the limits of what I'm capable of (little), the condition of the rock (is it really solid?), and the quality of the gear (I mean, after all, a harness is nothing more than woven thread). But it's mostly fear of falling. Not fear of heights; heights don't bother me. [*Remember in your dad's office on the sixty-seventh floor, looking out over Manhattan and you didn't dare come a step closer to the windows than six feet away? So cute . . .*] I always say, if you're afraid of heights, you should never aspire to be an alpinist. But if you *aren't* afraid of falling, you shouldn't become an alpinist either. It's that soupçon of angst that prevents you from doing reckless things and ending up as a page six report in the *Walliser Zeitung.*

In any case, a team is only as strong as its weakest link, so Augustin had to lower the bar to my level. So no technical wall climbing, but airy ridges instead, where you can always find solid ground under your feet in between challenging pitches. That's why I figured we wouldn't be climbing together again after last summer, but apparently he enjoyed my company enough to want to try it again. It surprised me a bit, but there you go.

A couple of days before we went up the Zinalrothorn, I asked him if he'd ever thought about the risk of a fatal accident. Augustin's answer was as plain as it was disquieting: "When I go, I go. Nothing I can do about it."

I think it was then that I got the premonition that Augustin would die young.

Our descent from the Zinalrothorn follows the same route as the way up. Carefully rappelling down the steeper pitches, deep drops left and right. The mountain harbors a cool indifference, and I become aware of its subdued power. There is always a moment when the descent starts to feel more like an escape. The solitude, pleasant at first, becomes brooding. Conversations become measured. Beauty becomes a somber threat. The mountain's spell is gone; you want to get down as quickly as possible. Fatigue starts to take its toll, but it's essential to remain fully concentrated, because the grim reality is that most accidents happen on the way down.

It happens on Le Bourrique, the donkey's back.

Le Bourrique is a horizontal traverse about fifty yards long, where the ridge is so knife-edged you have to straddle it with one leg in the Zinal basin and the other in the Zermatt basin and inch forward. Minor detail: the glacier on the west side is about 2,500 feet down at the base of a steep-sloping, hostile-looking frozen mess of snow-covered rock. The glacier on the east side is right below you, 4,000 feet down, overshadowed by a perpendicular bulwark of granite. I remember soaking up its fatal beauty on the way up; now the pitch fills me with dread.

Augustin takes the lead. I carefully belay him till the halfway point; there's a fixed anchor in the rock he can secure himself to so he can haul me in. When we sit facing each other, both secured to the bolt between us and one leg dangling on the west face and the other on the east face, it reminds me of the poster of those ironworkers on the Empire State Building. You know the one. New York, 1930s, they're lunching along an I-beam, leisurely puffing a smoke, the streets 1,000 feet below. That's how I feel now. Only it's not New York beneath me but 3,000 feet of nothing.

Augustin coils the rope into loops in order to belay me as I go ahead, and in doing so, he looks to the right, into the abyss. For a second, I think his head rolls off his body, as if the tendons in his neck simply let go of it. Then I realize it's his helmet, instead.

He'd taken it off at the summit, and when we were preparing for the descent he must have forgotten to buckle it under his chin.

"*Fuck . . . me!*" he yells.

Both of us watch it go, refusing to believe what we're seeing: a red dot getting smaller and smaller as it sails down the east face. Somewhere on the way down it hits a buttress and bounces off, blurred by its speed, then disappears.

It isn't difficult to imagine what it would look like if a body were attached to the helmet. The image is suddenly shockingly vivid. Like a child's rag doll, it tumbles away from me; a wild, desperate cry of disbelief rises out of the depth, till it too smashes into the wall. And then? Do all the bones break? Does it simply rip apart?

I look away, afraid of losing my balance, suddenly nauseous from the abyss's hypnotizing magnetism. I stagger, feel an irrational urge to flail my arms. Because there is no looking away here, there is no comfort. The drop on the left is just as disenchantingly deep. We are at the high point here; front and back is just this balance beam stretching out over certain death.

I try to pull myself together, make a vain attempt to erase the image from my mind.

"Did you forget to strap it?" I ask.

Augustin shakes his head in disbelief. "That was so fucking stupid."

"Jesus."

"No! How could I forget that!"

I shrug, more matter-of-factly than I actually feel. "Oh well, it's gone. Nothing you can do about it now. Focus, man, we've still got a long way to go."

Augustin can't get over it. That he could be so stupid as to make such a mistake. Eighty euros, that helmet had cost him. I chuckle. Ask him if he wants to go and get it. Augustin stares into the precipice, as if he's seriously considering the possibility. No way—far in the distance, the glacier lies glistening in the sun, torn and beyond reach.

I make it clear to Augustin that I want to get the hell out of here. The air is still and vigilant, the light dazzlingly bright. Far below us, the shadow of an alpine chough is circling, and I can't help feeling that we're prisoners here, above the world and isolated from everything. The image of a person falling is still imprinted in my mind. I feel my stomach clench at the thought that this is the same abyss I have to lower my legs into shortly in order to traverse the last stretch of Le Bourrique. Right now, I've gotten used to the ridge's solid comfort and I'm not looking forward to trading it in for the depths.

I wiggle back and forth, stare intently at the anchor, familiarize myself with the rock's grips. I triple-check the clove hitch and figure eights Augustin has tied into the rope. Yes, I want to get going, but a big mistake like not buckling your helmet only happens when you're at the end of your focus. And the image of me becoming that red dot disappearing into the abyss is haunting me a bit too vividly.

Two hours later we reach the shoulder: an eagle's nest on the mountain's northerly corner where the crest breaks off into the steep north face, coated with overhanging ice seracs. That's where I discover what will seal both our fates.

Our track from the way up bends to the left over a knife-edged snow ridge that is the sole access to the glacial basin below. It's almost three and the early morning's cold has made way for a lazy summer heat, which brings new dangers. In the blazing sun the snow has become mushy. It requires utmost concentration on the ridge. Our track is boot-wide with gaping drops to the left and to the right. Mushy snow means you can slip with every step.

So it's not surprising that Augustin urges me to hurry up. As he shortens the rope, I gaze at the overlapping mountain ridges in the west, gradually curving

doesn't reveal its secrets any longer. One time I lose my footing in the mushy snow but manage to retain my balance just in time with a swing of the arms. I curse myself. Concentrate, damn it. One slip and you're dead.

We quickly lose elevation, and when we finally reach the glacier, the place where the Maudit should be has disappeared behind the Grand Cornier. But the mountain has called us, and we are its subjects. We can only heed its siren song.

* * *

The plan starts to crystalize the following day around noon, when we've settled down to a typical climbers' day off.

"*Extrem brüchiges und heikeles Gelände,*" Augustin reads out from the SAC guidebook. "*Die Touren sind alle sehr langweilig und nicht empfehlenswert.*" In English: brittle terrain, very dangerous, boring and not recommended. The entire lower mountain ridge west of Moiry condensed down to a single-sentence brush-off.

Augustin remarks, "You don't need more than that to stay away."

I study the 1:25,000 Landeskarte der Schweiz unfolded before me on the grass. The description corresponds with what I see: exposed flanks, the remains of the ancient glacier, almost completely melted away, no noteworthy peaks. And what about the Maudit? The guide doesn't even mention it.

"Let's google it later," I say. I roll over and squint. "There's got to be something."

Our tent blazes in the sun in the campground in Mission, in the middle of what you might be tempted to call a battlefield. The site follows a series of terraces that gradually descend toward the brook. In the grass, the rope is drying next to the provisionally scattered crampons, ice axes, carabiners, and backpacks. The trunk of my Ford Focus is open. Augustin made fun of me because of the three corners held together with aluminum tape: two from the pileup on the Amstelkade last year and one because I'm just a lousy parker. In the car, more bags, crates, camping equipment. Our soaked thermal shirts, gloves, Smartwool socks, and Gore-Tex trousers hang from a washing line we stretched between two larches. The rest of our stuff is spread out on the grass between breakfast plates, water bottles, an empty carton of orange juice, and a piece of Swiss sausage wrapped in paper. It's chaos, but the kind of chaos I love. A chaos I can find myself in.

Languidly, we lie in the midst of it on the Therm-a-Rests we've dragged from the tent, both of us in shorts, both of us blocking the sun from our eyes with a lazy arm, enjoying the heaviness in our bodies. The whispering of the water and the buzz of the cicadas join in a wonderfully meditative chorus that rises from the valley floor. Later, a time will come when we feel up to forcing ourselves to rise and clean up the mess, and maybe then we'll repair to the campsite bar for a cappuccino or a Coke. But for now, the ground is good enough. The grass will do.

I know it's unfathomable to you, but to me, this is the epitome of relaxation.

"Can't you at least rent a chalet if you're that intent on going to the mountains?" you once asked me. "I mean, I get it, totally retro, that back-to-nature spirit, but do you also have to go cuddle the grass and load up on fungus infections? I'll pay for it, if I have to."

But that's not the point, of course. You know how antsy I get after a couple of nights in one of your favorite resorts or hotels. I need this simplicity when I'm in the mountains.

[*In my mind I hear you protesting that luxury is not the only thing that makes you tick, and then I'd say,* Really? *and then you'd say yeah okay, but that you can also be very pure, and then I'd say* Yeah, lying on a pristine, bleached five-star hotel sheet and smelling of Dior body lotion you're very pure.]

You know I enjoy our juxtapositions, our squabbles and edges, the fact that at first sight, our worlds seem so incompatible. If there's anything you can point to as to why we love each other, then it's that, and I've been treating it for three years now as an unexpected gift. There's nothing more damaging to yourself than trying to mold your lover into your own image. Instead, I respect the fact that our differences empower us, and I see each hitch as an exploration—each quarrel as a new, unconquered peak.

The mountains and you, they're two completely different worlds, and if I could lay them both bare, I'd be perfectly happy.

I admire you for letting me go up every time again, because I know how much it frightens you. The day before, as soon as my iPhone had a signal on the way down, I texted you that we were safe and sound, and then again when I was lying in my sleeping bag, too exhausted to speak: *We'll call tomorrow.*

And we did; we spoke that morning. [*That was the last time, right? Incredible, it seems so long ago.*] You ask when I'll come home. You tell me about all the things you're doing in Amsterdam, now that you have the place to yourself, about the friends you go out with. You demand that I be careful and think of you when I go climbing again and what it would do to you if my ass fell off a mountain. Subtlety was never your forte, but I think it's kind of cute. Your ways of demarcating: this is *your* obsession and this is how it affects *me*.

It was nice to hear your voice again. Especially after what happened that night.

I thought I'd go around the clock in a dreamless sleep after our climb, but I don't.

I kept seeing Augustin fall.

The red dot of his helmet, getting smaller and smaller, disappearing into the east face, his flailing limbs. What's scary is that he doesn't scream. He's absolutely silent.

I reach for him every single time, but I'm too late. Every single time my innards dive down with him.

And then suddenly I'm the one falling.

Somehow, I get disconnected from the rope, and I see Augustin's astonished face up on the ridge, I see his extended hand groping for me, but I've already gone too far. I disappear with blinding speed into the cold, shadowy mountainside, I spin into the darkness. I try to scream, but a weight crushes down on my chest, making it impossible to breathe. A primitive denial tears out of me, and in a panic I flail about. I'm trapped in my Gore-Tex coat; I struggle to extricate myself, to do something there's no point in doing—

And then I'm sitting upright, completely disoriented, my body hot and feverish and drenched with sweat.

I have no idea where I am.

What I do know in my half-asleep state is that there is a great menace looming, but at least I'm no longer falling. The pressure on my chest and arms is the down sleeping bag, which is wrapped around me like a cocoon. Only after I have thrown it off in a panic do I realize that the swishing sound is the brook, not the wind over a gaping mountainside. Shining through the tarpaulin is the light from the toilet block. The shapeless heap next to me is Augustin, safe and sound, asleep.

I need to pee. I usually hate the works: struggling out of the comfort of your sleeping bag, trying not to wake your climbing buddy when you unzip the tent, then into the cold, not to mention rain or snow. Now I don't mind. I want to be outside, away from the petrified silence of the fall. Incredible, it was so real. I look away, shake my head, but can't shake the afterimage from my mind.

Woozy, I crawl out of the tent. My calf muscles are screaming, and cold dewdrops from the tarpaulin trail down my bare back.

I stagger a while away, don't feel like walking all the way to the toilet block. I search for a spot by the embankment, pull down my boxers, and do what I have to do.

I stare at the night sky. The mountain ridges framing the narrow valley are contours. There is no moon but there is an astonishing number of stars. A solitary orographic cloud slowly weaves its way through the night. Above it, you can catch glimpses of the Milky Way. Normally, it's an endless, breathtaking scene, but now it makes me shudder involuntarily. The universe seems like a cold and hostile place, not meant for human life. Just like all these rocky and icy stairways to heaven that we keep trying to ascend. In the daytime there's a deceptive calm and a sense of security, but then, when the sun disappears behind the horizon, the isolation descends on you, the clammy certainty that if you scream, there will be no one, absolutely no one, to hear you.

The Maudit is back on my mind, the horned peak, the mountain we saw in the distance. Here and now, half naked under the chilly starry sky, I have no desire at all to climb it. Rather, the thought of it seems repugnant.

Back in my sleeping bag, I rub myself warm and fall in and out of a restless sleep. The dream doesn't come back, but at a certain point I am awake, because Augustin is sitting up and appears to be looking for something. He mumbles something in German, growingly agitated. I realize he's sleep-talking.

I sit up too and say, "Hey, it's okay. Go back to sleep."

He mumbles some more and lies down, seems to sink into sleep right away. I pull his sleeping bag up over his shoulders so he'll keep warm.

I suddenly have a strong urge to be with you and to hold you, you and your wonderfully warm body, because if I have you in my arms it's in a different place, a different time—between clean, white sheets and away from the loneliness of the mountains, in a place where I don't feel compelled to conquer them. And when we wake up, it's in each other's arms in a spacious, luxurious room awash with blazing sunlight.

THE TURN OF THE SCREW

NOTES BY SAM AVERY

The story had held us, round the fire, sufficiently breathless, but except the obvious remark that it was gruesome, as, on Christmas Eve in an old house, a strange tale should essentially be, I remember no comment uttered till somebody happened to say that it was the only case he had met in which such a visitation had fallen on a child.

—Henry James

1

'Course you never told them the whole story.

What you didn't tell all those flawless faces in the rooftop bars with floor-to-ceiling windows and color-changing mood lamps, what you didn't tell all those meticulous mugs in the underground East Village hangouts with their electronic music and killer cocktails, is that you only ever were looking at them cuz you had no choice. The so-called metrosexual offspring of media moguls and venture capitalists, with their clean-shaven jawlines, marble cheekbones, and depilated eyebrows, their protein-shake pecs and designer-clothes-clad abs, sipping mojitos and cherry blossom 'tinis—you didn't tell them you were addicted to them for all the wrong reasons. That the upper-class ass-essment was no more than your pathological trauma therapy.

One call from the Police Cantonale, one time I go into the hospital room at the wrong/worst/WTF moment, just when they're changing his bandages, and I become dysmorphophobic. The day before I didn't even know what that word meant.

So there I am in New York, sipping my Absolut Elyx Cup: vodka/cuke/mint/lime/prosecco. Within spitting distance, my baby sister, Julia, jigging with some stud who's so full of himself his LV sweatshirt doesn't even show any armpit stains. Mr. Flawless Face 1, 2, or 3 philosophizing my balls off: "Ya think people have the right to take on challenges so they can discover their true potential?"

Oyster breath, Paco Rabanne aura, thinks he can get me laid with his brazen IQ spiel. Can't get it through his thick skull that all he was to me was a mental one-click-away porn. His immaculate Ultra Brite smile a living sex-vertisement for everything gone from between *my* sheets.

What you didn't tell them is that you loved someone, someone on another continent, another bed, faceless, breathing through tubes and eating with his veins. That, for the time being, romantic candlelight dinners meant slurping Gerber through a straw. That you should thank whatever it is you believe in that the hole in his head was gone, so the food can't ooze out of it.

Or that he pushed someone off a mountain. This someone you loved, gone to all ends to discover his true potential.

No, you didn't tell them that.

Utopic/fairy-tale-ic/make you jealous till you're sick, that's how they told their stories online. Josh Fonesca, who bought his girlfriend, Sarah Hilt, a diamond-studded ring when she was lying in the ICU. Sarah Hilt, pumping music into her ears from her iPod while speed cycling the second leg of a triathlon; she didn't notice till it was too late that she'd ridden smack-bang into a wildfire. Her face and sixty percent of her body burned. Three CPRs, two hundred operations, and a proposal in Bora Bora later, she was on the cover of *People*. Like a melted human candle, saying, "Beauty Is Self-Confidence."

Or Gordon Duvall, who'd had a little accident with a buzz saw. A little accident that splattered one of his eyes and most of his nose away. A year later he hooked Billie Hamilton—blond bimbo, lingerie model—on a dating site. Bilbo, who announced on *The Ellen DeGeneres Show*, "I don't even see it when I look at him." And Gollum, sitting next to her on the couch, his one eye glancing askew from the remains of what was once a face, Ellen clearly wondering where Bilbo's seeing-eye dog was. The dating site where they met was Plenty of Fish, not exactly your hunting ground for credit card pervs. Or for the blind.

What no one ever told you is that reality is way different. All those lifestyle magazines, all those human-interest websites, they never published the stories no one wanted to know about: "I Dumped My Partner After the Fire" or "My Affairs After the Pit Bull Worked Her Over." All those message boards, all those discussion sites, all those hypocrites who declare, strictly hypothetically, "Sure I wouldn't leave him; it wasn't his *looks* I fell for."

All those PCs who forgot what it's like to be twenty-four. They pounce on you like a pack of wolves when you say mutilation sucks all the sex out of a person.

That New York retro club jam-packed with walking Tinder portraits—Mr. Flawless Face 4, 5, or 6 infiltrating my personal space, throwing one of my chakras out of whack, thinking he'll wake up next to me the following morning, probably never experienced disappointment his whole life, Nietzsche-ing me: "Your future. Tell me about your future. Today is only tomorrow's story."

And I was digging into my Good Evening Spitfire: Ancho Reyes/mezcal/coconut milk/cold coffee. God knows where Julia'd disappeared to, but at this stage nothing could faze me, not my walking/talking cover boy/Descartes's menthol mouth fumes, not even that Julia had gone AWOL on me to get speed-dated by semi-bi Lenox Hill. The booze buzz started to do its thing: spin my head, hot flash me. Buddha-Bar Breakbeat or whatever trance bass they were playing shoved into the background and my future, in all its conceivable contingencies, into the limelight.

I couldn't deal with it.

I tried to, I really did. Confronting myself with the grotesque, the tragic, in all its deformities. I googled it all. Facial disfigurement. Orogeny. Scars. Crevasses. Burns. Eroded rocks. Trypophobia skin conditions. Pit craters. Elephantiasis. Mountain streams.

I couldn't, just couldn't bear to look. Seeing those pics pop up made my flesh creep. I had to get up and pace, cover the screen with my hands. Know what I mean?

All those deformed faces.

All those deformed landscapes.

Zap: *Nick's* mutilated face the exact wrong-time split-second I go into the room. The mountains across the lake from the hospital window.

Mountains had bitten Nick's face off.

And then you thought it was over, that life wouldn't kick you when you were down, but then came the reaction to your reaction, and then the reaction to *that*: an avalanche of emotions that swept away everything in its path. Was I really that superficial? Such a degenerate dick? Why wasn't I more Josh Fonesca-ish? Why couldn't I be more like Billie Hamilton? Fonesca bought a Tiffany ring while the love of his life was fighting for hers like a smoldering ember, and what do I do? Flee to New York. My crib, my crowd, my crew. My urban watering hole for the dry spells. I came here to wallow in my comfort zone but, instead, was engaged in a futile attempt to escape my discomfort zone. The avalanche thundering behind me, hurtling off the mountain at me, dogging me even here in the streets of Manhattan. Even here, even here, even here.

As Mr. Flawless Face 7, 8, or 9 oozed his sweat on me, I chugged my Sunset Spice: rum/curacao/pomelo/tarragon/orange chili pepper. My own sweat dripping from my forehead into my eyebrows, from my neck hairs down the collar of my T-shirt, coloring the cotton with hot, damp stains.

Julia emerged from the crowd and said, "Easy on the cocktails, baby brother. You don't look so good."

I said, "I'm okay."

And Mr. Flawless Face number whatever, Harry or Niall or Liam, who cares: "Tell me about the most crucial moment in your life. The one defining moment that sparked all others."

So here's Julia eyeing me, secretly relishing the possibility of me spilling my guts. Knowing the most crucial moment in my life was also the most crucial moment in hers.

"Come on, let's go," she said, when she realized that if I opened my mouth it would only spew bad stuff. The kind of bad stuff you get from too many cocktails, head spins, and stomach cramps. Not even Zayn's or Louis's snazzy L'Envin sweatshirt deserved that. "Jack off on someone else," Julia said to the flabbergasted stud as she tugged me to the door. "This one's mine."

Score. Next to my sis, I'm a total bush leaguer.

This is why I came to New York. Even if I fuck everything up, when the smoke clears, there'll be Julia Avery. My sister, my panacea.

You know what they never tell you about New York? That the city borders on an enormous wasteland. The Big Apple's skin is an illusion, a thin layer of cultivated civilization, right behind which rises the wilderness of the Highlands, the Catskills, and the Adirondacks. Few New Yorkers are aware that, at this exact spot, two completely different worlds converge. The eternal north wind whistling down Fifth Avenue? Updraft caused by the skyscrapers, was what you always thought. Till you realized that the city is an island in the estuary of a primeval glacial valley. From Ellis & Avery, my dad's office on the sixty-seventh floor, I now saw for the first time that the mountain range of bricked architecture flows seamlessly into rocky precipices that tower above the Hudson, just beyond the George Washington Bridge. That the rocky mantle inching closer and closer underground had suddenly torn through the soft upper layer, forming outcrops here in Central Park. Eons-old geology smuggling the wilderness back into the city. Like it was growing. Infiltrating the city. Taking it over.

And behind that? Endless woods of rotting scrub you could stray through and lose your way in, endless hills where who knows what could happen. Okay, not exactly virgin territory, not exactly Manifest Destiny, but what they never tell you is that a coupla years ago, just two hours out into the wilderness, three people were killed by a mountain lion. What they never tell you is that a coupla years ago, just two hours into the wilderness, a complete village had disappeared—Black Rock or Black Hill or Black Spring or whatever it was called. And then you in turn never told anyone that the most crucial moment in your and Julia's lives had happened up there, in those hills, in that wilderness. You never told anyone that the last time you were in the Catskills was the last time you'd ever wanted to be in the Catskills.

You could cross an ocean, you could be fifteen years older, but the wilderness always catches up with you, because it's inside you.

2

So, next day, I drove north, out of the city where I'd spent only five days. At least, the moment I was sober enough to muster up the courage to have my dad's top-down Corvette Grand Sport valeted out of the garage on East Sixty-Seventh and to slip behind the wheel without the risk of a $60,000 insurance claim.

This was *before* Nick and I'd gotten back in touch—before CNN reported, the following day, about all the people killed in Amsterdam and I'd texted him, all het up. I missed him so much right then, it made my stomach turn. Not the Nick lying in the AMC, all wrapped up, half his face gone, not the stranger I was afraid of, but the alive-and-kicking Nick from three weeks back. Nick, filing the spikes of his crampons in the epicenter of a maelstrom of climbing gear that covered just about the whole top floor of our rented house in Amsterdam-Zuid. Early August, hot, Nick the shirtless-all-day type, broad shoulders bronzed from our ten days in Ibiza in July and *aye-aye-aye*, more eye candy for me. Me with my e-reader in the door to the roof garden, a pillow tucked behind my back, iced tea in the shade. Ramses, who'd snuggled up on Nick's down sleeping bag, gazing at us with his inscrutable poker face, managing to look simultaneously bored, annoyed, and self-satisfied.

"The question is," I said, "why would you *not* appease me with a Ted Baker bag?"

"Appease? I thought you were so independent."

"Oh my god. Those shades . . . Is that what you wear up there?"

"Uh-huh."

"Sometimes it's better to shut up. To just shut up and let the moment settle over you. Hear that, Ramses? The silence?"

Ramses looked away with a snigger and twitched his ears. Nick cracked up. "What's wrong with my sunglasses?"

"Can't you see?" I put down my e-reader and threw up my arms. "They're *so* . . . 'Come one, come all to our lovely and quaint hiking club.' But you're kind of the hiking club type, too, to tell you the truth. You probably got a pair of khaki shorts and Nordic walking poles."

"I've got my Black Diamonds, baby," Nick said with a deep Elvis baritone, as he expanded his chest and showed me his poles.

Nick, Ramses, our pad in Amsterdam—crystal clear flashes in an otherwise endless universe.

"Boy!" I laughed loud, mocking. "You're so provincial, don't you think?"

Shrug.

"Aww," I said.

I reached over the crates packed with camping gear and patted his arm. Nick pretended to lash at me with his poles.

"Yeah," I continued, "resort to physical violence. *So* alpha. Sly way of shifting attention from what this is really all about: whether or not you'll pay me back with a Ted Baker bag, for the fact that you're abandoning me again and laying your life on the line for that stupid hobby of yours."

"So, if I got it right, I can buy off my climbing vacation with a bag."

"Uh-huh," I said, nodding firmly.

"Like a kind of life insurance."

"Exactly."

"Because that will alleviate my death."

"You got it."

"Because then you'll have a Ted Baker bag."

"I wouldn't want you to miss seeing me being profoundly happy, even for a bit."

"Jerk," he laughed. "You're bad, you know that?"

My parents in New York, Pa and Ma Avery, you don't have to be Sherlock Holmes to have deduced by now that they're more than just a tad affluent. Although a large chunk of Hugh Avery's capital is in real estate and equities, he still made sure Julia and I had an ample scholarship that didn't exactly allow us to lead a jet-set life but sure brought us pretty damn close. "But it's a one-off," he had said, when he bestowed it to me on my eighteenth birthday. "It's enough to get you through your whole study, and if you're smart, a lot longer, but if you squander it all in one blow, don't come crying to me. I want you to plan your own finances and be more sensible than your dad was."

Wealth is riskier than poverty for your average eighteen-year-old—that was the trap he'd set for me. The only trap obscenely rich parents can set for their children in order to make them independent and not irreparably asshole-ish. I fell into it with my eyes open. For two years I was totally out of control. You can probably imagine what those two years musta looked like, and if not, picture Curaçao and Cannes and Macao, then picture 'tinis in casinos, trippy sex in limos, and you're getting warm.

Then I met Nick and he managed to tame me. Three months in Amsterdam turned into a year, and a year turned into indefinitely. Hugh Avery's scholarship was so dried up that I was then forced into a strict multiyear planning regime, but thanks to my savings account, I could afford not only our house in Zuid, where we've been living together for almost a year and a half (Nick, since working for Lonely Planet, persistently paying his share of the rent—nice of him, ain't it?), but also, when the mood struck, every Ted Baker bag that tickled my fancy. Still, one of my favorite pursuits was seducing Nick into showering me with expensive gifts, especially to get him thinking he could prove his love for me by buying me pricey goods. Men get a kick out of that. Even men so way up on cloud nine they're oblivious to social protostandards like these—even men like Nick.

"Still, it's not so cool of you to confront me with it like this," I said, pointing to the chaos in the hall. "Repeat after me: 'It's not cool of me to desert you again.'"

"It's not cool of me to desert you again," he repeated obediently. "Even though in April you couldn't wait till my flight left. And when I came back home you beat Ramses's gloomy-face record."

"Yeah, well, it's my right," I said, feigning hurt. Cute, comparing me with the cat. "And anyway, the thing that worried me most then was that you'd forget your MacBook charger somewhere and miss your deadlines. What worries me now is that you'll plummet to your death."

"You know how careful I am."

"And you know that not all the risks are up to you. If you come back dead, I swear I'll spit on your grave."

Nick pushed away his backpack and looked at me. "I wish you'd join me for once. That I could share what I'm looking for up there with you."

"'Hey, Sam, wanna go see some boulders? No Wi-Fi or mochaccinos, and when we get to the top I'll hold you up like Simba and everything the light touches is our kingdom.' Sure. Wanna go snorkeling with piranhas?"

He tilted his head. "Hakuna-matata."

I smirked. "That's not enough."

But that gaze, I saw something in it that threw me off. His eyes looked into me, distant and aloof. I shivered suddenly, despite the heat. Those eyes, bright green—there was a major loneliness in there, but next to it happiness too, so profound it almost blew your head off, so profound I could never reach it, would never be part of it. I'd seen that gaze before, and it always shook me up, because it shoved the question in my face: *How well do we actually know the one we love?* Like every time Nick was getting ready to go to the mountains, this creature would awaken in him, not a person but a force of nature, an entity that was always hiding and that, now that I'd caught a glimpse of it, I didn't want to let slip through my fingers.

And to tell you the truth, it got me hot. Much as I hated Nick's climbing sprees, after three years together, the first honeymoon more or less behind us, this elusive creature in him felt powerful, forbidden, like a secret lover I could hook up with for a quick, heated affair.

So, before I knew it, Nick had heaved me up and pressed me against our bedroom's doorpost, my hands around his waist and his hands—check this out—gripping both ice axes, gently tweaking the back of my neck with the spikes, forcefully pulling me against his body, those cold, metallic teeth digging into my neck, and goose bumps, oh Jesus, all the way down my spine.

"Those axes make you *so* unsexy," I breathed into his lips. But I was bullshitting, and he knew it.

"You can't mount me without them."

"No way, Nick. That line is even worse than E. L. James."

"A hundred million readers can't be wrong."

Ramses sauntered down the stairs, tail in the air, but he didn't need a sixth sense to know what was about to happen. As always, he made a show of letting us know he had better things to do.

3

I drove along the Hudson and through rolling hills I remembered only vaguely, till I was close up to the Catskills. Suddenly they were there, rugged and depressing and unchanged. It was like I was driving back in time. My memories of Huckleberry Wall had blurred with the years, but when I turned off the interstate and followed the Onteora Trail westward, they came back with a cold clarity that caught me by surprise. These mountains were less rugged and sinister than the ones I'd left behind in Europe, but even with the August sun doing overtime, they gave me the chills.

Back then the mountains were white, not green. It was the dead of winter and the storm was wailing around the house. The clouds and the blizzard had obscured the mountains and that only made matters worse.

I thought, *Turn back. Don't disturb the past.*

Thought, *Fly to Amsterdam. Buy a Tiffany ring.*

But I drove on.

I wondered if I could still find the place, but it was like I was on autopilot.

I got off the main road at Phoenicia, crossed the creek, and drove past the old lodge where Grandpa and Grandma always took us for a blueberry waffles breakfast, every time we came to stay. Weird, since Grandma made them better than anyone could. After that, the road curved sharply upwards through the woods, cottages concealed on both sides, and gradually transformed into a track. I remember it always looked like it would dead-end farther up, but it never did.

Past the last lot that marked the beginning of civilization, the track took a sharp curve to the left onto a dirt road Grandpa always called the Panther Mile. It climbed all the way up to the end of the world, to Huckleberry Wall.

The Cabin in the Woods.

The Last House on the Left.

A mossy wooden beam was now suspended over the sharp left in the track that always forced us to almost stop before continuing the jolty crawl up. The path beyond that was overgrown. Duh, because there was nowhere to go to up there anymore; the Panther Mile had dissolved into the Catskill Park trail system. I parked the Corvette at the edge of the lot and wondered what to do next.

Last time here was fifteen years ago, but nothing about my spoiled New York experience had changed. The sounds in the woods a low-rent "Sounds of Nature" meditation mix. The smell a discounted Fairway Market toilet freshener. My nature savvy drip-fed by Spotify and pine-scented cleaners.

I was going to do that movie-macho move where someone leaps over and out of the sporty convertible, but my hands were trembling like crazy, so I just used the door.

The grounds were exceptionally green and the farm was in good repair. I didn't know if the same people were still living there after all those years, but the apple tree was still there. I didn't have a plan, not even a name, just a memory. In that memory, they were already old. But that didn't mean much. When you're nine, anyone older than your mom looks ancient.

I halted halfway across the lawn because I heard the prattle of a local radio station. The screen door opened and an elderly lady holding a transistor radio came out on the porch. She was preceded by a house dog that first almost tripped her, then came pattering toward me, barking inquisitively.

The lady must have been in her seventies, but I recognized her immediately by her apron and long silvery hair. She turned off the transistor, telescoped the antenna, and slid it into her apron. "Down, Zeus!" she called. "Don't worry, young man, he won't do anything as long as you don't either. Can I help you?"

Zeus was medium size, brown; anything else, you decide—I'm no good with breeds. I patted his head, then hooked my shades in my shirt collar. "Maybe you could give me one of those apples from your tree, like you always used to."

She squinted her eyes and walked down the veranda stairs. "Yes, I know you . . . Remind me?"

"I had a little sister. And a grandfather and grandmother."

"Heavens! You're Herb and Dorothy Avery's grandson!"

I smiled. "Sam. Sam Avery. Happy to see you again."

She clapped her hands. "Sam Avery! My god, you sure have grown! Last time I saw you, you were still a little tyke." She approached me and not only shook my hand but also clasped it tightly. I could feel the bones and fragility in her fingers. I realized the woman was probably in her eighties instead, but those fingers were distinctly peppy. Zeus wagged his tail. "I wish I could give you an apple, Sam, but I'm afraid they won't be ripe until September."

"What's your name again, if you don't mind my asking?"

"Abigail Bernstein, but—"

"Auntie Bernstein! Of course! That's what Grandma always called you!"

"Bingo," she smiled. "Unfortunately, Uncle Bernstein left us six years ago, but I still keep my own chickens. What brings you all the way up here, Sam?"

I didn't know exactly what to say.

"I'm living in Europe now. I can't often . . . Well, I happened to be in New York. I thought maybe I'd go for a ride."

It was lame, and old Mrs. Bernstein saw right through it. She tilted her head and gazed at me. I felt like a doofus, ashamed because I wasn't really sure myself why I had come here.

Eventually I came up with, "I haven't been here since . . . well, since ages ago."

"I still remember when your whole family came here to scatter Herb's ashes—your grandfather's ashes, I mean. I was really glad I could take part, because I'd only seen his obituary the day before. I think your grandparents must have been living in Newburgh for three years at the time, and we weren't that much in touch anymore, like most old neighbors." Her face showed genuine regret, the kind you see only in people at the epilogue of their lives and after they've been given some kind of SparkNotes clarification of all that came before. "It was a beautiful ceremony. The woods were so full of life that day; all the birds were chirping. Remember?"

"I wasn't there," I said softly.

"You weren't? Why not?"

Hot flush behind my face.

"Heavens. Oh, heavens. That means the last time you were here must have been . . ."

"After the fire."

"Goodness gracious, I didn't know." The old lady's expression became firm, and she wiped her hands on her apron. "Know what? How about I quickly change, then walk with you to where the house used to be. That is, if you don't mind walking slowly. I'm afraid I'm not as strong as you are, at my age."

I wasn't sure I even wanted to go up there. Just the thought made my guts turn. As far as I remembered, the track stretched up the mountain for miles and miles before it brought you to Huckleberry Wall. Miles and miles back into the past. Nothing I looked forward to. I vaguely recalled we used to go up there only in Grandpa's 4WD . . . except for that last time.

That last time, when we sleighed down the mountain.

I told her the path was way too long for walking.

"Not at all. I walk there every day with Zeus here. Usually I turn back halfway, because it's quite a climb. But it shouldn't be a problem for you. It couldn't be more than a mile."

"The Panther Mile," I said.

She looked at me in surprise.

"That's what my grandpa always called it."

"Ha, I forgot that! The Panther Mile. That's a good one. It's been a long time since we saw any panthers around here. Sooner or later, they all go back into the mountains, Sam."

We both stopped talking and I mulled over her words.

Then Mrs. Bernstein said, "No wonder the track looked longer that night. Maybe it *was* longer—that's how those kinds of tracks tend to behave when it counts. Wait, I'll be right back."

She hurried inside, leaving Zeus with me. The dog panting at my feet, tilting his head, gazing at me, tongue hanging out. Smiling. Insinuating I must be really stupid.

4

To say I worked up a sweat keeping up with Mrs. Bernstein would be pushing it, but I gotta admit, checking my pace was no option either. It wasn't just her hands that were peppy; it was her total constitution. Zeus trotting half a football field ahead of us, filling the woods with barks. The whole time I'm thinking, *Where are we* really *going?*

"Tell me how it all started," she said.

With a story, of course. Everything always starts with a story.

The last time I was in the Catskills, the last time I was in Huckleberry Wall. The night it burned down. Picture it: the perfect mountain cabin, the perfect sleepover jaunt at Grandpa and Grandma's. Snow clinging to the windows. The snow on the windows, the storm screaming to get in, and my sweet ol' Grandpa telling ghost stories by the fire. The fireplace fire, I mean.

I told Mrs. Bernstein that when the hearth was burning it got so hot in Huckleberry Wall that it totally zonked you. Julia, only six at the time, flaked out on Grandma's lap. Grandma knitting her scarf, and all you could hear on a night like that was the needles' cozy tapping and the crackling of the fire. The wind battering the roof. My grandpa's oldster voice. They say you forget the voices of the dead first, but I know exactly how my grandpa's voice sounded.

It's his face I don't remember.

Every time I try to picture it, I can only see a black hole. Smoke coming out.

What I didn't tell Mrs. Bernstein, cuz I couldn't find the words, was that my childhood up here was loaded with stories. Walking up, me and Mrs. Bernstein on the Panther Mile, mounting the trail to Huckleberry Wall, these stories surrounded us in a wide circle. I remember when I was a kid, I could see hidden faces in the wooded hilltops around Huckleberry Wall. The hilliest and highest of them all, enshrouded in snow in winter, resembled an attacking bird of prey, the lower peaks to the left and right the tips of its spread wings. The spying bird eyed our backs when Julia and I were sledding down the slope behind the house or when I was helping Grandpa chop wood.

There were secrets and stories buried in these mountains, but basically they were *good*.

The havoc that one flame, one spark, one story can wreak.

"Tell us a real ghost story, Grandpa," I said that evening. That evening of snow and wind. Snow and wind and fire. I was sitting at his feet, on the carpet, a deep pile and *highly flammable* carpet, in my PJs, stuffed animals in formation, spouting some groundbreaking supplication for mansions with blood-dripping ceilings, manors in which nonexistent babies cried all night, manses where a body covered in stab wounds would materialize on the cellar stairs. My healthy American taste even then shaped by HBO and the six o'clock news.

I said, "Julia's asleep, so now you can make it *really* scary."

But Grandpa told me a totally different type of story, and those are the ones that leave the deepest impression.

"Once upon a time, long ago," he commenced, "in Phoenicia, at the bottom of the Panther Mile, as the sun hung large and red on the horizon, a party was under way."

"Is this a true story?"

"Sure it's a true story," he said. "All the stories I tell you are true. Everyone was invited, even the Hermit, who lived right here, high up the mountain. The townspeople didn't know if the Hermit would come, since he was an odd one and nobody had ever penetrated these woods on the slopes high enough to reach his house. Scroungers and berry pickers swore that they had never come across any living soul up in those mountains but had seen only fleeting shadows that skimmed over the treetops and obscured the sun, and had heard only the sound of mighty wings."

And fifteen years later, Mrs. Bernstein recited, "*There is a Catskill eagle in some souls, that can dive down into the blackest gorges, and soar out of them again to become invisible in the sunlight.*" She said, "I'm not sure I'm quoting it right, but it's from *Moby-Dick*. It goes on, something about it always flying higher in the mountains than the birds in the plains. But I think I like that first bit the best."

"Are there still eagles around here?"

"Oh, certainly. Sometimes I give them a morsel of liver; that's their favorite. From my hand. Aren't the woods lovely today?"

And I thought, *A morsel of liver.*

And we were higher now, Mrs. Bernstein's farm no longer in view. Walking the mile that, fifteen years ago, had determined that I couldn't be with Nick today. My forehead wet with sweat, my head full of a sound like wind clattering a sail, the sound of beating wings. Thinking, *Better not look back.* Thinking, *Do* not *look back.*

Mrs. Bernstein asked, "Are you all right, Sam?"

And whaddya think? 'Course the Hermit came, in Grandpa's story. Grandma was knitting her scarf, her lips curled in a vague smile. Julia fast asleep. Me listening to Grandpa's words: "He was an old man in a dark brown cloak, snow-white hair, though the funny thing was that no one could actually see his face. But no one cared, because the Hermit had given the townsfolk the gift of fire. You should know, all this happened in a time before humans had discovered fire. Before that, the people in Phoenicia had lived in clay, and fire made it possible for them to rise out of it, and what's more, now the party could go on all evening.

"Before long, torches and hearths were lit in the banquet hall and the delicious smell of roasting meat wafted through the air. The townsfolk had also prepared a gift, but among them was a handsome and strong young man called Prometheus, and he played a trick on the Hermit. Prometheus served him two dishes, one with a delicious tender steak hidden in disgusting-looking ox tripe, the other with the ox bones hidden in glistening roasted grease. Naturally, the Hermit chose the latter. The townsfolk ate up all the meat, laughing and slapping each other and Prometheus on the back.

"A shrill scream pierced the hall. Wind blew from all sides and it became dark all at once, because the torches and fireplaces had been blown out. A woman screamed, 'Dear Lord, he is the mountain! He is rising from the ashes!' And in the pale moonlight no one could see exactly what she meant, nor did she ever utter a single word about it again. But the furious Hermit was gone and had taken the fire with him, and he kept it hidden from them forever."

A gnarl or an ember must have popped out of the hearth and caused the rug to catch fire, I told Mrs. Bernstein. That's what *their* theory was, at least. I said, "We were all sleeping. By the time the smoke alarm had woken us up, we only had enough time to save ourselves. The living room was ablaze, and within a minute you could barely breathe because of the thick smoke, and the fire was already spreading to the roof. The cabin was lost."

"How awful! So fast! Fire is such a dangerous thing, Sam. There's a reason they say, 'If you play with fire, you get burned.'"

"Grandma screamed. I'd never heard her do that. Can you imagine what it's like to hear your grandma scream?"

"My god. Poor thing! It must have been terrible. And was it your grandfather's idea to put you on the sleigh? To put all three of you on the sleigh and drag you down the mountain?"

"Yes. He tried getting the car out of the garage, but it was too late."

She shook her head in disbelief. "He was as strong as an ox, your grandfather. It was an act of heroism that he managed to bring you all to safety before you froze to death. Because, my lord, that night was freezing! Many people would get lost in that kind of cold."

I shrugged. "All he had to do was follow the mile down."

"Oh, but there are other ways of getting lost up here. I still remember what you looked like when you knocked on our door. It was like there were four snowmen on the porch, two big ones and two small. My, it was such miserable weather, with all that nastiness falling from the sky! The snow, the birds . . ."

"There weren't any birds," I said.

"Oh yes, there were. They must have been drawn by the fire, dozens of them, big ones too, and they spiraled above the place where Huckleberry Wall was burning. Like they were searching for prey."

"There's no way you could have seen that," I said, hearing how unsteady my voice was. Something was wrong. With a shock, I realized that Mrs. Bernstein was neither muzzy nor senile. "You couldn't even see the treetops, you know. Because of the blizzard and the dark. And you were never up there, that night."

"Are you sure? That's not how I remember it. Some nights I'm still there."

And Mrs. Bernstein walking beside me. Walking beside me on the Panther Mile, and wild horses couldn't have dragged my gaze in her direction. Only her bony silhouette in the corner of my eye. I stared dead ahead, to where Zeus had preceded us, but if he was there, I couldn't see him. The path through the woods was silent as the grave.

Prometheus didn't take it lying down. No way. Fifteen years ago, in Huckleberry Wall, just before it went up in flames, Grandpa told me, "One day the crafty Prometheus said to the other townsfolk that he was brave enough to venture climbing up there and stealing the fire, so he could give it back to mankind. Of course, he was ridiculed, but Prometheus still clambered up the mountain, and when he got to the Hermit's house he found it empty. The Hermit was nowhere in sight. But the fire was burning in the hearth, and Prometheus stole it in a giant fennel stalk.

"When, holding his torch, he had reached the base of the Panther Mile, the people of Phoenicia flocked around him. The crowd broke out with a cheer and carried him in celebration into the town. Prometheus had become an instant hero. For days, they feasted, because with fire they could now roast meat and forge iron and heat water, and civilization rose up from the clay.

"But in the midst of it all, they didn't notice the pitch-black shadow soaring down from the mountain. They didn't hear the bird's hoarse croaking, not until handsome Prometheus was nabbed by razor-sharp talons and, legs flailing, carried into the sky, higher than the tallest trees, higher than the church's spire. It was a giant eagle called Ethon, and Ethon took him to the top of the highest mountain. There, Prometheus was left exposed to the elements. Wearing only a loincloth, he was chained to the rock, and the eagle ripped out his liver and gobbled it down with gulping, birdlike jerks of his head. And—"

"Herb, you'll give the boy nightmares," Grandma broke in, giving him a piercing look over her knitting.

"But that's how it went, Dorothy. You know that. And not just once, because Prometheus's liver grew back every night, and the next day the eagle would return and rip him open again with his claws and devour the bloody organ. Sometimes he only used his beak to tear the flesh from—"

"Herb!"

"It's okay, Grandma. I don't mind," I said, not mentioning that my mind was still on the loincloth, the loincloth I saw my handsome hero wearing, chained to the rock.

The loincloth. That's what did it.

And that's how I remember the end of the story. Prometheus was punished forever for messing around with powers greater than himself. Then we went to sleep and the cabin burned down.

Like so many stories, the Prometheus myth is a tale that's destined to pop up in your life at different occasions, and the next two times it happened really got to me. The first time was during Ancient History at Wagner Middle in New York, because it dawned on me that there was apparently an original that *didn't* take place in Phoenicia. The second was during Ancient Greek, my linguistics optional during my sophomore year in Amsterdam, because I was old enough to recognize the metaphors.

But that wasn't the reason why, both times, my heart was thumping my ribs to smithereens in class. Not the reason why here, fifteen years later, almost at the top of the Panther Mile with Mrs. Bernstein, almost at the place where Grandpa's story ended, sweat spouted out of my fingertips and earlobes, as I whispered to myself, "Don't look back, Sam. Do *not* look back. Believe me, you don't want to."

But I did look back, and when I saw the Panther Mile disappear downhill through the tunnel of trees, I remembered what it had been like.

That night, that epic plunge, the night Huckleberry Wall was burning and the Panther Mile stretched out for miles and miles. Grandma at the back of the sleigh, whimpering softly, her arms wrapped around me, my arms wrapped around Julia, holding on tightly, bundled up in woolen blankets against the biting wind and the snowstorm. We plowed on for hours and hours, till my cheeks were frozen numb and I was scared like never before. All I could make out was that large, dark figure tugging us down the hill—black, pitch-black, so black it was a blotch in the night, not a real person. It wasn't Grandpa,

I knew, because it had no face and smoke was rising from its shoulders and skull. It was the Hermit who pulled the sleigh down the mountain that wintry night. The Hermit was the devil. And yes, there were birds, great, mythical birds you couldn't see, only hear. Any minute, I expected them to swoop down, unimaginably fast, right through the bare branches. Then I would see eyes glowing like hearth embers and the ripping would begin, the ripping and the flapping and the screeching and the gorging.

And that's why I never went back into the mountains, I told Mrs. Bernstein fifteen years later.

That descent, that night, it was the darkest night of my life, and it was a descent that went a whole lot deeper than back to the civilized world.

Mrs. Bernstein, the woman who, together with her husband, had taken care of us back then at the base of the Panther Mile, the woman who was old even then, I still didn't dare look at her.

It was safer to hold her in the corner of my eye.

Her voice, I could still hear it. But it's the faces you forget first. What if I looked and she had no face?

"It was extremely cold that night," I heard Mrs. Bernstein say, a trace of sorrow in her voice. "When you get older, once that cold settles into your bones, it never really goes away anymore. Now I'm always cold. How's Dorothy these days, by the way?"

My grandfather died three years after the fire in Huckleberry Wall; my grandmother five years ago, in 2013. I don't know when Mrs. Bernstein died, but judging by what she said, it must have been sometime in between.

5

"Grandma still walks the Panther Mile," I said. "Don't you ever meet each other here?"

I turned around. I wasn't surprised to see that Mrs. Bernstein was gone. The path was still. So still I wondered whether she'd been there at all. Somewhere in the woods, a woodpecker was tapping. For a brief moment, I felt a primordial chill in the marrow of my spine, then I shrugged it off.

I decided it didn't matter.

What mattered was not what I'd find if I walked down the mile again, or whether the Bernstein farm, on the edge between wilderness and civilization, was empty or had been sold to new owners.

What mattered was where I ended up: just up ahead, the trail would reach a piece of fallow terrain, which in fifteen years' time had probably been retrieved by nature. Where Huckleberry Wall's foundations had once been, budding spruces would be growing, taller now than me. Nature would have obliterated any traces we left, and that thought was more frightening than the idea that I had walked up in the company of a dead woman.

Suddenly I had trouble breathing. My throat got so tight no air came through.

I didn't want to see it. I stood there, frozen, told myself it was now or never. Then I ran. I whizzed down the Panther Mile. I fled my childhood's ghosts, and with each step I imagined them becoming less real.

6

Cuz what I told Mrs. Bernstein—don't tell me you thought that was the whole story. Reality check: not even half of it. Back to Huckleberry Wall, the night of my grandpa's story, that night fifteen years ago, the nine-year-old me as restless and tormented as the tempest howling around the roof. The night that Prometheus haunted me and I wanted to, dunno, make him come alive. Prometheus, carrier of fire, my proto cult hero, my first role model, my inaugural man crush.

The last night of li'l Sam Avery's innocence.

Or maybe not so innocent after all, cuz there I was, solo and out of the sack, Julia and Grandpa and Grandma dead to the world; butt naked, barring the two pillowcases I'd knotted together as a loincloth. Prometheus in my fledgling fantasy. There I was, identifying myself with my object of desire. Giving my overdue, twisted Oedipus complex free rein, cuz let's face it, my mom couldn't hold a candle to my superhero image. The loincloth so tight it didn't matter I hadn't discovered jacking off yet.

Hail Prometheus, a scrawny, nine-year-old, sexually aroused little narcissist.

And Nick wonders where my penchant for role-play comes from. Or bondage. As a nine-year-old, I'd already pined for the scene in which I'd be chained to the boulder, at the eagle's mercy.

Didn't happen.

Wide-awake in the middle of night, I sneaked into the living room, which was still warm from the smoldering hearth. The orange glow flickering over Huckleberry Wall's gleaming pinewood panels. My retinue waiting in attendance on the carpet: Dr. Jingles, Twig, and Porcupiny. My teddy bear, my cuddled-to-rags indefinable whatever, and my what-the-name-implies.

This was my version of humanity.

And woe betide mighty Prometheus, addressing his cortege with open arms, doing his best not to cringe every time the gnarly branches struck the roof outside: "Worship me, oh subjects, that I will raise thee out of the clay!"

Totally full of himself, totally tripping on his rig-out. As early as that.

All those child psychologists, all those behavioral therapists they dragged you to, you didn't tell them that story, cuz even though you still couldn't understand those visceral feelings of incipient sexuality, you did savvy that this was the kind of secret you'd better keep to yourself.

I said, "I, the mighty Prometheus, shall bring you fire."

You think you know what's coming? It's way worse. Trust me.

So I'm poking the ashes with the tongs, staring at the cinders swirling up the chimney. Show me a kid who isn't at least a bit obsessed with fire. I pick up a charred log, observe it, blow on it till it starts flaming, the glare immediately flickering in my eyes and on my smooth, bare skin; me, an imp in the night.

Humanity watched as I brought them fire; it was the last they'd ever see.

As I held the log above them, it disintegrated with a *pffft.* Porcupiny was the first to catch fire. I swear I tried rescuing her, but I was so much in shock that I beat the stuffing out of the poor thing with the tongs, which only caused the embers to sputter all over the place.

One spark and your childhood needs a completely revised, limited edition republication.

One spark and not a single story you ever tell is the whole story.

The moment the fire took over, I realized that Prometheus would have to face consequences, the consequences for tempting powers greater than himself. That was the moment the embers ignited Dr. Jingles and Twig. And the carpet.

I didn't only give humanity the gift of fire. I cremated them on the spot.

And possibly, if I had acted quickly enough, I could still have done something. If I'd beat the flames with one of Grandma's embroidered pillows, if I'd alerted Grandpa and he'd grabbed the extinguisher from the kitchen, maybe we would have gotten off with just soot damage and a fire-and-brimstone lecture. But I was nine. Paralyzed. And practically in the buff.

Even now that the flames were spreading lickety-split through the carpet's dry deep pile and clambering up the curtains, even now, the first thing I wanted was to somehow get my PJ top on.

Go figure, but the fire didn't scare me out of my wits half as much as having to explain my drag to everyone.

Didn't tell Mrs. Bernstein any of that. This kind of thing you didn't even admit to yourself. Even after all those years.

I pattered as quickly and as quietly as I could to the hall, past Grandpa's and Grandma's bedroom, expecting the smoke alarm any minute to obliterate nine years of my family's love.

I couldn't untie the loincloth.

In my bedroom, hopping from one leg to the other, picking at the knots, tugging on the pillowcases, my limp teeny weenie spraying panic pee into them. By now, a hot, orange glow peering under the door. Prometheus, my manliness, my pride—clean forgot them.

Finally, I pried that soiled rag open, and once I was drip-dry, could pull my PJ pants back on. Top and slippers. I shook my sis awake and she started screaming at the precise second the smoke alarm started blaring.

Then, the chaos. Grandpa and Grandma too old for this kind of action. Us too young. By the time everyone had got out of bed and sized up the situation, it was out of control. Grandpa yelled at us to go outside, tugging Julia and me with his hands, our own hands covering our mouths to keep from inhaling the black smoke. The large room a rampant inferno, I was grateful to note that no traces of Dr. Jingles, Twig, and Porcupiny could be seen through the wall of fire. Relieved that the fire had destroyed humanity before it could expose me.

"A gnarl must have popped out of the hearth," Grandma cried, as, teeth chattering, we stood in the snow watching Huckleberry Wall burn. Grandpa came back from the conflagration, his arms loaded with blankets to save us from freezing. And Grandma cried, "That's what it probably was. An ember that sparked the carpet."

And for me, the father of the fire, this was my second chance to fess up. I coulda said it was me, coulda said I couldn't sleep and had flung a log into the fireplace, that the cinders spattered onto the rug. That it was an accident. No one had to get wind of my escapades.

What held me back was Prometheus.

That the birds would come and get you if they knew you were the culprit.

That's not how I had wanted it.

The denial, the repressing of the memories, the refusal to go back upstate: for your parents, your therapists even, it was all normal enough behavior, after all you'd been through. Julia had nightmares for years, scratching on the walls till she was ten. Squeezed empty a bottle of Lysol Power cleaner into the tropical aquarium. I told tales of sharp beaks and talons that visited me nightly to gore me. Didn't dare set foot outside the city, shit-scared of wilderness and anything that sloped away from man-made structures.

But what really defined the most crucial moment in your life was that you never again dared to be around Grandpa.

That, three years later, when he finally snuffed it after a CVA, you cried with the crowd at his funeral, but they were whew-tears. That's what you *really* didn't tell anyone.

That night's scene, branded in your brain, the epic plunge in the snow back to civilization, the bulky black devil dragging us on the sleigh, smoke rising from his skull and shoulders—closer to the truth than you think.

Grandpa musta had devilish powers to rescue his wife and grandkids after what *he'd* been through.

He wanted to get the car out of the garage. Grandma told him don't do it, no point. But he wanted to, for our sake. It was January and cold; he was afraid we wouldn't make it otherwise.

Ya see, that figure coming out of the explosion, stumbling toward us out of the wall of fire that had just been the garage, that wasn't my grandfather. His robe burned away to the seams, the blanket a smoldering lump falling from his hands, all that white hair barbecued away, and the fuming face like a Freddy Krueger mask that *resembled* my grandfather's face but wasn't: soot and blood and charred flesh and two gaping bewildered eyes.

That's not how I had wanted it.

All those deformed faces. All those deformed landscapes. That's why I couldn't face Nick now. That's why I came to New York. Didn't Prometheus get punished over and over again?

Grandpa took one more step toward us, then keeled over, that face buried in the snow, and there was a hiss as he slowly melted it down.

7

Back to that day in Amsterdam-Zuid, a coupla days before Nick left for Helvetia. The landing upstairs a jumble of climbing gear, us entangled in exhaled exclamations and spiraling aspirations. I'm tall, six feet, but with Nick's six four I could disappear in his arms and feel the air stream into him. I said, "Promise you'll come back."

"I promise everything."

"It's important," I said. I turned around, as much as the climbing rope permitted, and looked him straight in the eyes, imploring. Ice axe cold steel between us, his skin suddenly granite hard. I imagined something terrifying approaching from on high, something that propelled itself with powerful wing beats and against which I had to protect him unconditionally. "Seriously, you gotta promise me, Nick."

He pecked my eyelids. "Come on. You can't control the whole world, Sam." Coupla seconds later, "Of course I'll come back, you know that. I always come back."

I buried my face in his chest: my alcove, my breathing earth.

After a pause, I said, "Do you promise me everything?"

"Everything."

"Good, cuz I already ordered that bag."

"Seriously?"

"With your card."

8

Late the next evening, CNN reported a possible terrorist attack on the AMC. Ten-sec paralysis while watching the livestream; deep inhale, deep exhale to steady my heartbeat. Then I texted him.

> Jesus fuck Nick u ok???

Sometimes you need thirty-two killed to break the ice.

But we got talking, and a coupla days later, the evening before they removed the bandages, Nick emailed me over a hundred pages of manuscript.

He'd been productive. Anything better to do while lying there waiting for your face to regenerate and whitewashing your guilt about a death you caused?

I read it and put it down.

A haunted mountain, a descent routed by birds. We all tell stories when we can't face the truth.

THE STRANGE CASE OF DR. JEKYLL AND MR. HYDE

NOTES BY SAM AVERY

It was but for one minute that I saw him, but the hair stood upon my head like quills. Sir, if that was my master, why had he a mask upon his face?

—Robert Louis Stevenson

1

The front door wouldn't budge. Fucking door. Abnormally chilly draft from the house cramping its style, and me, whaddya think, flesh creeping shivers. My backpack's KLM label flapping around, and I'm thinking, *It's a sign.* I'm thinking, *The door, it's giving you a hint. Take it. Go back before it's too late.*

Last twenty-four hours major rewind: head wonky, I step out of an uncomfortable night flight, six time zones earlier I get in fresh and frisky, gulp down the lump in my throat as I wriggle out of Julia's arms, the overlong clinch at the security checkpoint after she could say, "Take care of yourself, okay? I'll come to you if you need help," embrace her, get out and into an Uber, open Ma's case on the bed, take my clothes out, hang up, say I'll think about it, pick up, hear my phone ring—a +31 number.

Why did I have to pick up? In every Hollywood movie, every Netflix series, every fucking Greek myth, bad news travels via long-distance calls. Black sails or smartphones, only diff is the medium.

Don't pick up and you never come back. Don't pick up and it's your ticket to a life behind the counter in some fast-food joint somewhere in the Midwest, your date a bitchin' hot Tinder Romeo who maybe's still in the closet but ain't never been in the vicinity of a mountain either.

Can't argue with that.

Louise Grevers, waiting patiently on the line, four thousand miles away, probably still picking up my doubts, right through all the Apple electronics and Vodafone frequencies. Probably even sympathized, too.

No judging, no reproach for leaving Nick in the lurch. Zilch. Just asking if it was okay at my parents', and if I've had time to collect my thoughts. They miss me in Holland, she said, asked if I considered going back home.

"On the other hand, maybe New York feels more like home to you now."

Major throat lump again. Knockout sweetness, this woman.

So twenty-four hours later I'm in Amsterdam, struggling with that damn door. Shouldered it full-force, stumbling over the doorstep. You know you made the wrong choice when even your house doesn't like you anymore.

Flung my backpack in the dusky hall, held back the urge to shout "Honey, I'm home!"

It was an uncanny moment, sun already crouching behind the houses, tomblike silence everywhere. Life invisible. Like I was the only human living and breathing for miles around. Our house also seemed unfamiliar after all this time. Had a foreign smell, like hospitals and cream. Not talking Dior here, I mean that antiseptic wound cream. Not for softness of skin, but for supple scar tissue. At the stairs, I listened to the silence upstairs that somehow seemed unusually deep, as if while I was away all sorts of rooms had been moved around or added.

It was obvious the house had to get used to me. And vice versa.

And Louise, twenty-four hours ago, long-distance: "I think Harald and I are losing our grip on him. Things haven't been the same since they removed the bandages."

That's why she called: Nick.

What even my Catskills epiphany couldn't supply, what even—get this—*an ice axe through his face* and thirty-two bodies in the AMC couldn't supply, was the catharsis I so needed. Even surrounded by Times Square's cultivated pixel-built reality, Starbucks mug in my hand, seeking serenity among as much nonwilderness as I could absorb, I was scared that some nonexistent birds would dive at me from the video walls and skyscrapers and rip me apart with their pointed beaks.

Death birds in Nick's story.

Ethon in my grandfather's story.

My taloned and feathered guilt complex.

You weren't there when your boyfriend got to see the ruins of the face that was to be his future. Consequence: you edited yourself out of said future.

Even after all the running, after all those planes and cars and never looking back, where you ended up was the epicenter of your own wilderness.

Now, twenty-four hours later, silence upstairs. The house was holding its breath. Get Well Soon cards on the kitchen table. Dishwasher full but off. Typical Nick. Blender in the wrong place on the counter. Next to it, a pack of Quaker Instant Oats. A can of Mott's applesauce. Trash can full of empty soup tins, semolina pudding, Nutridrink, Beech-Nut. And straws. Sure, straws. That's Nick too.

Next date night criteria: Is there a juicer?

I kicked off my shoes, went upstairs, and twenty-four hours ago, Louise had said, "I knew nothing would ever be the same, because he immediately put the bandages back on." She said, "Because he didn't want anyone to see his scars, not even us. And I knew because of that picture. The one where Augustin has no eyes."

Nick had stayed with his folks for a few days after he'd left the hospital. Louise had found the picture when she was putting the laundry into the closet in his room. "It was taken in the bivouac," she said. She described the photo but didn't need to. I knew exactly what it showed, cuz Nick had talked about it in his manuscript. It was the last pic he took of Augustin.

"Nick had them printed. He's really sinking his teeth into it. I think it's his way of processing it. Anyway, I didn't think looking at the photos could do any harm, because Nick had already shown them to us on his iPad in the hospital. And I thought this would be more of the same. But it wasn't. That particular one. Augustin was smiling in that photo, Sam. Only, Nick had scratched up his eyes with a ballpoint. He scratched them so hard they looked like black tunnels."

And there's more. He'd pierced the corners of photo-Augustin's mouth with scissors and cut open his cheeks all the way to the ears.

Nick found out his mom'd seen the snapshot. She didn't know how, didn't have any evidence of it, but didn't doubt it for a second. "He was downstairs with us that evening, and the way he was looking at me, Sam. I didn't recognize him. It was like I was sitting next to a stranger. And . . . he wrote a note. I was so taken aback by it that I threw it away and didn't even show it to Harald."

What it said? She wouldn't say.

She'd called Nick's psychotherapist behind his back. The shrink said you couldn't rule out Nick bearing grudges, if he blamed Augustin or anyone else around him for his mutilation. And aggressiveness. Delusions. OCD. Best thing that she could do was re-create normality as well as she could.

That's what she was trying to do. By calling me home.

"I think he needs you, Sam. And you want to know something else?"

"What?"

"By the sound of your voice, you need him too."

Louise was right, of course, but I still thought of what Cécile Métrailler had said: *If there was violence, it had to have been between them.*

2

Nick wasn't in bed. Didn't know where he was. The bed looked untouched, curtains drawn, gently swaying in front of the open window. I had a vision of them billowing like a drifting specter in the empty room when I came in the front door. The odor of antiseptic was much more pungent up here.

So I go back to the landing, call out his name. Nothing. Surprised, but not yet worried. My homecoming was unannounced, and maybe, despite everything, Nick had stayed the night with the folks or gone to the AMC for a checkup. But I kept my ears open, psyched out by the silence. Even no Ramses pit-a-patting from one of his hideouts, which probably meant he was nestled on the bed at Adelheid's, in number 47—a statement no doubt. I decided to call Louise at a godly hour and take advantage of the time in between to smooth out my jet lag.

Showered. Loved the awesome water pressure, splattered my face for at least twenty minutes, eyes shut, Spotify bouncing against the walls. Muffled sounds. Almost dropping off to the rhythm of my daily mix and the streaming water.

Towel skirt on, I went into the dark bedroom. Halfway there, all of a sudden, *wham!*

Nick was there, sitting on the edge of the bed.

I tottered, felt like I was falling face-first into the Grand Canyon or something. Still, I somehow managed to compensate. *Don't let him notice.* It was a matter of life or death, I knew. Something told me I shouldn't let on how much he shook me up. After a short, involuntary shoulder spasm, I came to a halt and just stood there, halfway between the bathroom door and the bed, while my face almost popped off my skull and my brain worked overtime to find solid ground under my feet. I'd stopped breathing. Good thing, or else I woulda screamed.

Nick was a specter. Could just as easily have been a pile of discarded clothes dumped on a chair in an accidentally humanlike form. I couldn't see his face.

"Surprise," I said shakily. He musta been in the cellar when I came home. Heard the boiler kick in.

Yeah, right. Seven a.m. and he's in the cellar. Doing what, exactly?

"I didn't know you were home," I said. "I wanted to surprise you, that's why I didn't say anything."

I just stood there in the middle of the bedroom. Both feet on the ground but the whole room reeling. Jesus, why did I become so unglued? Nick hadn't budged. Looked like he was staring at me in the semidarkness but without recognizing me. Something moved next to him. Well, blow me down! Ramses, curled up on the covers. Purring too, dammit. Nick's inert hand on his neck. That unglued me even more. I was sure Ramses wasn't there when I'd looked into the bedroom before. Or had he been? Suddenly, I wasn't sure about anything, except that I was feeling really vulnerable and naked.

"Damn, don't be so creepy," I said. I strode to the headboard and switched on the bedside lamp.

Shock. Nick raised his arm to block the light, concealing his face in shadows, but in that second, I saw it was still all bandaged up. Less elaborate than those first days in Lausanne, but enough to rattle me. The whole bottom half of his mug was swaddled. One band across the bridge of his nose and his cheekbones, another on his forehead to keep everything from falling off. But around his eyes was a sunglasses-shaped patch of bare skin, the tip of his nose was poking out, and tufts of messy hair popped out on top of it—dimly visible behind the bandages was Nick, all the way.

I twisted the lamp away to put him out of the spotlight and he slowly lowered his arm. Ramses jumped off the bed and stole out of the room, cold-shouldering me.

I tried to smile. "Weird, seeing you up. After lying in the hospital for so long, I mean. Makes sense, though. Duh. Still hurting?"

Blabber, blabber. "I thought they could come off," I said. "That everything's all . . . closed up and stuff."

Nick reached for the notepad and started writing. For so long it got me all jittery. At one point, his pen hovered above the pad, trembling, and he jerked his head from left to right like he was listening to sounds only he could hear.

When he was done, he ripped the sheet out and handed it to me.

I knew you'd come back. I knew you would from the moment you walked out of the CHUV because I saw it in my head. They say people who go blind can suddenly smell and hear better. It's like that. Only I don't smell or hear more, I see more. Much more. Sometimes I see so much I think my head will explode.

O-kay.

Freak talk. Psychobabble. I wasn't sure I was up to this. When I looked up from the note, Nick was staring at me again.

I walked to the closet, grabbed a T-shirt, and pulled it on. Made me feel stronger, but then I thought, *There are holes in the ice. They look just like eyes.*

Right, so now I had a T-shirt on, but I was back in the exact same spot in the middle of the bedroom. Didn't know what to say. Nick on the edge of the bed, his eyes big and cloudy under all those bandages—they *looked* like they were Nick's, but how could you know for sure when you couldn't see his face? How could I be sure it really was Nick sitting there and not some other being impersonating him, some thing that *looked* like Nick, had the same hands, wore the same sweatpants, but was actually something totally alien? It didn't use words Nick would use. Didn't *smell* like Nick. And when the mask came off, it wouldn't even have Nick's face.

"I wish I'd stayed," I blurted out. "That I didn't split. But I was shit-scared. I didn't know what to do."

Nick gave me a long look. Those dull eyes under the dressing practically clinging on to me.

"I just hope we can somehow get through this together. You've been through something terrible. And to top it off, that business in the AMC. I want to be there for you, okay?"

He nodded slowly.

"I love you."

He started writing again:

Something bad is happening to me. I can't stop it.

He leaned over to the headboard and switched off the reading lamp. It got dark again. Only a faint light shone through the heavy curtains, turning everything and Nick into outlines. But Nick was much more than an outline. He was an expectation, a fear, a memory, and his presence in that dark room filled my lungs and weighed on my shoulders and made me dizzy again.

"Does the light bother you?"

I could only just make out a nod.

"Okay."

Silence. So long I barely got up the nerve to ask the question.

"Can I see it?"

This time I couldn't tell if he nodded or shook. Just sat there, the shadow at the end of the bed. My heart was in my mouth.

"Nick. Can I see it? Without the bandages?"

He started writing again and ripped out the sheet. My eyes were adjusting slowly to the dark and I had to strain them all the way.

I love you too. I just can't show my face yet.

Alarm bells ringing. But Nick beckoned to me, so what was I supposed to do but to go to him? And fuck almighty, there's the room reeling again. Or was it Ramses purring? Couldn't see straight. The bed bobbing and heaving like I'd downed the umpteenth Sunset Spice in NY and I'm thinking, *Compensate, hotshot. Compensate, if you don't want to give yourself away*, and then I was plopping down on the edge of the mattress.

I grabbed something to stop the reeling and, shit, it was his leg. He wrapped his arm around my shoulder. Did he notice me flinch? Or that my body was whirling so much I'd go *kablooey* if he got any closer? But that's exactly what he did. Pulled me to him, pressed me against that big, feverish body of his. The antiseptic odor so overwhelmingly near, so penetrating, I had to hold my breath. But under it I smelled blood and sweat, and under that, I smelled Nick.

And something else. I honestly don't know what that smell was. Something old. Something that sure as hell *wasn't* Nick.

I tried not to moan when I surrendered to the embrace. We dropped sideways onto the bed and I was forced to raise my legs onto the mattress and lay them against his. I shut my eyes in an attempt to escape the dizziness, but even behind my eyelids the darkness kept twirling. Thank fuckness Nick couldn't see my face in the dark—my unconcealable expression of hollow disgust—and thanks, too, that I couldn't see his when I felt those rough bandages scraping my neck, and that gooey, unfamiliar topography rubbing my skin. His breath on my cheek wasn't hot like the rest of him but ice-cold.

3

Didn't think I'd ever be able to fall asleep, but looks like I did. When I woke up, the curtains were open and the bedroom was awash in warm sunlight. No Nick. The clock radio said 3:30 p.m. Jesus. Jet lag versus Sam Avery, 1–0.

I didn't have my T-shirt on. Couldn't remember taking it off, and that tangled up my insides. Did Nick do it when I was sleeping? Without waking me?

I suddenly had an image of him kissing me in my sleep, those damaged lips hidden under the stiff bandages, and I went cold all over.

When I sat up, a folded note slid off my chest. I read:

It was nice to hold you. I looked at you all morning while you slept. You seemed so small in my arms! So small I felt I could have squashed you like a bug, I only had to close my arms and all your bones would break. Little, fragile Sam!

It doesn't matter that you went away. All that matters is that you're here now. Don't be afraid of me, we'll get through this.

xXx Nick

4

When did the idea first pop into my head that Nick's trauma in the mountains had awakened some dangerous thing in him? Some thing that was actually some *one*, not him, or—way creepier—some thing that had always been there inside him? Well, right then. One of those first days in Amsterdam.

Maybe it was that evening, after all that went down when I found Nick on all fours in the cellar.

Or maybe it was later that night, when Julia said the word *schizophrenia* on FaceTime, which hit me like a bucket of ice-cold water in the face. She also went on about split personalities and Freud's Doppelgänger, after which I said "Please," after which I said "Stop it," after which I said "I get the point." My Nick, Jekyll *and* Hyde. Whatever—in your face that the birth of the *someone else* came right around the showdown between him and Augustin on the edge of the crevasse. I finally had to bite the bullet: Nick was responsible for Augustin's death. And it looked like his mind had not only got fucked up but also *dualized*, like, *ding-a-ling!* Good versus Evil, let the battle begin.

And that, that was the exact last thing I could use during my first night in Amsterdam. Wide-awake and straight up in bed, losing a hopeless fight with my jet lag, me in bed with my MacBook and shitloads of psychomedical terms, as far away from the cellar and the thing prowling down there as geographically possible without going through the roof or running outta da house: the exact last thing I could use.

What I *could* use was Vicodin and glitch-free Wi-Fi.

"I'm so glad you called, bro," Julia said, her face stuck in a choppy blur—her digital complexion, cyberspace skin damage. "Mom and Dad said you would."

"How the fuck do they know? They're top of the list of people I've kept in the dark all these weeks."

"That's why." Her face frozen in a zombified 2.0 of her ideal Snapchat selfie. "They said give him two days after he gets home. I thought their estimation was generous."

I pictured my parents and threw in a locust plague and tornado for good measure. Don't wanna sound like a jerk, but the last thing you need is to fill your parents in on all the details of how your life went south. Last coupla weeks in New York, I was about as transparent to them as reinforced concrete. Not that I'm ungrateful. As the apple of their eye, I had the right to unannounced visits in times of crisis, but that ocean suits me fine most of the time.

Julia, that night on FaceTime: "Talk a bit louder, okay? Why are you whispering?"

Can't, I said. Cuzza Nick. Where he was? In the cellar. But what did I mean when I said I was scared of him? Did he threaten me? I said, I *dunno* if he threatened me, that's the thing. I said, the cellar, that's his sanctuary now. "The cellar," Julia said. I said, he likes to be in the dark. At least, that's what he said. Julia echoed the sentence and, gotta admit, it made my first day back in Amsterdam sound hell-hectic, and now the image froze on big eyes and curled lips that didn't exactly look like they were expressing understanding.

And how could you make it clear to Julia that you were so shook up you were scared to even whisper about Nick?

One AirPod in, the other clamped in my fist, my free ear perked at the bedroom door crack, the inert gloom in the landing, straining to detect the minutest sound creeping upstairs, heralding Nick . . . or *someone else*. Shit-scared that Julia's way-too-loud voice would break right through the noise cancellation, down through two stories of stagnant air, to be picked up by whatever was lurking down there like a mega black hole in the cellar, a black hole that sucked in all sounds, thoughts, and doubts and even seemed to bend the house's gravity out of shape. Abs and pecs: check. The phantom of the opera: check. A million times the sun's mass's worth of everything I didn't dare mention: check.

I said, "I mean, what's he even *doing* down there?"

"Dude, cut him some slack," Julia said. "The guy just survived a serious mountaineering accident *and* a terrorist attack. I'd also be fucked up."

I said, "It wasn't a terrorist attack."

"Yeah, okay, but everyone *thought* it was. And no one knows what it was. CNN calls it an 'unknown medical anomaly.' That's just as traumatic."

Her face stuck in a seriously-not-making-this-up expression. "The AMC thing, on io9 they're trending that it was a kind of Captain Trips outbreak that they managed to isolate just in time."

Her face stuck in a seriously-don't-shoot-the-messenger expression. "Infowars says it was nerve gas but they're keeping it under wraps. That explains all the broken bones."

"Who by?"

"Duh, Zionists. It's Infowars." She said, "I only mean you're lucky he's still alive."

I said, "You don't get it. It wasn't a mountaineering accident, either."

And Julia's pixelated face frozen in expressions six time zones away, but still feeling closer than she'd been in weeks.

"Sam. The time to talk? It's now."

So I gave her the whole ball of wax.

Told her about Nick's manuscript, and the more I told her, the more it all seemed to disperse before my very eyes. It just became a story—not a true story, not anything that ever really happened. A haunted mountain, a possessed valley, almost funny.

Not funny was Cécile's conclusion that there musta been violence up there, and that it was mutual, and that Nick was alive even though Augustin was dead. *Dead.* I said all I wanted was to believe it was self-defense cuz Augustin attacked him with a fucking ice axe, but *why didn't he just tell me then? No one woulda blamed him.* Denying it was the real killer, because now I knew nothing. Now there was Augustin's photo that Louise'd found and what the fuck was that? What the fuck, sis?

Frozen screen again, Julia's peepers piercing right into me like no other pair had done this summer, saying, "Tell me what happened today."

5

Know the feeling? When you're thinking something so terrible you're ashamed of it, and you try to abort it out of your mind with all your might but it's stuck there and won't budge, no matter what you do? Like a jack-in-the-box, a tiny, eternally smiling Mr. Hyde at the end of the umbilical cord of your conscience.

The day had already got off to a bad start, as is often the case when your day starts at prosecco-and-roasted-macadamia-extravaganza o'clock. I was still wobbly, still feeling I would trip over my feet as I trudged down the stairs, not what you'd expect after *x* many hours of sleep. What you also didn't expect was Nick's parents waiting downstairs on the couch. Harald and Louise Grevers, not knowing better at this stage than that Nick's face was smashed off by rockfall, brought some of those chocolate cream puffs. Me discombobulated; me thinking, *The whipped cream—no way you can suck it out with a straw.*

Till I registered that they were for me, duh. A bomb belt bursting with calories for the long-lost son-in-law. They wanted to fatten me up. Create a monster to compensate for their misshapen son.

Sam Avery, Bride of Frankenstein.

The Creature himself was sitting, elbows on knees, in the shadow under the drawn curtain, iPad on lap. If I gauged his expression right, while Louise covered me with kisses (she tiptoed, me hunched, cuz if Nick makes you think basketball, Louise makes you think midget tossing), then *he* was now wishing they lived on the other side of a deep-sea trench.

In it, for all he cared.

They also brought Nick something. A plastic cup full of blended permaculture. Avocado, I guessed. Wheatgrass or some other hip stuff.

"I'll get a straw," Louise said, and strode kitchenward.

Despite everything, I was relieved Harald and Louise were there—said that to Julia, later that night. To Julia on FaceTime, whispering out of fear Nick would hear us. Not only did this postpone the inevitable talk—what was I gonna say to him, anyway?—but their being here helped a bit to get used to the whole new ballgame. With his parents around, Nick was plain Nick. Right then, I could almost kid myself that Nick was recovering from some prosaic accident, and I could almost pretend my suspicions didn't matter.

Okay, so I go down to him, give him the most awkward nonhug in my repertoire. Sit next to him, clench my eyes shut, tighten my throat. Oh, Jesus, wishing someone would beam down a cup of ginger tea, materialize something that'll decentrifuge my stomach, cuz I know right there if I stand up I'll have to puke.

And Harald and Louise giving me the third degree. How it was in NY. Whether the separation gave me the space I needed. Me wishing the ground would swallow me up, me feeling guilty, as if each extra word about me would undermine what Nick had been through. I reluctantly fessed up that my classes had already begun on the first of September and that I'd requested a postponement from my tutor. In-laws' sympathy or not, I sidestepped their questionnaire, because it suddenly dawned on me that it wasn't love; it was inability. Louise looking so tormented. Harald's eyes constantly straying toward Nick, shaking his head in confusion, as if it all made him just as dizzy as it made me. Nick's open eyes staring into space through the strips of bandage, holding them hostage. That was the shift that had taken place. Harald and Louise would never have control over their son again. Nick would define *them*, not the other way round. Those bandages, the concealed scars, they had his parents in their power.

All Harald could say was "Here, have a cream puff," handing me a plate.

These chocolate puffs, I'll be saying to Julia later that night, they're a culinary conundrum. Whatever you do it ends up in a pig's breakfast. No matter how hard you try, each bite makes it look more like a bomb fell on a dairy farm.

They tried, really. Louise asked Nick how his recovery was going. If he was taking good care of himself. Harald asked what the logistics were for the coming weeks and if Nick was keeping his appointments with the shrink and speech doctor. They tried stuffing the distance between them with questions. But Nick didn't wanna talk. In his face, his old man turned into an old man, his old lady started crying, and Nick, if you ask me, getting a kick out of their desperation. God-awful thought, but true. That desperation was *love*, and it was all Nick had left.

Fingers trembling, Louise removed an envelope from her purse. It had clearly already been opened and was taped shut again. She wiped her eyes and said, "Augustin's parents wrote us." She said, "Uwe and Bettine Laber. Did you know them?"

Nick shook his head sluggishly. Louise spoke slowly and cautiously, wanted to make sure she didn't say anything wrong, cuz Augustin's photo, the pic she'd found when she was putting away the clean laundry, was the elephant in the room. "They're deeply mourning their son. They wish you a speedy recovery. They're aware you can't talk yet but would really like to talk to you about what happened when you can."

Here it comes. Now she's gonna say they asked if you took any pics of him. And then we all know what happened to the Augustin bivouac photo. We all know, but you don't know I know.

But she didn't. Louise put the letter on the coffee table next to Nick and said, as calmly as she possibly could, "Read it when you're up to it."

And that's when it happened, I would later say to Julia. It struck me like lightning. I thought, *Small, fragile Sam.* And I could see Nick on the glacier, his arms around Augustin, so tight his ribs cracked and blood shot out of his eyes. When he let go and Augustin's lifeless body fell into a crevasse, Nick took his Swiss Army knife, shoved the blade into his mouth, and slashed open his cheeks from ear to ear.

It was like someone'd smashed me in the face. Me sitting up straight, a forkful of whipped cream on its way to my mouth. And Harald asking, would it be helpful if I joined him at therapy? Louise asking, when do they expect him to be able to take solids?

And my hands, I'd say to Julia, my hands all covered in chocolate fondant and cream. The silence, I'd say to her, made it impossible to surreptitiously wipe them on the throw pillow.

And all of a sudden Harald lost control. Jumped up, knocking the tray with chocolate balls to the floor, shouting, "Dammit, Nick! You're going to have to start talking at *some* point! You're going to have to take off the bandages and confront your new face!"

Everyone shut up. Everyone froze, a Mannequin Challenge for people looking at ruptured chocolate choux. One with a faceful of cream.

And Nick started typing:

Sam, by the looks of it you need to be drip-fed too. I can put them in the blender for you, but I don't think ma would approve . . .

And that changed everything. I remember I looked at him sheepishly, then burst out laughing. Louise and Harald laughed, too, Louise right through her tears. Nick was startled, then gazed at me again with big, clear eyes through those strips of bandage, and I coulda *sworn* those eyes belonged to the old Nick, the pre-mountain Nick, and how could I think all that about him, Julia? How could I have thought all those terrible things about him? The scar had not only his parents under its power but me, too. I was so wrapped up in my own fears and doubts that I didn't give a moment's thought to what it was like for Nick. Instead of standing by my man with his PT-fucking-SS, I'd turned him into a monster.

"And he was *trying*, sis. To be sweet. He squeezed my thigh, tried putting his arm around my shoulder, and the whole time I'm thinking he *murdered* Augustin."

"Come on. Don't be so hard on yourself," Julia said. "What else? Tell me everything."

6

I was up and down all evening. At least after Harald and Louise'd split and Nick had withdrawn to the cellar with Ramses, my dizziness went down a coupla notches, but I couldn't erase that image in my noggin. The image of Nick clenching his arms and blood spouting from Augustin's eyes.

It was after ten before I could muster up the courage to go down to the cellar. You probably have a good idea of what a cellar smells like, but this was like going into a drugstore after an explosion. Each inhalation sucking in enough antibiotics for a lifelong immunity to pneumonia. Every breath consuming enough wound malodor and stench of human degradation to make you barf. It was the same miasma emanating out of Nick this morning when he hugged me, but stronger. More cellary.

The stairs dipped down into the dark. No, not pitch; way at the end there was a glimmer. The cellar looked bigger than it shoulda been. Too big. Optical illusion big. And the glimmer, it was obscured by something in front of it. A black, amorphous mass. Down by the ground. Extricating itself from the gloom. Something horrific, something that *crawled*, its limbs moving all wrong and stuck all wrong to the body. Seeing it made my scalp crawl, too. Every hair on my head at attention, hurting like it was being pulled out by the roots, because I suddenly knew for sure that the thing there in the dark would *crawl over to me* if it noticed me.

Then the darkness collapsed, its shape became human. To my shock, I recognized it as Nick. It was my imagination that had blown him up to the stuff of nightmares. But accepting that it was Nick who was crawling around on all fours at the far end of the cellar was equally weird, and for a minute I was scared he'd *still* crawl toward me.

"Nick?" I said, flicking on the light switch.

Nick shot up so abruptly I almost jumped out of my skin, even on the other side of the cellar. And he was *moaning*. It was the first sound I'd heard him make in more than a month. Goose bumps galore.

Ramses scurried between his legs, giving me his unfathomable poker face, vigilant tail aloft. Enough light to see Nick had dragged half the household down here. Desk, Arezzo rug from his study, studio couch from the attic: check, check, check. He was crouched over an open map of the Alps, haloed by a desk lamp. Next to it, between toolboxes, crates of food, and tins of paint, books about mountains. Photos of mountains. And man-made mountains of empty beer bottles with straws.

Made me nauseous. Nick in the basement, absorbed in his obsession, the gothic novel cliché incarnate. Only thing missing was Augustin's ghost floating around doing the revenge thing cuz he got tossed into the glacier.

"Jesus, sorry, Nick. I didn't wanna startle you. Good to see you've moved. When's the housewarming party?"

He turned to look at me, and, man, chills up and down my spine. On the bandage strips, where his mouth shoulda been, he'd Sharpied a smiley mouth. A black, half-moon curve, crossed at the edges for round cupid cheeks. Coulda been innocuous, but wasn't. Cuz his head was moving and the smiley wasn't, giving his face the grisliness of a puppet come to life.

But the top half was real, and that was Nick. He made a muffled sound, looked happy to see me.

Smile!

he typed on his iPad.

This way you'll always know it's me and never mistake me for someone else. When I smile, you don't have to be scared of me, okay?

I couldn't tell if he was joking or not. I smiled to be on the safe side and said, "I'm not scared of you."

But I was.

I nodded at the studio couch and asked, "Have you been sleeping here the last coupla days?" Asked, "Why'd you wanna do that?"

Nick shrugged and looked away at the map, which was all covered in black scrawls. Ramses hopped lithely into his lap and nuzzled up against him with abandon. Squirming that lean feline body of his to try to get to those bandages and rub his snout against them. That was neither cute nor funny. It was creepy. Ramses usually hates smells.

"Pretty big score," I said, nodding at the pile of empty beer bottles. Nodding at empty La Chouffe crates. "Is that a good idea, with all the meds you're taking?"

More shrugs, more looking away. The white knuckles of his folded hands. The taut tendons in his neck.

Last thing you want is to sound like his mom, but the last thing Nick could use was a habit. The brewskis filtering through the hospital stench. Nick may like to bend the elbow at parties, but this wasn't exactly Sugarfactory, no Club AIR or any other night on the town.

That smiley mouth on the puppet face. Kept grinning at me, but Nick's eyes didn't join the party.

"Listen, I was wondering maybe you wanna come upstairs. Watch a movie or something." I hesitated, then added, "Maybe have a beer together."

And me sweating bullets while he typed, so bad my hands were doing the jitterbug.

He handed me the iPad.

You go watch a movie. I still have to get some stuff done here.

"Right," I said, after staring at his text for about as long as the movie would take. "Stuff. You need to get done. All more important than me."

Nick's head turned to me vehemently, and it looked like everything under those bandages was moving, everything beneath that mask was turning inside out, as if something that'd been in hiding was now creeping out.

New optical illusion: this time, that the floor under me had disappeared. Windmilling my arms, teetering IRL. This time, I felt like I was falling. Everything in the cellar, the shadows and highlights, the surfaces and empty spaces, twisted proportions. I reached for the edge of the desk, missed, grabbed again, got it. Took a few secs to get what happened, but the desk looked like it was *far away*. Like it was way deep in a void or something.

Suddenly, there's Nick, real close, clamping my wrists like some kinda stony vise, peering into my eyes. *You okay?*

"Kinda dizzy," I heard myself say. "Don't know what's up; been feeling woozy all day. Tipsy. Topsy-turvy. Whatever."

The sound of my voice crystal clear, reverberating like an echo against hidden mountain faces, but Nick's encased face seemed to be twirling away from my bulging eyes. Fine by me, cuz I couldn't bear to look at that smiley mask any longer.

"Dude, you're hurting me. I'm okay now."

Nick's grasp loosened and he let go. As he took the iPad again and slumped behind his desk, I tried to focus on fixed points in reality till the giddiness went away.

Sam, go upstairs. Go to sleep. Leave me alone.

And all of a sudden, I was sick of it.

"No," I said, and *felt* him tense up. "No, Nick. I'm sick and tired of avoiding you, and I'm sick and tired of you avoiding me. At some point you're gonna have to go out there. At some point you're gonna have to face it. It isn't going to go away if you shut yourself up, and definitely not if you shut yourself off from me." I took a breath, knew I had to push on. "I want you to tell me what happened. What *really* happened. Dude, did you even read your own story? Got any idea what it says? Like that mountain is some kind of—"

Slamming the table, he jerked upright. The desk chair clattered to the floor, hitting a pile of soup cans that rolled over the cellar floor. Ramses let out a serious screech—at me, no less. Curved back, puffed tail, bared teeth, then slunk off into the darkness. But not Nick. Nick towered over me in the gloom like a bare willow in November, and his presence forced all the air out of my lungs. I hadda keep myself from stepping back. If I did, he'd slash at me with those bare branches.

I kept talking, as composed as possible. Meanwhile, Nick snatched the iPad off the desk and started tapping so fast I could barely see his fingers. I said, "Listen, you've had an awful experience. I want you to know I'm there for you. *Whatever happened.* I'm with you. You're scared of that mountain, I get it. You went through hell up there. Fuck, maybe you were even hallucinating because of blood loss, or from shock or something. But that doesn't make that place the Twilight Zone. You're confused. Come on, where's the Nick I know, the one who laughs at ghost stories?"

He'd stopped tapping but didn't look like he was planning on passing me the iPad. Just stood there. Staring at me. Left eyelid quivering. I yanked the iPad from his limp fingers and read what he'd written.

Stop yapping and shut up! Your mouth just keeps going on and on and on. How would you feel if it couldn't do anything but spout a black river of blood that melts right through the snow and ice because your life is still hot when it flows away from you?

The silence lasted an eternity. Then I said, "No need to bitch about it. Yeah, I left, but I also came back."

And did it ever occur to you that maybe I don't want you to be back? That I don't want you to see me like this? Did that ever cross your mind? I'm a freak, Sam, and I disgust you. Please go away, go back to New York or whatever, just GET THE HELL OUT OF HERE!

I hadda swallow before I found my voice again, but then said, very collectedly, staring at the screen, "No, you don't disgust me. But if you don't let me see it, I'll never get the chance to get used to it, get it?"

When I looked up, I saw him slowly swing his right arm and put his hand on his Sharpied smiley mouth.

'Course the temperature didn't *really* drop by fifteen degrees in the cellar. It just felt like it did.

And Nick didn't *really* get bigger. But the shadow, when it slid over me, was no willow but a landslide, and if I questioned whether Nick—not *my* Nick, but this unknowable Nick—was capable of murder, that shadow removed all doubt.

"Nick."

He didn't pull his hand back.

"Nick, talk to me."

He didn't pull his hand back.

Slowly, agonizingly, he laid the iPad on the desk. Turning around took all my willpower. I braced myself so tensely I barely made it up the cellar stairs. Any second, I expected his hands on my neck, hard as rock. But that didn't happen. When I looked back from the top of the stairs, he was still standing on the same spot, one arm hanging, the other still raised, but, like his face, invisible behind the stairwell's walls.

And hours later, triple-X o'clock, middle of the dimly lit night, in bed, staring at the frozen FaceTime blur you'd pinned all your hopes on, you said to Julia, "So whadda I do now? Tell him what I think? Confront him with what I think he m—"

"No, of course not," Julia said. "Even if you're right, and you can't be sure, that would be the stupidest move." She said, "Listen, I'll tell you exactly what to do."

But that's as far as she got, cuz at that moment all the lights went out. This time not only the image stuck, but the sound too. My MacBook was on battery, so it took a while before I realized it wasn't a Wi-Fi glitch.

The bedside lamp was out.

The clock radio, all black.

And on the landing, an immense darkness was bulging.

7

I had no idea how long I'd been in the dark; all I knew was that Nick was in the room.

I couldn't see him. It was more the sound of air that had awakened me, an invisible eagle sailing above, the breath of something huge, so close it made the sheets flutter up, then down again. And now he was here, lost somewhere in the same darkness. No, not lost. There, in the corner. Staring at me. The Hermit. And me in total sleep paralysis, me Prometheus, panicking, limbs frozen.

He approached the bed.

Oh Jesus. He approached the bed.

It was like he was strewing more darkness with each step. A spreading ink cloud. An abyss rending the room apart. Incredible, so big, that thing coming at me! Maybe he really was the Hermit, broken loose from my grandpa's story, escaped from Huckleberry Wall before it burned down, and now here in the guise of an incubus. *Naked* as an incubus. In my half sleep, that thought was as terrifying as it was exciting.

I must have fallen asleep; no other way. After the power blackout, I lay in the dark, staring, perplexed, unable to bring myself to go downstairs and find out what had caused it. The things he'd *said.* That gesture, the way he slapped his hand onto the smiley mouth. *Schizophrenia*, Julia said. *Split personality*, Julia said. *The classic, violent doppelgänger, stemming from hidden yearnings and suppressed subconscious thoughts*, Julia said—she got that from Dr. Phil.

And makeup sex not one of the options that came to mind. Makeup sex not the *first* thing to come to mind when you were wondering if your boyfriend's gesture was meant to be a threat. But that was what I was thinking about *now*, as he slunk toward me on the bed.

I felt the mattress sagging under his weight. And it *kept on* sagging, making me sink between mountains of down. That shadow, it crawled over me. What a powerful creature! My hands went up and felt skin. I knew that skin. Could dream that skin. I could just make out the intense, possessed gleam in his eyes, right above me, hungry as a bird of prey. This creature, this demon, the face was wrapped in bandages, but it didn't smell of antiseptics now, it didn't smell like something medicinal. It smelled like stone. Like earth. Like something that came from earth itself. There was also no smiley mouth drawn on the bandages. Maybe Nick forgot to, after changing them. Maybe not. I couldn't care less.

Good or bad, I wanted to be under his power, wanted to be Prometheus at the mercy of the eagle's claws.

'Course I wondered how his mutilation would affect our sex. A dysmorphophobic like me, a facial focus like mine (no pun intended), and stuff gets into your head. Like Josh Fonesca, for one. You know, the one with the bushburned girlfriend and the engagement ring. Banging clouds of ash from that carbonized carcass every time his dick is raring for action. Or Billie Hamilton, the one who said on *Ellen DeGeneres*, "I don't even see it when I look at him," which, technically speaking, is only possible if she wraps Gollum's face with both her legs, like she's the buzz saw, while he holds his breath and sucks her wet insides with his face in stitches—and I don't mean he's laughing.

First time he's on top of you again, that divine, sweat-wet body. The transplant scars on his arm and thigh, they look like zippers. Pull on one suture and—*zip*—all the insides come gushing out. Or imagine Nick starting to groan and—*snap*—all the stitches behind that mask pop open, the mask first yellow, then brown, then red.

I mean, sex is about body parts, but this was overdoing it.

Believe me, thinking like this could really put a damper on your nighttime fantasies in New York.

So there's me, lying there, trying to surrender to him, desire and disgust entangled in a death match. Clutching that luscious body and pushing away the horrors behind those bandages. I shut my eyes, tried to bundle my energy, felt I had to prove something. If I could, we'd pull through it together. If I could, I wouldn't hurt him again. The eagle, my grandfather, my guilt, all bought off with a single shtup with my biggest nightmare.

And it went well. It went well. Till I looked down my sweat-soaked body and saw that swaddled head down there, his hands on my hips and, yep, me *buried* in strips of gauze, disappearing into that unknown, damp heat inside.

And I thought of Billie and Gollum. Seriously, fuck Bilbo and Gollum, but I couldn't help it.

I'll tell it like it is. I went limp. No matter how I tried. Or how Nick tried. Never happened to me before, not with Nick, my Nick, my walking Sexual Healing. Felt like I was falling through the covers, plunging till I'd disappear, and I only understood the emptiness I felt when I realized Nick had gotten up and was vanishing into the darkness.

"Nick, wait . . ."

But he was gone. Drifted away like a ghost, cuz I heard no footsteps, no creaking stairs, no cracking floors. Zip. Like he had never been there.

Only heard him once he'd reached the cellar, cuz that's where the screaming began. Numb, paralyzed, dead scared, I listened to Nick go apeshit. The crashing of stuff being dashed. The screaming, muffled, tortured, wordless, went on forever. Worst of all, despite all previous doubts, there was no doubt about it now: it was Nick who was screaming down there.

8

As often, I dreamed about Prometheus.

In the dream, it was me, me in the loincloth on the rock, only Ethon wasn't an eagle but an enormous, faceless shadow pitted with abysmal depths. I felt it engulfing me. *Smile!* it said, with a mouth that wasn't a mouth but a chasm. *When I smile, you don't have to be scared of me, okay?* And it smiled, and a chasm did open. It chained me to the rock, not by my wrists, not by my ankles but by the corners of my mouth, with iron rings pounded through my cheeks. And me in a panic, trying to turn away but lying there helplessly, the metal giving no quarter, me tasting it on my tongue . . .

Till I realized I was awake and *still* tasting metal. And in an instant, wide-awake, I shook my head wildly and felt stabs cut my cheeks and neck. I was ensnared in something. A ferocious, half-conscious panic rushed over me, but I immediately stopped moving, afraid my whole mouth would be ripped open. Reached for my face.

Felt *barbed wire.*

No, steel wire.

The kind Nick had used this spring to fence off the garden hedge so Ramses wouldn't be digging his escape to the neighbors' yard.

The kind of steel wire that was rolled up and waiting in the cellar.

Nick.

Oh, Jesus, was Nick in the room?

Even in my state of disorientation, it was clear to me that if he was still in the room, if he was watching me wake up to discover that *my whole face was entwined with steel wire, pulled tight from the corners of my mouth and fastened behind my neck,* that something much worse was about to happen. The fear was razor sharp and hot and turned my vision inward. It was like my senses had kick-started a life-support system strictly limited to my immediate surroundings. Beyond it, the room was vague. Beyond it, the light an unreal, shimmering gleam, like you're underwater and staring at the sun. Dark blotches were swimming in the light, but none of them were Nick.

But the shock still came, mean and cold, when the first wave of panic ebbed away and the spots at the edge of my vision began to take shape.

Everywhere on the walls—left, right, above the bed—there were drawings of hideous black birds.

9

Nick stared at the walls for a long time. His hand absently brushed the smiley mouth on his bandages, his face exhibiting disbelief, dejection, and utter exhaustion. Finally, he tapped:

I'm really sorry. I don't remember doing this.

"Don't remember?" I said, my voice shaking. Almost rammed that twisted piece of steel wire into his face. "You don't remember doing this?"

I pointed to the streaks on my jaw, the bloody pits in my neck, where the tips had pierced my skin.

"Don't *fucking* remember?"

Almost shoved my iPhone down his throat, the selfie of me before I managed to free myself, the horror selfie that ain't never gonna be your new profile pic.

"I mean, breakfast in bed, I dig, but this shit? You're overdoing it, Nick." Almost shouting now, drool splattering on his bandages. "So I googled the symbolism of your boyfriend wrapping your whole fucking face in steel wire and the experts are as yet undecided. But none of them recommend it as constructive couples therapy, *Nick*."

Me spitting his name out, it made Nick flinch like I'd whacked him.

His gaze drifted back to the birds, those birds on the walls. Drawn with a thick marker. Probably the Sharpie Magnum from the same set as the one he had used to draw the smiley on his bandages. Some no more than strokes, coarsely rendered Vs representing distant flocks. Others were life-size and shockingly in-your-face, pitch-black nightmares with shrieking beaks and spread claws that looked like they were coming straight out of the walls. What fucked-up zone was Nick's mind in to make him do that? And was it really possible he couldn't remember jack shit? It was pretty clear his horror wasn't sham. In some twisted way, that was encouraging. A sane Nick, a Nick who, just for a flash, was *himself*, was capable of understanding my rage. And believe you me, I was raging. Man, it felt good.

"You've gone too far, Nick. Way too far. Remember or not, same diff. Except that it *does* make it worse. What if next time you write 'I love you' on the wall, wrap my neck in steel wire, and strangle me in my sleep? What if you wake up to *that* without remembering it?"

I flung the steel wire at the biggest, most grotesque of the birds. It bounced off and landed in the corner.

Nick looked like he was going to type something, but he didn't. Once again, all sorts of movements were going on behind that mask. But now it was only pitiful shivering, that broken face's final protest. Nick started to cry. Collapsed, sat on the edge of the bed, shoulders shaking, hand clasped over his bandages.

And I faltered just for a sec. Tried staying indifferent. Can't deny getting a little kick out of the role reversal and now being in charge. Even my aversion to him contained a dash of relief, cuz it wasn't coming from fear of his behavior or his mutilation. It stemmed from power. I'd always admired and idolized the pre-accident Nick cuz he had power, not only in his looks or because he never lost control, but because he almost never seemed self-conscious. This little bitty bit of human, sobbing uncontrollably on the edge of the bed, had none of that power. It was too sorry for itself. Nick had diminished into a mini Nick to me.

With shaky fingers he tapped between the tears splashing on the screen.

You're right, it's inexcusable. I've lost control. What's the matter with me???

"What's the matter with you? Jesus, Picasso, if you really can't remember going into the bedroom and scribbling all over the walls and fencing up my face, it's spelled *psy-cho-sis*. And maybe you went through some god-awful shit on that mountain, but that means you need some serious help, cuz I'm not safe around you anymore. And neither are you."

Suddenly my skin started burning. I rubbed the cuts on my neck and thought, *And you. How come you slept right through it?*

Too creepy to dwell on, so I pushed the thought out of my head.

A shadow slipped in and jumped onto the bed. Ramses. I'd already resigned myself to not being forgiven by the cat for leaving him in the lurch for all those weeks, didn't expect him to toss any crumbs of reconciliation my way anytime soon, but I was still surprised that he didn't hesitate to rest his paws on Nick's thigh and start sniffing his tear-soaked bandages. *Prrr, prrr.* Traitor.

There it was again, the schizo voice in my head. *It's one thing to think Nick can take your shirt off while you're sleeping, without you waking up, but what's your hypothesis about him tightening a length of steel wire around your—*

Whoa. Hold on. Don't go there.

And what about Lausanne, right after the accident, when he started talking to you out of the blue and the bandages started bleeding? Big, blooming flowers of blood, practically black against the backdrop of the lightning in the mountains—

Knock it off! And BTW it was a delusion. I was stressed out. Elementary, my dear Watson.

But the voice was relentless. *Delusion. A delusion that made you vamoose all the way to New York.*

I suppressed it, and everything else too. My mental archive, my repository of forbidden thoughts; when the floodgates break, take cover.

I looked at the cat and mumbled, "At least someone around here isn't afraid of you."

Nick let out a strained laugh that ended in a sob. But he was through crying, tears all used up. And me, my anger was gone, replaced by uneasiness. With Ramses circling him, Nick started typing:

> You're right to be afraid of me, and you have no idea how much that hurts. Only, I don't think it was a psychosis. Because what I said isn't true. Oh God, it isn't true.

And me, awkward, "Whaddya mean?"

> I remember it, Sam. I remember drawing those birds. Only it wasn't me. Like I was watching myself through a window when I took the roll of steel wire and started wrapping you with it. I didn't mean to hurt you. But that person on the other side of the window did. And I couldn't stop him. It's really hard for me to tell you this, but I have to be honest, or you'll never trust me again. That person really did want to wind the wire around your neck and pull it till your face went red and your eyes bulged, and I couldn't control myself, like I was pounding on the window and he didn't hear me. If it can let me do things like that, if it can let me do such terrible things, where does this end?

I almost asked about Augustin's photo. Almost posed the question that'd been waiting to be posed for weeks, the core question, the essential one: What did he *really* do to Augustin?

But I didn't. His dissociative demeanor was giving me the willies. The warning on Wikipedia was clear-cut. When people with a personality disorder have a psychotic episode, they can be dangerous. To others *and* to themselves.

An icy hand suddenly clamped my balls.

If I don't succor him now, he'll start thinking really black thoughts. Hara-kiri type of black.

"Listen." I spoke slowly and clearly. "There's nothing that makes you do things. No possession. No other person. You're not yourself, that's all. And you *could* control yourself, because whatever you were thinking, you didn't let it come to that. See? You were in control. Like it or not, I'm still here. And I ain't about to leave."

Those big red eyes between the bands of gauze, they were clinging to me.

"But we're gonna make some changes around here, Nick. Your strategy for dealing with this, whatever it was, it obviously isn't working. We're going to call your shrink, and you're going to go there today. The psych unit, if necessary. You're gonna tell them all that happened, and maybe they can help you."

If I tell them this, they'll commit me.

I gazed at him for a long time and decided to risk it. "And is that so bad? Maybe you'll unwind a little. Jesus, Nick, look at you. You're a wreck. You need help."

I know, but I don't want to be committed, Sam. Please, I'll accept any help, but please let me stay home. Let me stay with you. It's all I have left.

"Okay, but things are gonna change," I snapped. It was the pleading; it got on my nerves. Sorry, pal, plead and you lose my respect. Granted, I'm not much of a psychologist. No Prozac, either.

I said, "No more freaky shit in the cellar. No more smileys. I want you to get a prescription for meds. Lithium, antidepressants, whatever. If they give it to you, you take it. And no more booze. I want you on a normal sleep cycle. Here in bed, next to me. Party's over. Cold turkey."

Nick nodded, lowered his eyes. "And I wanna come with, to your therapy. This week. I don't wanna cramp your style or anything, but I also have the right to know how to deal with you." I thought, *And I want a fucking Frappuccino.*

Please don't be mad at me.

"I'm not mad at you," I sighed. "But that place, the fucking mountain where it all went down, you're totally obsessed with it. I saw what you're doing in the cellar. And look." I pointed to the walls. "Is that freaky or what? I know what you wrote, Nick. I know what the birds in your story mean."

Those stops while he typed gave me the jitters. Gave me too much room to let my thoughts run, and lemme tell ya, they were sprinting, beeline to those floodgates, to full-frontal-assault it.

> It's like I never left that place. Sometimes I can still hear the wind wail. In the distance, just beyond the real world. I know that wind. It's the wind that blasted over the glacier, high above the crevasse we fell in. And above the wind I can hear Augustin laughing, only, after a while he isn't laughing anymore but screaming. Wherever I go. Here. The cellar. The AMC. It follows me. I can't shake it.

"No shit," I said.

That mountain, I thought. *It's got into you. You* are *the mountain now, only not like you think. That's the exact definition of obsession.*

I said, "Talk about it, Nick. With your shrink, with me, whatever feels right. I'm not gonna force you to take that mask off. You're gonna have to do that yourself. But that's the only way you'll find release. Anyway, time for coffee. But I got one more condition."

Nick tilted his head.

"I'm gonna a buy a bucket of latex and you're gonna paint over those walls. Today. I'm not gonna sleep here another night with those creepy things in the walls."

10

Major fast-forward to the night I sneaked a look under the bandages. This is two weeks later, Nick fast asleep, my heart in my mouth on overdrive and me trying to pinch the elastic bandages apart. The shapes under them strange and foreign like a fossil not yet dug out. And all this without waking him up, of course. Shit-scared, but eventually you *hadda* look, cuz if you didn't, you'da gone nuts.

This was the new normal in our world. Me staring at him, me on one elbow on my side of the bed, holding my breath. Ramses vigilant and upright at the foot, staring at us wide-eyed. Nick's chest rising and falling with a deep, sluggish rumble, a sound he'd never made before. That body, Michelangelo's *David* undone, meticulously constructed and deconstructed, crunch by supplement by bench press by skin transplant.

I swallowed. I cleared my throat.

The bandages didn't give. Too tight.

So there you were. Picking at the strips concealing your BF's ravaged face. Hoping the two extra oxazepams you spiked his chamomile with were enough to keep him out cold, cuz him OD'ing would be too much of a good thing.

All you hadda do to get here was wake up in his arms and in a tightly wound roll of steel wire, listening to freak talk about Mount Doom and say *Whoa*, say *Stop right there*. You only hadda take charge and say *This is what we're gonna do*, say *This*, but then it was late September and he still hadn't shown his face. Get fed up with it all and you'd see him as nothing more than one big scar. Your trauma, your grandpa, the eagle that came to rip open your old wounds every night—it all culminated in Nick, and if you didn't accept him now, you never would.

So it was time for a face-to-face. Midnight, masks off.

Nick was sleeping, and fuck almighty was I scared. Felt like Jack and the giant. Bilbo and Smaug. David and Goliath.

There was a clip. Behind his neck, near his hairline, in the pillow. I fumbled with it and unclasped it. The bandages loosened immediately. Nick didn't stir. Only the rise and fall of his chest, the subterranean rumble.

I pulled the wrappings and exposed some of his right cheek. I was told that even if the corners of your mouth are ripped halfway to your ears, the flaps of skin will meld in a week, if properly stitched. Inside it takes much longer, inside a cleft orbicularis oris, and a torn-off pterygoideus lateralis, mumbo jumbo for enough muscle and tendon trauma to make it take months before he can articulate a decent *a* or *i* or *e*. Not to mention the scar. A month and half had now gone by, and I was prepped for peeling scabs. I was prepped for a black-and-blue, bloated cheek, a stiff, leathery balloon the color of sweaty Cracker Barrel country ham.

But I wasn't prepped for what I saw.

Nick's skin underneath the mask was gray and hard. Cracked. Crumbly edges. Almost like rock. Around the loose strips of gauze was a dark residue. I rubbed it between my thumb and finger, and it squirted onto the mattress.

Granite shards.

And I'm suddenly not so sure I wanna take a look under those bandages.

Nick moved. My hand shot back and froze. Ramses's back twitched and he scampered away, a black flash of edgy energy. On my side of the bed, I'm mute, adrenaline speeding through my veins.

Nick's head rolled slowly on the pillow. Loosened another strip. More gray, more grooves. Hard to see in the dark.

I counted. Ten. Twenty. Thirty.

Approached warily. My hand trembling with the urge to pull the rest of the bandages right off and expose his true face.

Too late I realized that the dull thump I'd heard when I peeled off the last wrapping wasn't in my head. I'd heard it in *his* head. A profound, dark sound. As if deep inside him, the earth's crust had caved in.

Dizziness back, more intense than ever. My growing feeling the past weeks that it was somehow issuing out of Nick, that Nick was a kind of walking Ménière's disease, cuz come close or even look at him and you got all wobbly.

Like the sight of him yanked the ground away from under you. I didn't dare think about the implications. But now everything was reeling too much, and there was no turning back.

I pulled off the last wrapping and didn't even get the time to recoil.

My Romeo's flawless Gillette face, Nick's smiling, infomercial Adonis face, it lay before me like a scarped, eroded landscape. Under his cheekbones a wasteland of dead skin and fissured rock, ravaged by the elements. A vast canyon, deeper and more jagged than the rest, cleaving it in half. Stretched all the way to the abyss of the corner of his mouth. I'm saying "canyon," I'm saying "all the way," I'm saying "abyss," cuz even if I can still see myself sitting on the bed, the strip of gauze in my hands and everything whirling around me, *I was in that landscape too, like I'd tumbled into it and was clinging on to a giant's jawline.*

Incredible! He was humongous! And me so tiny! Under my hands, the rock shook with his breath's constant rumble. Echoing like a distant avalanche. The world strained and released, and I felt I was going to throw up, but then I got it: I was facing Nick like he'd faced the mountain, and I was experiencing *vertigo.*

But still, that canyon before me, that canyon where the ice axe smashed right through Nick's face, I hadda go there. Hadda look inside. Like I had a choice?

As I crawled to the edge, a blast of icy wind punched me in the face. Total-body shiver session.

Under my fingers, rock turned into ice.

It cracked, blue and hard and hostile. The cold took my breath away. My eyes bulged, the corneas seemed to freeze. The moonlight fell through the bedroom window, illuminating the vertical walls of ice as I peered over the edge of Nick's face into the crevasse.

The depth! Oh, god, that chasm! The most dizzying my eyes had ever seen.

The abyss was full of shadows, full of darkness from a pitch-black place so deep no light could reach it, full of dancing echoes.

And it was alive. The echoes were alive.

Something was climbing up out of the crevasse.

I saw it. A horror, darker than all others. Like a spider, clinging to the wall. Straight beneath me.

It was staring upwards. Staring at me.

And me, total panic. Outta here. Away from this insanity. Behind me, the spinning bedroom; behind me, the loose wrappings of gauze on the pillow; but wherever my hands groped, they found only air. Grasping in a vacuum. Nick's abyss sucking me in. I wanted to scream, but it was like the air had frozen my lungs.

The thing in the crevasse was nearer. It was human-shaped but its movements weren't human at all. The limbs were all wrong. When I looked, it stopped moving. Like I could confine it with my gaze. But if I blinked . . .

Oh Jesus fuck, the arm, *the arm*, it shot up! Fingers riveted into precipitous blue ice. Right under me. Cracks forming where they'd slammed in. The face, it was shrouded in shadows, but I saw red, outdoor-sports-jacket-type red, and shaggy hair.

Fuck Nietzsche and his abyss. The thing climbing out of Nick's face was *Augustin.*

This time, I did scream. With all my might, I biffed myself back into reality and pushed myself away from the edge. I was suddenly thrown back onto my side of the bed. Next to me, the dark, silent figure that was Nick, only not quiet now. His body shuddering, twirling, a fluttering sound, a shriek, it filled the bedroom and bounced off the walls, which seemed more distant than I thought possible.

In a flash, something shot past me. It spread its wings. I flailed around, screaming. Three coal-black birds were circling the bedroom. One hit the ceiling light, tumbled down, then flew on, screeching.

There were birds coming out of Nick's face.

And there was more. An arm protruded from the exposed scar. Five frozen zombie fingers stretching, seeking heat. Seeking me. Around it, the sleeve of a red Gore-Tex jacket.

Augustin.

You wouldn't believe it if it came out of your own mother's mouth.

Nick jerked upright. Literally roaring. The shock wave blew the window out and threw me off the bed. I mean, there I was, literally flying through the room and thudding against the wall. It walloped the air out of me. I rolled onto the floor, coughing and doubled up with pain.

I didn't know what had just happened. Nick was thrashing his arms about and seemed to be struggling with something under the covers. For a minute I thought I *saw* something under the covers—a twisting shape, the illusion of something horrifying. But then it was gone. Nick ceased his eerie, inarticulate shrieking and stared wide-eyed at the circling birds. Feathers fluttered through the bedroom. They found the burst window and disappeared one by one into the night.

Silence.

Nick reached for the bandages on the pillow, and his eyes sought mine. I straightened up and raised both hands. "Seriously, before you start chewing me out, this I didn't know. I couldn't have."

But Nick wasn't pissed. He was shocked. Shocked, and by the look of it, dead scared. His body soaked with sweat. His hair stuck to his forehead. He pulled the covers up to his eyes, wiped them with it, and, with trembling hands, started wrapping himself with the bandages.

"What the fuck just happened?" I said.

Something had blown me across the room.

Only now I saw the havoc surrounding me. There was a crack in the wall.

Not from my impact but from the same shock wave that had blown the window off its hinges. The linen closet doors were dislodged, drawers cast away. Our framed picture on the floor. Neighbors musta thought it was a gas explosion. My mind said landslide.

I looked at Nick and said, "Birds came out of your face."

The new normal in our world.

"Birds. Birds came out of your face," I repeated.

And something else too, I thought, but didn't say. Didn't wanna upset him even more.

I walked to the bed and pulled off the covers.

The foot of Nick's side of the mattress was soaked. The hairs on his legs were standing on end. Grit between his legs. *Ice* grit.

My mind went to what I thought I'd seen under the covers.

I was chilled to the bone.

"Sorry," Nick said.

It was the first word I'd heard him say since the accident. I looked at him in disbelief. It sounded muffled from behind the bandages and the articulation sucked, but it was unmistakable.

"Dude, everything's different now, don't you understand?" I sat next to him and closed him in my arms.

Something had blown me clear across the room.

Birds had come out of Nick's face.

That meant it was real.

My boyfriend possessed. By the supernatural.

And I was Bella with balls. My boyfriend no pussy werewolf or sparkling vampire but a fucking mountain god.

LOG OF THE DEMETER

PASSAGES FROM NICK GREVERS'S DIGITAL DIARY

Written 18 July, things so strange happening, that I shall keep accurate note henceforth till we land.

—Bram Stoker

1

September 22, 2018

I brought something down with me. Can't deny it any longer. I brought something down from the Maudit.

What was that thing in our bedroom last night? The thing under the covers?

And the birds, you saw them too. So much for the *delusions* Ms. Claire the shrink keeps referring to. Your look was priceless. "Birds came out of your face," you kept saying. You must have repeated it at least fifteen times. At some point, you even laughed. And what else could you do but laugh? If you can't laugh, you either cry or go stark raving mad.

Because they were alpine choughs. No doubt about it.

And the thing under the covers, it was Augustin.

I dreamed about him. Dreamed he was dragging himself up from the crevasse, right onto the foot of the bed. I fought with him under the covers, because I was dead scared he'd drag me back into the crevasse. So that I would be with him in the dark. And he was cold, Sam, so terribly *cold*, because he had been stuck inside the glacier for so long. I remember flailing about, and suddenly I was back in the bedroom with those screeching birds everywhere, and he was gone. But the ice was still there, at the foot of the bed. The ice he'd kicked loose as he climbed out of the crevasse. Augustin I may have imagined, and you say you didn't see anything. But where did that ice come from? That was no more a figment of the imagination than those choughs.

Still, despite everything, there's one shimmer of light, and you have no idea what a relief that is. You believe me now. There's nothing worse than when your loved ones think you're crazy.

Okay, so you've seen it. Seen what has become of my face. I'm not happy that you looked after I asked you not to, but I'm thankful you at least didn't run away screaming. That would have been a conceivable reaction. Sometimes I want to run away from it, and Claire Stein says that's exactly what I'm doing by insisting on putting the bandages back on. But I think that I'm only now starting to understand that there's more to it than shame.

At breakfast, I asked why you aren't afraid of me anymore. I'm sure you want to understand—though "understand" may be an overstatement in this case. *Wiyah na affway ami anymoa?*

"I was afraid of you the whole time," you said. "Now I'm more afraid than ever, but not of you. I mean, like my mother always used to say, 'When birds start flying outtaya face, that's where I draw the line about what I'd hold you responsible for.'"

"Because before, you *did* hold me responsible." *Beecaw beefaw, yu-dud homi wisponsabah.*

"Uh-huh. Now you're a victim, too. We can be afraid together. How romantic is that?" And then, typical you, "Let's face it, what you did was totally badass."

Not even close to badass, if you ask me. But more importantly, *I wasn't the one who did it.* Ask me to throw you across the room and I wouldn't be able to. I don't have superhuman powers. But there's something inside me that apparently does . . . and I can't control it. Sure, the glazier's been around. We can patch the tiles back on the roof where they were blown off, and we can plaster up the crack in the wall. But what are the implications for me, Sam? And what are the implications for *you*? Last time, it wrapped your face with steel wire. And now this. If it's capable of this, what else can it do? Not such a badass idea, if you ask me.

Even now, we keep avoiding the issue, because that's easier than facing the truth. Because we don't *want* to face the truth. But I've known it from the moment I woke up in the CHUV in Lausanne. I brought something down with me from the Maudit, something that's living inside me like a parasite. And it isn't Augustin, despite what I saw under the covers last night.

It's the Maudit itself.

This is the story of a possession.

"Okay," you said, when you'd sipped the last of your cappuccino. "How do you exorcise a mountain?"

I have no idea.

2

September 23, 2018—private notes

Told Dr. Claire Stein, my psychiatrist at the AMC, everything this morning. Big mistake. Worried I did something terrible.

For a month now, I've been talking to Claire every Monday and Thursday between ten and ten to eleven. The Medical Psychology department has referred me to her. Suits me well. Psychiatry is in another building, a much more modern building across the street, connected to the hospital only by a footbridge. Glad I didn't have to wander through those endless corridors anymore. The AMC has in no way recovered yet from the blow. The employees are constantly on edge, walking around the hallways with their gazes fixed to the floor, only looking up briefly when you walk by, but the looks on their faces are like they're always in a hurry to be somewhere else. The atmosphere there is eerie, *dead.* I notice I don't want to be reminded about it, maybe because I was so close to death myself.

Anyway—Claire. At first it was the standard song and dance about trauma therapy, PTSD, EMDR, but before my sessions with Sam last week, I let her—at his urging—read my manuscript. She naturally doesn't believe much of it, but she's polite enough to not make me feel like I'm crazy, while not acknowledging what she calls my delusions, either. Early in today's session, she looked at me from under a framed quote by Sigmund Freud—"Sometimes a cigar is just a cigar"—wearing her typical psychiatrist's poker face, as friendly and inscrutable as you can get.

"It's quite a claim, Nick, saying you're possessed."

I reached for my iPad, but Claire put her hand on it and said, "Try saying it out loud."

I felt uneasy. Vocalizing something like that out loud is even harder than writing about it. "Listening to me isn't that much fun, you know?" I mumbled. *Wissennee a-mee i-in eahma fu, yano?*

"I can understand you fine."

"Fine, if you insist." (Not going to write it phonetically to prove how horrible I sound.) "I can't expect you to believe me. I don't believe that kind of crap myself."

"You don't come across like you do, either. You told me you're not religious. But the term *possession* is religious by definition."

"True, but religion has nothing to do with it. There's no devil or demon. No evil spirit or *anything* that can impose its will on me in a mythical sense. There's only the mountain."

"The mountain you're so obsessed with," Claire said.

Something tightened under my bandages. "I know what you're getting at."

"In psychiatry, we also use the term *possession*, but only in the context of *obsession*. We talk about being possessed by an idea. It isn't unusual for obsessive thoughts to arise after a traumatic experience. You can't get them out of your head, and you become incapable of seeing anything outside the context of the obsession. Then you behave accordingly."

"So it's me. My behavior is triggered by my obsession."

"Don't you think that's a more feasible explanation, at the very least?"

"I discussed it with Sam. But the birds change the equation. They were real. Sam saw them too."

"Are you really sure?"

I was about to say something but promptly fell silent. That came like a kick in the guts. In our three sessions together, Claire had got a pretty good picture of Sam. Now she thought I was pulling him into my delusions in order to make them seem more plausible. Or worse, that Sam wanted me to believe he'd seen the birds too, to keep the chasm between us from getting even bigger.

The death of my sanity. Christ, I can't go any lower than this.

"Let's assume for a minute that it all really happened," Claire said. "Your flashbacks, the possession. How does that work, exactly?"

"Sam said it like this: 'Possession is obsession with capital penetration. That mountain fucked you up pretty good.'"

Claire smiled but didn't digress. "In your manuscript, you say you believe that mountains have souls." Stressing the word with air quotes. "A conviction like that doesn't pop up out of nowhere. And I have difficulty imagining someone whose convictions are firmly anchored in science and rationality thinking like that. How did you come up with that idea?"

3

(Italy, 2006)

Claire was right about one thing: my obsession with the mountains had already existed long before I set foot on the Maudit. It was born on the day of my coming of age. That's not what I literally told her, but as I'm writing this, I know that it's not only true but also that it's more relevant than I'd dared admit before.

I'm convinced that in every life the passage from childhood to adulthood isn't gradual, but that instead there's a single, distinguishing moment that marks the transition, like a stoneman, a pile of stacked rocks on the col between two valleys. Often you don't see it while it happens—maybe you become aware of it only years later—but good mothers do.

I'll never forget the look in my own mother's eyes when I came back to the campground in Gran Paradiso that midafternoon in August 2006 and plunked my sweaty backpack in front of the tent. I was fifteen years old, and my rite of passage had been to climb the Punta Rossa. When I came down, she must have seen something in my face, some kind of toughening, an aloof expression she didn't recognize. But what she actually saw was that her son had grown up. He was older than the boy who'd left that morning and who, in the weeks before, had scoured the fields and built dams in the creek. It broke my mother's heart, but that didn't bother me. Every son breaks his mother's heart sooner or later.

The previous day, during a trek with my parents through the Parco Nazionale, the mountain spoke to me. It wasn't a particularly high mountain, and at first glance, not so attractive either, but it was attractive to *me*. More importantly, with my limited experience, I thought it was within my reach. Even when the path looped in the other direction, I could still feel its presence in my back, as if it were magnetic. At that moment, I couldn't have put into words what I already knew instinctively, that the mountain possessed a primeval form of life and was speaking to me: *Come up, Nick. I'm waiting for you.*

Harald and Louise Grevers were hikers, not climbers. They felt drawn to the alpine pastures, the highland grasses and the panoramas of the slopes and the valleys. Dad wore his Borsalino panama to fend off the blazing sun, and Mom picked flowers. In the mountains, they were just like an Italian couple from a

Fellini movie. The peaks didn't interest them in the slightest; no reward awaited you at the top.

"Only a point from which you can't go any further," my dad would say to me. "It's much nicer to end up at a lake or at a *rifugio*. Up there, everything seems small."

I didn't get how he could call that scintillating landscape of ice castles in the distance "small." Maybe he couldn't bear feeling small and insignificant *himself*, beneath such grandeur. Me? Call it nihilistic, call it teenage anxiety, but I *wanted* to disappear in the immensity of it all. Up until then, my life had been a succession of bland events from which I couldn't distill any noteworthy meaning. Higher up, life seemed more rugged, more pure, unpolished by time. The mountains were a world devoid of the varnish of civilization, and I felt the irresistible urge to lay them bare.

But my father was unyielding. "Absolutely not," was his answer, when I begged him to take me up to the Punta Rossa, or at least allow me to go alone. "Much too dangerous. If you're so intent on climbing mountains, you can take a course with the mountaineering association next summer. Now you're coming back down with us."

And so I did. I took that course a year later. But the Punta Rossa had come first, and that's where it all began. The mountain had opened a door, and now, after all these years, I'm afraid much more has slipped through the crack than I'd like.

The next morning, I set out before dawn. I left a note on the tent: *Went to look for ibex horns and build a dam further up the valley. Back before dinner.* I told Claire that, looking back on it now, the whole undertaking seems pretty rash to me. Fifteen years old, all alone in the mountains, and no one knew where I was. But at the time I didn't see the dangers involved. The mountain was all that mattered. Maybe it's an integral part of growing up that you constantly walk a tightrope over death. The test is to make it to the other side alive.

The valley was still dark and damp with dew. The morning chill gave me goose bumps on my bare legs. Wisps of mist covered the slopes, giving the landscape an eerie character. The forest above the campground seemed riddled with secrets. If you solely regarded it as the gateway to the upper world, then the only respectful way to pass through it would be to do it quickly and quietly, with your eyes lowered to the ground.

I started running, had the feeling I was being chased by something. But that changed the minute I found a rhythm that I felt I could endlessly keep up. The air between the larches seemed strangely charged, electromagnetic energy that made my teeth and fingertips tingle and the slopes buzz with life. No matter how steep the trail got, I didn't stop. Not to catch my breath, not to drink, not to look around. Running with my eyes to the ground, my heart in my mouth, and focused on my breathing, I seemed to be getting lighter. I felt like I was flying. Maybe I was.

It was only far beyond the tree line that I became aware of my surroundings again. The sky crept from deep purple to a pearlescent glow that faded the last stars. The day before, it took my parents and me three hours to reach the point from which you could see the Punta Rossa. Today it had cost me merely an hour. Dramatically, it rose into thin air before me, a mighty pyramid of rock, interwoven with a web of ribs and gullies that glowed bright red in the first sunlight. Somehow the mountain seemed bigger than the day before. I was in a hollowed-out combe of grasslands where yesterday we had seen a herd of ibex grazing, but they weren't there now. It was as if the mountain wanted to reveal itself exclusively to me.

Come to me, Nick. Up here there are no limits to who you can be.

I ran on, past the point where my parents had turned back. The mountain had chosen me, and I had answered its call.

I'm coming. Here I am, and I'm here for you only.

Everything that happened after that has the tangled consistency of a delirium, in which I strayed further and further from the path and pushed on through the wilderness with increasing recklessness. I remember that, at the base of the rib, warmed by the sun and craving things I had no understanding of, I threw off my backpack and attacked it head-on. Without a plan, straight up, guided by a primitive, animal instinct. What I didn't tell Claire is that something self-destructive had been awakened in me. And I *loved* it. It was overwhelming. Ecstatic. I was consciously severing the bonds that tied me to the lower world and trading them in for a detached existence in stone. Up here, the only thing alive was the mountain.

It was staring at me. Right into my soul.

It wouldn't take its eyes off me.

I can still see myself standing on the summit: head thrown back, eyes shut, arms outspread, one knee raised. My body engaged in a perilous balancing act with the wind, my spirit wavering in a thrilling deadlock between life and death.

One step to the left. One step to the right. I can be eternal too.

Now, twelve years later, that thought still gives me shivers.

4

(In the psychiatrist's office)

"How dangerous can I become? I need to know before it's too late."

I stared at Dr. Claire Stein with hollow eyes. I was painfully aware of how she was likely perceiving me, my drooping shoulders, face in hands, and the eyes between my fingers undoubtedly bloodshot. I was the epitome of the psychiatric patient. A *disturbed* patient. But I was also aware of the skin under the bandages, and it was dry and hot and throbbing.

Something was brewing in there.

"Have you ever felt the urge to hurt Sam?"

"No. Are you kidding? No way!"

"No impulse to?"

"No."

"Not even when you lie awake at night, and bad thoughts about your mutilation sneak up on you?"

"I love Sam. I want to protect him."

"And you still threw him across the room. You wrapped steel wire around his face."

I started to stammer. "I . . . I already told you. It was beyond my control."

"Because you believe it wasn't you, but that the mountain operating through you made you do it. What about Augustin?"

I didn't know what she was getting at. "Augustin is dead."

"That doesn't necessarily mean you don't hold him responsible for what happened to you. Last week, Sam told us about the photo he found, the one where you scratched Augustin's eyes out and tore open his cheeks. You said you couldn't remember doing that. Is it too far-fetched to conclude that you acted in a fit of resentment?"

My pulse went up and I felt sweat break out in my neck. "I'm not a violent person. I wouldn't harm a fly."

"He maimed you for life."

"That wasn't *him*. Because . . ."

"Because the mountain operated through him, too," Claire finished my sentence. She laid her Parker pen down on my pile of notes. "Okay, I can follow your reasoning till here. But what I don't understand is why it causes such extreme outbursts of violence. Why did it get Augustin into such a rage that he attacked you with the ice axe?"

I didn't answer her right away. I heard what Claire said, but my own words kept echoing in my head: *I'm not a violent person. I wouldn't harm a fly.*

"He was no match for it," I finally said. "For the Maudit, I mean. No human is able to resist such a primal force. It opens doors in your head that are best kept shut. It awakens . . . urges."

I expected that would elicit a reaction from her—it certainly did with me—but Claire remained impassive. "And still, here you are. Talking to me as yourself. I don't see any mountain. Why are you able to control it now?"

"Thinking I can control it is the biggest mistake you could make. I made the same mistake when we reached the summit. Until then, the Maudit had complete power over me, but suddenly its spell was broken. That's why Augustin turned against me. I wanted to get him away from there. I wanted to save his life. But I was naive." I swallowed with difficulty. Talking with a semi-ruined mouth plays havoc with your salivation, I'll tell you that. "That axe slammed a big, black hole in my face."

"And that brought it back?"

I nodded. From across her desk, I looked at Claire with sadness. "Tell me the truth. You think I'm crazy, don't you?"

She smiled. "'No great mind has ever existed without a touch of madness.' That's what Aristotle said. No, I don't think you're crazy. But I do think that right now these thoughts are dominating and disrupting your life, and we have to do something about that. So I'd like to propose a different way of looking at things. I read a case study about people who climb mountains. Don't take this personally, but according to that study, on the whole, mountain climbers aren't exactly the nicest of people."

I didn't say anything, didn't have the zip for a snappy retort.

"They were characterized as egocentric and obsessive loners whose eyes are solely fixed on the summit and for whom nothing else matters. Something you just said made me think about that. You said the Maudit had lost its magic for you when you reached the summit. Don't you take the summit of every mountain you climb back down with you for your collection?"

I nodded, again not fully sure where she was going with this.

"They're the trophies of your conquests. They say: this mountain is mine; I rose above everything and everybody. The article typifies that experience of transcendence as a mutual mainspring for many climbers. But the inherent danger is it becomes like cocaine. You constantly want more. Each next summit has to be higher still, more beautiful, more challenging. Each successful climb enhances the illusion that you are becoming invincible. But that's the thing. You're not invincible in the mountains. In the mountains, you're Icarus, flying closer and closer to the sun. And we all know how that ended."

Her fingers fluttered downward, and out of the blue, I heard a voice in my head: *And you will also find out what it's like to fall. To fall . . . and fall . . . and fall . . . and fall.*

The hair on my neck stood on end. What had gotten into me? Where did that come from?

In her office, everything was still the same. I looked at Freud's framed words on the wall: "Sometimes a cigar is just a cigar." Yet everything felt different now. It was as if a sudden wind had come out of nowhere and gently, almost imperceptibly, rocked the building. I'd swear Claire felt it too, because I remember her looking up at precisely that moment, and a shadow coming over her face.

She immediately pulled herself together and resumed. "What I'm trying to say is that when we have such a deadly fascination with something and, at the same time, it makes us feel so powerful, we may start believing that we are what we aren't. The article quoted an alpinist who claimed to literally change identities in the mountains. Normally, he wrapped butter in a factory, but while climbing he became a god. His words. Well, I don't want to imply that you—"

"You are *so* off the mark," I said.

Claire shut her mouth with an audible *plop*. A strange thing happened: I felt a painful stab behind my face and, alarmed, raised my hand toward the bandages. At the same time, I saw Claire flash an inquisitive look at me before lowering her eyes and picking up her Parker, which she started clicking absently in and out with her thumb.

Something was amiss.

"Are you okay, Dr. Stein?"

"I . . ." She hesitated. *Click-clack, click-clack.* "Sorry, I . . ." She put the pen back down, squeezed her shut eyes with her thumb and index finger, then looked up at me, smiling somewhat dazedly. "Sorry. I got dizzy there for a second."

She took a sip of water. When she put the glass back down, it was with such a bang that water spattered over the rim, forming a ring on her notes.

I'm not a violent person, I thought. *I wouldn't harm a fly.*

Yes, something was amiss. Definitely. I couldn't figure out her expression, but it wasn't her typical psychiatrist's poker face anymore.

"Let's leave the subject for now," she said. "I think it's time for you to confront yourself. I think it's time for you to remove your bandages."

"I can't do that, Dr. Stein."

"Why not?"

"Because they're not bandages. It's a mask." I leaned in and, with the middle and index fingers of both hands, touched the wrappings under which the shape of my face was strange and unrecognizable. "It's hidden behind it. As long as I wear the mask, I can contain it. But if I take it off, it will come out. And it will come out with the force of an avalanche."

5

(Italy, 2006)

It awakens urges.

What I didn't tell Claire was that when I reached the summit of the Punta Rossa that day, the electrostatic energy I felt throbbing in my body during the climb was discharged in the form of explosive sexual release. I had just enough time to pry the button of my shorts open before climaxing so uncontrollably that my ears buzzed and I had to grab the sagging iron summit cross to keep from literally falling into the abyss.

Maybe I didn't tell Claire because I reckon my adolescent escapades are none of my shrink's business, but I'm pretty sure that's not the reason.

Because I also didn't tell her about the ibex.

I had stumbled on it during my descent through the boulder fields below the pass. Here, no longer on sacred ground, the trance of the climb had worn off. I felt exhausted, deflated like a balloon. If the ibex hadn't bleated, I probably would have walked past her without ever knowing she was there. Now

I jumped to a stop. It was a doe, judging by her small, ridged horns. She was wounded. She dragged herself across the boulders, almost impossible to see against the backdrop of gray and brown. When I got closer, she tried to limp away, but she wasn't fast enough.

I stared at the distressed animal, not knowing what to do. She had been left behind by her herd after apparently breaking her hind leg from a fall off an outcrop. I could see the bone protruding and I smelled the sickly, gaseous stench of inflammation. Happened days ago, by the looks of it.

A shrill cry. High in the thin air, a golden eagle was circling, or maybe it was a bearded vulture. I immediately understood what that meant. She had been marked.

I knelt next to her. Her mild, almost human eyes looked back at me, and she bleated again. "Easy, girl," I shushed. "I know it hurts. Easy."

I shuffled closer, heart thumping. The wounded ibex tried to get up on her front legs, but she had lost all her strength and slid sideways over a rocky slab, falling with her sinewy posterior on top of the wounded leg. She cried.

"Shh," I whispered again. "Relax. I won't harm you. Poor girl."

Without breathing, my eyes open wide, I reached out my hand and laid it on her back. I was fifteen, from downtown Amsterdam, and until then had never touched a wild animal. When I did, the reality of the situation hit me, and I wished I'd never gone up the mountain that day. It would have been better if I'd gone and built a dam in the creek. The ibex doe would have died a lonesome death up here, maybe tonight, maybe sooner if the birds dared to set upon her. It was cruel, but the mountains *were* cruel. Now things were different. I *was* here, even though I wasn't completely convinced I had gotten up here of my own free will. This made her my responsibility. She was the toll I had to pay for the panorama of myself that the mountain had offered to me.

A flash in my head: I *wanted* to pay the toll.

The doe stopped trying to crawl away from me. Apparently she no longer regarded me as a danger, or had decided it didn't matter anymore. I touched her small, sturdy horns. In a gesture of submission, she laid her head on my thigh and closed her eyes. I kept caressing her and whispering to her softly, as if it could delay what I had to do.

The sun was blazing on my shoulders and my body was sticky with sweat, but the heat burning behind my face was coming from within.

I must have already been holding the boulder in my other hand. I don't remember picking it up. What I do remember is standing up and lifting the rock above my head with trembling hands. My windpipe was closed, breathing no longer an option.

The doe tried to stand up again. Later, I tried to convince myself that that's why things unfolded the way they did. The animal had moved and her head was no longer lying on the ground. But it was me. Her horns were blocking the way, and I was afraid that her skull was too thick at the stem. That a single blow wouldn't kill her. When I swung down the rock with all my strength, it was too much to the front.

Horrified, I looked at what I had done. The blow had crushed her snout. It was awful. The animal bellowed and rolled her eyes. Hair, foaming blood, and bone splinters stained the rocks when she scrambled to her feet, and now, with the strength of the dying, she managed to hobble away. Her ravaged snout dangled from her head on a strip of flesh and she was twitching with her horns. For a second I stood rooted to the spot, not knowing what to do. Then I ran after the trail of blood, looking in a panic for another rock.

Seven yards ahead, her legs gave out. Without hesitating, I started bashing in her head with the boulder. After the second blow she stopped bellowing. After the third she only quivered. After the fifth she was dead. But I kept on hitting her. I raised the rock and swung it down. Raised the rock and swung it down. I thought of relentlessly turning cogwheels, thought of tubes spouting smoke, thought of heavy machinery that, once in motion, couldn't be stopped. My hands, my arms, my upper body were covered in blood. I felt it spattering on my cheeks and in my hair. The blood was a hot, red haze in front of my eyes.

Later, I covered the carcass with boulders. The following day I could barely lift my arms up to my shoulders, but during the descent there was only heat flowing through my body. I found a steel-blue pond in the combe above the tree line and dove into it. The water was so freezing that my heart skipped a beat or two and the blood in my veins seemed to clot, but I stayed underwater as long as I could hold my breath. It was the only thing that could extinguish the fire in my body.

I reached the campground in the late afternoon. I threw down my backpack and was about to crawl into my tent without a word, but my mom, who was cleaning carrots, called my name. Our eyes met for an odd, charged moment, and when she spoke, I heard something ill at ease in her voice.

"Hey. Did you find anything?"

"No," I said. "There was nothing up there."

6

(In the psychiatrist's office)

"Why are you afraid to show your face?" Claire Stein asked.

The pressure. Oh, Christ, the pressure behind the mask.

"Because that's the heart of the matter. You were mutilated up there in a terrible accident. And let's be honest, till now you were always the kind of guy that could turn heads. On the street, in the bar, at the gym. You have many more followers on Instagram than the number of people you know, and that isn't because of the articles you write for Lonely Planet."

"I wouldn't want to say . . ."

"You don't have to be embarrassed about it. Anyone blessed with good looks is to a certain extent aware of the advantages it offers in life. But eventually you start taking it for granted. Not out of arrogance, but simply because that's how things are. You get used to your perceived self-image, and mutilation doesn't fit in with how you pictured your life at twenty-seven. So you tell yourself stories that distract you from that reality. That, Nick, is the actual mask you're hiding behind."

There was something wrong with her voice. What was it? I still couldn't read her look, and the uneasiness, the feeling that everything had been unsettled, was growing.

Okay, she was right. My mutilation *did* play a role in how miserable I'd been feeling the past few weeks. But the true reason was different. I felt it pressing from behind my face against the tightened bandages.

I heard Sam in my head. *Kinda dizzy. Don't know what's up, been feeling woozy all day. Tipsy. Topsy-turvy. Whatever.*

It was the voice that spoke those words—the voice of a frightened little boy—that finally turned memory into realization. Suddenly it made sense.

Claire was afraid of me. She had known something was off, and she had every reason to. Because it was back. That's what the pressure building up behind the mask meant . . . a pressure that had now risen beyond a critical level.

My throat tightened, and although I tried to resist it, it was like my face was being pulled apart by two invisible ice-cold hands.

"Take off your mask, Nick," Claire said, voice hoarse. "It's time for you to confront yourself."

"Can we please stop for today?" I heard myself say, starting to get up. "I know it's early, but I'm really, really tired . . ."

"Stay in your seat! Sit down and take that mask off."

"It would really be better if—"

"Take that mask off!"

She belted it out, her voice a squeal that pierced my head. Suddenly my head was full of echoes. They bounced against my skull, thin and mysterious, as if in my imagination I'd heard someone scream in the mist on a glacier. But was it really imagination? Because I could see it now too: shreds of turbulent, rushing snow, high walls of merciless ice, and a mouth of darkness opening out under my feet. The wind rising out from the depths was icy cold.

And the wind was carrying something.

The glass covering Freud's framed words cracked.

I felt it happen, my consciousness turning inward, the window in my mind opening up like an eye, from behind which I couldn't do anything but powerlessly watch as the mountain stared at her.

It saw her.

Disoriented, I realized that I had gotten up and that my chair had fallen back against the bookcase with a dull thud. I couldn't say a word, had absolutely no control of my movements. It was as if my suffocating panic was holding me prisoner behind that window. I could rap against the glass for all I was worth, but no one could hear me.

"Nick, go away." The fear in her voice was now unmistakable. "We're through for today. Please get out of here."

"Are you sure you want to see it, Dr. Stein?" the Maudit said, as it slowly walked around the desk, unwrapping the bandages from my face. "Do you really mean it?"

"Nick, go away!"

"Because I *can* show it to you. I *can* show it to you. But it's cold behind the mask. Cold. So cold that not a single person can survive there for long. So, are you sure?"

But all of a sudden Claire didn't want to see it anymore. She now wanted only one thing: to flee, till she was far away from the dominant shadow that was spreading over her.

But her chair didn't roll back any further than the window, and behind it, a fatal forty-foot drop onto rock-hard concrete.

The mist in my head became impenetrable, and the last thing I saw was that it was leaning over Claire and peeling away the last strip of gauze.

Claire screamed.

After that, all I can remember is the image of Augustin's tumbling helmet, falling and falling and falling, a red dot that kept getting smaller, and the worst thing about it was that the falling never stopped.

7

(Home, evening)

That happened this morning. When I came to myself again, it was late afternoon, and I was shocked to discover that I was home in the cellar, with the summit of the Maudit clenched in my right hand. I dropped it like a burning coal. The stone fell on the cellar floor and bounced off into a dark corner. In a panic, I touched my cheeks, as if I'd walked through a cobweb. The bandages were in place. Thank God. At some point during my blackout I must have put them back on.

Sam had gone to the UvA, and I found a text on my phone saying that he wanted to go over to Fazila's after that to binge a bunch of stuff on Netflix, so thankfully I didn't need to cook up an explanation for why I was in such a state. Because it took ages for my panic to subside. Eventually, the worst ebbed away, but the despair and the guilt remained. Even now, after having spent the entire evening writing everything down in an attempt to make sense of my whirling thoughts.

For fuck's sake, what have I done? What damage did I inflict in Claire Stein's office?

No matter how hard I try, I can't remember what happened after it stood in front of her and took off the bandages. The hiatus in my memory is elusive and awful. There is no doubt things went badly off the rails, but how bad? *How bad?* I'm sitting here in my Pages document's pale light, staring blindly at the wall and trembling like a stray dog in a thunderstorm, because Augustin's tumbling helmet isn't the only thing I remember when I try putting the pieces back together. Every time Claire pops into my head, I think of the ibex doe.

About how she bellowed when I threw that boulder down.

"I'm not a violent person," I keep whispering. "I wouldn't harm a fly. I'm not a violent person."

But who am I kidding? It has happened before, and if I don't do anything about it, it will happen again. Because it's getting worse. It's getting worse, that much I know for certain by now.

My iPhone is next to me on my desk, with Claire's private number open on the screen. "Call me if you need me," she'd said after our first session. "Day or night. If you feel the need, call me."

I can't count the number of times I almost did, tonight. But I'm too scared. I'm scared of what's waiting for me on the other end of the line. Afraid of hearing the ringing go on and on when she doesn't pick up. I imagine Claire lying in a pool of drying blood while her cell phone rings in her purse, and on the wall, behind shattered glass, Freud's words remain silent: "Sometimes a cigar is just a cigar." I try with all my might to dispel the image from my mind, but I can't.

It's now 1:26 a.m. Too late to call, even though Claire said *any time*. My nerves are crying out for it, but I can't do it. Maybe it won't be as bad as I think. When I came to, my clothes were drenched with sweat, but they didn't have blood on them. Maybe my fantasy is running wild. Suppose I *did* imagine the whole thing, I don't want Claire to think that I'm crazy. That my file would have "FEIGNS SCHIZOPHRENIA" written all over it. All caps. Big circle around it.

No, it'll have to wait till morning. But I doubt if I'll call her then.

A neutral email. Yes, that I can do. Just ask at what time the next session is scheduled. You can deduce from her answer . . . what, actually? *That she's still alive* I wrote a couple of times, but I deleted it. Of course she's *alive*; don't get yourself all worked up. You're being ridiculous. Just wait for her reply.

If she replies, of course.

One time, the screen lit up by itself. I jumped so hard I almost screamed. It was just before eleven, and it was Sam. It's cats and dogs out there and he said he'd rather spend the night at Fazila's than have to bike home in the rain. I think I managed to make my voice sound neutral, despite his asking a couple of times if I was okay. He's worried, sure. But he also needs his own space to cope. I get it.

Sam must never find out what happened today.

Anyway, I sat and wrote all evening, faster and faster, as if the act of writing would exorcise it out of me. But my writing failed to deliver the answers I was looking for. I'm tired and I'm afraid. I can hear the hail battering the roof incessantly. And then I can't help but wonder what it's like up there in the valley right now. In the valley above Grimentz. Season is over, the first storms of fall are battering the mountains. People have stopped coming, and at the foot of the Maudit only the wind is howling. The echoes of the storm sound just like screams from a crevasse.

Can a mountain be haunted?

Can a whole valley be cursed?

The photos of our expedition to the Maudit are spread out here before me on an open map of the Val d'Anniviers. The way Augustin is smiling into the camera belies how awfully wrong things went. If only we'd kept to our original plan of going to Italy after our ascent of the Zinalrothorn, Augustin would still be alive. Why did he have to die, while I was able to get back down? But we could never have foreseen *this*.

I'm not unique in attributing superhuman inspiration to the mountains I climb. All over the world, numerous mountains slumber with spiritual relevance, and entire religions have evolved at their foothills. The Olympus in Greece. Mount Sinai in Egypt. Mount Taranaki in New Zealand. Mount Fuji in Japan. But the Maudit is different. Augustin and I both knew it. The Maudit wasn't slumbering. It was alert, restless. And *hostile*. Like a soul embittered by an ancient and unimaginable event.

It didn't want us there.

And it isn't going to go away.

God, please let Claire be okay.

8

September 24, 2018—private notes

Pressure behind my face is gone. Feel much better. Canceled my appointment with the speech therapist anyway because I don't dare remove the bandages.

Worried sick all day about Claire. Searched AT5 and *Parool* for reports about the AMC. Didn't find anything. They say no news is good news. But man, the doubts. So I ended up sending an email only now. Got one of those out of office replies, with the attached adrenaline rush of false hope. Why do people even install those frickin' things? Anyway, the bits and bytes say she can be reached during office hours and will respond to my email ASAP. So I'll have to wait.

S. surprisingly cheery today. We didn't talk about it. You'd think it would be practically inevitable, right? Sometimes he seems to pretend the whole thing never happened. It's refreshing, in a way. It offers a glimmer of hope about how our life together could be when all of this is over. That I've managed to overcome my shame and am now talking with him definitely helps to restore normality. Conversations are exhausting with the constant delay of having to type everything on a touchscreen. Worse, Sam stopped reading my messages—he was *playing* them. He downloaded one of those stupid speech apps that make me sound like Stephen Hawking. When I said I loathed hearing myself like that, he installed the voice of Schiphol Airport's announcer lady. I think that nudged me to give in and finally open my mouth.

No pain now, but pretty high on a double dose of antidepressants and muscle relaxants. Feels like it tones it down, or that I'm at least more on top of it now. Let's hope I can keep on top of it. For good.

September 25, 2018

Why isn't she emailing me??? Not knowing is driving me crazy!

9

September 26, 2018

Disturbing developments.

Finally got a reply, but it came from the office administration. They wrote that, as of now, due to personal circumstances, Dr. Claire Stein would be unavailable for giving treatment and that her patients will be referred to other, "equally qualified" psychiatrists. My Monday session is scheduled with one Dr. Han Freriks. Wham. Just like that. No explanations. I finally got up the nerve to call Claire, but her phone didn't even ring. I immediately got a recording saying the number was out of service.

I should be relieved. My worst fears have turned out to be unfounded, but this doesn't bode well. The Maudit *saw* her when the mask had been unwound. Stop kidding yourself believing there's no connection between what happened in her office three days ago and the fact that Claire has suddenly canceled all of her appointments.

So what did it do to her? I'm scared even to think about it.

"Something's up," Sam said, loading the dishes into the dishwasher after dinner. "You're being weird. Has anything happened?"

Apparently, you can't deceive the one who really loves you. I obviously can't tell Sam about Claire, because I don't want to scare him more than necessary. But fortunately I had something else on hand, so I wasn't forced to lie. Not blatantly, at least.

"I read the letter from Augustin's parents," I said. "It's in German. You can read it too, if you want. And I think you should, actually. There's something in it that's pretty weird."

That much was true, at least. I hadn't wanted to read the letter until now, afraid that it would be too painful. Can't tell the Labers the truth about their son anyway. But you want to give them something. Some sort of narrative. So I opened it last night and read what they had wanted to tell me.

Uwe and Bettine Laber were divorced on good terms, Augustin once told me, but it appears that she's kept her married name. I've never met either of them, but they both seem to be nice people. Their grief is enormous, and they have many questions about the last days of their son's life. Seeing as the Police Cantonale couldn't give them a body, they had at least wanted to have a place to mourn.

"So they went to Switzerland," I said to Sam, after getting the letter. "And guess what, they were lied to! Get this." I showed him a passage that I'd highlighted with a yellow marker. "They say they visited the glacier where the authorities told them the accident had happened. *'Man könnte sogar mit dem Auto hin, am Stausee Moiry entlang.'* So they say they could get there all the way by car. The weather was *'wunderschön,'* the glacier was sparkling in the sunlight. Incredible, the things we went through up there. And incredible that their Augustin is still up there, in the mountains he loved so much . . ."

At first, Sam didn't understand what that meant, because he wasn't familiar with the region's geography.

"Not only did the authorities send them to the wrong glacier, but to a completely different valley. The Moiry glacier lies in a branch of the Val d'Anniviers, if you take the road up from Grimentz past the reservoir. That's the Stausee they're talking about. The Maudit's glacier, where it actually happened, is much smaller and lies in a secondary valley, much higher up and invisible from Grimentz. And absolutely impossible to reach by car. Remember how hard it was for us to even find the entrance to the valley?"

"Yeah . . . but wouldn't it make *sense* then that they'd send his folks to a different place? At least that way they can mourn without, like, falling off a rock or somethin'."

I gazed at him in disbelief. "But then why would they lie to them about where their son's body really is?"

"Okay, got a point."

"If it had been any other mountaineering accident, they would have said, 'We're sorry, Mr. and Mrs. Laber, but that area is very inhospitable and we would strongly advise you against going up there by yourself. But if you do wish to visit the location in order to say good-bye, there are many reliable mountain guides in the area . . .'" I was getting worked up and had to force myself to articulate, in order for him to understand me behind my bandages. "But they didn't do that. They lied. What for?"

But Sam wouldn't have it. Said an administrative error could have been made in any number of links in the chain. You know how quickly mix-ups occur in crisis situations. Doesn't have to be bad intent, he said. I don't get how he could ignore the whole context! Because it sure looks like the truth is being covered up. The Labers were sent to a different location. To keep them safe? But then who's lying? The Police Cantonale? Or have they been lied to in return, by the mountain rescuers?

The million-dollar question, of course, is *Who is aware of what's amiss on the Maudit?*

"And there's something else," I said. "A couple of days ago I sent emails to three mountain guide agencies from a fake Gmail account. To disguise any link to me and to Augustin, I presented myself as an English alpinist wanting to climb the Maudit. I said I couldn't find any information online and was looking for a guide to take me there."

"What did they say?"

"The agencies in Grimentz and Zinal emailed back that the Maudit is scenically uninteresting due to its boring, strenuous approach and crumbly rock, which also makes it dangerous. Those are verbatim quotes from the SAC *Bergführer*."

"The what?"

"The guidebook. They offered me alternatives on other mountains in the area. The Alpin Center in Zermatt wrote that they don't operate in the area at all. Which is bullshit, because they also list the Grand Cornier and the Dent Blanche, and those are practically around the corner. I followed it up by offering all three twenty-five hundred francs to guide me up the Maudit anyway. That's a lot of money even by Swiss standards, and they usually only charge that for the most challenging undertakings. Zermatt never replied. Zinal wrote only 'Too dangerous. Choose another mountain.' Initially nothing from Grimentz, but when I kept insisting, they sent me a pretty tetchy email back."

"What did it say?"

"Would I please refrain from any further contact."

"How friendly."

But even Sam, who knows money can buy you anything, had to admit it was strange. What if the locals *know* about that place and keep it secret? I keep fretting over the difficulties Augustin and I faced that morning to even find the access to the valley. The fence with barbed wire, the ACCÉS INTERDIT sign, the absence of trails, and the overgrown timber that looked like an old barrier. And then there's that surgeon from Lausanne, whatsisname? Why was he so intent on sticking to the conclusion that it was rockfall, despite it being so obvious to Nurse Cécile that I was attacked?

This could be huge. I need proof that can't be attained from afar. And even though this whole thing screams *Stay away, stay out of it*, I just can't look away, because I am personally involved . . .

(later—to Sam)

Just wanted to say how happy I am that I have you. It was sweet, what you did tonight. We're going to get through this together.

Curious, though, how Ramses suddenly won't have anything to do with me anymore. He's never shown me that puffed-up tail before. And sucking up to you the whole time. Traitor.

10

September 27, 2018—private notes

No! It came back. Back! Every time it seems to be getting better, and then *wham*, smack-bang in the face. Twice as hard as before. That ugly, mutilated fuck-fuck-fuckface. Can't go on like this!

Sam is too scared to come anywhere near me. Says his head literally reels when he's around me, ever since we came back to Ams. I asked why he never said anything and he said he thought it was him. Or that it would go away. He can be so fucking naive! How could he keep shit like that from me???

Today it was worse than before. Said I'd suddenly fallen back into Mr. Hyde mode, as he calls the *other*. That I kept staring at him this whole time, so intensely it made him all giddy. And that he felt something else staring at him, through me. That's why he walked away, only he tripped over his own feet and fell. That's how dizzy he was. Couldn't put it any other way than that he experienced—here it comes—*fear of heights*. His words.

Can it be true? Can he feel the Maudit through me?

I feel it, that's for sure. Didn't tell S., but I *remember* it staring at him. Again, the spiritual cramp, the window that had opened behind my face like a big, leering eye. It came through it! The transformation within myself is terrifying, but I can't say it was altogether unpleasant. I looked at S. and saw his life in all its insignificant, ephemeral puniness and felt so powerful in contrast, so infinitely dominant! Like a perfect, eternal state of *being* within which I could do literally anything with him I wanted to. I could throw his soul into a bottomless pit, into everlasting darkness, without batting an eye.

That thought scared the hell out of me, when I had recovered. Because it was *mine*.

(later)

S. went to UvA (he says, but he's avoiding me). Had the sudden urge to go out myself. Pulled my collar up high, hat on, sunglasses. Moved through the crowds like a shadow. Didn't know where I was headed till I'd taken the ferry from behind Central Station across the IJ river and saw the A'DAM Tower looming up.

On the observation deck, towering high above everything, I could feel the world shift from one solstice to the other. Summer is over, winter is coming. There were birds in the sky. Migrating to the south. Far beyond the horizon lie the mountains. Felt them pulling at me with destructive power. Still, as I write this.

Pressure behind my face is building again. Oxa seems to alleviate it, but only temporarily. Urge to tear off the bandages almost unbearable.

(later)

Took the Maudit's summit from my collection and now carry it with me. No need for Sam to see it. It's *my* summit.

11

September 28, 2018

Barely able to think clearly today. Constant blackouts. Excruciating, the loss of control. A shadow has fallen on me and has me trapped in my own body. It's pushing my mind away into an oblivious, ice-cold Null.

(later)

Oh fuck fuck fuck fuck fuck fuck fuck

(too late)

Afraid I've done something terrible again. Had another of those blackouts. This time it happened when I was in front of the bathroom mirror. Sorry, Sam, sorry world, sorry sorry sorry, but I took the bandages off. Telling myself I needed to rub in scar cream (which is BS, because I usually just glob it in between the strips with two fingers). But I had to release the pressure. That was the real reason. Couldn't bear it any longer. And that disgusting face, it's worse every time I look at it. I'll never get used to it. Couldn't bear the sight of my own reflection, so I cracked the mirror. Just like that, no touch involved. Like a fucking fairy-tale cliché.

And that's not all. My fingers, white-knuckled, clawing the sink, got cold like it was December. The porcelain burst into a *craquelure* under my fingertips. Next, I was back in the crevasse, hearing Augustin screaming against walls of ice. The cold. The echoes in the dark. And then the Maudit, coming up from the deep. So enormous; so *alive*. After that, only Augustin's falling helmet. Exactly like it happened in Claire's office. There was no end to it, that was worst of all.

Must have come to an end after all, because I came back to myself on the street in front of the house, with Loes Timbergen from a few doors down freaking out on me. Rosalie wailing out loud in her arms, little face buried in her mother's breast, tricycle on its side. What was I thinking, scaring a child like that? Maybe Loes was just referring to the mummy mask, because I had it on again. Maybe she thought I was playing a prank. But I don't think so. What if something worse happened? Something terrible, like with Claire? What if I hurt a *child*?!

Anyway, I raised my arms in apology and walked away quickly. Cleaned up the mess in the bathroom. A good mosaic is no eyesore, if you know what I mean. Seven years of bad luck, right? At least I was myself again. Pressure gone. Took an even bigger dose of oxa and slept through the rest of the day. Resisted the urge to take them all and be done with it.

Won't do it. For S.'s sake.

Little Rosalie's frightened face, I can't get it out of my head. It gives me the jitters all over.

12

September 29, 2018

Just heard the doorbell. Sam got it. Loes Timbergen. Heated discussion. Couldn't make out what L. was saying, but heard Sam when he blew up. "Listen, if you wanna take that tone, he wasn't wearing a mask, he's recovering from an accident he barely survived, and we've got more important things on our minds than your kid losing a night's sleep over it. It's not Nick's fault she's sick, got it?" And slammed the door.

So the girl is sick. Sick. Sam's right. Get it out of your mind. Not your responsibility.

But. But. But.

(later)

Still haven't heard from Claire. I can surmise till kingdom come, but I simply don't *know* what happened to her after she faced that horror. The horror I carry within me. But what happened to that girl Rosalie—that I *do* know.

I can't deny it any longer.

What if it's contagious?

13

September 30, 2018

Sam, what's the matter? Is it about the bathroom? Or has something else happened???

(later)

What did I do? Please talk to me!!!

(later)

Sam finally talked. Said my phone rang last night. Almost had a stroke, because he knows I put it on Airplane Mode at night. Maybe I forgot to yesterday evening, no knowing now. Didn't give it any thought this morning, because I slept through the whole thing. Anyway, it was Augustin. Name and portrait on the screen. Sam scared, not knowing what to do. Then he thought that maybe they'd found A.'s body and the police were going through his recent calls, so he picked up.

You could hear only static. Like someone was calling very long distance, Sam said, or a strong wind was blowing into the speaker. But then he heard a voice. Had to strain to understand what it was saying, because it was whispering. Realized it was a single word in German, being repeated over and over: *kalt. Kalt kalt kalt.* Went on for almost a minute. The whispering got more and more intense. Then they hung up.

Maybe he dreamed it. Nothing from Augustin in my Recents; no other numbers, either. S. got mad when I asked if it could have been a dream. Probably rightly so, but had to ask.

Now drained and scared. Real, real scared.

(later)

The die is cast. Decided to go to Switzerland. Can't go on like this. Sam, the sweetheart, it was his suggestion, even though it's the last thing he wants.

Wish I knew if this is the right thing to do.

14

October 1, 2018—to Sam

Dear Sam, sorry about everything. Everything I said and everything I've been putting you through. I'm responsible for this misery. I had to go up that mountain at all costs. I can only hope you'll forgive my stupidity one day.

The longer I think about it, the more I see that you're right. It was a good decision to search for our answers at the source. But let's promise each other one thing: we *will not* go up there. Not even to the valley. Whatever happens. I understand what you said, but truth is I don't believe in all that psychological crap about confronting your demons.

That mountain is *dangerous.*

So promise me. Forget about seeing it with your own eyes. We stay away from it.

(later—private notes)

Some good news after all. Sam just came up to me. Managed to get his father to agree to rent a chalet in Grimentz for a month, with some spiel about trauma alleviation and couples therapy. Unbelievable—it must have cost a fortune. I don't even want to know how much the rent is.

"Your dad's a hero!" I said, hugging him tightly. "When this is all behind us, we'll fly to New York together and take him to a Yankees game. He's always wanted to do that with you, right?"

Sam raised his eyebrow and said, "Go ahead and take him to the stadium, if you want. I, on the other hand, have an appointment in a lounge bar on Seventh Ave, where they know how to fix a mean mojito."

We leave day after tomorrow. We're finally taking action!

15

October 3, 2018

Found an eleventh-hour reference. A couple of years ago, Pieter and I spent a rest day during our climbing vacation with his uncle, Frans Wijngaards, who owns a chalet near Zermatt. I remembered that he had shown us an old little book with legends and local tales. It was called *Walliser Sagen*, from 1963. I emailed Frans last week, asking whether it said anything about the Maudit, but he couldn't find anything. But turns out today he emailed me a scan of a passage about the pastures above Grimentz. One of them, located behind a place labeled "Col Maudit," is apparently called the Valley of Echoes, and the valley dwellers have shunned the area since time immemorial, because the devil is said to reside there.

16

October 4, 2018

Just left the Rhône valley at Sierre to head south. No rain all the way through the foothills, but cats and dogs as we got higher into the Val d'Anniviers. Slept most of the way on the German autobahn—oxys and chronic pain are wearing me out—while you were driving. Relieved you could keep it up for so long, because my stamina has hit an all-time low.

Too worked up to sleep now, though. Low-hanging clouds block the view of the higher slopes. The waterfalls of the Navisence at the bottom of the valley are hidden under a second layer of clouds, which means we're passing through a gray, hovering no-man's-land. I didn't fail to notice that you turned down the music. That you lick your lips every time we round a new turn. You don't like it one bit, do you? Minor consolation: this time, you're not alone. I've driven here so many times before. And always with the same familiar feeling of a homecoming. So different now!

At the end of this road lies the Maudit. If what I think is true, I'd be crazy not to question what's driving me to come back here. Because it may turn out to be very dangerous. But still, the events of the past few weeks have made it sufficiently clear that the answers to our questions cannot be found in the Netherlands but are buried at the foot of that mountain, in Grimentz. At the mouth of the valley where it all happened.

Sure, I have my doubts. How many times have I asked myself whether all of this isn't just a figment of my imagination? I know you have been thinking the same. Maybe you still are. But even if I'm fooling myself, it's still not such a bad idea to go to Switzerland to confront the trauma and continue my recovery process. Who can tell? There's a reason they have so many spa retreats here. The fresh mountain air will boost both our spirits. Even the scar revision I can probably get done here, if we decide to stay longer. Medical care in CH is top-notch.

The GPS says it's twenty more minutes to Grimentz. The road winds past ravines towered over by steep cliffs. I admire your determination and your patience, seeing as, to you, this habitat is so hostile. Your ability to take the sting out of difficult situations with edgy humor. I don't know how I could have survived the last two weeks without you. You not only watched over my mental health but you also gave me the strength to fight back. And after all I made you suffer through!

Ramses is in the back in his travel carrier, half-closed eyes focused on me, with a look on his face that says we can all go to hell. Bundle of laughs. He'll never forgive us for this trip. I realize I have a responsibility. In this all-encompassing chaos, cherishing a drowsy, angry cat and my love for you may be quick, ephemeral flames, but to me, they are all that matter.

And that, I realize as I'm writing this, is why I am so scared. Because I *know* we should get the hell out of here. The mountain is waiting for me, up there, in the mist. I can feel it all over.

It's drawing me like a magnet.

It's calling me home.

THE HAUNTING OF HILL HOUSE

NOTES BY SAM AVERY

All I could think of when I got a look at the place from the outside was what fun it would be to stand out there and watch it burn down.

—Shirley Jackson

1

That. What Shirley says. Times a million.

The rain clattered down so hard on me it was personal. Poured on my hunched head and shoulders, streamed down the hood, elbows, and bottom of Nick's spare Gore-Tex coat—fashion fail deluxe, pratfall supreme, I call character assassination. Jeans pasted to my thighs, Ralph Laurens sloshing in muddy rivers of rainwater that flowed over my feet to the side of the driveway. Visibility nada. Me standing there, lips sputtering water, blinking like a drag queen on speed to drive it out of my eyes. Staring at the chalet, whispering, "Ho. Ly. Mo. Ly."

The chalet was attractive like something dropped from the *Enola Gay* could be attractive. It lay there at the bottom of the valley by the brook, which for the occasion had morphed into a swirling, seething tempest, swollen and roaring like a ravenous brown monster. The Moiry dam, its source, according to Nick, out of view behind a claustrophobic clusterfuck of insanely steep slopes that enclosed the cabin. It lay there in a glade in the pine forest, against a solitary rocky outcrop that jutted out of the landscape like a festering boil. A festering boil topped with a cross and a lady chapel.

Picturesque, they said on Airbnb. I'd say Dam Collapse Catastrophe Ground Zero.

All you ever woulda wanted in a home was here: classic Swiss-eaved saddle roof, larch wood walls on a stone base, snow shutters carpentered by Heidi's grandfather himself—

Oh yeah . . . and a hellish flashback-wormhole to everything you ran away from as a child.

Someone's idea of a sick joke. Huckleberry Wall, take two.

My iPhone vibrated. Text from Julia.

> How's mountain boy doing?

And me, huddled in that yellow outdoor garbage bag, thinking of what they said on Airbnb: cozy living room with panoramic southern view, fireplace, and polished paneling. Thinking of what they said on Airbnb: three bedrooms, king-size double, and a color-therapy Jacuzzi. What they didn't mention was the possessed subtenant in the basement with crows inside his mutilated head. The German spirit boy who called you out of bed at three in the morning to tell you how freezing the crevasse was where he'd been stuck. Notwithstanding the absence of a sauna, five-star ratings guaranteed.

The ride over here had been a nightmare, but this was the ninth circle of hell.

For a second, I thought about just standing here and surrendering to the elements, letting the river and the storm swallow me up. Then I turned around and walked slowly back to the Focus. I opened the door, slumped behind the wheel, dripping, and shut the door. The windows fogged up in nothing flat.

Nick looked at me.

Seconds ticked away.

I said, "Not a word."

Asked him to fish the keys out of the glove compartment. The thick leather instruction folder we got from the owners, a couple down in Sion. Without their map, we'd still be looking for the access road. A mile of bumpy dirt road with rim-deep puddles just beyond the village. Downhill this time, but the resemblance to the Panther Mile was uncanny. There was supposed to be a campsite somewhere along it, but we didn't see it. Here at the end of the world there was nothing. Less than.

I held the key, felt it weighing down on my soul, and sighed, "Welcome to Hill House."

Nick typed on his iPad. Stephen Hawking comes on: "It's not that bad. It's got a certain curb appeal."

"Dude, the House of Usher had more curb appeal. When we're outta here you owe me a penthouse."

2

It was still light when my panic attack struck. This was after the dripping bags I'd put in the hall to dry. After leaving Nick in the living room to cocoon on the couch above the under-floor heating with a steaming pot of chamomile tea, after I'd sized up the room and said, "Can't get more Swiss than this, not including raclette and tax evasion." This was after Ramses jumping out of his travel bag the second I unhooked the latch and, offended, pretending to suss the place out, but never wandering too far, because nowadays, he's actually a scaredy-cat, too chicken to be alone with Nick. After my text to Julia: One guess where I am—with any luck they serve fucking pflaumenschnaps and after her reply: Bro, seriously??? BAD IDEA. This was after my hot shower, after my soaked clothes in front of the radiator, after sweatpants and white T-shirt, after, after, after.

You gotta hand it to me. Up until then, I was coping fine. Despite the chalet's old-fashioned cuckoo-clockish woodwork and beams, it was surprisingly modern, almost clinically clean, and if you pushed me, maybe I would even pronounce it "snug," if only to tickle Nick.

But then I found myself in the master bedroom on the basement floor, unsuspectingly hanging up clothes, and suddenly the whole house tumbled on top of me. Suddenly my head itched, my T-shirt was too tight, my skin the wrong size. Ruffled my hair, spun around, felt like I was heading in all directions at once.

What'd gotten into me? Everything around me suddenly felt abysmal and terrifying. I looked around, seriously rattled. Only the patter of the rain on the roof. The indistinct rocking of the house in the wind. Maria crying in her little chapel.

That feeling you're trapped, that you can't get out—they didn't advertise that on Airbnb.

So there you were, incarcerated in the *Eurotrip* version of a house you'd spent your whole life running away from. Twenty-four and life focused solely on escaping the boy in the pee-soaked loincloth, the boy who brought fire to humanity and set his family tree ablaze with a single spark. Twenty-four and life spiraled you back to where you started, where the piles of ashes were still smoldering.

All you ever wanted to forget but couldn't.

No one winds up in a house like this by accident.

I walked to the bathroom and splashed my face with cold water. Stared back at my bloodshot eyes, thinking, *What the fuck are we doing?*

Responsibility. That's why I was here. Still, everything that was so logical before we'd left now seemed deranged. And the disquieting feeling crept over me that the line between chasing shadows and fighting lunacy had become so fine, so unclear and fluid, that you could hardly call it a line anymore. Maybe there was some sort of general condition Nick suffered from after all. Maybe I hadda U-turn back to Amsterdam and spill the beans to Nick's shrink or some other AMC doc who'd finally shed light on the whole deal.

But the birds were real; I saw them with my own eyes. (*And you saw something else too*—Whoa! File it behind the floodgates.) The birds were real, and that's why I was here.

Plus, I was responsible for Nick. We all know how the last mutilated face on my account ended up.

All kids have scars. All kids have stretch marks, cuz the skin grows too fast. We all suffer from soul striae. I was here to iron something out.

Still, back in the bedroom, I couldn't shake off that uneasy feeling, and I saw my grandpa emerging from Huckleberry Wall, all ablaze, but this time he didn't do a smoldering face-plant into the snow. This time he wobbled toward me through the wailing wind and took me in his arms. Only when I felt the force of his grip on my ribs did I realize it wasn't Grandpa but Nick, and I heard him say, "Little, fragile Sam!"

The Catskills or the Alps, Phoenicia or Grimentz, the Hermit or the Maudit. Every house was buckling under shadows.

Every house was haunted.

3

"There's absolutely no reason," I said, as we climbed up through the valley, "no reason why we *shouldn't* take you back to New York and start an escort service. Facial disfigurement is the new buxom. You aren't deformed, you're differently abled. You've got a whole new career ahead of you in the States. Political correctness alone will do the trick."

He was doing his best, but I could see Nick was having trouble keeping a straight face under those bandages.

"Think about it. No one wants perfection anymore. Beauty calls for insecurity. From a certain age, we all start using profile pics from ten years ago. No one'll admit it, but they *want* pay boys with progeria. Playmates with psoriasis. Everyone wants to compensate."

"So it would actually be a kind of social therapy."

"You got it."

"And you'd exploit my handicap without any remorse."

"Not me. *Us.*" I stopped walking so he could catch his breath. "And I haven't even gotten to the merch. Imagine, the first ever life-size Nick Grevers sex doll. The hole in the mouth fits all sizes, baby."

Nick shoved me and said, "Cut it out, asshole. It hurts like hell when I laugh."

It was a crystal clear moment on a crystal clear morning. Nick's laugh, it has the power to pump me with instant happiness.

I missed that laugh. Even now, when I could see only part of it, it was like a supernova in a vacuum of dead stars.

Before all this business, it was one of our favorite things—to shamelessly roast each other about our flaws. No limits, no taboos. Our way of marking out each other's territory. Saying you're mine and I'm yours. It was our relationship's defibrillator. Pecs: check. Pads. Clear. Aaand . . . *zap!*

It was great being *us* again. Made me feel the wounds of the past coupla months were healed, and I'm pretty sure same goes for Nick.

More important, the mountains seemed to do him good. Hadn't seen him so upbeat since the accident. The Maudit seemed further away than ever. The rain had stopped during the night and been replaced by a bright, crisp fall morning that was so invigorating it almost floored you. Cuz you were practically strong-armed to spit it out: it was magnificent around here. Slopes gleaming with blinding colors. Air so organically pure and filtered your lungs collapse from cold turkey CO_2 withdrawal. Cowbells tinkling idyllically in the distance. Nick doing his exercises on the rock next to our house, which, for obvious reasons, I'd dubbed Castle Rock. Seeing him stretching on the plateau, those luscious lungs sucking in mountain air, radiant white shirt, body brought to you by shakes, liquid baby food, and pills, pills, pills, it hits me how clear-cut his sexiness is. Even in bandages. Clear-cut—get it? (*Da-dum-dshhh* *cricket sound*)

And with that, I even surprised myself. Ever since that fuckup in Amsterdam, we hadn't been intimate anymore. Not really. Couldn't get it up. The nerve, I mean. Maybe some things that seemed fucked up beyond repair could still be fixed.

Anyway, Nick suggested going up the trail behind the house. So he could finally show me his beloved mountains. And his talking . . . well, he wasn't exactly rattling on, sounded more like an amateur ventriloquist having a bad day, but hey, who needs articulation when you got willpower?

"Okay, forget the handicap. If you can learn to control your superpowers, I see a golden future in the film biz."

"I don't have superpowers, Sam."

"Don't be so conservative. What you did with me in the bedroom, that was telekinesis. Imagine. Every FX studio in Hollywood rendered obsolete. No action or horror movie without your name in the credits. You could be the first real-life Carrie White. And I'll be your manager. Even if we only demand fifty percent of what the studios save on CGI, we'll be raking it in. You just need a bit of practice. Here. Lift me off the ground."

"Say what?"

"Lift me off the ground."

"I can't."

"Willpower, Nick. Believe in it. You don't want it enough."

"That's not how it works."

I took out my iPhone and said, "Want me to film it? It'll get a hundred million views on YouTube."

Those explosions in his eyes—I couldn't get enough.

We took it easy and rested whenever Nick's body said so. One step, ten steps, a hundred steps. In front of us a huge brown cow was chewing on alpine grass. A gray cow was trying to scratch her rump with her horns, soundtracked by the jingles of a massive bell. A third cow was blocking the trail, squinting against the sun. Chewing their cud, the cows didn't budge, only their tails swatting their ass flies.

And me, I stood still, cuz those cows, those horns, not what you want shish kebabbing your painstakingly built abs.

"Relax," Nick said, hands raised. "Alpine cows are gentle as lambs. They wouldn't harm a fly."

"I dunno, Nick. A wise man once said, 'Never trust anything that lives on a mountain.'"

"Which wise man?"

"Me. Don't you know some kinda spell to get that critter to move outta the way?"

Nick approached calmly. Deferentially. Like he was some kinda swami. And the cow, it just gazed unfazed. Couldn't tell by her look whether she was super smart or incredibly dumb.

"If she freaks out, CinemaSins will troll the hell out of us," I said. "Animals-sense-supernatural-presence-before-humans-do cliché."

Nick giggled. "Come on. She's harmless."

"You mean she'll harm me less?" I said, but I swerved behind Nick, keeping a wide loop, as far from the trail as possible without falling into the creek. Expecting a stampede any minute. Or the cows to crowd in a procession around Nick.

But none of the above. Clarabelle didn't give us a second glance. It was almost a letdown.

About a mile past our house, the trail climbed through a narrow valley to above the tree line, and not much later we reached the top. In front of us, right in the middle of the upper valley, rose the massive gray wall of the Moiry dam. Above it, the shimmery reflection of the sun on a mirage. A jagged line of shark teeth. The mountains' ivories. Glaciers, snowcaps, the works.

My stomach was on tumble-dry, a feeling that, geometrically speaking, was a hundred and eighty degrees diametrically opposed to the wild sparks in Nick's eyes.

"Wow," he said.

I didn't say a thing.

A solitary curl of cloud brushed one of the highest peaks. Those mountains, they had something hypnotizing about them, but not in any dreamy or salutary way. I couldn't help feeling that the dam formed a barrier. It emanated unseen menace. I wasn't prepared for it, and it freaked me out. Also cuz of what I saw in Nick.

"See that ice face right above the dam? Pointes du Mourti. I climbed it."

"Motherfucker," I said.

"With Pieter. Our first north face. And that high one there in the distance, too. That's the Dent Blanche."

He musta seen something in my face, cuz he touched my hand and said, "Aww."

I looked away, wished I had my shades with me. Said, "And now you're gonna quit climbing, right?"

"Um . . . I haven't really given it much thought yet."

"You need to think about it?"

Nick shrugged. "The Kazakhstani climber Anatoli Boukreev survived a blizzard on Everest that killed eight others, and six days later he soloed Lhotse, the fourth-highest mountain in the world."

"Eighth, sixth, fourth, who cares?"

"Joe Simpson started climbing again after he broke his leg high up in the Andes and almost died."

"Cuz he's a fool."

"Your fools are my heroes. Maybe they went back to the mountains to come to terms with something."

But that wasn't the main reason and we both knew it. I thought of Nick's manuscript, what he had written in it: *If you, the climber, hear the mountain's call, it will bewitch you, it will intoxicate you, and you will realize that you could fathom her only if you succumb to it—if you go* up.

And Nick, again that intense look when he sniffed the cool air. He tousled my hair, which totally pisses me off most days, but I let him now, cuz I suddenly felt really shaky.

"Why don't you like it here, Sammy?" he asked. "The mountains always make me feel so peaceful."

Why didn't I like it here? The mountains bit your face off. They almost killed you. They always make me wait at home, frozen with fear, every time your yogi yearning comes calling and you need to observe the whole karmic cycle of life from some elevated spiritual perspective. A jaw operation and two scar corrections coming up, and even so, your face will still be marked for life. How's that for peaceful?

But I didn't say that. And I couldn't tell him about the Catskills, either. About Huckleberry Wall.

"Something about the way they block the horizon just gives me the jitters." I made a wide gesture. "They make the world too small. Like everything behind them is a secret. And with every step you take, one disappears behind the other and then another one appears. One sidestep and your whole world looks different. How creepy is that?"

"Know what's creepy?"

"What?"

"That hospital. They're all so terribly unanimously positive, with their good intentions and carefree smiles and blah blah about how everything will be all right, but all around me people were dying. All those fathers and mothers and sons and daughters that couldn't take their loved ones home, and I was ashamed because I was feeling miserable about my *face*, about how everything would be different when I got out."

"I'm sorry I wasn't there."

"That's not what I meant; you know that."

"I'm still sorry. It feels like I let you down by not being there for you. Even here. Even on this fucking mountain. I shoulda been there for you."

"That's stupid."

"But it's true."

We walked in silence for a while, unspoken words between us. A treasure of raw, white Tiffany pearls strung on the horizon.

"I'm not sure I can take you climbing again, Nick."

I know, he said. *It's okay*, he said. But everything good about this morning suddenly seemed out of balance. Disrupted.

"Where's the mountain where it happened?" I asked, hoping it wasn't too much of a bet.

"You can't see it from here. It's on the other side of that ridge." He pointed to the eroding scree on the right, steep and incised by avalanche gullies. "When we go to Grimentz, I can show you the col at the entrance of its valley. The col where Augustin and me made the stonemen."

Hearing Augustin's name, here, so close to where he died, gave my guts a nasty squeeze. Since we got here, we'd shut up about the incident and the real reason we were here.

"So if you go all the way up, right here, you could look down into the valley?"

Nick's brain machinery churning. "I don't know. The main crest is higher, I think, out of sight. But theoretically you're right, yes. Only . . ."

"Only what?"

"I'm not sure what you'll see. We trekked through the valley for hours and hours before we reached the glacier. When the clouds closed us in, you know? The valley couldn't have been that long. It didn't make sense. It didn't jibe with the map or the surroundings."

"You guys were disoriented."

"Yes, that's true."

We didn't say anything for a while.

And me, totally Sam Avery: "We can book a helicopter flight. That way you can see it."

I saw Nick go stiff. "I don't want to. Too dangerous."

"*Looking* at it is dangerous?"

No answer.

And I gazed at the mountains and thought about teeth again. And in my thoughts they were all rotten.

AT THE MOUNTAINS OF MADNESS

NICK GREVERS'S MANUSCRIPT (PART 2)

Our sensations of tense expectancy as we prepared to round the crest and peer out over an untrodden world can hardly be described on paper; even though we had no cause to think the regions beyond the range essentially different from those already seen and traversed.

—H. P. Lovecraft

The morning after our ascent of the Zinalrothorn, we woke up refreshed, and any premonitions and irrational fears we might have felt seemed frivolous. Our muscles were warmed up by the sun, our spirits nourished by the light. In the distance, at the end of the valley, the mountains were beckoning, sparkling like rough diamonds on the necklace of a new day.

Plus, by then I already realize that there's something strange going on with the Maudit. But instead of taking it in as a threat, it magnetizes me.

The mystery calls.

Google is of no help. Connected to the campsite bar's wireless, we try different searches, but nothing. Neither on Bergtour.ch nor on SummitPost, Camptocamp, or Hikr. Strange, since those websites are more or less the modern alpinist's bible. But the signal is crappy, and after sitting around for ages waiting for a couple of low-res pics of the area to load, we lose our patience.

We swipe through our own pictures from the last two days instead. There are a couple of really good ones—like the one with Augustin dangling in midair from Le Rasoir you saw on Instagram.

[*At that moment, we didn't give it much thought, but if you think about it, it's striking. Even a bit creepy. The AMC has a fast 4G network, so this morning I googled the Maudit again and it's remarkable how little has been documented about it. Try for yourself. It's mentioned in passing in a number of French descriptions of the crest that curves to the north between the Val d'Anniviers and the Val d'Hérens, but there isn't a single trip report to be found. I also can't find any good close-ups. There are a couple of panoramas taken from the north, but because of its unfavorable geographic location, most of the peak is either hidden behind the ridges that frame the Moiry reservoir, or it's practically invisible against the Pennine giants on the border with Italy. The only concrete reference I found is in a scan of an old (and actually quite sinister) clipping from* Le Nouvelliste *from 1957, about an accident on the Maudit in which seven alpinists lost their lives. It's in French and I can't completely figure out what it says. I saved the JPEG; maybe you can translate it for me when you get back.*

I don't know why it didn't register that sunny day in the campsite bar. It's not a total surprise that my internal blueprint of the Alps appears to be incomplete, but the fact that the internet is of no avail in a time when practically every molehill has been plowed up and has its own hashtag is more than a little alarming to me.]

We ponder all day on what to do. When evening falls, we drive up to Grimentz, precisely the sleepy town with luxury chalets and closed-for-the-season ski lifts I'd expected it to be. A sanctuary for timid mountain folk and affluent summer visitors. From the narrow alleyways of the village center, flush against the slope, we can see the entrance to the Moiry valley, where the paved road winds upward toward the reservoir. More to the west, almost imperceptible, lies the col to the much narrower, higher-situated basin from where we should be able to access the Maudit. The mountain itself is invisible from here. The evening is brooding, the colors vivid; the twilight brings out faceted, deep-blue and green hollows in the densely wooded slopes.

In an inn smelling of brick oven and melted cheese, we get two foaming steins of draft beer. The only other guests are a couple of old-timers from the village who nod curtly when we walk in. Above the bar hangs an old-fashioned birdcage. As I drink my beer, my gaze is constantly drawn to the dark shadow shuffling inside it. A crow. Or a chough.

Neither of us can make a decision about tomorrow's plans. Until Augustin goes to the washroom, returns, and gives me a smiling jerk of the head toward the downstairs. I follow him to the lower level, where a series of framed photos and old engravings adorn the walls. Chalets with snow-covered roofs, panoramas taken from the ski runs above the village, men in traditional attire in front of a crevassed glacier.

"Here, look at this," Augustin says. He points to a yellowed, framed engraving between the doors to the men's and women's. It's entitled "Val d'Anniviers 1878." It's hard to tell from which angle it was drawn. I recognize the peaks, but they're coarsely sketched with brown ink, pointier and rougher than in real life, as if the artist unconsciously associated them with the crooked teeth in the mouth of a wolf. A reflection of the zeitgeist, I realize, in which the mountains must have been a hearth of dangers and local superstitions for the valley's dwellers.

At the top are the names, in the same faded ink: Cervin, Dent Blanche, Garde de Bordon, Pointes du Mourti. The glaciers bulge out of the valleys, mightier and longer than in the twenty-first century. The reservoir of Moiry doesn't exist yet. Where it is today, the drawing depicts a desolate, U-shaped valley, from which the glacier curls like a split tongue. And on the right, on what must be the west side, is another valley. Higher, with more rigid contours, smaller, but there it is. At the end of it, a dark, sharply crosshatched peak. A horned summit: a bull, a devil. The inscription above it says "Pointe Maudit."

"That's it!" I call out. "You see? It looks exactly the same here as when we saw it from the Rothorn, don't you think?"

"These old names are pretty amusing. Cervin is now Matterhorn, even in the French-speaking cantons. And Gabelhorn is now Obergabelhorn."

"But that basin, it seems to open up right above us, right over Grimentz, just like the map says. Weird, this engraving clears up more than all those pictures on the internet."

I keep looking at it. The Maudit seems indisputably hostile. Something about the way the peak has been rendered larger than it really is, and the way the summit seems to lean forward, or how the valley, whose name isn't mentioned on the map, seems to be full of shadows.

"What do you think? Should we just go?" Augustin asks. His eyes reflect the subtle fascination I see every time he thinks up a new project, a fascination that is the seed of obsessive possession.

"With zero information?"

"Old-school. We take some bivi gear and I can take your spare helmet from the trunk, which will save us a trip to the outdoor supply store. We search for a way up along the stream that comes down from the valley and climb that mountain, without any route planning. Should be cool, right? Like we're pioneers."

It does sound enticing.

It's his kind of plan. Augustin's heroes are the Edward Whympers and Geoffrey Winthrop Youngs of this world, erstwhile alpinists who performed their heroic virgin ascents without any trails or Gore-Tex gear.

"MeteoSchweiz says there's only a chance of some local thunderstorms in the afternoon, so we could bivouac," I suggest. I notice I'm getting excited. "Would make a big difference, if we leave the tent in the car."

"And when we're up there, we'll decide on the best route. Neither of us knows anything about the Maudit. Where in the Alps can we still pretend we're first-ascenters?"

"You sure you don't want to go to the Jorasses?"

"We still have loads of time for that. There probably really is a misprint on the map, but there's no way the Maudit could be higher than eleven five, twelve K at the most. If we set out from the bivi day after tomorrow and leave early, and if it isn't too difficult, we can be back in the early afternoon. Evening at the latest. We'll wind our way to Italy after that."

That was the plan in a nutshell. Unprepared but determined, sure of our abilities, invigorated by the brief but intense bond that is forged between climbers during a delicate enterprise high up in the mountains, even if they aren't friends in real life. Such a bond goes deeper than sea-level friendships. You pledge yourselves to each other's lives, make a binding oath that, even in the most unthinkable circumstances, you will come back down together and alive.

It's unfortunate that neither of us had a good command of French and therefore didn't know what *Le Maudit* means.

* * *

If this were a fiction, a sequence of increasingly confusing diary excerpts would now follow, detailing the approximately fifty-six hours that our expedition to that forlorn, forsaken place lasted. That's the classic approach in these kinds of stories, because authors think that the tone of the firsthand narrative adds a dimension of realism. But it is in fact completely unrealistic for two reasons.

First, alpinists never take a diary in their backpack. Every ounce counts. When you frantically maneuver your way up a ninety-degree dihedral, eight yards above the last bolt, while your muscles are pumped full of lactic acid and the weight on your back pulls you further and further down, you thank yourself for chopping the handle off your toothbrush or for removing the labels from the zippers. I once had a mountain guide who always took a mass market paperback to kill time in the huts or bivouacs. When he'd read a page, he'd rip it out and use it as toilet paper. Wiping your ass with Tolstoy! Talk about efficiency.

The second reason is that you simply lack the time to write. A bivouac up in the mountains is time-consuming, cold, and uncomfortable. The only thing on your mind in those circumstances is staying alive, keeping warm, and preparing yourself as efficiently as possible for the next day's climb.

So a diary entry is a no go. But I do have the photos.

[*I uploaded them after all, Sam. I didn't trust myself to be able to fully recall what happened up there without them, because my recollections were still confused and fragmentary. I thought the photos would at least trigger something. And fuck yeah, they did.*]

They're taken with the GoPro. I rarely shoot video in the mountains because I've noticed that photos have more impact and do a better job of representing their scale. The photo report of the Maudit consists of sixteen pics, all taken on the first day, during the approach and in the bivi. Of the climb itself I have none. The battery was dead by then. [And my iPhone? *I hear you think. Yes, it was still working, but from the moment we entered the valley we lost the signal, so we had no way of calling the emergency services. And by the time the GoPro's battery went dead, I was so busy keeping myself alive that taking pictures with my iPhone never even occurred to me.*]

The first pic shows a barbed wire barrier in front of what looks like the beginning of a steeply descending trail on the densely wooded slopes above Grimentz. A yellow sign says ACCÈS INTERDIT and Augustin is posing in front of it with a silly grin on his face, his rolled-up sleeping pad buckled to the side of his North Face backpack.

Our problems have already started, shortly before that, when we try to find the access into the narrow basin. According to the map, obscure tracks go from the village's higher section to the brook that streams down from it (TORRENT DE MAUDIT, it says in blue letters), but the dotted line stops before it even reaches the stream. From Grimentz, where we parked the car in front of La Poste, the steep slopes are a mess, and we can't find the track. We lose forty-five minutes by following a brook above the village, which eventually leads to the abandoned ski slopes to the west.

Only once we escape the woods and arrive at a rustic alpine pasture with a few crude, weather-beaten sheds do we see we're not where we should be. More to the south, the narrow, V-shaped notch in the mountain range we are heading for now appears to be visible. Map check makes matters only more confusing, because we don't see the obvious landmarks on the map anywhere physically around us. No wonder there's so little info about the Maudit, I think. They haven't exactly made it a walk in the park to get there. In the oh-so-cultivated, well-trodden Swiss Alps, this seems like a piece of virgin wilderness.

For a moment, I consider abandoning our whole plan, because instinctively it feels *wrong* that I have allowed myself to be fooled by my usual sense of direction. But Augustin cheerfully proposes to walk back to the village and search for the more southerly gully. I envy his carefree attitude and ability to find pleasure even in such a mistake, without any complaints or doubts.

That is how we end up in the place where I've taken the first GoPro photo, the one with the ACCÈS INTERDIT sign. No wonder we couldn't find it at first. The trail begins outside the village, on the far side of a sloping meadow, where supply sheds made of larch balance on round granite stones and corner posts. But by counting the farms and chalets on the map, we get back on track. The upward spur is practically indistinguishable and overgrown with dense vegetation, but this must be it.

Only then we stumble on the enclosure, which probably stakes out a private reserve for grazing cattle. Crossing the barrier isn't that easy. A precarious tour along the barbed wire on the left brings us to a cliff above a waterfall that must be the Torrent de Maudit. This side, impassable. A ten-minute search leads us to a place in the woods further right, where the barbed wire is looser. By holding it up for each other and stepping on the lowest strand, we manage to worm our backpacks through, and then ourselves. It takes a while before we're back on the steep path on the other side of the fence, but now we can get moving.

The second picture is taken much further up and is subtly more disturbing. Like the third, and then the fourth. You see, the photo report of our expedition to Le Maudit is fragmentary and incomplete, unlike all the other series of climbing photos on my external drive. It's not your usual succession of action shots, sunset snaps, and obligatory summit panoramas.

[*I didn't attach them, but I don't mind showing them to you if you insist, once you're back. But I'm not sure it's such a good idea. This morning I showed them to my parents. Dad asked me to, but I really didn't want to, because I still haven't told them any of what I'm telling you now—and I'm not planning to, either. But I gave in in the end, because there's so much they don't know as it is.*

Both of them felt uneasy about looking. Mom didn't finish the whole series; she pushed my iPad away before she'd seen them all, and turned away, unable to put into words why the blood had drained from her face. I think I can. It's the same reason so many people find it difficult to look at the Schiphol selfies circulating on the internet of people about to board flight MH17. It's in light of what happens just after the photo is taken that makes looking at it seem wrong. Selfies of the just-about-to-die. You know it, they don't. It's too intimate, a breach of privacy in the last, most transitory moment of their lives.

And there's more. When you look at the pictures, you can't help but think that you're looking at the report of two doomed individuals who are more and more losing their grip on reality.]

Photo 2 is taken maybe two hours after the first. We're now pretty far above the tree line and the sun is scorching the exposed slope. It's a selfie of me, with Augustin higher up the slope behind me, in short sleeves and with a bandanna holding his long hair off his face. Photo 3 is taken another hour or so later and facing down. Much lower, Augustin is trudging up the slope against the background of the mountains across the valley. Photo 4 is another selfie, and by then, the sky has become overcast.

What's disturbing about these pictures is that all three of them are crooked.

The sunny selfie is tilted to the right, and it's only thanks to the GoPro's wide-angle lens, which bends the horizon on the edges, that you can see, in the upper corner behind Augustin and me, the notch that is the entrance to the valley. But when you think about it, it's strange, the angle from which I apparently took the picture. I don't think I could have done it deliberately. Sport cam selfies from below and at an angle are one thing, but so crooked? In the next picture, the mountain range horizon is tilting sharply to the left, and in fact you could say that, as a photo, this is a total failure. And the second selfie is leaning to the right again. If you focus on these photos long enough, you'll feel a bit nauseous, as if not only the photographer but also you are standing on the bobbing bow of a ship, without any landmarks, because everything around you is bobbing too, until you feel like you need to vomit over the handrail. [*This is where both Mom and Dad fell silent while looking at the photos.*]

Something else that's disturbing is the way our faces and body language change.

What the photos don't show, not directly at least, is the effort it took us to gain elevation. Even before we pass the tree line, the trail has simply ceased to exist. The only practicable passage in the jumble of intertwined spruces and larches is often blocked with piles of overgrown, decaying trunks. It looks like the logging took place years ago and has simply been left there, exposed to the elements and serving as soil for new life. Still, I can't shake the thought that these are barriers, and that they are deliberate. An obstacle? Of course, it suddenly occurs to me—old avalanche dams. It makes the ascent grueling, and we lose more time. But that's not the only thing that shows from our expressions.

In photo 2, you see my face in wide-angle perspective. My brow is furrowed in an undirected smile, bronzed by the sunlight, cheeks flushed from the physical exertion. Wisps of hair cling to my forehead, my lips are slightly parted. Augustin is standing higher up and looking down, past the camera, stone-faced. Nothing out of the ordinary here—a slight tension perhaps, because we're trying to find our way through unknown terrain.

In photo 3, Augustin is lagging far behind. He's hunched forward on his Black Diamonds like an old man, although the high angle seems to somewhat enhance the impression. His face is barely visible. The only remarkable thing about it is that from over here the shadows make his face seem deathly pale, with holes instead of eyes.

And on photo 4, he's above me again.

He seems strikingly gaunt here. At the exact moment I take the picture, he turns away from the camera, and his disheveled hair stands out against the pale, overcast sky. My own face is now center-framed, and that is maybe the main reason why this photo feels so eerie. I look ashen, skin stretched tightly around sunken eyes and more-than-obvious uneasiness written all over my face—or call it numb fear, though you can see I'm doing my best to conceal it.

Because at that moment we'd just done a third map check, and this time we got into an argument about it. We can't figure out where we are on the map. According to the altimeter on Augustin's Seiko, we're at 9,200 feet. I ask whether it's possible the watch gives an overly high reading due to the reduced atmospheric pressure, but Augustin says it's a GPS sensor. GPS communicates with satellites, and they are never wrong.

"But where are we, then?" I say, as I thrust the map into his hands. I'm frustrated, because I can't understand it. If I look back down into the valley, I couldn't wish for a better view of the surroundings. Still, the contour lines don't seem to tally with the actual situation up here. The map says the nameless basin at the end of which the Maudit rises starts at 8,800 feet, but the col is still above us (from here it no longer looks V-shaped; more a flat, plateau-like pass). Or did we follow this gully too far up, and is the Maudit valley beyond another rib, more to the west? But then why doesn't the shape match up?

If I look at it too long, I see spots before my eyes and notice that my head seems to float ever so slightly. I don't understand it. I've never had any problems with orientation.

My doubts irritate Augustin. "What do you want to do about it? Half an hour tops and we'll be on the col. We should be able to see the Maudit from there and then we'll know where we are."

"But look at the map. Can't you *see* that it doesn't add up, that we're too high?"

"Can't *you* see that the valley is up there? Look!" He swings his Black Diamonds at the notch.

"It doesn't make any sense."

Augustin laughs scornfully. "Dude, what are you talking about? We're just a little lost because there are no trails. Let's go up, we can see better from there."

He's right. You climb, you see. You descend, you no longer see, but you *have* seen. I gaze past him at the col, at the steep, uninviting slopes that enclose the valley behind it, and at the sky, which is growing more overcast. Three choughs circle high above us on an invisible thermal. I notice I've got goose bumps on my neck and arms. I'm cold, now that I'm standing still, wearing only a sweaty thermal shirt. "Okay," I finally say.

But I don't *feel* okay; the chill has gotten into my head, and that is when I take the fourth picture, that is the chill the photo conveys to the viewer.

What the photos obviously don't document is what goes on in my head during the last thirty to forty minutes before we reach the col. At least, that's how short it must have been, even though it felt longer, much longer. Every time I look up at the col, I notice that I see spots before my eyes again, and it's starting to make me feel dizzy. I suck my lungs full of air and try to clear my head, but before long, the sensation sinks down into my stomach. I lose my spirit, because I know this feeling all too well.

One of the greatest physical discomforts about mountaineering is the necessity to set off at night, when it's cold and pitch-black, under the hypnotizing light of your Petzl headlamp. You have to take advantage of the colder-than-daytime temperatures. It's vital to be off the glaciers around noon at the latest, when the sun turns firm snow bridges on invisible crevasses into lethal pitfalls. Every year, climbers—sometimes entire teams—disappear into deep glacial voids and die in their frozen darkness. If the mountain is merciful, the drop is deep enough to smash them into silence in one go. Most victims, however, are trapped between blue, narrowing walls of ice, and as their body warmth melts the ice, they slowly sink into it, slowly deeper and deeper, until they die very consciously of asphyxiation.

So you set off early. But my stomach, still asleep, always rebels when I have to perform great feats at three o'clock in the morning. I can't take food; I throw it up right away. But if I don't eat I get nauseous, because my body lacks fuel. Both options are equally bad. That's why these days I swear by metoclopramide, which I take to calm my stomach before a climb.

This morning we left at a decent hour, and now it's almost noon, but still my stomach is in knots, and with every step I take it feels like it's swinging in its own greasy hammock. I try to concentrate on my breathing and find a rhythm in my footsteps' steady stride. My heart is beating so hard that I feel it thumping not only in my chest but also behind my temples. This is starting to look like altitude sickness, damn it. But that's BS. We're well acclimatized, and the effects of the altitude shouldn't kick in until well above 13,000 feet.

I stand still and jackknife, leaning on my poles. We're halfway up a steep boulder field and I stagger a bit to keep my balance. The horizon in the north is rolling. I raise my hand to my chest, as if trying to calm my heart. I feel miserable. Maybe I should stick my finger down my throat and make myself throw up to get rid of the nausea, but somehow that prospect scares me. I don't want to go there. Stupid, looking back, how your judgment deteriorates in such circumstances. Alone, out of breath, and under the influence of . . . of what, actually?

I stand upright and scan the scree field. Augustin roves steadily up the slope [*roves steadily? did I really think that?*], back and forth, back and forth, and for a moment he looks like a hanged man on the gallows, swinging gently in the wind.

"Stop," I groan. I rub my eyes with my knuckles, smell the salt on my fingers. I try to breathe more slowly, thinking about getting a metoclopramide from my first aid kit, but I don't feel like taking off my backpack. When I lower my hands from my face, there are only spots, but most of them disperse and I can see clearly again.

Go. Climb on for a bit.

The mountains in the north are still rolling.

Not the ones across the valley but those in the far distance, beyond the Rhône valley, where you can see the Berner Oberland range. The snowcaps expand, contract, expand. The air seems thin, as if I'm hallucinating. I shake my head violently and moan. Hearing my own voice should give me confidence, but its sound is peculiarly distorted by the alluvial fan, as if thousands of mouths, hidden behind gray boulders, are moaning back at me from below.

With a jolt, I look around me. To the left, to the right, up and down. Nothing; it's my imagination. The choughs are gone. Deep silence reigns, aside from the gurgling of the brook, somewhere far away.

I see moisture in the air, a single drop breaking free from the steel-colored sky. Suddenly worried about lagging too far behind, I get going again. My nausea has subsided but resurfaces five minutes later. When I look up sometime later, I'm surprised to see Augustin resting under a big, thumb-like rock.

"You okay, buddy?" I ask when I reach him.

He smiles at me; the air has been cleared. "Weird, isn't it? The spatial effects of this place," he says.

I nod and lumber on, not prepared to disrupt my cadence, because it'll cost me the energy I'll need to pull myself up after a rest. Thinking back, I can clearly recall how bad Augustin is actually looking as I pass him, but I apparently don't notice it at the time. What he says doesn't even register. I don't know what's come over me.

"I think there are death birds here," he says confidently. "I keep hearing them. Behind the mountains."

I laugh—*concentrate on your rhythm*—and then I pass him. I start counting my steps. To ten, over and over again. If I focus on it, I don't feel my dizziness, don't feel the heaviness in my limbs. My hold on the handles of the Black Diamonds weakens, the backpack gets heavier. There's a pressure just behind my ears, growing constantly, as if I'm sinking deeper and deeper underwater, through a hole in the ice. A hole in the ice or a crevasse. Stupid thought. Why did I just imagine seeing Augustin dangling from a gallows, swinging slowly in the wind, back and forth, back and forth?

I think there are death birds here.

They aren't behind the mountains. How could he think that? They're in the crevasses and will come and eat the life out of you, if you fall into one.

"Al . . . most . . . there . . ." I pant to myself. "Step . . . step . . . step . . . just a few more . . ."

[*With hindsight, it's clear we weren't in our right minds anymore by then. I don't have another explanation for our behavior. How else could we have assessed the situation so poorly? Or kept making the wrong decisions time and again and, despite the glaring red flags that we should turn back pronto, kept right on going?*]

One thing is certain: even before we reach the col, I feel the mountain's presence at the end of that valley drawing us in and yet, even so, repelling us, as if there is a magnetic field up there that for some unearthly reason keeps changing poles. It splits me in two. I feel that something is terribly wrong, I feel it everywhere, and at the same time I *have* to go there. The mountain is a seducer. Its mystery an obsession.

And all at once, just before I enter the pass, it's gone. My horror, my dizziness and nausea, and the way the elements and the forces of the wild suggested the unimaginable, it's all suddenly gone. The mountains are just mountains—dead rock, solid ground under our feet.

The valley opened up, and we entered it.

* * *

It's an anticlimax.

The Maudit's summit is in the clouds and refuses to reveal itself. That's the story of photo 5. By the time we get to the col, it's twelve thirty [*I remember, because after pulling a fleece out of my backpack, I tried checking the weather on my iPhone, but by then there was no data network anymore*], and all the surrounding ridges are shrouded in clouds. But despite that, we have a clear view of the valley, as can be seen in the photo.

The valley is a scree basin of gravelly moraines and old snowbanks, mottled by the stream's muddy outwash. Except where we are, it is enclosed by steep slopes and imposing cliffs. Maybe three miles further up lies the retreating embranchment of a compact glacier. Couloirs of snow rise into the clouds from its higher flanks on both sides of the mighty, uncommonly dark wall that must be the Maudit. At its extremity, where the ice mass's tongue breaks into a maze of transverse crevasses, is where the glacial lake must be, watching over the valley like a cold eye.

"Bummer, huh?" I comment.

Augustin looks around in clear disappointment. He had expected something more impressive, a view of the summit we came here for. He spreads his arms toward where it should be—forming a capital Y with his Black Diamonds—and whoops as loud as he can: "*Heeeeeeyo!*"

Instead of his voice echoing and resounding off the cliffs, his call sounds peculiarly flat and quickly dies away. The valley is too big for the echo. We're too small. There's a loneliness here, but it's not the kind of loneliness we're looking for. The dead silence, the complete absence of trails, and the desolation of the scree fields give the impression that human civilization has turned its back on this place.

With my stomach in knots, I turn around and look to the horizon. Behind the Berner Oberland massif, a dark bank of clouds has formed, and it seems to be building quickly.

"I'm not too happy about the weather changing, to be honest. Do you think it will hold?"

Augustin shrugs. "They said there was only a chance of local thunderstorms. It'll probably be okay."

We hear a shrill shriek, and I look up with a start. An alpine chough glides on the rising wind above the valley's mouth and then nose-dives from on high. I suddenly see there's a whole flock of them. They're coming from everywhere, a dark, blotchy swirl like leaves in the wind. I hear their hoarse squabbling and screeching, which sounds almost human but, like Augustin's whoop, falls flat in the changing atmosphere. The birds perform their wild acrobatics, but suddenly, as if to a signal only they can hear, they hover above the plateau, their weird little feet dangling under their tilting bodies. One of them lands about ten yards away and steps jauntily between the rocks toward us. It folds its wings, pokes a long, bright yellow beak between its feathers, then looks warily at the unexpected visitors on the col. I wonder how long it's been since they saw a living soul out here.

Augustin grins and kneels, reaches his hand out to the bird and calls to it. The chough stays put, distrusting yet brazen.

Even without looking at the barometer, I know what the coming of the birds implies. Alpine choughs flock to the valley and abandon the mountains to the storm as soon as the atmospheric pressure drops.

As if in confirmation, the bird gives a grim cry, flies up, and dives down with the entire flock in a single turbulent swoop.

[*And of course we should have followed them. Of course we should have done the only logical, the only reasonable, the only responsible thing and followed the birds to the valley. But we didn't. I wish I had an explanation for that, but I don't.*]

"Wow, what a sight," Augustin says.

We follow them with our gaze till they disappear.

"So these are your death birds?" I ask with a faint smile. The question pops up unexpectedly, as if it had been waiting at the back of my mind all this time, but I'm taken aback by the way it seems to hit Augustin.

"Death birds?"

"A while ago, when we were walking up here, you said you heard death birds behind the mountains."

"Oh yeah, I said that, didn't I?" Augustin looks away, and his voice sounds strangely remote. It's as if he's allowing the words to hover between us, as if he'd rather read them from a distance before he'd be willing to accept that we'd lost control for a while. "I don't really know."

He remains silent and I think that's all he has to say on the matter, but all at once he resumes. "Don't you know the stories? Death birds are said to guide the souls of fallen climbers out of this world. If you believe what the old guides and mountain folk say, at least."

"And do you?"

He smiles. "Did you know mountain rescuers often find fallen climbers without their eyes? By the time they find the bodies, the birds have already gotten to them. Ravens, jackdaws, crows; they pick out the eyes and swallow them up."

"Jeez, really?"

"Ask one of those guides. They say the birds do it so the soul is free to escape. Otherwise it's doomed to stay and haunt the place it was found in. But sometimes the soul doesn't want to leave and it lingers inside the bird for a while. They say that if you listen, you can hear their screams coming from the mountains at night."

Neither of us speaks. I suddenly feel a strong urge to text you, but when I take my phone out of my pocket, I again see that there is no connection. That's often the case in these remote valleys. The steep slopes surrounding the intermediate dales block the signal.

I turn off the screen and put it away. "Should we look for a place to bivi around here or keep going some more?"

No, let's go back, I think. *Back down to the valley.*

Augustin nods. "Let's set up camp by the lake. The terrain is almost even, an hour's walk at the most. We can make it before the storm. The ground there should be softer, and when it clears up tonight, we'll have a good view of tomorrow's route."

It doesn't take long before we've hoisted our backpacks, but before we depart, Augustin does something unexpected. He piles up a dozen or so flat stones, creating a stoneman. I hesitate for a moment but then follow his example. Marked territory. This is our valley. Before you know it, two stonemen stand on the col, overlooking the valley together, at the mercy of the mountain.

One for Augustin, one for Nick.

Then we're off, and the stonemen dissolve into the gray mass behind us.

THE VALLEY OF UNREST

NOTES BY SAM AVERY

Now each visitor shall confess
The sad valley's restlessness
Nothing there is motionless—
Nothing save the airs that brood
Over the magic solitude.

—Edgar Allan Poe

1

It was dark the first time we went to Grimentz, cuz Nick hated people staring at him. Nick totally Claude Rains in *The Invisible Man*, shoulders hunched deep in the Hilfiger parka, collar at attention, and a felt hat he normally didn't wear, over those bandages. It left only a narrow open strip through which his eyes peered, dark and watchful like a deer's.

Unwrap him and there'd be nothing underneath. A pitch-black void. His deer eyes two poached eggs in the air. Ghost eyes. A hovering hat.

His wanting to show me the Maudit, or the access to it at least, ended as a letdown—or should I say relief? As the day progressed, the sky became overcast. It even rained. Now the pine tree shapes pierced the low-hanging clouds. Your million-dollar mountain view obliterated by a black broth that dissolved into the highest branches.

During the walk to the village, Nick told me his own ghost story. What it was like for him to have his self shoved aside and the mountain take charge.

How he saw only his pale reflection staring back at him through that imaginary window. The mouth a dark, gaping well. The eyes two gazing dark pits that reached all the way into the distant night. And in those holes, the tumbling red dot that was Augustin's helmet just kept falling and falling and falling and falling.

This story, Nick told me the whole thing without looking at me even once. Both of us staring ahead at the road, Grimentz's lights looming up in the mist ahead of us.

Nick said he'd been reluctant to tell his story cuz it brought Augustin back from the dead. Especially here, so close to where it happened. Nick looked up into the mist, and I wished he hadn't. He looked in such a specific direction that it seemed like he thought that up there, behind the invisible mountains, Augustin was still waiting, clinging on to some mute semblance of life from which he couldn't be saved but couldn't completely die from either. A sad, lost soul frozen into the glacier.

"The good news," said Nick, "is that I haven't felt it here yet. The pressure seems to be gone. Did you feel anything about me?"

I lied.

I mean, why make him feel bad? Buck him up, even if you know better. Go Nick! A million years of power, spray it with some fresh mountain air and—*wham!*—you're cured.

We strolled into the village, past the dark, idle cable car terminal. Motionless steel cables suspended in the mist, reaching for the abandoned pistes on the higher slopes. There was a Coop here. A boulangerie-pâtisserie. There were outdoor supply stores, an école de ski, a guides de montagne, an Office du Tourisme. Shopwindows loaded with twenty-four-karat-gold-inlay Cartier watches. And of course chalets for rent. Chalets for sale. All the elements a luxury Swiss resort needs to be a luxury Swiss resort. And still, it all felt wrong. The mist weighed on the village, compressing its air, silencing it. No sounds. No burbling water, no barking dogs, no tourist voices. Grimentz was in limbo, an interseasonal purgatory, silently awaiting the arrival of winter. And it was waiting for something *else*. That feeling, that certainty, I couldn't shake it.

I said, "I don't like it here at all." Slowly climbing the steep street, I said, "I feel really lousy. Uncomfortable."

"The mist is kind of gloomy, isn't it?"

"It isn't the mist. It's just . . . creepy. Don't you feel it?"

Nick shrugged. "Last night, you slept at an altitude of over 5,000 feet. The mountain air may be differently charged, maybe that's what you feel. But I don't think so. Usually, a tangible difference in pressure comes only before a storm. The air is still now."

"Stiller than still. That's the thing."

Nick tensed up noticeably when a group of men started making their way down from one of the streets higher up. They were speaking a dialect I couldn't make heads or tails of. When they saw us, they shut up, sized us up, ignored us, and walked on toward one of those hotels-slash-inns. One of those cribs-slash-crime scenes. One of those storm-beaten buildings with projecting eaves and empty flower boxes hanging down from dark window alcoves. Hôtel du Barrage, it was called. The kind of local hangout where they don't mind if you bring your grandmother, even if she's been residing in formaldehyde for years. When they pushed open the door, it *smelled* like someone's grandma in formaldehyde. That, and melted Gruyère. The men hurried in, heads hunched, but one of them snuck a look at us. At *Nick*. Nick's mummy mask.

I said, "If you think I'm gonna mingle with orthodox mountain pygmies to find out what the local superstitions are, you got it wrong."

This hotel, Nick said, this was where he and Augustin came up with the plan to go to the mountain. In the cellar, he said, next to the toilets, that was where they found the old etching that pictured the Maudit.

"In the mood for a *Pflaumenschnaps*?" Nodding to the door, I said, "My treat."

Nick, eyes hovering under the tip of his Claude Rains hat, shooting daggers at me.

Once past the inn, you only hadda walk into the old village center for the anxiety to pounce on you again. Houses of blackened larch wood, moss-covered slate roofs, and big, sooty chimneys. Old granaries leaning so heavily they'd collapse without struts. And all so cramped that the streets looked more like tunnels. Bending in all directions, connected to each other by narrow stairways along the housefronts. Not a single sign of life. House doors bolted shut. Latched shutters. Upside-down flowerpots against the walls. The village had been winterized . . .

And was *waiting.*

Look at it, and your sweat glands jump into action. Look at it, and it is big-time claustrophobia.

So you're walking, and suddenly it's there. The feeling that forced you to look around skittishly. As if the still air were being disturbed by minuscule electromagnetic pulses, imperceptible except on the very edges of your retina and by the tingling in your fingertips. Just by looking around, you'd swear something had moved just outside your line of sight. That, just out of earshot, someone had called. A shadow. An echo.

"Nick?"

I cleared my throat. My voice sounded unusually thick and raw. Nick didn't answer. Stood there under one of those gables, under those eaves, looking.

Then I saw it too.

The shadow that hung there, that hung on *all* the houses, it wasn't someone's grandfather's frayed climbing rope. No Walliser cuckoo clock or satellite dish tuned to SFR or RTS. It was a birdcage. In the cage, a crow. Nope. A jackdaw.

And I thought, *Birds.*

Thought, *Birds came out of your face.*

The birds that flew through our bedroom in Amsterdam. The birds Nick had painted on the walls. These birds here were exactly the same. And they were all over thc place.

There were cages hanging from all the roofs. No wonder I didn't notice them before, cuz those creepers within were black as death and perched perfectly still in the dark. Even when I walked up to one of them, brought my face right up to the bars, I hadda convince myself it wasn't stuffed. It *looked* stuffed. Feathers dull and dead, like the animals in those dusty display cases in a museum of natural history. But then the smell hit me. Musty, malodorous, pungent like rotting textile and raw flesh. The bird was alive, and its glassy, indifferent eyes looked out of the darkness directly into mine.

Rust? Fuggedaboutit. Spiderwebs? No way. The cage was practically brand-new, spick-and-span.

A shrill cawing made me jump back, but it wasn't the jackdaw in my cage that'd stirred. It was the one in the cage Nick was in front of. Other side of the street. Nick, he took a few steps back too. Our shoulders touched. We spun around.

In Nick's cage, the shadow was pacing restlessly on its perch, hampered by a leather strap around its leg. Spread its wings. Cawed again, louder this time, a melodious yet chilling *spreeeh.*

The daw that'd just gazed at me now also stared past me at Nick.

All the daws were staring at Nick.

And me, my heart lub-dubbing in my throat, I said, "Did you know about this?"

Nick's eyes shot from cage to cage to cage. "No."

"They're the same ones, right?"

"Yep. Alpine choughs."

"The animals you called death birds."

"That was superstition."

"Dude, *this* is superstition. Don't you see?"

'Course. What else? All those birds in their cages, on every single house in Grimentz. Superstition incarnate. Old wives' tales from the mountains. Alpine choughs: oracles' birds, messengers of the Old Testament God. Fate-fending fetishes. Animal barometers for reading the air—not temperature or pressure, but something else in the black night.

But what?

From the mist came a weak cry, probably from higher up in the village. Hard to tell if it was human or animal. Maybe one of those choughs. Something wasn't right. Something about the way the echo vibrated inside my head made me wonder whether I'd really heard it.

Again, the thickening air. The strange shimmering in the corners of my eyes. The set of electric shocks, as a warning.

I looked around me. Looked up. Listened.

"Did you hear that too?"

Nick asked, "Hear what?"

But before I could say anything, one of the birds shrieked, and then all hell broke loose. All at once, all the birds went into a frenzy. Hopping up and down on hooked claws, dusty wings beating, chains clattering, cages rocking. One of the shadows—I saw it giving its primitive rage free rein, taking it out on its cage door with all it had.

Nick grabbed my arm and *wham*, adrenaline rush, head spins. But it was still Nick, and he said, "What was that again about CinemaSins?"

"Animals-sense-supernatural-presence-before-humans-do cliché. Jesus Christ, Nick, let's get outta here."

We hurried away, but all over the place the birds reacted to our presence. A cacophony of caws from swinging cages in the mist, heralding some impending doom.

Up the road was a courtyard with a trough, a church on the other side, which under different circumstances you'd label idyllic. White stucco walls, wooden bell tower, the whole Lonely Planet secret marvel thing. But next to the heavy wooden door was a curly copper fixture, and hanging on it was another cage. Bigger than all the others. This time, five imprisoned choughs, flapping around in a mad frenzy, pecking each other's mangy bodies with their nasty beaks.

A swelling growl made my hair stand on end and chilled me so much it felt like my skin was sinking into my body. I clung to Nick. From a dark corner of the courtyard, a big black dog appeared, with a bell on its neck. Barking, snarling, drooling. On a leash, okay, but his owner, this little dude with a pale and soulless face, still a kid basically, was having trouble keeping it at bay. Shrill voice barking orders. By his side, two more kids, staring wide-eyed at the caged birds' tumult. One of them, arms spread, ran to the church's cage as if he wanted to hush them, but his little friend shouted something and he turned around. When he caught sight of us, the expression on that dorky face switched from concern to such demoniac mortal terror it was almost comical.

That kid is also someone's son, I thought. Someone's son *and* nephew, by the looks of it.

The first little dude, the one with the wolfdog, tightened the leash, choking it just a coupla steps before Nick and me. Shouted something. The beast panting behind his white breath, black lips curled away from its snout. Teeth like little bunched nails, forepaws thrashing the air.

And the two of us in that narrow alley, my hands tight around Nick's arm, Nick's body hot and shaky, a feverish tension behind that mask, as if the scar tissue under it was sliding over the bone. His eyes intense and sunken, and in those eyes I read escalation, in those eyes I read that we hadda get the hell outta there before something *really* bad happened. Something terrible.

The kid shouted something again, but his dialect didn't even come close to French.

"*Que se passe-t-il ici?*" I tried, but the only reply I got was a stone. Granted, not perfectly pitched, cuz it bounced off the granite splint of a shed this side of the courtyard, but a stone nonetheless.

I raised my hands and called out, "*Arrêtez! Qu'est-ce que tu fais?*"

And all around us, the choughs freaking out in their cages. All around us, black feathers and slick blue flashes. All around us those beady eyes staring, and groping claws, looking for us. And the kid gesturing. Calling. The other one, the little dude in front, siccing his dog. All around us, serious trouble brewing.

The next stone knocked Nick's Claude Rains hat off his head. A second later, blood. Nick's knees buckled, but he rebounded and his body stiffened, his body hardened, *something took over*, and who knows what woulda happened if I hadn't given him the biggest shove of his life right then, so hard that he fell backwards, hands up, splat against the Walliser supply shed.

Somewhere a light went on. Somewhere a shutter opened.

Nick stared at me, spluttered out a WTF, and I pulled him by the sleeve, making a run for it. A barrage of stones came at us, one hitting my shoulder, but I didn't wanna give those little motherfuckers the satisfaction of seeing me flinch.

We ran till we were past the cable car terminal, past the edge of the village, where Nick staggered, had to hang his head between his knees, me holding him up.

But we were invisible there. Those little dudes and the birds and the dog, way back behind us. Swallowed by the mist.

"What the fuck was that?" Nick panted.

"A fucking hate crime, that's what it was. A fucking stoning." Screaming, "A *fucking stoning, fils de pute!*"

A weak cry seeped through the mist and Nick gestured, "Shh. The birds, I mean. Those boys. I *scared* them."

"Jesus, Nick, you okay? Your head's bleeding."

He looked up at me. Blood dripped over his eyebrow to the edge of the bandages, seeped in and spread like merlot on a napkin.

I wiped it off and kissed his forehead. The kiss, he must have sensed some of my rage in it, some of my zinging adrenaline, cuz Nick laid his hands on my shoulders and said, "Seriously, you need to calm down. I'm okay now."

"No way. We were shooed away like animals! They took your—"

"It doesn't matter. Come on, Sam. Let's go home."

But it wasn't until we'd reached our side of the valley floor, and Hill House's dark outline and the rock formation behind it were looming up in the mist, that the essence of the word *home* really hit me.

2

First chance next day, I got Julia on FaceTime and told her the whole episode. Picture it: Me pacing up and down in front of the chalet's big windows, the woods and rocks in front of the enormous sunny V of the valley, Grimentz's bell tower chiming two o'clock in the distance. Woods and rocks and me pacing, iPhone in hand, Julia on full-screen killing her straight-out-of-bed look in New York, still stunning, but that's just good genes, as I always say.

"Dude, what a story," Julia said. "Remember Grandma's rhyme? She always sang it when the crows stole the bread crumbs from the cardinals in the garden. *One crow sorrow, two crows joy. Three crows a letter—*"

"*Four crows a boy.* Oh my god, I forgot it! *Five crows silver, six crows gold—*"

"*Seven crows a secret never to be told.* How many did you see, bro? Maybe we could tell your future."

I said they weren't crows but choughs, and Julia retorted minor detail for the superstitious, and I said there were way more than seven, and BTW I'm not superstitious, but A for effort.

Oh, and did I send Pa and Ma a postcard? The chalet was on Pa's card, wasn't it?

Julia sitting cross-legged over her steaming mug of Teatox Skinny Morning, asking why the hell I went to Switzerland with Nick, away from his psychologists and medical treatment.

Nothing new about sis worrying about me. We look out for each other; always have. The epic descent on the Panther Mile, that frozen night in the snow—if you only had each other the moment your life started and the rest went up in smoke, you bonded. Us standing hand in hand in the snow, teeth chattering, watching the inferno consume our childhood, and our grandfather running out like a human torch—it's safe to say we've never really let go of each other since that day.

"I really love Nick, you know that, but you're not safe around him. You don't know what he's capable of. I read that delusional people can—"

"He isn't delusional, Julia." My voice subdued, listening to make sure I didn't wake Nick while he was sweating out an oxazepam in the bedroom downstairs. "There's something real creepy going on with him. And this village is totally creepy too. You can feel it everywhere; it gets under your skin. Ramses is totally weirded out by it too. And the valley . . . Here, check out how fucked up it looks."

I flipped my iPhone to the window and Julia rolled her eyes. My sis may have poisoned her tropical fish and pissed her bed till she was ten, but she had no mountain traumas. She's the type who could go down a black diamond run in Aspen or Banff or Calgary with her eyes closed.

Smoke was what triggered *her*. Smoke and flames. Sandalwood-based oil.

I never told her I was the one who burned down Huckleberry Wall.

Now, Julia, six hours earlier in NY: "That makes it even worse, dumbass! Whatever you think you saw there, what good will it do to rake up things that should stay buried?"

My point exactly.

Pacing up and down in front of the window, AirPods in, Julia in my hand, I told her about the doorbell ringing that morning. Us just up, last thing we expect after last night is visitors, so I say to Nick to keep still.

At the door, this whole delegation. Three strong, from Grimentz, led by some guy with one of those collars, a white jabot-type thing, some church rep. I'd come up with the name if I was born two generations earlier or three states to the south. They looked simultaneously intimidating and ill at ease, staring at me in the doorway. The one dude with Nick's hat pressed against his jabot.

They'd come to apologize for *le petit incident* yesterday evening by the church, they said. *Les enfants* had owned up to it all and had gotten a good whupping by their folks. They'd been taken aback—did one of us maybe wear a *masque de bandages*?—but that was no excuse for their disgraceful behavior. And now they wanted to set things straight. To *bienvenue* us to Grimentz.

"It was like the most awkward conversation ever," I said to Julia. "No way were they here to say sorry; they came here to check us out. Seriously, it was totally weird. And who were those dudes, anyway? This is a fucking Airbnb. How the hell did they know we're staying here? And question after question. Who we are, where we come from, what we're doing here. And this dude keeps looking past me into the hall, like maybe there's someone else he can talk to. When it was clear to them they'd have to deal with me, they said they wanted to apologize directly to my *copain* and would I *peut-être* go get him?"

"Ew, that really is creepy. Then what?"

"I pulled the hat out of his hands and slammed the door."

"Wow," Julia said. "Subtle, bro."

"What else could I do?" Ramses, who was nervously licking his forepaw in the window, flinched. I lowered my voice and hissed, "The whole situation is fucked up. Those creeps didn't leave the door, cuz I heard muffled voices. And even when I thought they were gone, I wasn't sure, cuz I thought I heard something outside the window on the other side of the house, and now I'm scared to go check and I'm going totally crazy here in this fucking house and this fucking country where all those fucking mountains keep coming at you and—"

"*Sam.*" Julia's blueberry eyes bored into mine through my iPhone screen. She said, "What you need"—poking her finger right through six time zones—"what you need is a team."

I fell silent.

She said, "An ally. Eyes on the ground."

Julia was right. I needed reinforcements.

Six hours earlier, New York, but for always hand in hand in front of that burning house. "I can be your home base. Your hotline. Your long-distance consultant. But who do you know over there, Sam? Who do you trust enough to call?"

I swiped to my second screen.

"Bro? Hello? The picture just froze."

I opened WhatsApp, scrolled like crazy through my chats.

"*Hello?*"

"Justaminute!"

There. End of August. That +41 number. I opened the chat and read my last text:

> Cécile, WTF?

And hers:

> Sorry. He was right, he's a monster.

3

Fast-forward to two days later, Friday afternoon, the kitchen. The thick leather instruction folder we got from the owners couple in Sion said the cleaning lady comes on Friday afternoons. The cleaning lady in question, Maria Zufferey-Silva de Souza, Portuguese but married to some Swiss guy from Grimentz. The resulting gene mix was MoMA material, I said, when she showed me a pic of her son. The son, *Men's Health* cover boy potential, now quartering in a barracks in Andermatt. Maria, beaming in her apron, she and her thundering laughter, didn't stop talking about her offspring, all in French, with a delectable Swiss-Portuguese accent, of course. She was a walking thesis in linguistics.

Don't lecture me on South European moms. Want something from them, just ask about their sons.

"He must be happy to have left the valley," I said. "I mean, it's really beautiful and all, but I can imagine life here can be pretty cramped for someone his age."

"Not at all," Maria said. This was a woman who could fervently bewail her lot while scrubbing the kitchen tiles with the furious routine of someone who does nothing else, not missing a single spot. "Anton grew up here; he feels at home in the valley. Every time he has furlough, he comes back. I always say go to Bern, son, go to Geneva, or farther, over the border. I prayed to God for war, that they'd dispatch him to Syria or Iraq or Yemen, because that's the only way he'll see something of the world. But he'd rather go skiing all winter with his friends. Home, where he grew up. Can you imagine?"

She stopped to take a sip of the ristretto I'd brewed for her. Sweat on her big boobs, she winked at me confidentially and said, "I can't. I've been living here for twenty-three years now, and the only thing that keeps me going is visiting my sister in Lisbon every January for a month. Being snowed in the whole winter . . . what a disaster."

"It can't be all that bad."

"Yes, it is. The cold seeps into your bones. And it's not only the cold. It's the storms from the mountains that drive you crazy. My husband didn't understand it the first time, but I said, 'Pascal, if you don't let me go, I'll never set foot in this village again.'"

"Good for you, girl," I called, and fisted the air.

"Ah, *querido*." She blew me a kiss.

Maria, I liked her right off the bat. Her purity. Sleeves rolled up to the elbows to show the whole world her age spots. An immigrant in Grimentz's insular community, she'd always remain an outsider in their eyes. Maybe that's why she was so candid with me. That and the caffeine jolt I dealt her, the perfect setup to grill her.

"What's the deal with all those birds, by the way?" This behind the chalet, where I'd just brought her a self-brewed Black Insomnia, Maria sweeping the needles off the patio. "All those birdcages hanging under the roofs in the village."

"So you saw them," she said.

"Not only saw." I told her what had happened when we visited the village. The birds going berserk, those asshole kiddies with the stones, that Godzilla dog with its small, grinding teeth.

And Maria said, over the swishing of her broom, "Don't take it personally. Those rascals aren't used to strangers in the off-season. It's all pretty small-town here." Leaning toward me over her broom, theatrical sotto voce hand: "Some are a bit slow, if you ask me."

"But what's the idea behind the birds?"

Ils sont des something-or-other. Dialect word, not French or Portuguese anyway.

"Lucky birds," she then said. The only English words I heard Maria utter. Those dark brown eyes, a sparkle in there.

"Lucky birds," I said.

"They are birds from the mountains. The old folks believe they bring good luck. Legend has it they carry our forefathers' souls and should therefore be worshipped. But that's all ancient superstition. Many of those customs fade away with time. Nowadays it's mostly for the tourists."

"Do you believe they bring luck?"

Maria crossed herself. "I believe in our Blessed Lord. But these people have been living here for generations. Life up here is different. Tougher. It makes you believe in your own things."

Which didn't exactly answer my question, I figured. A more marketable version of the truth. A rhetorical evasion. With all her purity, maybe there was more to that Maria than met the eye.

"Tell you the truth, I thought it was kinda creepy when all of them went wild at once."

"Oh, they do that sometimes. They sense a change in the atmosphere, a break in the weather coming up. They set each other off and then all hell breaks loose. And what racket do they make! But it's no big deal."

And sometimes they fly out of your boyfriend's face in Amsterdam, I thought. *No big deal either.*

Ramses appeared out of the bushes on the side of the house and settled in the old larch's shadow, eyes half closed. Maria stopped sweeping and looked at him the way someone would look at a very sick opossum.

"You brought a cat." Maria, she stood the broom against the wall and brushed the hair off her face. "I wouldn't let him out. We're not too keen on cats in the village."

I wanted to ask her what she meant by that, but Maria's barrage dried up from one moment to the next. Mumbled something about having lots to do and hurried inside. Strange. A break in the weather. Call me paranoid, but I got the impression she'd said too much.

Maria didn't stay long after that, but the rest of the time that she was there: cold fish. In the Jacuzzi bathroom downstairs, she said no to my self-brewed Arabian Death Wish. On the landing upstairs, I caught her mumbling to herself. Pretty sure it was a prayer.

Even when I asked her if Anton, Boy of the Alps, had a Heidi, she evaded me. Right, don't lecture me on South European moms. Back to the drawing board.

Just before she left, Nick came back from his walk. I noticed he was looking better. Stronger. Arms, nose, and forehead bronzed by the October sun, gleaming with health. But you could see Maria was taken aback when she saw him.

He had an accident, I said. That's why we're here. To recuperate. Maria nodded politely, shook Nick's hand, but she didn't lift her nervous eyes from her bosom.

"This is Maria, Nick," I said slowly, in French. "She comes from Grimentz. She does the cleaning."

And Nick, spouting his full French repertoire: *"Ah, oui. Bonjour!"*

Maria couldn't split fast enough. Snatched her bag from the kitchen table and—grudgingly, you could see—said, "Okay, I'll be back next Friday." Followed her out the door, Nick and me trailing behind her. He nudged me. Could I ask her what she knew about the mountains above the village. So I interpret.

At the bottom of the steps she turned, eyes gliding briefly over Nick's face, grasped the rail, said to me, "I don't know anything about the mountains." Nervous laugh. "They're pretty to look at, they dictate life down here, but nuh-uh. I like the valley. I know there's a whole world up there, but it never appealed to me."

"Has she heard of the Pointe Maudit?"

That name, even unarticulated, even muffled by bandages and smothered by Dutch, had its effect. Maria went pale and tottered. Impossible to define her expression. I wanted to ask if she was okay, but just then a Peugeot in obsidian black bumped over the wooden bridge crossing the creek and turned into our yard. It gave Maria the chance to hurry to her Nissan and step in without a good-bye.

Which was, like, totally unweird.

"Are we expecting visitors?" Nick asked.

Maria's Nissan drove off in a cloud of dust, and the Peugeot parked in her ruts. Nick and me, together in the doorway, watching the car door open. Nick's face in total confusion. A leather women's boot stepped out of the Peugeot's open door. Followed by tights. No runs. Full head of dark, curly hair.

What Nick saw coming up to him was a specter from his first days after the coma. A ghost from his delirium.

"Bonjour," said Cécile Métrailler.

And I said, "Saprize."

4

Turned out it wasn't that hard to get Cécile here.

Two texts. Two texts was all it took to get her to leave Lausanne for the weekend and drive to the mountains. The first:

> You were right too, he really is a monster. But he doesn't do it on purpose.

The second:

Monster & Me are in CH. Wanna talk?

And what else? Turned out that the bar-slash-inn section of Hôtel du Barrage wasn't so bad after all. Sure, they didn't serve any Captain Collinses or caipirinhas, there was no black light or backlight, but their Cardinal draft was pretty drinkable and there was a humongous fire in that humongous stone hearth that radiated an almost hypnotizing heat.

Cécile and I had a table all the way in the back. Cécile's eyes, they didn't let go of me for a single second. Leaning in over the woven tablecloth, she asked, "Did you know that no one in Wallis flies out for a code thirty-three eleven? It's common knowledge between the rescue services. It's a miracle Nick was saved, Sam."

That's what I call infiltration. The inn full of townsfolk, us the only outsiders. Pretending we belonged.

In the kitchen, the chef was singing Italian songs, so loud you could hear it in the dining room. The chef with his flapping white apron, serving the guests roasts from the spit: pork loin/jacket potatoes/Gruyère gratin/stewed apples. A chunky barwoman, dark fluff on her upper lip, brought foaming tankards of beer to the tables, or *génépy* to the fogeys smoking pipes around the fireplace. The smell of beer and tobacco embedded in the carpet and the beam-propped ceiling.

You'd almost miss it, but in the semidark above the bar, a birdcage. A big one. In it, something dark shuffling about.

Cécile looked at me and said, "A code thirty-three eleven is a missing person on the Maudit or in the mountains near what the locals call the Valley of Echoes. It's always a missing person, because they're never the ones who call. That's why it was so surprising that Nick *did*."

Cécile Métrailler had done some detective work. Dug up some hidden facts.

The reunion today went as well as could reasonably be expected. Five days in Switzerland and it was a major relief to see a familiar face. Cécile being here felt good. Cécile Métrailler, Nurse Cécile, the only beacon of hope those first days in the CHUV. Still, one step over the threshold, initial courtesies out of the way, and you could feel big stuff brewing.

Cécile was here to help, I'd said to Nick. Said I'd asked her to come cuz she was the one who knew there were holes the size of glacial lakes in the official account.

You need an infiltrator, I said. Someone who knows the 'hood. That's her: Cécile Métrailler, secret agent. We had to confide in her.

And Cécile on the couch in our chalet, legs crossed, hands fidgeting with the throw pillow. Wary eyes. Pupils pulsating every time she looked at Nick, like someone was shining Morse code in them with a penlight. *Dot dash dot dash, open shut open shut.*

While Nick talked—me throwing in French when Cécile didn't understand his English—I kept my eye fixed on her expression. I'd picked up on the way people reacted around Nick before. How they could feel the mountain in him. I'd seen it with Harald and Louise Grevers, with Claire the shrink. Even today, with Maria. It was subtle but unmistakable. The subconscious aversion to being around him for long. The instinctive disgust causing them to turn away. How they licked their lips the entire time. How they suddenly staggered or clung on to something. And they didn't even have to *see* him.

For obvious reasons, Nick avoided having friends come over when we were in Amsterdam, but one Saturday morning Fazila came by to pick me up for a shopping spree and we were having lunch in the kitchen. Nick was upstairs in bed. After half an hour, Fazila said she felt dizzy. Said she needed some fresh air, wondered maybe her period was too early.

Yesterday it suddenly hit me.

Dry mouth. Nausea. Dizziness and headache. *All symptoms of altitude sickness.*

I googled it: hypobaropathy. Exposed to it too long you get pulmonary edema and cerebral edema and then you croak.

All of them symptoms I didn't have . . . *cuz I was acclimatized to Nick.* What I had was fear of heights. Can't acclimatize to that.

But what if someone was exposed to Nick for too long?

This all zipped through my head as I stared at Cécile. Nick talking and Cécile's fingers digging like claws into that pillow. Her eyes, they looked away from him, practically popped out, and her pupils pulsated their SOS to the world like it was her last cry for help.

What was wrong with her? Was *this* altitude sickness?

When Nick was through talking, Cécile's face was ashen. Was it okay if she lay down for a bit? Said she'd had the early shift that morning at the CHUV and was tired from the drive up. I showed her the bedroom Maria'd prepped for her in the attic. Clean sheets, aired mattress—only disadvantage, there's no en suite bathroom. Doesn't matter, she said, her body language screaming *Get out now!* Voice hoarse, lip quivering as she shooed me down the stairwell and shut the trapdoor behind me. I called up did she need anything, herbal tea or something, and she replied no, all she really needed was rest.

Once I was back downstairs, Nick, looking at me miserably, said, "It's me, isn't it." Outside, twilight had conquered the valley, and Nick said, "Something's wrong. It didn't look like she came here for fun. Or for us."

And me suddenly thinking, the way she kicked me out of the attic, it had looked like she was in a *hurry*. Like she was late for sundown and would change into an ogre or something.

Now, at our table in Hôtel du Barrage, I grabbed her hands and asked, "What happened to you?" Those eyes big and brown; now it was my turn to hold her in an eye lock. "You ran out of the hospital in the middle of cleaning Nick's wounds and you left them all exposed. You texted that he was a monster. What did you see when you were changing the dressings?"

"What did I see? I . . . An ugly wound. Bloody."

I told her the nurse in charge said she ran outside screaming. That couldn't be from seeing a little blood. What's so bad it could make her scream and run?

"It was nothing," Cécile said. "I was under a lot of pressure at work. It just got over my head." Plucking at her hair, she said, "*Juste une dépression nerveuse*."

I thought, *Pull the other one. You wanna tell. That's why you're here. But you can't get up the nerve.*

"Okay," I said. "Fine. Full disclosure here. I looked too. Under the bandages."

"That was unavoidable." Another sip of beer. "I remember you said you were afraid to do it. Could you bear it?"

"Birds came out of his face."

Cécile blinked.

I pointed past her to the thing shifting around in the semidark above the bar. "Same kind as the birds in all those cages everywhere." Lucky birds, per Maria. Ancestors with claws and beaks. "I was prepared for a lot, but that was overdoing it. Your turn. What did you see?"

"I'm not sure I understand what you're saying, Sam."

I asked, "Do you believe in ghosts? In spirits?"

"Yes," Cécile said bluntly. By the look of her, she wasn't bullshitting.

"I don't," I said. Pause. "But there was something else."

"What?"

"I thought I saw Augustin. Nick's climbing buddy, the one who froze to death in the glacier. When I looked under the bandages, his hand came out. Gore-Tex jacket sleeve, fingers all stiff and blue from the ice . . ."

What came looking back at me, over the beer glass, were those big, brown eyes, which, now that I was so far into the story, sucked the rest of it out of me. The mise-en-scène hadn't changed. The customers' laughing, the crackling of the fire. The chef's singing. The outside world a moonless black, the escape route to the valley a single narrow lane in the October rain. All of it was there, but the only thing that mattered was the story I told Cécile in order to pry hers out of her.

The dizziness, the vertigo, the whole shebang. I laid my cards on the table.

"I know," I said, when I was done. "I musta imagined it. But it seemed so real, ya know? It seemed so real."

On Cécile's arms, all the hairs stood on end. Sweltering, oppressing heat in the inn, but all Cécile could feel was the cold mountain wind.

"You felt something too," I said. "I saw it on you when Nick was telling his story today. I saw it in your eyes; something was up. What was it?" I dropped another silence and, as if on cue—*bang!*—a gnarl exploded in the fire. Cécile jumped. The only thing you could see in that semidarkness was the customers' hollow faces. The dark shadow in the birdcage. My mouth, forming words she didn't want to hear: "Something happened to you when you looked under the bandages. You saw something. Did he hurt you?" I asked, "Why are you here, Cécile?"

And Cécile said, "I'm here to help." A heartbeat later: "And I'm here because I *can* help."

5

So here we go.

"I grew up in the mountains," Cécile said. "Not in the Val d'Anniviers, but in the Val d'Hérens, on the other side of the chain right above Grimentz. As the crow flies, it's less than ten miles from where we are, but for all intents and purposes it's a different world. The valleys here are isolated; each has its own course and its own stories. The mountain folk don't need more than that. They know their valley like the back of their hand.

"Of course we heard the stories of the highlands, when we were kids. Ghost stories. Strange things that happened in isolated valleys. You didn't give it a lot of thought. When you grow up in the mountains, the world outside is full of secrets. You know the exact place by the brook where the old herdsman from Fourcla was caught in a spring tide and swept away. They say that at high tide you can still hear him screaming on that side of La Borgne gorge. You know the exact places around the village where wolves and lynxes come during the winter months. The snow there was always tamped down with four-toe paw prints. At night you could hear the wolves howling at the moon. But there were places upstream where the snow always remained untouched. As if the animals shunned those places, see?

"Well, there were also stories about a mountain that was always covered in clouds. About a valley that was full of echoes and where no one would go anymore, because the devil had put a curse on it. Here in the mountain villages, the Roman Catholic Church still leaves a heavy mark on what people believe.

"Anyway, when I was twelve, we moved to Lausanne. You get older, you lose touch with the mountains and forget the stories you were told as a child. I hadn't thought about that mountain for very a long time. Until last August, when Nick was flown in by the rescue team."

She paused, but I didn't dare to break the silence. The inn, the people, the fire—clean forgotten. The way Cécile told her story, I was nine years old all over again. Back in Huckleberry Wall, back in my PJs, listening to Grandpa's ghost stories, goose bumps all over.

"I felt sorry for you. For both of you. I knew what was in the Police Cantonale's report couldn't be true and that Dr. Genet's diagnosis of Nick's wounds was a lie. Why would he lie about something like that? Something wasn't right. There was such a strange atmosphere in the ward; nobody wanted to talk about it. Remember the night we met, that I blatantly lied about what Nick's note said?"

'Course I did.

"Well, that's why. It kept haunting me, even after you'd left and Nick was repatriated to the Netherlands. So I started nosing around. And when I read in the report where the mountain rescue had found him, all those old stories came back to me, and I sank my teeth into it. I felt I owed you. Because I ran away that night. I regretted it.

"And yes, you were right. Maybe I did feel something weird when I was changing Nick's dressings. Even though he was maxed out on morphine. I thought it was pure intuition that got me so scared all of a sudden, but after everything you've told me, it's reasonable to assume I sensed the same as everybody else. That I sensed the Maudit in him. But I didn't know that at the time."

"Sink your teeth into it" meant tracing the clues back to the source. That's why Cécile drove up to the Air-Glaciers base at the Sion airport to talk to one Benjamin Crettenand, the guy who signed off on Nick's report.

Turned out Benjamin was the pilot who flew the chopper that day. After Cécile told him who she was, after she told him the Dutchman they picked up was her patient and that she *knew* that mountain cuz she grew up in its valleys, *he* practically begged *her* to let him answer her questions. Turned out he'd been waiting for someone to spill his guts to all along.

"Seriously," Cécile said, "you don't know how much of a miracle it was that Nick was rescued. When he made his call, he was unable to speak, but he did have the presence of mind to text 1414—the Swiss 911—his GPS coordinates. Plus 'HELP' in all caps. Benjamin told me that when he and his team saw the coordinates precisely lined up with the col of the Vallée Maudit, they looked at each other and got cold all over. Because no one had apparently called from up there before."

"How's that possible?" I asked.

"For one, because Benjamin claimed hardly anybody ever goes up there. He said you won't find any hikers or climbers or cross-country skiers in those parts. Not even hunters. I found that hard to believe, because the Swiss Alps are overflooded with tourists and explorers. But Benjamin was adamant. One valley up north, right here above Grimentz, flocks of students tear down the slopes in winter. One valley down south, swarms of mountaineers crawl up along the ridges in summer. But this particular valley, nobody. Because those who know about it—the locals and the guides—apparently work very hard to *prevent* people from going up there."

You couldn't close a mountain, this pilot of hers said. But you could keep it under wraps. Discourage its ascent in the guidebooks. Fence off the access. Loop trails the other way. And the ones who *did* find it, either by accident or by otherwise unlucky fate?

They ended up as code 33–11s.

"Code thirty-three eleven stands for the Swisstopo's official metric elevation of the Maudit, but Benjamin says they've got it all wrong. The valley's dimensions, too. Satellite images make it look like the glacier that used to flow through it has mostly melted away, but he says that doesn't tally with what it looks like up there, either. He says no one knows exactly how big the valley really is. Bigger than assumed, in any case. And the mountain, it's higher."

"Most of the time," Cécile added.

And I said, "Most of the time?"

"Hey, don't shoot the messenger. I asked what he meant by that, but Benjamin just laughed. He said I'd never been up there. Said the place does something with your head. The available information is inconclusive, because most code thirty-three elevens are never found. A worried call from the family to the emergency services or the Police Cantonale, and that's it. Then a funeral—after a while. Only once they've been declared dead. The coffin is always empty. As if the mountain has swallowed them up."

Cécile, a pale face hovering in our dim corner of the inn, said it didn't happen very often. Once every two years, tops. Consider the 120 hikers and climbers that die in the Alps each year and you could call it statistical noise.

"And even then, they're never sure. It's hard to know, with the little bits they dig up. Where the car was parked before they towed it away. On what page in the guidebook the ribbon was—it's all basically detective work."

But *they* knew. The mountain rescuers knew. Because they were first in line to hear the *really* sinister stories.

Mrs. Marjorie Hatfield from Tintagel, England, for instance. Some twenty years ago she left Grimentz for a stroll in the mountains. Zigzagging her way up for less than half an hour, a cold mist came down the trail. One wrong turn and she was off course. Another and she was lost. Marjorie decided to keep descending in order to find her way back to the village, but after hours and hours, and much to her shock, she reached the edge of a ginormous bulging glacier. It wasn't supposed to be there. She slipped and fell off a jutting patch of bedrock. The following day, hikers found her in the woods above Grimentz. Missing her eyes, she couldn't stop screaming.

Cécile said, "I asked how they knew all this, and Benjamin said they must have deduced it from her screaming. With bandages on her empty eye sockets, she died five days later in a bed in Hôpital du Valais, blind and still screaming. Apparently, her heart muscle tore between two gasps."

Or Alexander Rüegsegger's call, Cécile said, pausing only to bring her Cardinal draft to her lips. Her words vibrated in the semidark like some ancient, forgotten childhood fear.

"Benjamin got the call a few times, but he says he never gets used to it. The first time it happened, it was after dark and a storm had grounded all helicopters, but the radio at the base in Sion suddenly crackled and it was Rüegsegger. He said he wanted to return to the base but couldn't find his way out of the valley. Over his voice, Benjamin said he could hear the chopper's turbine. That and those squeaky disturbances, like he was on some wrong wavelength."

Benjamin had told Rüegsegger he had to keep looking. That he'd eventually find a way out. Telling this to Cécile, he was all rattled. "You do what you can, you know?" he'd said. "Am I wrong to give a soul some hope?"

Everyone on the base knew that Alexander Rüegsegger and two of his coworkers had crashed their helicopter during a search flight on the Maudit back in '78. The wreckage was never found. Benjamin said it hadn't been the first incident, and no helicopters have apparently gone up since. Not theirs, not the Rega's, and not Air Zermatt's.

"He said if you disappear up there, you disappear for good."

Except Nick hadn't.

Benjamin Crettenand, he was the real hero of this story. After all, it was his decision to fly out that saved Nick.

"His coworkers asked him if he was sure," Cécile said, "and Benjamin said they still had an hour's daylight left. Didn't they ever want to see with their own eyes what was up there? So they agreed to go as far as the col and not a single foot beyond. If Nick wasn't there, they'd turn back. But he was. Even though they flew into a whiteout, they spotted him through a break in the clouds. First they thought he was dead. He was lying flat on his stomach and showed no sign of life. The fresh snow around him was infused with blood. He was still clasping his cell phone with his bare hand. And . . ." Cécile hesitated but pushed on. "According to Benjamin, there were crows' footprints in the snow all over the place."

The inn felt like it got twenty degrees colder.

"Anyway, they plucked Nick off the col and returned him to Lausanne, where Dr. Genet operated on him the same evening. Apparently he regained consciousness long enough to make it clear to them there was a second climber involved and that he'd fallen into a crevasse on the glacier. Still, Augustin Laber was considered a tragic death, not a missing person. Benjamin spoke with the Police Cantonale and they wrote up a report. The whole thing was fabricated, because no one flew back that evening. No one saw an ice axe on the edge of some crevasse. Contrary to regulations, no representative of the Police Cantonale ever accompanied them. Someone had looked the other way."

As in any good story, Cécile had saved the best for last. As in any good story, I had to ask her if Benjamin had seen something strange up there.

"No," she said. "But when he'd let the paramedics out to get Nick ready for transport and was hovering over the col, he claims the place had started to hypnotize him. Like he'd lost track of time. And when suddenly one of the paramedics' voices came blaring through the headset, asking him what the hell he was doing, it turned out he'd strayed hundreds of yards into the valley. Hundreds of yards away from where he thought he was hovering."

"No . . ."

"Yes. And he swore he'd made only small corrections with his stick and pedals, so he would stay put. He said nothing like that had ever happened to him before. He thinks something must have pulled him in. I asked if it could have been the wind, but he said wind doesn't do that. And he added one more thing. One last thing, before he didn't want to talk anymore."

"What was that?"

"He said, 'Now I know: all those stories are true. It's a *bad* place, and no one can make me think otherwise.'"

6

Fade in to Hôtel du Barrage, late evening. In the past hour, more people had gone out through the street door than in; the remaining dinner guests were now drinking schnapps. No more "O *sole mio*" from the kitchen, only the clatter of plates going into the dishwasher. In the semidark above the bar, the black bird shuffled quietly in its cage. Opposite me, Cécile Métrailler, secret agent, lit a cigarette, fingers trembling like she was playing invisible castanets.

And I said, "D'you believe him?" Staring at her, two empty beer glasses and smoke and darkness separating us, I said, "D'you believe all those stories?"

She sighed. "Maybe something strange really happened to him, or he thinks something strange happened to him. I wasn't there, but I was there when he told me, and I'm convinced *he* believed he was telling the truth . . ."

Cécile, she was musing. Pulling up a smoke screen of words. Tempering the disclosure that she really did believe the story. I've seen it before; I've done it too.

"There's just so much." Probing the air with her fingers, face swimming in the half-light, she said, "So many incidents can be attributed to that place, if you start adding things up. And the implications are dead serious. People disappear up there. There are two parents in Germany who were lied to about what happened to their son. Imagine how they must feel."

The barwoman came to our corner, asked if we wanted to order another drink. I saw Cécile hunch her shoulders when the woman leaned over and wiped the rings off the table, like she was caught leaking classified information. I smiled and said, "Two more of the same, please."

When she was gone, I asked, "Okay, but what are we talking about, Cécile? If it's all true, what are we dealing with here?"

"I can't explain what's wrong up there, but it scares me. Didn't you notice how similar Nick's and Benjamin's stories were? Didn't Nick also say the valley looked bigger from the inside?"

"Yeah, sure, 'course I noticed. But that was disorientation. Delirium. At least that's what I thought *before* that pilot of yours started claiming you might as well chuck your map, up there. And that the mountain is higher. I beg your pardon; it's higher *most of the time*. What the hell does *that* mean?"

Cécile said softly, "That's exactly what scares me, Sam. I don't know."

I do, but what I was thinking was too wacky to say out loud: a valley that somehow morphed . . . that was *alive*.

Admit it, if the mountain could possess Nick, this was just origin.

Baby steps in the hierarchy of the supernatural.

The barwoman returned with our beers, but my mouth suddenly dried up. Nick had survived, that much was certain. He'd lain up there, lost, alone. Bleeding in the snow, thinking he was gonna die. Hairsbreadth diff and they wouldn't even have gone searching for him. He must have been so unimaginably terrified. So fucking lonely.

Realizing he'd been that close to dying turned my stomach. I hadda stop thinking about it. So I was sitting there, sweating up my shirt. Looking around, dizzy, suddenly convinced that something enormous was coming. Something enormous, with big, hollow tunnels for eyes.

The water inside freezes and thaws, freezes and thaws . . .

It was like a slap in the face.

"Sam, are you okay?"

"No," I said. "Actually, not." I drained my beer and banged the glass on the table so hard that the fogeys by the fire looked up. "You say that place scares you; it gives me the fucking creeps. Because it *changed* Nick. What came down that valley, what was picked up by the chopper and was operated on by your doctor, that wasn't Nick. Not *just* Nick, at least."

"So you really believe that. That he is possessed by the Maudit."

"Yep. Yeah, I do. Don't you?"

She nodded slowly, reluctantly.

"And I don't know how, but his mutilation has something to do with it. Like he's hiding it under his bandages. Maybe you can convince him to show it. Offer to give him a checkup or something, and then . . ."

Cécile visibly recoiled.

And I said, "You're afraid of him, huh? You're afraid of Nick."

And she's all uneasy, like *I, uh*, like *I'm not sure if . . .*

"Yeah, you're afraid of him." I leaned forward, took both her hands. "Cécile, there's something you're not telling me. I saw it today, in the chalet. I saw the way you looked at Nick. How nervous you were. This is no time for secrets, Cécile. If there's something I need to know, I'd rather hear it now."

And she, snapping at me, the scapegoat: "And you wouldn't be nervous? The way I left him behind? The way I left *you* behind?"

"What did you see under the bandages?"

"I already told you."

"You sensed the mountain in him."

"Yes, but I didn't know what it was."

"And nothing else?"

"No."

"But what was it you felt?"

Same old. Dizziness. The proximity of something enormous. Difficult to describe. Fuck, her stony face. Impassive, a statue. Still, cracks. Behind it, a glimpse of something uncontrolled, almost hysterical. A lie? Or was I chasing shadows?

"Cécile . . . *Why are you so afraid of him?*"

Her trembling lip.

"Cécile?"

Her voice, only a sigh in the dark: "Because Dr. Genet killed himself."

I practically jumped out of my seat, so violently that the people in the adjacent tables turned to look. "No shit!"

"I didn't want to tell you with Nick around."

"Holy shit." The image that popped up in my mind was Dr. Genet frowning and turning the police photos upside down and right side up again. Louise Grevers raising her hands to cover her mouth. "What happened?"

"No one really knows, it was hushed up in the ward. But it was all so strange. There had been no signs that he'd had any depressive tendencies. There's a panoramic terrace on the CHUV's roof, where the hospital employees sometimes have receptions in summer, because you can see the whole city and the lake. Early in September, Dr. Genet went up there, climbed over the rails, and jumped. He was found on the plaza, twelve stories down."

"Jesus Christ." Trying to find my composure, I said, "I'm really sorry. But what's that got to do with Nick?"

"Can't you see?"

"No. He wasn't even around when it happened."

"No, he wasn't around. But he also wasn't conscious when I changed the bandages. And what he showed me was heavy-duty enough to make me drop everything and run away."

Oh boy.

Cécile, she said, "That place mutilated him, Sam. That place in the mountains. On this, I agree with Benjamin: it's a *bad* place. And don't get me wrong, but I'm not sure Nick was supposed to come back from it. Dr. Genet may have been a bit arrogant, but he was a good man and an excellent surgeon. I worked under his supervision for a year and a half, and he was always cheery, always joking around. As far as I know, he had a happy marriage. They had three children and were going to go to Mauritius in September. He had no reason to do what he did. Until Nick was flown in, straight from that place in the mountains, and everything changed. *Everything.* Dr. Genet operated on him, looked straight into his mutilated face. A couple of weeks later, he killed himself."

I coulda said a thousand things but I shut up. Didn't dare cut her short now.

"I saw him a couple of times in August, between that night and his death. He'd changed. We all saw it. He looked pale, his hair was straggly. It was so bad the head of the ward, Martine Guillarmod, even summoned him to ask whether he was ill. I can still see his expression. He didn't say anything those couple of weeks, but something was going on behind his eyes. Beats me what it was, but it upset me. It was like he was consciously letting go of life."

"That's terrible," I said. "But again, I don't see what Nick's got to do with it. You looked under the bandages; so did I. We're both here."

Cécile, her breath a nicotine/beer cocktail: "The smack when he fell was awful." Her bottom lip trembling, she said, "The sound . . ."

"Oh shit. Were you . . ."

"I was outside, smoking. It was sheer coincidence I witnessed it. And at the same time, it didn't feel like a coincidence at all. Paranoid, huh? But yes, I was the one who checked for a pulse, before the Police Cantonale arrived. As if I somehow expected he might still be alive." Some cheerless sound, more a sob than a chuckle. "I was the one who found his suicide note in his coat pocket. The note he had found the answer to."

"What did it say?"

"*I had to find out if the falling would end. Whether I'd ever hit the ground.*"

My body cramped, a major total-twitch, one humongous elemental chill, so bad I started to shake all over. Dunno if Cécile noticed anything, cuz all I saw in front of me was the hospital bed in Lausanne, the mummy mask pulled tightly over that hideous grin, and Nick, who totally shouldn't have been capable of talking: *And you will also find out what it's like to fall. To fall . . . and to fall . . . and to fall . . . and to fall.*

Immediately after that, the cellar in Amsterdam. Nick covering the smiley mouth on his wrappings with his hand.

Smile! This way you'll always know it's me and never mistake me for someone else. When I smile, you don't have to be scared of me, okay?

Little, fragile Sam.

It all started to hit home, and it revealed such a somber panorama that I fought against it with body and soul. Okay, you accepted the fact that that place up there in the mountains had entered your boyfriend. You accepted the invasive erosion of the soul. Your parasitic orogeny. Your base camp possession. But each cocktail had its own ingredients.

And *mountains* don't wish people dead.

It was in Nick's words that it had spoken. Filtered by Nick's thoughts.

Nick's fears. Nick's remorse.

Nick's hands. Nick's teeth.

Nick's will.

Was it really possible that Nick, drowsing, comatose, *possessed*, had catapulted Dr. Genet straight to his unfortunate death?

I didn't buy that. Didn't wanna buy that. *Couldn't* buy that.

"Listen," I said. "I'm so sorry you had to witness that. But Nick is not responsible for it."

But who was I really trying to convince?

"Promise me you'll ask him about it," Cécile said. Almost *begged*. "That you'll gauge his reaction."

"I promise. But don't forget, Nick means no harm. He's trying to resist it. Let's help him get rid of it. And let's call it quits now. We're both dead beat, and that desperate look of yours doesn't suit you one bit, girl."

She didn't think that was funny. "Please be careful. I don't want anything to happen to you. I don't want it to harm you."

"Nick would never allow it."

But I thought again, *Little, fragile Sam.*

We paid the bill. While waiting for my change, I asked what our next step was, and Cécile said she wanted to take me to the Val d'Hérens, where she was born. That there was someone she wanted me to meet. But that wasn't the last surprise I got that night. As we walked out of the Hôtel, I looked back at the semidark above the bar one last time, to the spot that, like a magnet, had drawn my gaze the whole evening.

In the birdcage, the silhouette was not a chough but a man.

He was grinning at me.

7

Excuse the cliff-hanger, but after the info influx (info OVERLOAD—all caps, as Julia would say), I figured it's time to cut to the next scene. You're probably thinking, *Sam, WT-fucking-F?* I see you shiver with antici—But have no fear; you'll get the whole story. Soon. *Pation!*

First you had that chronically nerve-racking night when you tried to process the whole business and out of total exhaustion ended up in an hours-long textathon with Julia. One object of my concern lying asleep on the pillow beside me like an edelweiss and the other upstairs in the attic, probably cursing her own demons. All of us cramped in one chalet, a *Friends* episode on steroids, except no one was really "there for you" because we were all too busy plotting our own exorcism. So, insomnia *à gogo*, till sometime in the wee hours Ramses silently hopped onto my side of the bed, nudged me with his head, purring a whole Relaxation Therapy playlist. Nice to know there was at least someone you could count on, but it was a tad depressing, too, because Ramses is just a common stray, not even a Burmese.

Next morning, Cécile couldn't beat it fast enough. Puffy eyes from little or no sleep, trembling corners of the mouth every time she tried to smile. My breakfast only half consumed before she directed me to the door. And Nick? Totally oblivious, despite all his noble intentions. And his power smoothie.

"Tonight," I said, when he waved us good-bye, crestfallen. "I'll tell you everything tonight."

I kinda felt sorry for him. Standing there in the doorway, so alone. I didn't have a good spiel about why it was just the two of us, but I'd promised Cécile.

Nick gave me a short hug and whispered, "You're on to something, huh?"

"I've already sold the TV rights." *Tonight*, I mouthed.

"Okay, but please be careful. With her, too. I like her, but she's acting strange."

The *her* in question already sitting shotgun in our Focus, but then all our gazes were drawn by a movement on the other side of the road. Trotting along from the direction of the village, none other than Ramses, terror of the Nile.

Every cat owner tries to turn a blind eye to two hard facts about their cootchie-cootchie-coo darlings: that they're ruthless killers and that they lick their own assholes. About the former—once in a while in Amsterdam, Ramses would leave half-eaten mice for us on the doormat, and one time a mangled tit, but what he now had in his mouth, that really took the biscuit.

It was one of those big, black alpine choughs.

I shouted, "Dude, that's someone's ancestor!"

The limp feathered body almost half as big as the cat, red gore dripping out of his mouth—Ramses was dragging it, more than anything else. Looking furtively up the drive, giving me a cursory, stoical, arrogant look, like *Yeah, what? Wasn't me. Anyway, I deserve a medal for this*, and next thing you know, the bird's body shivers, the chough twists its neck and pecks the cat deep in his side, hacking short and fierce like a hawk. Ramses screeched with pain, leaped practically three feet into the air, and let go of his prey. It fell to the ground, spread its battered wings, hopped-stumbled a coupla fast yards, and flew away low over the ground, back to the village. And Ramses nowhere to be seen. Only a dark cannonball that shot past me into the chalet.

Cécile, sitting with the car door open, took her shades off and said, "Did he get one of those choughs?"

"Looks like it," I said in French. "Though I'm not so sure who got who." In Dutch, nodding to inside the house: "I think someone needs some aftercare."

"Not the killer he thought he was," Nick chuckled. "That'll teach him to play with his food. *Bonne chance aujourd'hui!*"

He waved to Cécile and we left.

That bird was dead as a dodo, I thought, as I turned the Focus onto the main road. Cécile staring silently out her window, wooded slopes throwing ocher autumn light into the car, and my thoughts going where I didn't wanna go. *In my version of what I saw, the bird's guts were hanging out of its stomach. In my version of the truth, there's something seriously wrong about what just happened.*

And that looped me back in a large circle to what I saw last night. Or *thought* I saw. Sure, it was a flash. It was late. My head was reeling from Cécile's collection of happy horror stories. But there, in the gloom above the beer taps, closely confined and pitch-black, I saw a person in the birdcage. A man. One bony hand gripping the bars, the other hand and two legs dangling out. Precisely how you pictured the way they used to cage thieves and leave them to starve, when that was still, like, a thing.

Precisely what you *didn't* expect above a Swiss bar, with a barwoman rinsing glasses and cold-shouldering her pet-toy.

It didn't fit, of course. The cage was way too small for jailing a dude. And yet he was there. But that wasn't even what made you feel like you'd stuck a wet finger into a wall socket—your heartbeat racing, sweat spouting, on the verge of hyperventilation. It was his face. You saw it for a nanosecond. Like he was wearing a mask. Like you were looking at a puppet's face that was staring into the distance, staring past you, but definitely seeing *something*.

And he was grinning. That was the worst.

That grin froze your innards.

Look back just once, search Cécile's gaze just once, and it was gone; you saw just a bird in a cage. One of those ancient mountain men gaping at you from his stool like you'd gone nuts.

Yeah, I was zonked. Had a head full of ghosts.

And nope, I wasn't absolutely positive Ramses's bird had been dead.

You only knew what you thought you saw.

We didn't exchange a single word the whole drive down the valley. One hairpin turn after the other, the blacktop could bring us to Paris or Milan or the Mediterranean and it wouldn't make a diff. Behind us was that mountain. We felt its power reaching for us with invisible fingers. Wherever we'd go, it would still follow us there, like glacier water that drips into brooks, flows into rivers, and ends up in the sea half a continent away, where you, a random swimmer, could suddenly be enveloped by a cold current that made you shiver with unease.

8

The person Cécile wanted to introduce me to turned out to be her grandmother, a blind woman who in her whole life had rarely if ever been outside the Val d'Hérens. Her name was Louetta Molignon and she lived in a slate-roofed house in the upper parts of the village of Evolène.

"*Mamie, c'est moi, Cécile,*" Cécile said loud and clear, when we found the old woman sitting in a wickerwork garden chair behind the house. "I've come to visit you, and I've brought a friend from America."

She hugged her grandmother, and from behind Cécile's body, wrinkled, liver-spotted hands appeared that probed her and read her like braille. From behind her long, yoga-stretched thighs, you could hear the muffled rasps of something antediluvian. Then she stepped aside and made room for me.

I said, *"Bonjour, Madame Molignon. Je m'appelle Sam."*

Louetta looked like she'd been spewed out by the big bang itself. White hair, so thin you could see her scalp. Large ears and crooked teeth, a flaky neck that disappeared into a hideously jolly pink floral vest that looked like it didn't contain even a carcass. But her eyes, the romantic poet muses, were still young, and you could see her whole life reflected in them . . . Just kidding. One was spooky white, and the other hung lewdly downward, like it was searching in vain for whatever had once filled her wiry old-lady bra.

No, with Louetta Molignon, it was her spirit that was peppy. Still hip and with it.

"Sweetie," she said, as she took my hand with her haggard claw, "why bother with a foreigner?"

And she started laughing so hard her face wrinkled like a cinnamon roll.

Madame Molignon would later tell us she had help for the housekeeping and the shopping but still lived self-sufficiently. A bit like how a fossil in a natural history museum lives self-sufficiently.

"As long as you make my granddaughter happy, young man," the old woman said, her fingers probing upward along my arms and shoulders. "A good specimen, by the looks of it. Exactly how you'd picture an American."

Cécile, her face flaring scarlet: "Ah, but we're not a couple, Mamie . . ."

Louetta, waving a dismissive hand: "You can't fool your old grandmother, child."

And me, with a winning smile: "Don't worry, Madame Molignon. For better or worse."

She said she had fresh milk and Cécile should go get it. The setting was so idyllic it made me think of Auntie Bernstein, who walked/didn't walk the Panther Mile with me. Weird how at a certain point old people's faces all start to look the same in our memory. What makes them unique is the stories they tell. And like all elderly ladies, Louetta had the greatest stories. She'd fused with the mountains. She talked about the mountains with such love, it even started to rub off on me. She made it seem like she'd been there when the youngest of them were born.

The milk really was the freshest and creamiest I'd ever tasted. I was surprised I liked it.

We'd been there a while when Cécile suddenly said, "Mamie, tell Sam about the Morose. About the time it almost got Grandpa."

"Dear Lord," Louetta said, and before you could say "Lucifer" she'd crossed herself. "Why would you want to rake up those kinds of things? They're bad; we don't talk about them."

Cécile said I had a friend who'd had an accident high in the mountains. That we thought the mountains had made him sick, that a *specific* mountain had made him sick, and that we wanted to know what we were dealing with so we could help.

The way she said it, I suddenly got a lump in my throat.

And the old lady goes, "Oh, that's not good, young man. No, that's not good at all." Like she was the Oracle of Delphi herself. "Anyone who goes into the mountains brings the mountains back with them." Louetta Molignon suddenly looked right at me with that opaque white eye. "You also carry a mountain with you, young man. A very old one. I can see it."

And before I could react, she started talking.

Everyone here feared what they called the Morose, she said, even though it never occurred in *this* valley. The winds blew differently here. In this valley, God had been merciful.

You had to strain to understand her dialect, but I knew what *morose* meant. Everything that's dismal and gloomy and depressing.

With blind eyes staring over the fields, Louetta told us, "It was a long time ago, a whole life before you were born, when your grandfather was still young. In the mountains above La Sage, there's a pasture they call Le Tsaté. In those days, there were a few old huts next to a chapel. That year, it must have been '48 or '49, we spent the whole summer up there, and we let the flock graze on the slopes above the alp. Every Sunday, Father Zufferey, priest of La Sage, came up to read the Mass and bless the cattle and the milk. He'd done that as long as we could remember, because everyone knew there was a place up there in the mountains that was defiled by the Evil One."

Louetta's gaunt shoulders shivered when she uttered the moniker. The foul place, as she called it, was on the other side of the chain, and you never went up there. The mountains were too steep; it was impossible to reach that valley from this one. What's more, she said, that place spelled doom. The wind that came down from there was disturbingly cold, and its night sky was said to be starless.

"I'm too old to remember much, but this I remember like it was yesterday. That year, when the days were getting shorter and the nights colder, the people from the alp left for the valley, one by one. After the last blessing, I too went down to the village with Father Zufferey. But your grandfather didn't, child. No, Jérôme loved the pasture. He always wanted to spin the summer out as much as possible, until the good days were up and the dark days came. High up in the mountains, there are only two seasons: the good days and the dark days. Nothing in between.

"In any case, Jérôme stayed behind with two other cowherds and the cattle, and it got me all nervous. Because something had stirred in the air. We all felt it. A shroud of unease had descended on the alp at the end of the summer. It made the cows fidgety. And we all knew what had brought it about.

"'You must go down, you hear?' I said to Jérôme before I descended. 'You know what dwells up there, and I don't want you getting yourself into trouble!' Your grandfather assured me that he'd come down within a week and that he'd stay away from the higher slopes. But once in the valley, I regretted that I didn't insist for him to come and join me. They were all alone up there. No one was going to go up again that year, and the alp was completely forsaken. Even by God."

Louetta said, "And then the dark days came."

The old mountain folk, she said, had older ways of telling when a storm was brewing. They felt it in their bones. Bones grated. Joints creaked. Teeth tingled. The layman's osteoporosis prophecy. Nature telling you that you don't need the AccuWeather app but good ol' witchcraft.

And there were more signs. Omens, when high in the atmosphere, the dense, cold air mass pushed its way toward the Alps. The corona around the sun. Great flocks of birds spiraling upward, then hurriedly descending into the valley. Lenticular clouds hanging above the peaks with deceptive calm. The mountains, you could read them, if you knew their language.

All of this, Louetta told us, was *before* you heard the Morose.

The Morose existed only in the Val d'Anniviers. And only downwind from the Vallée Maudit, which they called the Valley of Echoes around here.

When the Morose began, according to the old mountain folk, you heard the valley bewailing the death of the world.

"It was an October like this one," Louetta said, "and we'd known for days that the storm was coming. Any moment, we expected to see your grandfather and his cronies come walking into the village. But he didn't come. And I started to worry. On the last day, the wind grew stronger and stronger, and when you looked to the south, it looked like the night had already come! Outside, you had to struggle against the wind to make your way. Everyone in the village was up and about, fastening the shutters and closing off the fences.

"And then Ambroise Nicollier suddenly came running over the gravel road from La Sage, out of breath and wide-eyed with fright. Ambroise was one of the two cowherds who'd stayed up there with your grandfather. Such a nice young man. His daughter Marie-Louise used to play with your mother, sweet child. Died in '57 in a landslide in Ferpècle. It was quite a tragedy."

They'd planned to descend that morning, Ambroise said, so they could stall the cattle before the storm broke. But when he woke up, he had found himself alone in the cabin. No cronies. No cows. Everything obscured by mist.

And outside, the wind was bewailing the death of the world.

Ambroise, he knew the stories, Louetta said. That if you heard the Morose, strange things would happen to you. That you had to hurry for shelter before it lured you up like the singing of the Sirens. So he made a run for it and didn't slow down until he'd reached the valley.

"'It's *wrong* up there, Louetta,' Ambroise said, still panting. '*He* dwells on the slopes up there, and all we can do is pray for Jérôme and Nicolas. I heard the devil sing! The devil!' And he was gone. To his mother's house, we heard later, and it was weeks before we saw him.

"By now, I was in a state. I put on my coat and walked all the way up to La Sage, while the weather was deteriorating all around me. When I got there, I told Father Zufferey what had happened. I begged him to gather some strong men from the village and go look for Jérôme, but he said there was no point. Darkness could fall any minute. And as if on cue, the storm broke at that very moment. Hail drummed down on the chapel roof, and that meant the Morose had reached its peak in that accursed valley, and I lost all hope of ever seeing your grandfather again."

"Then what happened, Mamie?"

"Well, an hour later the chapel door swung open and there he was. Exhausted, soaked to the bone, and pale as a ghost. I rushed to embrace him, but Jérôme was shivering like an old man and didn't want to say anything before he'd prayed with Father Zufferey and had knocked back a glass of hot red wine. 'Never,' he then said, 'have I heard what I heard today, and I hope to never hear it again as long as I live.' And then he started talking."

When he'd woken up, it wasn't in the safety of the cabin but in a boulder field. Everywhere around him, mist. Everywhere around him, the whistling of the wind, a hair-raising singing, swelling in the unseen. He yelled to Ambroise and Nicolas, and everywhere, surrounding his yells, fanning out behind him and all around, he saw phantoms stirring. Horned, lumbering heads that rose out of swirling openings in the mist and fixed their gazes on him. Only after prolonged moments of absolute mortal fear did he realize he was looking at his own cows, restlessly snorting behind the subdued clanging of their heavy bells.

"Jérôme called his friends again," she said, "but only the wind replied. Panic struck his heart. Still calling out, he started to wander around the slope, but he didn't know which way to go. The mist drifted by him in cold ripples. In the distance, or at least that's how it seemed, he was *sure* he heard a cry. He stood and listened until he heard it again, from higher up the slope. It was such a grim, anguished howl, it caused the herd to run wild and disappear into the mist. But Jérôme had heard his own name being called, and he rushed up the mountain.

"'Ambroise, Nicolas, where are you?' he shouted, over and over. Then several voices answered, thin and distant and way up high. It still sounded like a cry for help, but suddenly your grandfather wasn't sure anymore that they'd been calling his name or that it was Ambroise and Nicolas who were calling out there. They kept on coming, the cries from the mist. Sometimes he thought he could see shadows, but every time he approached them, they vanished.

"Exhausted and shivering from the exposure, Jérôme eventually stopped.

He realized he'd been fooled, and it could now prove fatal. The mist had become impenetrable, his breath was vaporizing, and the wailing of the wind sounded like a choir of screaming souls. A dissonant melody brought forth directly by the devil himself.

"'Father Zufferey,' he said in the La Sage chapel that evening, 'I heard the Morose up there, and I managed to tear myself away from it only by the grace of God.'"

Because it had suddenly gotten louder.

That sound, it had pierced his soul, Louetta said, but it had also cut deeper. Much deeper. You knew it was the Morose when you heard it. And then?

No one knew. Because no one who'd heard the Morose had lived to tell the tale.

You see . . . Jérôme Molignon, Cécile's grandfather, he didn't *really* hear the Morose. That was raging on the *other* side of the crest, in the Vallée Maudit. Jérôme, he only heard the outer frequencies. Muted. "*Dans la marge,*" in Louetta's words. So close to it, it had almost killed him.

In Grimentz, Louetta said, dead in the valley's outwash, the wailing of the wind came shuddering down unhindered. There, your best bet was distance. Everything scatters in the end. Everything dies down.

Still, the cattle got sick. Men went crazy. Mothers had miscarriages. Children became mutes.

"*Sérieusement,*" I said, staring at the old woman in disbelief.

"Oh, yes," Louetta said. "I heard the story of a little girl who was hiding from her mother in a barn when the Morose hit, and she never spoke another word till she was on her deathbed, sixty years later."

So, once a year, they closed all the shutters in Grimentz. Once a year, during the first violent storm of fall, they hung crosses on the doors, and the locals played Ländler music in their chalets till the wee hours. Outside, you could hear the alpenhorns and the Schwyzerörgeli above the yodeling of the night.

A blitz of sound to drown out anything that could be worse.

Infertility, outbursts of violence, people who fell under the spell of the wind and disappeared into the night—there were worse things than Swiss traditionals.

According to Louetta, it still went on, to this very day.

Which they didn't tell you on Airbnb.

9

"I'm not going in there," Cécile said, staring at Hill House through the windshield. "Not with him around. Sorry. I can't."

Outside, the wind breathed through the pine forest.

"Awkward," I said.

Afternoon, Nick's Focus parked next to Cécile's Peugeot, Cécile not stepping out but lighting up a Lucky, and now we're sitting there in a *totally normal* situation. My black V-Wire Curves between us to ease me up, but when the silence was too drawn out, I plucked the Lucky from her fingers and took a good drag. Usually I only smoked in NY's most *Vogue*-approved drinking dens, and I'm not talking tobacco, so I basically erupted into a hacking aria.

"Ugh, ya really gotta kick this, babe," I said. I flicked the cig out the open window. Cécile didn't look like she even noticed.

"I want you to go in, get my stuff from the attic, and bring it out here," she said. "Please. Could you do that for me?" Begging: "Without him noticing . . ."

"Cécile, come on. You're overreacting."

"I mean it, Sam. I'm not going back in there."

"But we were gonna talk to Nick. You weren't gonna leave before—"

And that's as far as I got before Cécile threw the door open, stumbled out, and puked in the tall grass next to the drive.

So I got out. Ran around the car, laid a hand on her back. Felt how wet she was. Wet and *cold*. "Jesus, Cécile, you're really sick, huh?"

When she got up and wiped her mouth with the back of her hand, I saw she was crying. "Please, Sam, don't make me go back in there. I don't want to. I really don't want to."

She was scared. Real scared; panic attack scared. So I held her in my arms and said, "Shush. I won't make you do anything. If you really wanna go home, go home. You've already done more than I could have hoped for."

"I'm so sorry, Sam." Whimpering and shivering against my shoulder, she said, "It seemed such a good idea to come here and tell you all I know. But now I'm not so sure it was the right thing to do."

"Why?"

"I've only complicated things for you, and it didn't get you anywhere." Her whimpering got heavier, making her more difficult to understand. "I'm sorry I couldn't help you more. I'm really s-s-sorry."

"Hey, whoa, whoa. Nonsense, Cécile. Hey, look at me."

She looked up reluctantly, wet eyes red-rimmed, makeup running in dark streaks. "I look terrible."

"Who cares? You don't need to impress *me*."

Limp smile. "That's not what Mamie thought."

I danced my eyebrows. "For better or worse, sugarplum."

Now she laughed through her tears. "Only an American could say something like that to a woman and mean it as a compliment."

It felt good to still be able to laugh like, well, normal people, but her gaze soon shifted past me to the chalet, and the shadow descended on her face again. In that gaze, I suddenly saw the family resemblance between her and her grandmother.

Louetta Molignon, she'd finished telling her story, but I only picked up half of the last part. About how the grandpa, alone, lost and wet to the skin, had descended in the mist, bumped into his herd, and Nicolas, lower down the slope and upon arriving in the valley, had discovered he could still hear the wind's whizzing. But this time in his ears. An annoying hum that didn't go away and kept him up for nights on end. The doctors couldn't find anything. Made sense. The cause was the same as for Nicolas's sudden impotence. The reason cows suddenly stopped giving milk. They'd heard the Morose—muffled, the way you heard someone screaming behind a closed door and couldn't make out the words—and the Morose had left its imprint on them. For three months, the symptoms didn't go away, and then they suddenly disappeared. By then, the mountains were buried under a thick blanket of snow, and the valley was still.

And me, I listened to it all. Saved all her words to my mind's hard drive, but my brain got stuck on trying to process this story into something saleable. To downplay it as just a de facto superstition.

Something I could hoodwink Nick into buying.

When Louetta was done talking, I asked, "Madame Molignon, what did you mean when you said you could see a mountain in me too? A very old one?"

"Did I say that?" Smacking her thin lips, the old lady said, "Don't take it too seriously, young man. Sometimes I get a bit confused." She turned to Cécile. "Sweet child, will you please pour me half a glass of red wine? The bottle is on the shelf in the kitchen. I always say, 'Half a glass a day keeps the grim reaper away.'"

And she started laughing so hard her face wrinkled like a *bisteeya*.

As soon as Cécile was gone, Louetta gazed at me with a stern, milky-white eye, and I again got the chilling feeling that she was looking right through me. "Maybe you can be as old as me one day, young man," she said. "But you've still got a lot to unlock."

"What do I need to unlock?"

"The world."

Somehow, I knew she was right.

"There *were* birds that night, Sam. Big ones, with long beaks, looking for prey."

My face started to heat up.

"Everyone carries a curse. We can help others only once we've gotten rid of ours."

That staring white eye, the mist inside it—it felt like it was hypnotizing me.

She's just like Auntie Bernstein. Watch. In a second she'll disappear, and when we drive off it'll be like she never existed. Like we've never even been here.

She didn't disappear, but the moment was gone, and by the time Cécile came out you hadda admit to yourself that it was more likely you'd imagined the whole thing.

That was then.

This was now.

"What are you going to do?" Cécile asked quietly.

"Talk to Nick, I guess." I shrugged. "With all due respect to your mamie, I don't believe in the devil and omens and all that religious claptrap. But I do know there's a power up on that mountain that gives both of us the creeps. And that power is also inside Nick."

"You could go too," Cécile said. "Together. Away from here. Away from that mountain."

But I shook my head. "I wish that was so. I'm really scared a kind of Pandora's box will open if Nick stays so close to the source of it for long, but our only hope lies here."

Now she took hold of me, hard, her fingers clawing my arms. "Please be careful, Sam. He's dangerous."

All kinds of stuff was going on behind Cécile's face, but that expression . . . I couldn't place it. It bothered me. Only later that evening, alone in bed and thinking about dark days and a starless sky, did I realize it had been relief. Relief about what? Relief that Nick and me were staying in Grimentz? But why?

Apparently, Cécile hadn't seen I was telling only half the truth. Because whatever that power was, I didn't believe it had turned Nick into a monster. I didn't believe Nick had driven that doctor to jump to his death.

What I did believe was that it had *changed* him.

And it got me curious.

Wouldn't you be?

If Pandora's box opened, I wanted to be there with him and look into it together.

I did what Cécile had asked: got her stuff from the attic. Didn't see Nick anywhere. Probably sleeping downstairs. Even if he'd noticed me, I was outside too fast to hear him call.

"Now, girl," I said, back on the drive, "sashay away."

But Cécile just stared upward. "Look," she said. Pointing to the hazy sky.

I took off my shades.

In the west, low above the mountains, there was a perfect halo around the sun.

AT THE MOUNTAINS OF MADNESS

NICK GREVERS'S MANUSCRIPT (PART 3)

I was glad when the mirage began to break up, though in the process the various nightmare turrets and cones assumed distorted, temporary forms of even vaster hideousness.

—H. P. Lovecraft

Trekking in the mountains is an introverted affair. Not everyone is cut out for it. Despite your climbing buddy's company, most of the time it's you alone with the mountain, alone with yourself. Since you need to save energy for the ongoing physical effort, you fall into a silent, steady cadence from one step to the next, which may increase the distance between the two of you without you noticing it. Pretty soon you move in a disconnected, trancelike determination, a purely meditative state in which your head is empty and your mind is so receptive to the surroundings' hidden powers that you can feel the earth's pulse. It's the perfect mindfulness exercise; whenever I come home from a climbing vacation, my mind is fully recharged.

It's in the same sort of trance that we completely lose our grip on reality, during our hours in the valley, as we gain elevation.

I remember there are moments when I become aware of the changing surroundings. They are just like photos but snaps in my memory, images and fragments that I can still see clearly.

This first snap is not long after we leave the col. Behind us, in the north, it has become dark. The Berner Oberland has disappeared behind a purple-gray wall of clouds and it looks almost as if night has descended on the Rhône valley.

The next snap—I'm not sure how much later—the view of the valley is obstructed by shreds of clouds rolling down from the steep rocky slopes surrounding the valley's entrance, as forerunners of the storm. A wind has kicked up, which cools the sweat on my forehead and flutters Augustin's hair over his bandanna.

We follow the bed more or less upstream, although you can't really call it a bed all the time. One moment the brook winds through the valley in a broad, furrowed outwash, and the next it has disappeared under the scree and all you hear is the dripping of meltwater. The terrain is easy; it rises only gradually, and if you know how to move, it's an elegant dance, skipping from rock to rock, occasionally supported by your Black Diamonds but mostly relying unfailingly on your equilibrium and the welcome balance the boulders offer. At that moment I'm still convinced we're gaining ground well and will be able to pitch our bivi before long.

Then all at once I'm jerked out of my reverie when Augustin says, "It's further than it seems, huh?"

I look up and around. I ask him how long we've been going. Fifty minutes now. I can hardly believe it. We'd estimated that it should take us less than an hour to get there. The clouds, heavy with rain, have descended on the glacier under the Maudit's north face, but the glacier has barely gotten any closer. Gray-white and cracked, it holds its breath in the distance. Behind us, the col where we left our stonemen has now disappeared from view as clouds creep in from the valley. It makes it difficult to gauge distances. It had seemed so close from below.

"Let's walk some more," I say. Soon enough I sink back into my absentminded dreaminess.

The wind picks up and becomes beastly cold.

This isn't right, I think, who knows how much later. Augustin is up ahead and I don't want to disturb his cadence, and since I don't have a watch on, I worm my hand into my pocket to take out my phone. I see that it's more than an hour and a half since we left the col, and I know: *We should have reached the lake a long time ago.*

But we aren't even close.

Only the scree fields stretching away in all directions till they disappear into clouds or cliffs.

My sense of direction is all messed up. Around us unfolds an unfamiliar deception of space and motion, as if the horizon is moving away from us in all directions at full speed and the valley is engulfing us in all its magnitude. *Time is strangely viscous here*, I think in confusion. Then: *No, it's the valley.*

Then I see Augustin's helmet before me again, that red dot slowly shrinking as it drops out of view. I hear a scream—I know it's in my head, but I immediately look around anyway, my heart thudding, because the silence was ripped apart so suddenly, and the scream echoes so close to where I am that it seems as if it's coming from the clouds directly above.

I rub my face, contemplate whether I want to waste energy by taking off my backpack to drink some water. I'm startled by a mumble of words and look around again, but I see only boulders. Am I hallucinating? Is it purely disorientation? I can't answer that.

When I turn around, I see a detached cloud bank rolling toward us, quickly catching up. The cloud looks diffusely white in contrast to the leaden sky and is growing like some monstrous life-form. I call out to Augustin, but he can't hear me, so I whistle with my fingers. He looks back and I point with my Black Diamonds to what's creeping up on us from behind.

Augustin waits for me, and by the time I catch up, he has put on his Gore-Tex coat. I quickly follow his example. Just in time, because the cloud rolls over us and the mountain's cold breath slaps us in the face.

The world changes into a pale white cocoon in which nothing can be discerned anymore.

"Shouldn't we pitch camp?" I ask. The lack of confidence that I can hear in my voice embarrasses me.

But again, Augustin shrugs. "It's just a cloud."

Again, that enviable levelheadedness that makes it so easy to submit yourself to his self-confidence. If only I had a little more of that.

We move on, but now we stay close together and make sure to no longer lose sight of the brook. The sound of streaming water gives us something to hold on to. As long as the water can find the way back to civilization, we can too.

Augustin's coat is bright red—*Just like his helmet was*, I think. *His falling helmet*—and the strap dangling from his buckled ice axe is bright yellow, but even from up close the colors now look dull and lifeless. Visibility is less than thirty yards, where boulders and clouds melt into a bleak haze. It's a spooky sight. We're walking through a misty tunnel with an uneven, rocky floor. Now that the view of the valley is obscured, its presence oppresses us all the more. Anyone who has ever been down in a cave or a mine knows what I'm talking about. Invisible expanses can trigger suffocating claustrophobia.

And it scares me.

All of it scares me.

I can't help it. I think about the practically impossible access to the trail, about the ACCÉS INTERDIT sign affixed to the barbed wire. I think about the fact that there are no tracks here. I think about man-made obstacles, about inaccessibility for a *reason*. I think about the two stonemen we built at the mouth of the valley, swallowed up by the mist. The image casts the shadow of an enormous, ungraspable danger.

I try to force myself back into the walking trance, but I can't. Ice-cold precipitation starts to lash me in the face, numbs my cheeks, and pierces my eyes even when I squint. I pull my hood tight, but the flapping noise it makes in the wind immediately gets on my nerves. It's practically impossible to discern between mist and precipitation, and it takes a while before I realize that the sky is full of sleet. It whispers incessantly as it hits the boulders, like a soft patter stealthily following us.

"Hey, come on," I call to Augustin, when I almost slip on a boulder for the umpteenth time. He halts and looks back. "This is nuts. I don't want everything to get wet and then have to crawl into our sleeping bags. None of this shit will dry overnight."

Augustin turns it over in his mind as he looks around him. Snow has gathered on his nose and is dripping off it. Pitching a bivi now, with no idea where we are, doesn't sound like an attractive prospect to him.

"Listen, it's still okay. If we keep going for another fifteen minutes, we should get to the lake; it can't be further than that. At least the ground there should be . . ." He stops halfway through his sentence, looking at his watch. He taps it and presses a few buttons.

"What?"

"It says it's almost quarter to five. What time have you got?"

Quarter to five? That's impossible. I fish the iPhone out of my pocket again.

The screen is misted up, and as I try to protect it from the snow by keeping it under my coat, I wipe it dry with my fleece.

4:47 p.m.

"Impossible."

"Did we . . ."

"How is that possible?" I say it in Dutch, but it's all I manage to say. The last time I checked the time was apparently two and a half hours ago, when the clouds surrounded us. No more than twenty minutes could have gone by since then.

That means we've been walking in the valley for over four hours.

"Did we get it all wrong on the col?" I ask.

"It was twelve thirty when we got there. I know, because I remember thinking four and a half hours from the village was good time, considering there were no tracks and even despite our detour in the beginning. And we set off at eight. Nick, what's going on?"

I have no answer.

"It's impossible. We haven't had any serious rises since the col, right? Even by a conservative estimate we must have covered at least six miles. Fuck no, seven and a half." Which is impossible. Such a distance would have brought us almost to the border with Italy, and there's no way the valley could be that long. "What does the altimeter say?"

"10,000 feet."

"You see? We've hardly gone up."

"If it's right."

"Isn't it a GPS?"

"How should I know?" Augustin raises his voice, not much, but enough to alarm me. In this whiteout, all we have is each other, and that unity must be preserved. "I think we should go back, Nick. All the way down. I don't feel good about this."

"If it took us four hours to get here, it will be dark before we get to the col. That's if we don't get lost in the mist."

"But there's no way it could have been four hours!"

"Well, apparently it was!"

"Fuck!" His lower lip is trembling, and he turns away, looking into the snowdrift. I notice for the first time that he is upset. Apparently his self-confidence has its limits after all, although I would have preferred not to have found out.

And I see something else. The snowflakes no longer dissolve when they land on his hood.

"Augustin, relax. Let's keep calm. We have—"

"There's nothing here! Don't you feel it? Can't you *feel* how deserted this place is? How empty?"

Yes, I felt it back when we were on the col and observing the rolling plains of scree and the surrounding cliffs. *Dead* is the word that springs to mind. The valley seemed *dead*. You could tell even by the way Augustin's yodel had gone flat and died down in the expanse.

"Yes, and I don't like it either. I don't know how come we haven't reached the glacier yet. We must have gotten disoriented. I don't know what to say. The strain, the whiteout, the altitude, whatever. But hey, we simply made a miscalculation down there and the glacier is probably right in front of us, in the mist."

That sounds plausible. I think I can even feel its cold, massive breath. The valley may be dead, but glaciers are alive—dormant, watchful, ancient, and cold.

"Let's just bivouac. I'm cold and I don't want to find our way back down in the dark and in the mist. It will clear up tonight and tomorrow morning we'll be able to see where we are. Then we can decide whether to go up or back."

"Yeah, and what about this snow?" Augustin looks at his watch. "It's twenty-eight degrees. Was that the forecast?"

I shrug. We both know how incredibly local these things can be in the Alps. High mountains create their own laws and weather systems, and if you allow them to take you by surprise, they will render all your accumulated experience and technical skills useless. You can learn to read the weather, but you can never truly understand it. Even so, the sudden drop in temperature is strange. The past few days, the frost line had risen to 13,500 feet, and it was supposed to stay warm for the next couple of days.

"Come on," I say. "Let's look for a sheltered spot."

It startles me to realize that, for a moment, I don't know from which direction we have come, because the terrain is practically flat and the increasing snow is making visibility even worse than it was. More by luck than judgment, Augustin spies the bed of the brook and we hurry to it, relieved to have retrieved our landmark. The brook is our last resort. When even the birds have left and the water has fled, downstream is the only guide to the valley. We may have gotten disoriented, but at least we weren't lost.

That's what I thought, anyway.

* * *

About an hour later we settle down pretty comfortably—insofar as that's possible in the damp cocoon of a bivi sack in the middle of freezing nowhere.

The light is diffuse, as you can see in photos 6 and 7.

I call this pair "A peek into camp." The mountains have entered that strange, subdued phase between late afternoon and twilight. Although the daylight has not yet receded from the sky, the snowdrifts make it look like the evening has already frozen solid all around us.

The first of the two is a timer shot, but you can see I'm not in the space or the mood to pose properly. A bit further upstream, we had found a large, slightly overhanging boulder. The lee it offers is pathetic, but it's the best we can do, and with some mental gymnastics, you could call the ground somewhat smooth. We quickly set up camp by piling up boulders as a storm barrier, spreading out the bivi sack and cramming the Therm-a-Rests and sleeping bags in through the opening. The exertion keeps us warm, but the wind is getting stronger and lashes our faces with cold waves of snow. You can see Augustin behind me in the photo, sitting on the bivi sack. The Gore-Tex is billowing with trapped air and he's gazing intently, concentrated, preoccupied with taking off his light blue Scarpas.

The atmosphere in the second camp picture, photo 7, is cheerier. Augustin's smiling broadly at the camera over a steaming mug of lemon tea. He's propped up on his elbow, tucked under the bivi sack's hood and emerging like a caterpillar from the goose down sleeping bag. Like me, Augustin has put on his cap to keep warm. Our breath is rising in puffs and blends with the steam from the MSR stove under the sheltering boulder. We've just had Chinese tomato Cup-a-Soup and the tea and are now digging into Thai noodles with curry. And duck, the package says. It's amazing what culinary pleasures you can concoct with powder and melted snow.

[*Yes, photo 7 has an aura of positivity, Sam, but it is the last picture I would take of Augustin. If only we knew these kinds of things when they mattered.*]

We're lying down, pressed against each other, staring at the bivi sack's silver interior, as the day's rigors finally creep into our bodies. I try to adjust myself to the hard discomfort of the rocks under my pad and the shoes and backpacks piled up at our feet. When I gaze circumspectly through the bivi sack's opening, cold air and snow rush in. The weather outside has only deteriorated. It's a strange sight; you would think it was the middle of winter.

There are occasional gaps between the hurriedly passing clouds, which only reveal layers of more clouds hanging above them, gyrating in the powerful machinery of the drifting snow. It spreads a fan of powder on the bivi sack's surface and starts to pile up against the stone barrier. The Black Diamonds, which we planted between the rocks, stand out like guards, and I shiver involuntarily.

When are you going to ask yourself the questions that need to be asked? This goes through my mind as I pull down the hood and shut out the storm. *When are you going to ask yourself why it took you hours and hours to cover a distance that shouldn't have taken more than a quarter of the time? How could the valley seem to be growing with every step you took? And how come you couldn't find a single bit of information on this place online?*

Drops of condensation on the bivi sack glisten when Augustin looks at his cell. I ask whether he has a signal. "Uh-uh," he says, shaking his head.

"Weird, huh, how dependent you start feeling once you're off the grid? Makes you realize how on your own you really are."

Augustin shrugs. "I don't like them anyway. I have a prepaid so I can call 1414 in case of an emergency, but besides that, I only use the camera."

"Yeah, only, just when you need it, you get a mountain blocking the cell tower and there's no signal."

I ask him if he's ever had to call mountain rescue, and he shakes his head again. I tell him about the one time I had to. It was years ago, on a remote mountain called La Grivola, in Northern Italy. We unexpectedly got stuck in a thunderstorm and were forced to leave the ridge and descend through a disastrously steep labyrinth of unstable ribs and avalanche troughs. After hours-long precarious rappelling on self-made, flimsy anchors and a fall of my climbing buddy Wilco, whom I scarcely managed to hold, we were trapped. The rope was stuck in a crack somewhere above us and I didn't dare put all my weight on it to climb back up. The deteriorating conditions and Wilco's fall had shaken us. We decided to call a chopper . . . but had no signal. Eventually, the solution was at hand: I cut the rope, and we had just enough left to reach the glacier.

"Good job," Augustin says soberly. "In the mountains, you're responsible for your own actions. If you put yourself in a position where you're dependent on other people, you've made a mistake. You got yourselves in trouble and got yourselves out again."

Cutting that rope dug a 250-euro hole in my study budget that year, but at least I got my life back.

Wilco, not so much. After that summer, we lost touch, and three years later he made a mistake while rappelling in the Dolomites and plummeted 1,000 feet to his death. I felt completely hollowed out when I read the email.

We listen to the clattering of the cover, the whispering of the snow.

Why aren't we discussing the questions that so urgently need to be addressed? Instead, my mind keeps flipping back to Augustin's death birds. The birds that supposedly carry the souls of fallen climbers from this world.

Augustin never really answered my question about whether he believed in that story.

They say that if you listen, you can hear their screams coming from the mountains at night.

I think about the alpine choughs on the col, with their shrill cries as they came to ascertain our arrival before beginning their descent into the valley. The one that landed, it haunts my exhausted mind. The way it fixed its angry, lidless black eyes on us. If that's what's in store for the soul, then death robs us of all that is human.

The warmth from our bodies and the still, stuffy air in my cocoon make me drowsy. To my astonishment, I feel myself slipping away into a haze. I fight the urge to sleep, which suddenly seems seriously perilous in this place. But my fatigue gets the best of me, and as I relentlessly drift over the edge of consciousness, the last thing I realize, brief but highly alarming, is that I am not alone in this twilight zone. Something is pressing against the outside of my sleeping bag, raking its way toward the tight hole that hides my face. And for a second, I can almost smell the musty odor of feathers and the stench of carrion it exudes.

* * *

The silence wakes me up with a start. It's as if a great force that had at first held me prisoner violently flings me out of my reverie and pops all the synapses in my brain. My eyelids fly open on total darkness. *My eyes are gone,* I think, the dream's blind terror still swirling in my memory.

Then I feel the weight of the sleeping bag against my cheeks and understand where I am.

I sense that Augustin isn't there before I see it. The familiar pressure of his body in the cramped bivi sack is gone. Panic erupts from deep within, and I struggle out of my sleeping bag, yank the claustrophobic hood up.

For a second, I don't understand what I'm seeing, because it's still light out and the surroundings are bathed in an unearthly orange-yellow glow. Was I asleep for such a short time? The wind is still raging. Eddying dark gray and purple-black cloud banks are still obscuring the valley mouth, but it has stopped snowing, and a sudden gap in the clouds reveals where we are. We've come further into the valley than we realized. I see that we're in a rolling, rocky bed opposite a steep moraine bank. The blanket of snow has assumed the color of the disappearing sun, but the light lacks the richness and cold beauty of a normal sunset in the mountains. It has a feverishly pale sheen that imparts a feeble, sickly air to the surroundings.

"Augustin? Augustin!"

He is nowhere in sight. His backpack, his crampons, the stove, they're all there, untouched. Where on earth is he? *Why didn't I notice him leaving?* I look into the bleak northerly emptiness and thoughts of the unthinkable immediately start to haunt me. My vulnerability strikes me with terror. I grapple upright in order to look uphill behind the bivi boulder.

[*Sam, how can you put an image into words that changes your life at a single glance? A single moment, rising on the mind's horizon, that is so all-encompassing, that evokes so many frozen emotions and is so rich in monumental beauty and unimaginable horror, that any attempt at describing it would destroy it, annihilate it, render it formless, like the erosion of exposed landscape. Is it even possible?*

Okay, well, let me try.]

It turns out that we have set up our bivouac very close to the lake. In fact, we have gone partially past it; the brook's snowy bed curves toward the western basin and the lake is to our right, just slightly higher than our camp. Behind it, the glacier looms as a silent witness to our error. The tongue is twisted and fractured, causing hundreds of jagged cracks to form where the glacier and the moraine meet. Higher up, the wind blows up a ballet of spiraling cloud fragments and wisping powder snow—but higher still, there's a gap.

Through it rises the Maudit—shockingly close, amazingly grand, ablaze in the setting sun's dying light.

Its north face towers hundreds of yards above us, uncommonly dark, an impregnable fortress of majestic pillars that cast deep shadows in the intermediate grooves and are too steep for the snow to stick to. My god, what a mountain! The astonishing brightness of the evening light and the face's proximity suck me in and induce the dizzying illusion that I'm falling. Or maybe it's the mountain that is falling toward *me*, the cliff's chaotic labyrinth collapsing over me. It takes my breath away, and I can't help but stagger backwards, a few stumbling steps in my socks over the bivi sack. My gaze follows the razor-sharp crests high above. A perfect shape, crowned with improbable mushroom-shaped cornices hanging from its horned summits, the right one higher than the left. In the lee between them, the ice field, like an eye bleeding in the last of the evening sun.

This mountain, the Maudit, it is more phenomenal than a cathedral. It is a sanctum.

[*I hope I don't sound too New Age, Sam, but standing there at the foot of the Maudit, I can see right through to the mountain's soul. I'm not religious. I don't believe in destiny, in omens, in birds that carry the dead's souls to another world. But I believe in a mountain's soul, in the invisible power of the geological processes that pump life into earth's mountain ranges. You can* feel *their souls when you climb their flanks. Gurus, monks, and prophets came down from the mountains and interpreted them as divine revelation, but you don't need to be a spiritual seer to feel life in rock and ice. As a climber, you feel it anew every time: the significance of birth, life, and death spanning millions of years, during which the seasons tick by like our heartbeats.*]

There, as I breathlessly gaze up at the Maudit, I experience the immense power of that life, and set against it, I perceive my own story as a grain of sand in the palm of my hand. It is completely overpowering, it is stupefying and overwhelming, and it is terrifying at the same time.

And if that were all, you could say I had some kind of mystic, transcendent experience. Some sort of insight inspired by having faced nature and the immensity of her dimensions. But there's more, something that excites a terrible premonition deep inside me.

You know it as a climber; this "soulification" gives every mountain its own specific character. Mont Blanc is a sleeping giant. If you observe its massif and satellite peaks from the slopes above Geneva, you can even discern a head in it. Gran Paradiso is a gentle old lady. She admits hundreds of people to her snow-white flanks every day. Zinalrothorn is a young soul, rough around the edges, who viciously bares his teeth, but that's just a recalcitrant child's bravado.

As a climber, you connect briefly with that soul, and you make an agreement with it . . . but it's not a friendship. The mountain lets you in and the mountain lets you out, if it is well-disposed toward you. In the evening, you look over your shoulder one last time at the summit at the far end of the valley. You nod to each other in mutual respect—you got away with it this time. But you never forget that the mountain will always have the upper hand. Scorn it for even an instant and it will strike back mercilessly.

As I look at the Maudit, I realize this mountain's soul is *old* and *dangerous*. I see it as an evil, dark blot. A cancer spreading over the valley. I suddenly become dead scared.

We are unwelcome here. I can feel it all over.

"Augustin!" I shout, as loud as I can. I listen tensely for his reply, but the valley answers only with a ghostly echo that is blown away in the intensifying wind.

Then I see him.

About eighty yards ahead, a natural embankment stretches all the way out to the lake. On it, silhouetted against the decor of the gaping mountain face, sits Augustin. Motionless, with his back to me. Staring up at the peak. The scene I am witnessing seems to be proceeding in extreme, silent slow motion.

As on the Maudit's highest flanks, a layer of fine powder snow has gathered on Augustin's hood, his shoulders, and in the folds of his coat, as if he'd been outside in the storm for hours. And just as the snow, spit by the icy wind from the highest crests, swirls in a cloud of ice particles, *the snow swirls up from Augustin, too, perfectly mirroring the mountain.*

Augustin and the Maudit: it's like elves are dancing around them. A whirl of light borne on the music of the wind.

[*If I ever believed in souls, Sam, it was then.*] Not daring to breathe, I watch as, riding the spiraling snow, they break free—Augustin's soul and the mountain's soul. They commence their enchanting courtship, rising into the red sky. They make love. They become one.

I only barely recall putting on my shoes or grabbing stones to weigh down the bivi sack, but that's what I must have done. On stiff legs I follow a trail of snow-covered boulders. When I look up, the magical scene has dissolved. The day is coming to an end, the mountain is shrouded in shadows.

Augustin is still there, as motionless as before, but the glow is gone, the snow is no longer swirling. Now he is sitting in the dark.

"Augustin. Hey, Augustin."

I climb the moraine and approach him warily. I don't want to startle him. The wind has erased Augustin's footprints in the snow. *How long has he been out here?* I wonder. When I reach him and kneel before him, his face is lost in the shadow of his hood.

But I can see his eyes, the Maudit's horned summit reflected in their feverish luster.

I say his name again, but Augustin keeps staring inexorably at the mountain, as if it has him completely in its power. I feel a wave of nausea when I see that his eyes aren't blinking, not even from the wind blowing against his corneas. I take off my glove liners and snap my fingers in his face. The spell appears to be broken. He looks at me, but I still have the feeling that he doesn't see me, that he's staring right through me at something only he can see.

"There are holes in the ice," he says, and I think, *We shouldn't be here. Even the death birds have gone away.*

"Augustin, hey man, quit being so freaky, okay?"

I get the sudden urge to see his face. Without his face, with only those floating, possessed eyes, it could be anyone sitting there.

As I reach my hands out to carefully take off his hood, Augustin says, "*Augustin ist tot.*"

Even someone who speaks as little German as I do knows what that means. Dead? My guts turn, and I imagine that when I remove his hood there will be nothing underneath it, only the empty abyss of a crevasse.

"Augustin, cut it out. What are you doing out here in the cold? How long have you been sitting there?"

Just before my fingers touch the edge of his hood, he springs up. The force of his revival startles me, and I seem to sense something invisible shooting past me, something with the pulling force of profound depths.

"I think it would be best to take the east ridge," he says. He gestures to the jagged left skyline. "I think we can access it via the ribs or through the couloir back there, if it's in any condition. I think that's the least difficult route. We'll have a better view in the morning, but I don't want to wait till first light."

His voice sounds strangely toneless, and it takes a while before I realize that he's talking about climbing the Maudit. The concept seems so preposterous to me, I can hardly believe it. After what I just saw, after my epiphany, we're supposed to attempt climbing up those flanks? *Us?* The arrogance; the hubris! Are we to take on the wrath of a god?

"Augustin, listen . . ."

"Or do you want to try the west ridge? Looks steep, but it's okay with me if you think—"

"No way are we going up there, not today and not tomorrow."

"What do you mean?" For the second time in a short while, I'm startled. His words are venomous, caustic. Augustin isn't himself. Something about this situation is very wrong, and I can't put my finger on it.

His coat was completely covered in snow. That means he must have been out here long before the storm started to wane. When you couldn't see jack shit. How did he even know the embankment was here?

I have to clear my throat before my voice can say out loud what I'm thinking in my head. "I think it's best that we go down, Augustin—"

"Are you nuts?"

"And not tomorrow morning, but *now*. We can use the last of the light. After that, we have our headlamps. The weather cleared up some now, and if we follow the brook we won't get lost, even with the dark and the snow."

But that's what you thought on the way up. Until the valley decided to screw with your minds. Who says it won't do it again if you try to escape?

Augustin's voice sounds soft and icy, like glacial wind. "Go ahead if you like. I'm going up."

"Don't be an asshole. You know how precarious that terrain is. Can't you see? You have no idea what you'll find up there or how you'll come down."

"The Maudit will show me the way."

"Chilled to the bone" is just an expression, but that's exactly what I feel.

Who am I actually arguing with here? To my amazement, Augustin turns around and starts walking toward the glacier.

Now. With night falling.

I impulsively grab him by the shoulder. He flings his arm up, and before I know what's happening, a white flash explodes in my face. The flash bursts in the shadow of something unimaginable, a superhuman force that is much more than the elbow that hits me full in my cheekbone. In that flash, an avalanche of gigantic chunks of ice crashes down on me. Shock waves of pain shoot through my head, and with a smothered scream, I fall backwards against the rocks, both hands pressed against the left half of my face, causing me to roll over on my side.

[*But Sam, in that split second when I fall back, I fall much, much further. Straight into the illusion of an immeasurably deep void.*]

When I look up, I see Augustin towering over me. The wind finally gets a grip on his hood and blows it off. The face that is exposed is divided. On the one hand, I see Augustin, though I can't make out whether the expression on it is one of delight, despair, or detestation.

But there is also another face, one I don't know, have never known—and it is so alien and aloof that I involuntarily start to groan.

In this face, dehumanization reigns. It's the face of something ancient, and I don't need to look at the black tower behind it to know I'm looking directly into the face of the Maudit.

SLEEPY HOLLOW

NOTES BY SAM AVERY

His appetite for the marvelous, and his powers of digesting it, were equally extraordinary; and both had been increased by his residence in this spell-bound region.

—Washington Irving

Meteorologically speaking, fall had already been under way for a few weeks, but if you believed Louetta Molignon, if you swallowed the story that there were only two seasons in the mountains, then the last real day of that year's summer was the day after Cécile had tooled back down in her Peugeot, that Sunday, October 14. After that, the weather turned, but that Sunday, picture it: the sky one giant hug from the sun. A monkshood hug, a juniper kiss, and picture it: Nick doing his exercises on Castle Rock, he'd taken his shirt off, and the way he was stretching, the way he was overlooking the valley, the sun was sparkling on his bronzed skin like he was emanating light.

That place mutilated him, Cécile's voice said in my head, as I was looking at him, but what difference did mutilation make if you were a polished natural phenomenon?

Nick doing his burpees and his planks on his yoga mat. His lunges and his squats. Glistening body, radiating, shimmering like the peaks I'd seen on the other side of the dam. The bandages on his face so brilliant white in the sun it made you squint. This was Nick. So what was I supposed to do but to scramble up there with one hand and two feet, Ramses at my heels—Ramses, who stopped halfway up the rock and looked up at Nick with suspicion.

"Hiya," I said.

"Hiya," Nick said.

Holy fuck. We were back in first date territory.

"I brought you some grape juice. The kind you like, from the Coop."

"Thanks." He took the glass from me and the straw disappeared between two dressing bands. He sucked up half of it in one quaff, then put it down on the plateau. "Here; feel this."

He took my hands and pressed them to his chest. A nervous charge of maybe a million volts shot through me, a yearning that made my ears pound. Nick's skin was hot. Not workout-in-the-sun hot, but subcutaneous-microreactor-meltdown hot. Evaporating-star hot.

"Wow," I said.

"Bizarre, huh? Can you feel the energy?"

"Some people would call it 'fever.'"

"But it isn't. I feel great. No more pain. Actually, this is the best I've felt since I left the hospital."

He articulated better too, that's for sure.

"You're totally glowing."

Nick's eyes were burning. "It started the moment I climbed up here. It's like the sun is melting all my negativity away."

The heat in his pores musta evaporated his sweat, cuz his skin felt smooth and dry. He led my hands up above his shoulders, crossed around his arms. My fingertips, his skin—there was something predetermined about it, unavoidable, a this-is-the-end-of-the-universe-and-nothing-else-matters kind of quality. And the heat, you could feel it wafting out of his whole body. Even the implant scar below his biceps was quivering like the air above a hot blacktop.

"What?" I asked.

"You're staring."

And the space between us getting smaller. Me suddenly feeling that Nick is leaning forward to kiss me, *kiss*, breath and lips and oh god, a stab of pain and emptiness cuz I'd been forced to do without his lips this whole time and then *wham*, full-frontal crash against the wall, his eyes huge, the sparkle in his face deleted, as if the reality of his bandages touched down in both of us at exactly the same moment.

Like he'd been burned, Nick let go of me and, guess what, everything was reeling again. Everything was tumbling down. Three years together and everything turns topsy-turvy, coming to this moment, with Castle Rock tipping steeper and steeper down to the drop into the creek, the slopes swaying and spinning around us, and Nick towering up above me. He grabbed my arm before I could fall, and me, flailing my legs, a clumsy kick, hit something. Sound of breaking glass and the rock bleeding red grape juice out of slashed quartz veins.

There are holes in the ice, I thought. *They look just like eyes*.

"Sorry," he said. "Sorry, Sam, I didn't mean to . . . you know . . ."

"Yeah, I know. Same here. Please hold me."

Everything around me seemed deep and abysmal, the sound of the brook alternately close and far. Without Nick's arms, I was totally off balance.

"You okay?"

"You're doing it again." My fingers tracing circles next to my temples.

"Sorry. It's not on purpose."

Nick shut his eyes, the expression on his face intense concentration, like he was spiritually clinging on to something. Couldn't focus on him, everything too wobbly, too much light everywhere, my teeth tingling too weirdly in my head, so I shut my eyes too and surrendered to the dizziness.

No, I thought. *Not dizziness. Fear of heights*.

Did it ever occur to you that it could be you *who's doing this?* I heard Nick say, but his voice, it was in my head. No one here had said anything out loud. The realization filtered in slowly, and Nick musta felt me suddenly tensing up, cuz we opened our eyes at the exact same instant. Looked at each other. There was something different about the light. There was a brightness and a deepness to it that wasn't there before. Reality a real-life Instagram filter, an ultra-hi-res, gigapixel panorama, color intensity a spectacle beyond imagination. Nick's eyes in that light big and round and fascinated and unknowable. Bored right into me.

And I thought, *Telepathy. This isn't salubrious mountain air; this is LSD.*

"Come sit next to me, Sammy."

Did he speak those words out loud? Methinks. But hey, we were already wheeling to the ground and had sunk down onto his yoga mat, he on his side, me cuddling into him and he spooning me, and maybe alarm bells started ringing somewhere, but *without* his arm around me I had the feeling I'd fall, and *with* his arm around me I had the feeling I'd fall, so at this point, what's the diff?

Cécile and all her warnings, if she saw us now, she wouldn't understand. She wouldn't understand my intense and terror-stricken yearning for Nick.

Last night I told him everything. Everything I learned from Cécile. Everything bar how Dr. Genet had kicked the bucket. Some beans you didn't spill, cuz you didn't want to upset him. You chewed it over, couldn't find any relation between Nick and that dude's death, so decided it didn't matter.

Except that you were afraid of what you'd see in Nick's face if you told him. Except that you were afraid of the same confession in his eyes as when you asked him about Augustin, if he—

Whoa! Floodgates, file it, check.

Still. Those stories had brought us closer.

That's how horror stories work: they dull reality's sharper edges. Made the face hiding behind the bandages a little less frightening. Cuz it could always be worse. As evidenced by Marjorie Hatfield, who, eye sockets empty, had screamed herself to death. As evidenced by Alexander Ruëgsegger and Augustin Laber, who didn't have faces at all anymore and forever dwelled between frozen mountain cliffs. Nick wasn't gonna be one of those stories. Nick was alive. And the cliché turned out to be true: what didn't kill you made you stronger.

Now, spotlighted by the sun, Nick dizzying: "I thought that after all those stories you'd find me so repugnant that you wouldn't let me so near you again."

"It's standard procedure to face your inner demons before exorcising them, Nick. Possession 101."

"Am I your demon or is it the Maudit?"

I stretched and twisted my spine, like Ramses, who always makes it look like it feels so good. It did feel good. "Watch out or I'll exorcise *you* and keep the mountain. Lemme tell ya, I could definitely get used to that spin."

"And me thinking you never wanted to have anything to do with the mountains."

"I never met one that made me trip this wild."

For a while, there was only our breath and the play of sunlight on water droplets and little flying bugs in the air. My ear against Nick's chest, I listened to the earth's heartbeat. Deep and slow, it resonated through both our bodies. In my muzziness, I noticed that it beat five, six times a minute max, but who cares. My head refused to mold it into a single coherent notion. It was much more fun to just float above Castle Rock and rise and fall to the rhythm of the primeval life germinating in Nick.

I said, "Seriously." My voice dreamy, I said, "The new you. The mountain. Whatever. I never let you so near cuz I was always afraid of it. But now . . ."

"Near" meant more than just his arms around me. I saw the image of a delta of living streams of energy at the source of a glacier tongue. Winding streams, which didn't enclose only my soul but also the deepest essence of my being. I couldn't find the words to describe the image, but there was no need to. Nick shared it. I knew that.

In that new, creepy, sparking way we shared things.

His words drifted toward me, *And is it a good trip or a bad one?*

"Holy fuck, are you seriously in my head?"

So what are you going to do about it?

"Hello? I stash private info in there."

He roared with laughter, and the earth seemed to quake. I was pretty sure it wasn't only Nick who'd laughed. *Believe me when I say I know just about all your secrets by now, Sam. Why don't you come and join me?*

Can you do that? Testing . . . testing . . .

Are you kidding? Babe, this is peanuts compared to what I can do.

. . .

You see?

Damn.

How much further would I let myself get carried away? I didn't want anything more than to surrender myself to Nick, my Nick, the new Nick, but I was playing with fire. Something in there was on the rise and could reign over much more than just me. The question was not how long it would take for Nick's transformation to reach a point of no return. The question was what he'd be capable of when it *did.*

Cécile: *Please be careful, Sam. He's dangerous.*

It's a bad place.

I'm not sure Nick was supposed to come back from it.

He's dangerous.

It's a bad place . . .

And Nick: *Become one with me.*

My breath caught. "Wh-what did you say?"

You heard me.

Intense excitement. Manipulating hands kneading my mind, and the image I now saw before me, bulging avalanche dams about to burst. The dam in Moiry about to give way. The snow-white bandages on Nick's face pulled tighter and tighter over what was about to tear its way out . . .

Till an all-too-realistic buzzing wrenched me out of my reverie.

A dragonfly. A giant bug. No, a drone.

And me, I fell back into my body. Blinked my eyes. Nick, he'd already jumped up, staring, hand over his eyes, skyward.

"Are you fucking kidding me?" he shouted.

It was coming at us from the village. Silver and black. Four propellers. GPS sensors, a 4K spy cam.

I got up and stood next to Nick. "Are they serious?"

The top of Castle Rock looked down on Hill House's overhanging roof. The drone glided some thirty yards above us, circling slowly over the valley floor, where it stopped and hovered above the little bridge. The spy cam, a kind of mini periscope sticking out of its bottom, unabashedly aimed at the chalet.

Nick scratched himself feverishly under his dressings. "Maybe it's the kids from the village . . ."

"Doesn't look like a toy to me. That size drone costs at least a thousand bucks."

"Then it's those fuckers. Goddammit! They're the ones who came to our door, right? They know who I am, Sam."

"Jesus, and I'm thinking they still use Morse around here."

"Dude, they're Swiss. They built the Large Hadron Collider in Geneva. I think they can pretty much handle a drone."

The drone: the MI6 of the Alps. A DIY kit for every shamus.

Someone was plotting against us.

Fists clenched, Nick stared at the sky. His fingernails boring bloody grooves in his palms. Him standing there, shoulder blades flexed, the cables of his forearms bulging, that body big and erect like an alpha predator—he'd scare the shit out of you. His eyes reflected the sun; that *whole body* reflected the sun. Maybe I was still tripping, but the rays were literally spouting out of him and the wind that suddenly kicked up in the valley was an echo of the storm breaking inside him. What was standing there was no longer human. What was standing there was a Sun God. A Storm Maker. Furious. Mad. Deranged. A stranger, not my boy, not my boy.

The drone sped closer to the chalet to shoot it from a different angle. We were now fully in view to any controller with FPV goggles or a phone app, and the aircraft actually swerved a bit as if it was startled. Then it began climbing at breakneck speed.

And then. And then and then and then and then.

I heard the shriek first. Saw the flash first before I realized what was happening. A shadow eclipsing the sun. Flapping sound, like sails. Suddenly, he was there. Ethon. The Thunderbird. No, a golden eagle. It shot out of nowhere, as all birds are wont to do, and screeching, swooped down on the drone. Grand. Gracious. A bullet. Fearsome, the eagle of my nightmares.

I know it's impossible, maybe it was the confusion of the moment, but I'd stake Nick's mom on it that the bird had a wingspan of at least sixteen feet when, at the last second, it spread its wings and looped almost upside down to grasp the drone from below and pluck it out of the sky with outstretched talons, before the propeller could transmogrify it into a dark brown aerial pillow fight.

Poor drone didn't know what hit it.

The clawed remains of the lens flashed in a golden shower of falling glass.

Talk about efficiency.

With the drone in its claws, the eagle flapped southward over the valley. Its triumphant screech echoed against the slopes. It climbed higher and higher and disappeared off the face of the earth beyond the mountain chain.

And me, I cheered. "Amelia fucking Earhart!" Soon as I could muster it, soon as I'd regained a smidgeon of control over my voice: "MH fucking 370! Eat that, motherfuckers!" My arms in the air, I whooped, "See that, Nick?"

But as soon as I looked at him, I knew he didn't only see it.

He'd *done* it.

Like every mountain rules over its ecosystem.

Like every mountain rules over its valley.

Like every mountain rules over the weather.

Nick, he was sheer light and heat. Under those rolling muscles, his lungs pumped life into that body. Under the earth's rolling crust they pumped life into Castle Rock. Pumped life into the valley, into the creek, into the wind, like the Maudit pumped life into Nick. He stood there, serene and elevated, indifferently determined to rise above everything, higher and higher, locked in a constant battle with the elements that wanted to bring him down. This was Nick, throwing off his civilized identity, embracing the implacable, darkly alluring force of the wilderness.

And me, this is who I was. My past and my future, full circle. My hands clawed at his face, clawed at the strips of bandage and started pulling them off like a lover's clothes. Good or bad, I didn't care anymore. I peeled them off him like a skin.

I had a boyfriend who'd evolved into a god . . .

And I had fallen . . . and fallen . . . and fallen . . . and fallen.

Head over heels.

THE METAMORPHOSIS

PASSAGES FROM NICK GREVERS'S DIGITAL DIARY

But what now if all the peace, the comfort, the contentment were to come to a horrible end?

—Franz Kafka

1

October 28

I'm disappearing.

It happened again this morning. Had a blackout and came to in a field above the village, alone and shivering from the cold. No bandages, of course. When I got home, Sam was in a state. He'd searched for me everywhere, said I was gone for a day and a half. A *day and a half.* And I couldn't recall any of it. Brushed him off, took a long, hot shower and scrubbed my mutilated face obsessively. The scars were throbbing and pulsating. It's alive behind them. I can feel it. It's *pushing;* the pressure is almost unbearable. The bandages helped some, but not much.

So started writing. Need to get my thoughts together, because time's running out. The moments when I'm myself are getting scarcer.

Now, as I type this, I'm in a constant state of anxiety. Any minute it could strike again. I'm hypervigilant for any sudden draft, any thought that doesn't feel like mine. Every time, the pressure seems to increase. I'm sick of it. It's getting stronger, and if I don't do anything about it now, soon I won't be there anymore. But what can I do? When it comes, it hits me with the force of a hurricane and blows my consciousness into the glacier's deepest recesses. It's like I've never escaped. I'm frozen, stuck in eternal cold—till I'm suddenly myself again, somewhere, not knowing how I got there, how much time has gone by, or what I did in between. It's awful. The total loss of control is awful . . .

And it's *good* too. In some depraved manner, it's *good,* and I let it happen.

It awakens urges that . . . No, I won't write that down. But I'm not the only one who can't resist it anymore.

Sam has gotten hooked on it.

And that's when it *really* becomes dangerous.

Since that day on Castle Rock, he's constantly setting it free. He comes up to me and starts tugging on my bandages, craving what's behind them. Apparently, my mutilation no longer bothers him. I should be pleased, but I'm not. Because it's not me he desires. It's the *other.* He wants the wilderness. He wants the Maudit. And I try to stay away from him, say we're playing a lethal game because its force is constantly building, but S. gets all hostile. The look in his eyes is the look of a junkie. Calculating. He sees in me only something he needs, and behind that sly face you can see him thinking how he can wheedle it out of me.

I have no idea what Sam sees when he tears off the bandages and allows himself to be overpowered by the Maudit, but it's probably the same as when an addict shoots the needle in his vein. You know it's a path that leads you to the abyss. You know it's only a matter of time before you OD. But you do it anyway, because the liberation of the fix makes you forget all of that. Sam has a past of shit he'd be better off staying away from. So why am I being his dealer? Because I let it happen. The pressure behind my face gets unbearable, and then I *have* to rip off the bandages. I have to let it loose! It's *manipulating* me into letting it loose. But I *want* to, get it? I want to, and before I know it, I find myself with the strips in my hands, and then I don't know anything anymore.

It's not lust that's driving Sam, even though sex is a part of it. It's not love, either. It's something more fatalistic. Day before yesterday, he came to me in the evening and grabbed me tight. He looked a mess, and his whole body was shaking. He pressed against me and sucked the air all the way in like he was inhaling me. Pretty creepy, actually.

What he whispered in my ear got me all queasy: "When you go, please drag me down with you into the darkness."

My god, what have we set in motion?

So this morning I came to myself on the slopes above Grimentz. Downhill, three men in overalls were gesturing around a cow that was lying on her side in the mud. At first I thought she was calving, but it's not the time of year. Then I saw she was entangled in barbed wire. Along the entire length of the lower field was a torn-down fence. Trampled, muddy grass, cow pies. A herd had been grazing here. And it had clearly broken out.

The oldest of the three men saw me. Started pointing. Expression changed, became enraged. He shouted something and raised his pinky and index finger at me. Checked Wikipedia: the horned hand gesture is still commonly used by the old mountain folk to ward off the devil.

The youngest of the men took a few steps in my direction, revealing the sorry state of the cow's hindquarters. Her skin was completely stripped off. She must have forced her way through the barbed wire. Some of the herd had apparently managed to tear themselves loose and pave the way for the rest, because from far below, in the village, came the soft tingle of their bells. One cow was dead halfway down the slope.

I stared in disbelief. Was this my doing???

Then I forgot all about the cows, dead or alive, because the farmer's son raised a double-barreled shotgun. All my muscles went limp. Still, I managed to raise my arms and demonstratively stroll to the side of the field to show I meant no harm. Before I got to the edge of the woods, I lost my restraint and made a run for it. Almost tripped and fell when I heard the shot. It resonated over the slopes, but this bullet wasn't meant for me.

So here I am now. What kind of monster have I become? Those cattle farmers sensed it in me. Dr. Claire and Cécile sensed it in me. Even my parents sensed it, back in that early stage. It scared the hell out of them. And rightly so.

Because I know what it's capable of.

I still haven't heard from Claire.

And I'm very much afraid I never will.

I can't count on Sam to help me anymore. Have to take things into my own hands before it's too late. That place's poison is spreading through my veins. I have to make use of the moments I still have, but I sense them becoming fewer. If only I knew what to do!

2

October 29

Ramses is gone.

It's been dark for hours, and there's no point in looking for him anymore. S. is worried sick. I am too, to be honest.

S. says the last time he saw him was this morning, when he fed him. But Ramses never strays far from the chalet and never stays out for long. So far, he's been pretty much unmoved by his vacation in Switzerland, and in the evenings he even curls up and purrs in his permanent spot in front of the fireplace, though he always keeps one ear perked in my direction, constantly on the alert for me. He, too, senses the Maudit, and he doesn't like it one bit—hasn't since his flip, back home in Ams. But the thing is that R. is a city cat. This valley's boundless space is very un-Ramses-like. It turns him into a scaredy-cat. So, yes, it freaks me out that he hasn't come home yet.

We called him, rattled with his munchies. Nothing. S. walked all the way up the road and shined his phone's flashlight. Wanted to go with him, but he said no, stay home. Sounded resentful. Does he think it's my fault Ramses is gone?

Maybe it is.

S. wasn't gone for long. He was pale when he came back, and all jumpy. Said he hadn't seen a thing.

3

October 30

Found him. A fucking leghold trap! Asshole motherfuckers. Who would do such a thing? That trap had been put there deliberately.

Sam came home with him in the early hours. All teared up. Ramses a messy tangle in his arms, meowing pitifully, with fearful eyes. When I saw the iron chain dangling from Sam's arms, I immediately got the picture. He laid the cat carefully on the carpet so the under-floor heating could warm him up. Ramses twitched his tail and meowed again. It was his right forepaw. The trap it got caught in was made of dark, rusty iron and constructed particularly for small game. The jaws had sharp teeth, which had bitten deep into his flesh. Tufts of white fur were stuck to it. Ramses must have struggled to break free. Poor, poor cat! While Sam dried him off with a dish towel, I scratched his little head, and for the first time in weeks, he submitted to it without protesting.

S. said he'd found him somewhere past the bridge, in the tall grass by the road. I wondered whether the trap could have been set by poachers, for hunting rabbits or something, but Sam said no, there had been *cat food* on the iron plate. Ramses could have just as easily stuck his head in and got his neck broken.

"Assholes!" I shouted.

And there was more: Sam found three other traps, all containing cat food and teeming with ants. He sprung them with a branch and said they were so powerful that each of them had snapped the branch in two.

"They want to frighten us off," I said. "They're using the cat to get at us. Cowards."

But S. shook his head. "I don't think so. "I think they were really trying to get Ramses."

I asked how so, and then he told me what he'd heard from Maria, our cleaning lady with the pretty name: that they're not too fond of cats around here. Not Maria personally, but *the whole village*. Apparently she'd advised him not to let the cat out. When I asked what it was all about, Sam gazed at me—did I really not get it?

"Remember the bird he almost tore to pieces? What you call the death birds? The birds hanging all over the place like talismans on their front doors?"

I was about to say something, but my mouth plopped shut.

Anyway, took R. to a vet in Sièrre, who removed the trap. He was lucky, she said. His paw wasn't broken, but it was gashed almost to the bone, and badly swollen. There's damage to the muscles, but with a bit of luck Ramses will be as good as new within a couple of weeks, the doc said. She gave him painkillers and antibiotics and bandaged his paw. He seems to be a bit better. Since we brought him home and let him out of his travel carrier, he's been eyeing us and the world with his trademark fuck-off gaze, but he has been eating heartily, and right now he's sleeping by the fireplace.

But that word *talisman* keeps haunting me.

According to S., Maria said alpine choughs bring good fortune. They're said to carry the souls of ancestors, which is why the townsfolk in Grimentz keep them in or around their homes. A nice tradition, with obvious similarities to that other, more sinister legend, the one Augustin recounted: that they are death birds who free the souls of fallen climbers by pecking their eyes out.

A supernatural interpretation of a morbid, but perfectly natural phenomenon, I would have concluded *before* this whole business. But none of this is natural.

I can still see Augustin in the depths of the crevasse, rolling over on the ice bridge and reaching for me with frozen hands . . .

I don't want to revisit that memory. Let's just say the birds had gotten to him.

I'm so cold, Nick, he said. *So cold . . .*

Suppose it wasn't delirium. And suppose the legend is true. Then the thing I tried to hoist up and out of the crevasse was no longer Augustin. After all, Augustin's soul had already been set free. And yet it had been *alive*. In its own, frozen way, it had been alive.

Was it the Maudit itself? Or something completely different?

Because it knew my name.

(later, evening)

Had a fight with Sam. He suggested going back to the Netherlands! Said it's getting too dangerous for us here. That there's nothing much we could do around here anyway. I suggested he should maybe go back without me, because of the influence it has over him, but he didn't want that. I saw through the lie. It's the addiction talking. Sam doesn't want me to be rid of it anymore. He wants it for himself. It made me furious.

My vision got all hazy, and after that, there's a gap in my memory. Must have had a blackout. Just came to in pitch-blackness. Only when the moon broke through rushing clouds and dropped its light through the window did I realize that I was lying on the carpet in front of the fireplace. Ramses was staring at me over his bandaged paw, with sly, yellow eyes.

Face thumping. Unbearable. Before, the pressure was off for at least a while every time I let it out. Not anymore.

Sam. Don't dare go downstairs. What have I done?

Fuck fuck fuck goddamn motherfuck . . .

Okay, get ahold of yourself. Have to go look.

(even later)

False alarm. Sam's asleep. Naked though, so there's that. But I can't trust him anymore, that much is clear. Leaving is not an option. I *can't* leave. My only hope is right here. And S. would never leave without me.

Plus, there are practical objections. We just extended our stay in the chalet till December 1, and in a couple of weeks I'm getting my scar correction here in Switzerland. A private clinic in Montreux. The AMC sent them my medical file, because if there's one place where cosmetic surgery is top quality, it's got to be CH. Dad said just go ahead and do it; you're there anyway. He said he'd cover the costs.

They'll have to remove the bandages. They'll have to cut into my face.

Under anesthesia, it's *got* to be safe. Right?

If I have doubts, I can always cancel.

4

November 3

Spent days searching. Websites, maps, newspaper reports, online photos, and not a single new lead. Total fucking zilch.

In daytime, I don't dare show myself in the village anymore, so I only go out after dark. I drift through the streets of Grimentz like a ghost out of a Victorian novel: turned-up collar, face covered in bandages, and hat tilted forward. Only the choughs give my presence away. Every time they start screeching and their cages start to rock, somewhere a light goes on, and I rush away into an alley. I'm a scapegoat. A pariah.

What is it that I'm looking for? I don't know anymore.

Sam's dependence has reached new lows. I try convincing myself it will get better, but who am I fooling?

Sometimes I think I should let go and just let it all happen. Just so I won't have to deal with it anymore.

(later)

Okay, great, stumbled onto something after all, though not sure how encouraging it is. Tonight, just before midnight, I slunk across the courtyard in front of the church and, hidden by the shadow of an old plum tree, sneaked into the cemetery at the back. It lies on a terrace looking out on to the mountains across the valley. The moon had risen, and in its pale light you could see that the snow line had crept to below 8,000 feet. The last few days, the sky has been cold and clear. Gloomily *settled* weather. But lenticular clouds cover the highest peaks, which means that there's turbulence in the higher atmosphere.

All the graves are adorned by the same wooden cross, with two diagonal slats on top that make them look like little chalets. Frost, thaw, and blazing sunlight have apparently left them unaffected. Even the oldest graves, dating from the 1920s, are in perfect condition. In the moonlight, not all inscriptions were equally legible, but some gave out ominous messages, such as "Guide de Haute Montagne" or "Mort en Weisshorn." These affected me more deeply than I was prepared for. They are the mountain's dead.

Had they, like me, left the valley behind them without a single worry, death the farthest thing from their minds?

On some of the graves were flowers; others had birdcages. All empty . . . and that made me feel rather uneasy.

Someone cleared their throat, and I spun around.

It was the pastor. He raised his hands, and I was afraid he would burst into a tirade of French, but instead he said in calm and perfect English, "Please excuse me for startling you."

I felt my face throbbing behind the bandages but managed to keep it under wraps—for now. Judging by Sam's description, this was the same man who had come to our door with the other two, the morning we were chased out of the village by those stone-throwing boys. Black cassock, white clerical collar, and the gold cross the Catholics in Switzerland are still so proud of. His lantern's flickering candlelight reflected in his glasses. The eyes behind them seemed tense, but the expression on his face wasn't hostile. Rather, he seemed intrigued, and in some way, maybe even amicable. Yet he didn't come close enough to shake my hand.

"Mr. Grevers"—he pronounced it *Grévèrs*—"you must leave Grimentz immediately."

I was dumbfounded.

"I can no longer guarantee your or your companion's safety. Your presence has deeply upset the villagers and there is talk of a revolt. There have been worrying omens. The birds have sensed a change in the air, the cattle have broken out, and strange sounds have been heard up the valley. Your presence is disturbing the natural course of things. I prayed to God, but I can't help you. You *must* leave the valley!"

"And what exactly is the natural course around here?" I asked. "There is nothing natural or godly about your birds and that damn mountain. There is no God on the Maudit."

Upon hearing the mountain's name, the pastor literally shrank back and crossed himself. Turned deathly pale. But what was I supposed to do? He knew what was going on; there was no use in denying it.

He then went into an incoherent plea, which I could only partially make out. The days of doom were nigh. The *change* was palpable, as was the *presence*. He could feel it *now*, as he spoke to me. And the whole time, he kept staring at the bandages around my face.

Help me get rid of it and I'll be gone, I offered, but the pastor shook his head and whispered, "No servant of the Lord can exorcise what is living on that mountain."

I asked him to at least tell me what he does know. He must know *something*, I was sure of that. Said I was as scared as he was. That I hadn't asked for all this and that I wanted to prevent worse from happening—and that landed. The pastor led me to the rearmost section of the cemetery and showed me the graves of four men, who had all been in their twenties or thirties when they suddenly died in 1957. My heart started to beat faster when I read the inscription by the light of his lantern: PTE. MAUDIT.

The men had been members of the Andenmatten group, he said, a team of seven who had attempted to climb the Maudit that year, despite their fellow villagers' warnings. Of course! That's why the year had rung a bell. The article in *Le Nouvelliste*. Just opened the JPEG. It says that bad weather had taken them by surprise and that they never came back. The pastor said that there are two more tombstones in the graveyard in Zinal, but all the graves are empty. The seventh was Jorg Andenmatten himself, he said, the group's leader. To everyone's surprise, he had come wandering into Grimentz almost a week later. Weakened, hypothermic, but alive. The whole village flocked to hear what had happened, but Andenmatten couldn't remember a thing.

"But the minute we saw him, we knew it was a *foul* thing."

I looked at him in disbelief and said, "There's no way you could be old enough to have been there."

"I was a child, but I can still remember it clearly. Who could ever forget the horror that walked amongst us? Andenmatten had brought the Maudit into our midst and left a disgraceful stain on our community. We all had to bear the consequences, and for some, the burden was heavy. Much too heavy. And then came that endless night of October 29 . . ."

I wanted to ask what had happened, but the pastor raised his hand to his mouth and started tottering. The lantern in his other hand rocked and his face transformed into a mask of horror. I instinctively raised my hands. Was on the verge of running away, because I could feel the pressure behind my bandages build mercilessly. I didn't want to infect him, you know? To infect him like I had infected the others.

"Please," I begged. "Really, I don't mean wrong. Just tell me what happened."

But the pastor only stumbled backwards. Touched the cross hanging from his neck and reiterated his plea for me to *please* leave before it's too late.

"At least tell me if there's some way of getting rid of it!"

"You will not like the answer," was the last thing I heard him say, before he turned around and fled into the church.

The pressure receded. I walked home with my hands in my pockets and my head full of questions. They're still there. But I do know one thing now: it has happened before. Jorg Andenmatten. I have to find out what became of him. But I can't stop seeing that mask of horror on the pastor's face as he stands before me, and hearing his last words: *You will not like the answer.*

5

November 6

Stopped writing. Unable to. Never expected to open this document again. It's hopeless. The moments I'm still myself are becoming scarce. The very last of who I am will disappear too. The glacier is closing in on me and stretches out till infinity.

Oh, Sam, that soulless thing in the rocking chair . . .

I can't bear thinking about it.

Have to get Sam out of here. Protect him from himself *and* me. Can't put him through what's awaiting me. But that means I'll have to break with him, and I can't handle that. Oh, if only there were some way . . .

But I'm getting ahead of myself. I'll write it all down. For Sam. Maybe then he'll understand, when I'm gone.

Two nights ago, I woke up completely disoriented. Face throbbing something awful. It wasn't so much pain as a feeling of immense *hollowness*, as if something had dug its way out and left a deep cavity. It was the middle of the night, and it was snowing. The cold burned inside my lungs when I inhaled.

Something was shuffling right beside me. It stank of rot.

My hand shot to my face. No bandages. Skin frozen stiff.

Something brushed against my arms. Hopped onto my chest. Immediately after that, a sharp stab in my left eye. [*It was one of those birds, Sam, and he was pecking at my eyes!*] Screaming, I jumped up. Before I knew it, I had flapping wings in my grip. Its sharp, seeking claws were grasping my chin and ripping at my lips. In a reflex, I jerked my hands apart and literally tore the bird in two. The stench was sickening. Disgusted, I cast the bloody parts onto the ground, fell to my knees, and covered my eye with my hand. As I was doing this, screeching shadows flew up all around me. *A whole flock of choughs had gathered in the snow.*

The flock disappeared through the whirl of snowflakes, into the night, and only then did I look around me—and what I saw almost made me wish the bird had blinded me.

I was in a larch forest. The snow, which in places was sticking to the ground and by morning would color the valley white for the first time this fall, reflected the night's eerie light. This seemed to be coming from everywhere and nowhere. And I knew where I was. Up ahead, I saw the barbed wire barrier with the yellow sign that read ACCÈS INTERDIT. On the other side, I could vaguely make out the steep trail to the Maudit. This was where our ascent had started. This was where I had taken Augustin's picture, with him smiling into the camera, a lock of hair carelessly swept over his bandanna, Therm-a-Rest rolled up against the side of his North Face backpack.

Not six feet away from me, in a jumble of bird tracks, there was a crooked figure. Even seeing him with only one eye, there was no doubt in my mind it was Augustin.

He was turned away from me, motionlessly staring at the ACCÉS INTERDIT sign. It wasn't the Augustin from the photo—this was the Augustin from the glacier. He was wearing his red Gore-Tex jacket. The reason he was bent over in such a strange, impossible posture was that he had multiple fractures in both legs from when he fell into the crevasse. Yet, there he was, up on his feet.

His frozen hand hung limply from his sleeve. His index finger was trembling. Was it the wind? Or . . .

I wasn't breathing as I stared at him. One-eyed. Blood was trickling out the other, through my fingers. I could barely open my left eye. Had to constantly blink as tears flowed down my cheeks, but as far as I could tell, the damage wasn't serious.

Augustin, on the other hand . . .

I tried convincing myself that Augustin's projection had come from the mangled death bird. But I knew better. He had come out of my face. That's what had caused the hollowness. Part of him had always been inside of me, since that night in the crevasse.

Still, I instinctively knew that what was standing there wasn't the real Augustin. He was a *good* person. Full of joie de vivre. This thing *looked* like Augustin but was distorted. Like a negative. An echo.

A rustle shook me out of my daze. It was the chough. And—it was trying to drag itself through the snow with one mutilated wing. *At least, the part the head was still attached to.*

What shot through my head was the ibex doe . . . but the image was pushed away by a far more urgent realization.

The death bird had been cloven in two but was still *alive.*

It was then, I think, that I started to understand so, so much.

I snatched the wing with the torn-off piece of flank from the snow and wasn't surprised to discover dried glue stuck to the feathers. Thread. Flaxen straw. The other half of the bird struggled and pecked at my wrists as I picked it up and carefully buried it under my coat, but I didn't pay any attention to it. I was looking at Augustin. He hadn't budged, but then his image seemed to shimmer before me, and in the blink of an eye he had *turned around* and was now staring at me. Without hesitating, I ran the hell out of there.

I looked back once. About thirty yards lower. I wish I hadn't. Augustin's specter had turned back around to face the slope. Now I could see what it was that he'd been looking at all the time.

On the other side of the barbed wire barrier were many more human-shaped shadows in the woods. They were all staring down toward the valley.

(continuation)

I found the shop right away, on the narrow main street a few storefronts down from Boulangerie Salamin. It had stuck in my mind because of the stuffed chamois in the window and the golden eagle with its wings spread over a collection of minerals and rock crystals. The inscription on the shop window said TAXIDERMIE & CURIOSITÉS NATURELLES. One of those shops that are strictly for tourists. Now I understand that's just a facade.

I pounded on the door till a light finally popped on in the house behind the shop. I didn't care if I was waking the neighbors. The birds screeching in the storefront cages were betraying my presence anyway.

Locks and bolts were turned. When the door had opened a crack and the startled face of an elderly woman stared at me, I didn't hesitate for a second. I rammed the door with my shoulder and burst into the house. Letting out a yell, the woman sprang back, and before you knew it, I had her pinned to the wall, my free hand on her mouth to prevent her from screaming. I kicked the door shut with my heel. There was a brief auditory illusion, because I could still hear the screeching of the death birds. But one look into the shop and I realized it was coming from inside.

The shop was lined with all sorts of stuffed alpine fauna, but the choughs in the cages were alive. They were all attacking the bars.

"Quiet," I told her. "Don't scream."

I took my hand off her mouth. She looked up at me, terrified. I must have looked like a monster to her, so no surprise. Towering two heads above her, scars exposed, eye bloodshot and lip torn. But her appearance shocked me, too. Long gray hair draped over a battered face, covered in scratches. I immediately understood how she'd got them. They were the sacrifices that came with her line of work.

But it wasn't my looks that had frightened the old woman the most. She knew that the Maudit had entered her shop along with me.

With my limited command of French, I improvised, *"Je suis ne pas dangereux."*

But I was, and she knew it.

Gingerly, almost tenderly, I took the mutilated bird out from under my coat and showed it to her. The little creature had stopped lashing at me and was shuddering with stress, but it was still alive. The woman's eyes widened and filled with understanding when she took it from me. I took the dismembered wing out my coat pocket and held it up for her.

"Il ne pas mort," I said, probably redundantly. It was pretty clear it wasn't dead.

The taxidermist shot me a disparaging look and then, as she rushed past me to her worktable, said, *"Il n'y a pas de mort pour les oiseaux."*

That got me cold all over, despite the benevolent warmth emanating from the house. My French is good enough to deduce what she had meant: *There is no death for the birds.*

So it's true. It's all true. Of course. The bird I had ripped apart but that didn't die. The dead bird Ramses had shown up with, that somehow came back to life and scared the living daylights out of him. *They don't die, because the souls they carry with them don't die.*

But that doesn't explain how many there are, I thought, as I looked at the bird in the old woman's hands. *So many people couldn't possibly have died on the Maudit. Never.*

And it also didn't explain why Augustin was still *alive* when I found him on the ice bridge, after his eyes had been pecked out. Why didn't he pass into one of those birds?

Because that wasn't Augustin. It wasn't something alive. And what you saw tonight wasn't Augustin either. Not really, at least. You're missing something . . .

Increasingly anxious, I stared at the blindly attacking birds. Their cages were swinging on their chains. Feathers fluttered downward like pitch-black snow. Even the mangled specimen I had brought in was stirring. It tried to get away from the bright halo of light the floor lamp cast on the working surface. When the old lady slid it back, it let out a hoarse croak and pecked at her abundantly scarred fingers.

"*Allez, allez!*" she called, now more annoyed than afraid. She gestured for me to leave the shop. But I couldn't move. The whole situation was grabbing me by the throat.

Those hacking beaks. The talons clawing at the bars. What kind of creatures were these? Not dead, not alive. Bird phantoms possessed by the dead possessed by the mountain. They must feel drawn to human life, maybe that's why they fly back to the valley. Whatever tradition it had given birth to, they were kept in cages, and because the birds never died, they were associated with good fortune and a prosperous life.

And what didn't die had to be maintained.

With the skilled ease of a craftswoman or an alchemist, the taxidermist slid a leather hood over the chough's head and buckled the straps in place. The bird instantly calmed down. She poured alcohol on a wad of cotton and started to dab the bloody hole in its trunk. I tensed up. Turned away. Had a sudden need for cold, fresh air.

The old woman yelled something at me, but I barely heard. My eyes fell on a framed diploma on the wall. I walked up to it, and while the lady yelled again, fiercer this time, I read *Certificat d'Honneur et Mérite pour Votre Excellence dans l'Art de la Taxidermie, Marie Andenmatten—Canton du Valais.*

I noticed that my feet were leading me deeper into the shop, but I couldn't control them. The antlers, the dried flowers, the stuffed animals, everything was reeling. I looked back and saw the old woman jab a needle straight through the compressed, fleshy edges of the bird's body and the torn-off wing.

"I think I'm going to be sick," I heard myself say, but distantly, as if I were underwater. I stumbled past her worktable, into the dark hall, heading for the house. Bumped into the doorpost. The woman let out a startled cry, but her voice, the croaking of the birds, it barely reached me.

There was a staircase to the left, light shining down through it, but I started down the corridor, into the dark. I don't know what had gotten into me. But that name . . . that name . . .

There was a door with a bleeding Christ on the cross on it, but when I tried the handle it wouldn't budge. The door opposite was ajar. Air as dank as the air in the shop wafted out at me and made my stomach turn. In the hall's bleak light, I could see pelts hanging on brass hooks. A grimy bathroom with the odor of the elderly. A closet full of rock crystals. A thick curtain, and behind it one last door.

Mounted on the left wall was a framed black-and-white photo of a young couple standing in front of a glacier, which I recognized as the Glacier de Moiry, beyond the reservoir. In the gloom, the couple seemed to be grimacing more than smiling, he lanky with sunken cheeks and she with pale, colorless eyes.

Don't open the door, I thought.

But of course I opened the door, and I shrank back from the wave of thick, human heat. It was pitch-dark. I almost slammed the door shut again, but then I heard a gentle rustling. Something had moved. With trembling fingers, I took out my phone. Swiped up. Tapped the flashlight icon and aimed it into the room.

And in the naked light I saw.

It was a bedroom, but the made bed looked like it hadn't been slept in in years. In a rocking chair next to the bed was an old man with no eyes. He was smartly dressed in an ironed shirt and the embroidered gilet typical of the traditional attire of the Valais. His gaunt hands were folded on his lap and, at first, I thought he was dead . . . *but then I saw that his stomach was rising and falling with his breathing.*

At that instant, I saw the family resemblance. The man was many years older than the young man in the photo, his pasty face wrinkled and pallid, thin strands of hair hanging off an otherwise bald skull, but he had the same lanky figure and sunken cheeks. And the young woman . . .

The man in the rocking chair showed no signs of having noticed my presence. The hard light coming from my phone seemed to be getting sucked into his empty eye sockets and to disappear within them. I, too, felt irresistibly drawn to them, because despite my mind screaming *Turn around!*, I'd already taken several involuntary steps into the room. Who knows what would have happened if at that instant the monstrously ecstatic shriek hadn't come from the dark on my left. My body literally doubled up. I pointed the phone at what was coming at me. That broke the spell.

It was an alpine chough, but it was inside a big iron cage. Its bright yellow beak was piercing through the bars like a knife as it spread its shadowy wings.

I turned and ran, because that's when I understood what the pastor had meant with his last words: *You won't like the answer.*

The man in the rocking chair was Jorg Andenmatten.

7

(continuation)

When I ran away from the horror at the end of the corridor and left the dismayed Marie Andenmatten and her mangled birds behind, a small crowd was waiting for me on the street. About fifteen villagers. One look at their faces, their balled fists, and the clubs they were holding was enough. I wasn't going to escape this unscathed.

So I called on it. [*Sam, forgive me.*] Never before have I consciously summoned the Maudit, but I did now.

"Go away!" I shouted. "I don't want to hurt anyone, but I will, and I can't help it!"

The anger in their faces transformed into fear. I spread my arms, puffed out my chest, and turned my mind inward. I wasn't wearing my bandages, and it happened with relentless power. I only remember the sensation of *growing*, then my mind keeled over, and I came to myself only tonight.

Two days later.

I *hope* they got away in time. I hope so with all my heart.

I have no doubts that they'll come back for me. That's why it isn't safe for Sam to stay here anymore. For me, either, but what I have to do has to be done here; I know that now. Up to now, I could see only two solutions, both of which bode ill for the future. Either I let what the Maudit had started happen, and bring about total destruction not only of myself but of everything that's dear to me, or I stop myself to spare us all that fate. My stock of oxazepam is enough to get it done. And honestly, if it weren't for Sam, maybe I would have already tried.

Death or Pandora's box—but now I know there's a third option.

The old man in the rocking chair. That soulless, no-eyed thing. And in the dark, the birdcage with the chough.

I had stood face-to-face with Jorg Andenmatten, who had been possessed by the Maudit, and now I know how the exorcism works.

As I write this, I hear meltwater dripping off the eaves. The snow has almost completely melted away, but there's a storm brewing.

I can taste it in the air. Clouds are gathering up in the mountains. Before, I would have needed MeteoSchweiz to know that, but now I listen to what a deeper instinct is whispering to me, and I know it as sure as I know my own name.

Sam has to get out of here right away.

In the distance, I can hear the valley sing.

WUTHERING HEIGHTS

NOTES BY SAM AVERY

The intense horror of nightmare came over me: I tried to draw back my arm, but the hand clung to it, and a most melancholy voice sobbed, "Let me in—let me in!"

—Emily Brontë

1

The Morose came on the seventh of November.

It was everything Louetta had said, but worse.

You knew it was there when, that morning, a human cry descended from the clouds. A cry that shook the large window's glass in its grooves.

You knew it when the wind picked up and you felt the atmosphere's dense, cold air zinging in your teeth.

You knew because your cerebral cortex started to tingle. Because your bone marrow itched. You knew it the way rats and weasels know an earthquake is coming. The way fish swim away before a tsunami.

The fireplace going dark was just a harbinger.

The barometer's drop just prophecy.

Nick, he'd been pacing up and down in front of the big window all morning like a caged tiger. Gazing out, his eyes pulled like a magnet, drawn to that place behind the surrounding ridges where the Maudit waited. His feet excavating a deepening trench in the hardwood.

He'd gotten a little scary.

Fuck that, he was scary on a whole new level. Milly Shapiro in *Hereditary* scary.

Thing was, there was no getting through to him anymore. Couldn't find Nick in there anymore. Each time I said his name, each time I ran my tongue over my parched lips and came into his orbit, it was like he was looking straight through me. Like I didn't even exist.

Then you think you hear another cry, an echo, a reverberation, and your gaze shoots to outside the window.

The valley was on standby. Holding its breath for what was to come.

At ten past ten, the chamois exodus began.

All at once the woods were alive. All at once, black-and-white-striped skull snouts floating between the pine trees. Whole herds of *Rupicapra rupicapra*, their little horns swinging with their bowed heads, marching past the chalet without giving it a second glance and following the brook downstream into the valley.

Not exactly what *National Geographic* would describe as "natural behavior." Not exactly what the zoologically inclined intelligentsia would label as an "ecological anomaly," but Nick didn't even see them. This was where I drew the line.

Maybe Nick had taken me hostage. But now the Morose was taking *him* hostage.

2

For you to know how we got here, I have to take you back, way back, to almost a whole day ago—the moment I hit rock bottom.

Last night, FaceTiming with Julia for the first time in weeks, her voice in my Bluetooth earplugs: "I'm seriously worried about you, bro. Amy Winehouse's corpse looked better than you do. Why have you stopped answering my messages?"

Cuz I didn't wanna admit how in over my head I really was, of course.

Even when down in the pits, every boozer, every junkie, every addict comes up with "I got this. Everything under control. No prob."

'Course, I didn't tell her that I feared I'd been deliberately set up. Now, in one of my rare clean stretches, that I feared I'd been seduced under false pretenses. After all, I was the one who'd been enabling it. Empowering it by continuously tearing off those bandages and releasing the beast.

Me, his aphrodisiac; he, my cocaine.

Nah, I just said I'd been busy. Every rehab clinic will tell you that's the addiction talking. Cuz truth is, my fingers were trembling. Truth is, the cold sweat in my neck was a *withdrawal symptom*. Listening with one earplug out, trying to hear Nick downstairs, trying to make sure he didn't hear *me*, cuz everyone knew this was my cry for help. Now, taking advantage of one of my scarce clean-headed moments, this was the oh-so-necessary intervention in the making. Don't wanna kill the suspense, but at some point during this heart-to-heart, my mask was going to break. Even I knew that.

Even the little boy who'd set his childhood on fire and was shit-scared he'd get caught knew you couldn't hide forever.

You see, the way my grandfather told the story, Prometheus was left to rot. Chained to the mountaintop above Phoenicia, exposed in his kinky loincloth, with the eagle returning every night to tear out his liver. According to the ancient Greeks, the liver was the seat of human emotions. With that under fire and continually plundered, Prometheus's soul, over time, got more and more barren. His body no more than an empty shell.

Every night anew, the story goes, his guilt returned to feast on his emotions. Sound familiar?

My grandfather was never too fond of a happy ending.

Only years later did I discover a different ending to that story also existed. In it, a handsome hero called Hercules shows up one day to save Prometheus from his pickle. Prometheus, the princess in the highest tower; Ethon, the dragon to be slain. Hercules shot an arrow right through his noggin, and together they rode straight into the sunset.

Every story can spin an alternate ending. Every story can be rewritten.

What I needed was my detox-shake Hercules. My Rehab Hero.

Enter Julia Avery.

"Seriously, that place is poison to you," Julia said late last night, full-screen on FaceTime. "Your *guy* is poison to you. As long as you keep protecting him, it won't stop, Sam."

"But you don't get it. It's not Nick's fault. It's the mountain. It's the Maudit."

Silence. A coupla seconds too long for comfort.

"If you could just hear yourself . . ."

I couldn't tell her. I hadda *show* her.

I walked to the hall. Warily, I steadied myself on the doorpost, leaned forward above the stairwell, tilted my head to listen.

One earplug out, but still in the other Julia saying, "Seriously, you gotta end this, before it's too late. You gotta get out of there."

Silence.

Profound, monumental silence. Roaring on the lower floor. I tried not to move, tried to hold my breath. You could *feel* Nick before you could hear him. All at once, the stairwell's magnetic suction. The expanding depth. Wobbling. Shooting at me. The optical illusion of a terrible height. The cognitive experience of something unspeakable.

As quietly as possible I tiptoed back to the living room. Ramses, left forepaw all bandaged up, eyes wide, looked past me to the door. I tried to check the dizziness by fixing my gaze back on Julia, my tiny avatar-sister, but my eyes were burning and she was all blurry.

"Bro, what's the mat—Are you crying?"

And me with my iPhone at arm's length, I put it on selfie mode, just me looking at me as I put a shaking finger to my lips.

"*Sam, what's going on?*"

I put the phone on the mantelpiece and slid a tealight holder in front of it to keep it upright, with the cam's eye facing the living room. Checked the composition. I brought Louise and Harald's postcard and the vase with dried alpenroses closer. A cluster of domestic inconspicuousness. If you didn't know the iPhone was there, you wouldn't know the iPhone was there.

In my ear, Julia saying, "Where *is* Nick, by the way?"

The house shook. The screen glitched.

Ramses disappeared with a nervous hop, skip, and jump via the stairwell to the attic.

Julia said, "What was that?"

And me whispering, "That was Nick."

He entered the room.

Julia in my ear, "Sam, what's going on? *What's going on?*"

"Hello, Sam," Nick said.

He was smiling, a Cheshire Cat smile, stretching the complex puzzle of scars and fault lines on his face all the way to his ears. His left eye was bloodshot and there was an ugly, scabbed cut on his lower lip. I looked at it, doing my best to remain undaunted by the dramatic change in atmospheric pressure his arrival had brought about. My fingertips, my lips, my ears became numb. A dull pain was pressing against my eardrums and the backs of my eyeballs.

Something was wrong. This was not the usual way the Maudit affected me. This was worse. Way worse.

Julia was a gasp, a call, a gust of wind in the distance. "*Run away! Run away, Sam, now!*"

Nick came at me. All the hairs on my body jumped to attention with sizzling, static sparks. Everything in the chalet, every object and its spatial proportions, the shadows and the highlights, seemed to bend toward me, their glowing focal point. My instincts were screaming *Run!*, screaming *Get out of there while you still can!*, but I didn't run. Some kind of fatalistic metalogic took over and whispered to me what every addict knows: cold turkey is pie in the sky. Every shooter mainlines that needle one more time. Just *one* last time, then I'll quit.

Nick grinned. "Small, fragile Sam."

He put his arms around me, and just for a sec it was like I could look *through* the world and see the world *beyond* it, in which the chalet was spinning in a cold, inert universe.

And Julia, a screaming voice in my ear: "*Who is that woman? Who is that woman in the corner behind you?*"

But that caused me only a vague semblance of alarm, because there was no woman, there was only Nick, his aroma an overwhelming *Nick* in my nostrils, and I inhaled it deeply when—*kaboom!*—a new shock wave shook the chalet, foundation to roof. A high-pitched flash of electricity, Julia's scream amplified to a deafening beehive, and all the lights went out. My iPhone screen shattered. The microwave in the kitchen crashed onto the floor. A penetrating burning smell as the router shorted out.

Julia's voice had fallen still.

Nick, a storm front in the dark of the earth, he said, "You and me, Sam. We don't need anybody else."

3

That was yesterday, and that's why I was now tiptoeing my way through the hall. Bundled up in warm clothes. Pulling on my Ralph Laurens. In my head, Julia. I lay awake all night, wide-eyed in the dark, trapped under Nick's muscle-bound arm. He slept like a pit bull guarding a bone, or a dragon guarding a ruby. Me dead worried about Julia. Julia most probably dead worried about me, but no means whatsoever of sending her an SOS, with our Wi-Fi severed. My phone—dear, dear iPhone—RIP. The Maudit had cut me off from the outside world. Thank your lucky strikes there were spare fuses for the power unit or we would have been blasted all the way back to the Middle Ages.

And yep, despite everything, still worried sick about Nick, cuz where did he get those wounds? That bar fight lip, that zombie eye? Did the shock wave from the Maudit taking things out of his hands pop a vein in his retina? What if next time it pops a vein in his brain?

I must have fallen asleep after all, and when I woke up I knew it was too late. I knew, then, that up there in the valley, *something* had also been woken up.

Then I heard the wind and remembered what Louetta had told me.

I *had* to let Julia know I was okay—okayish—but that we needed help. And fast.

So I fish the SIM out of my iPhone's carcass so I can stick it into Nick's phone and use his 4G, except for the minor detail that it's in a pocket that happens to belong to his sweatpants, which are now pacing up and down in front of the large window.

No way was I gonna ask him could I please borrow his phone, with him like that. Like, *Hey, just wanna* Candy Crush Friends Saga *for a minute, cool?*

And no way was I going to pickpocket him, with him like that, either.

So I pulled on my jacket. Pushed out of my mind the thought that he might stop me. That he'd suddenly stare at me with those frigid eyes and demand to know where I thought I was going with that MacBook Air under my arm.

With the aftershocks of his intoxication still reverberating in my body, I wasn't sure I could keep *myself* under control.

Stood there for a coupla secs, my hand on the door handle, looking at him over by the window, hypnotized. Something on the inside of my heart was trying to gnaw its way out with its little teeth, but I staved it off.

Then I sneaked out, shut the door behind me, and locked it.

4

Outside it was worse. Way worse.

I hadn't even gotten halfway to the village before I wished I'd stayed home. The valley was on the verge of a panic attack. The mountains seemed to have been disjointed. The sky rocked. The cold unhinged. There are November mornings when the cold is clear, crackling, and crisp, but this cold was sticky, syrupy, clung to you. Like it was begging you for help. You, the first organism to have crossed its path, and would you *please* take it with you and protect it from what's about to happen, because that was much, much worse than the cold itself.

Jesus. The Morose hadn't even got started yet and my metaphors were already going haywire. I squeezed my eyes shut. Opened them. Hurried on.

And fuck.

Fuck!

Something was wrong with my head.

I stood still. Looked around.

Over there. Or . . .

I got the claustrophobic feeling that I was being stared back at from everywhere around me. The steep slopes, the gloomy sky, everything seemed nasty and horrid. My back was quivering with electricity. What had gotten into me?

My gaze shot upward. My whole body tensed up.

It wasn't my imagination! Again, one of those human cries. I was sure I'd heard it. I was sure I'd *seen* it. Something flashing through the sky in a straight line. Just beyond the peripheries of my perception—like my brain was one step too late in registering it.

I peered at the passing clouds, so antsy and intense it was like someone'd blow-dried my retinas.

There, again. And there.

The clouds were *laden* with cries, as if a massive downpour was coming.

What was it the old mountain folk used to say? *When the Morose began, you heard the valley bewailing the death of the world.*

And Louetta Molignon: *Then several voices answered, thin and distant and way up high. It still sounded like a cry for help, but suddenly your grandfather wasn't sure anymore that they'd been calling his name or that it was Ambroise and Nicolas who were calling out there.*

With an increasing chill engulfing my whole body, I was no longer thinking of local meteorological phenomena or how the tunnel-shaped valley functioned as a natural amplifier for the wind's fluctuating wails.

I was thinking of what Louetta had said, that no one who'd ever heard the Morose had lived to tell the tale.

Thinking: *Outer frequencies. Outer frequencies are what save you in Grimentz. Everything scatters in the end. Everything dies down.*

Still, I was thinking about people who disappeared in the night, under the wind's spell. About the eerie screaming from the valley, which, if its poison penetrated your spirit deeply enough, would start sounding as enticing as the Sirens' call.

About violence. About disease. About insanity.

About Louetta, who'd said: *I heard the story of a little girl who was hiding from her mother in a barn when the Morose hit, and she never spoke another word till she was on her deathbed, sixty years later.*

All those things were real.

Why didn't I turn around then and go back to the chalet, take Nick's Focus and clear out? Just beat it? I'd be lying if I said it didn't cross my mind.

But I couldn't do it. Because of Nick.

I loved him, even if I'd become addicted to his power.

That thing in the chalet isn't Nick anymore. The Maudit is stealing his show. Do you really think you'll get to see Nick again after today?

I shivered and pushed the thought away, but a new echo of a cry dying down in the wind made me flinch. Suddenly furious, I looked at the sky and yelled, "Fuck the motherfucking fuck off!"

Maybe chances of my getting Nick out of this in one piece were slim, but I was going to do everything in my power to make it happen.

As I walked to the village, face like a thundercloud, head hunched deep into my collar, the only answer to the only question bouncing around in my head lit up like a lighthouse in the mist: *Take him out. Take him out and take him down.*

5

In Grimentz, it was anything but the calm before the storm.

From the parking lot below the village, it was your quintessential exodus. A gridlock of snazzy Swiss cars even before the exit to Zinal, cuz some farmer was guiding his cattle to a safe haven in the valley along the only access road. The closed Office du Tourisme's canton flag was clattering with a restless, metallic sound against its pole. The folks brave enough to venture outside on the streets were frantically and loudly latching their hatches and fastening their fences.

The flapping of flags. The honking of car horns. The *ting-a-ling-ling* of cowbells and the mooing of cattle. The audial onslaught had already begun.

From higher up the slopes, the stately, harmonic tones of alpenhorns fanned downward.

I knew that the cable car terminal had been shut down for the season, but the boulangerie-pâtisserie's shopwindow had been boarded up from the inside with plywood, and that was news to me. The sheet of paper on the inside of the Coop's window with the handwritten message *Fermé Temporairement* was news to me.

The mountain made its power grab, and all of Grimentz's retailers had to take it lying down.

Even the ski shop was closed, I discovered a bit down the road. Major bummer, cuz I'd seen they sold cell phones there. No iPhones, but, hey, right now I woulda settled for a Nokia. Hell, a Motorola if I had to.

My mood darkening fast, I walked on. Suddenly it came to me what was missing. The birdcages. Apparently they'd all been taken inside. There wasn't a single one left.

Evacuated for what was drawing nigh.

I think that was when I started to get scared.

No one was on the streets by the time I'd reached Hôtel du Barrage. No one to hear me call "No, no, *no*," over and over again, when I saw that here, too, all the hatches had been shut. A fucking hotel. How did they even arrange this with the tourists?

I thought, *There aren't any. Schweizer Pünktlichkeit. They take care of it.*

Just for the hell of it, I tried the door. Sat myself down on the porch stairs. Took my MacBook out of its protective case, flipped it open. They had Wi-Fi, but only for guests. Password protected, of course. I tried "hoteldubarrage." Tried "Grimentz2018." Tried "*pute-de-raclette*," with and without dashes.

I tried it everywhere, in front of every dark restaurant, every vacant vacation home, every boarded-up chalet. But no go on the login.

So I banged on the Hôtel du Barrage's door. I banged as the wind whistled around the empty flower boxes and rocked the signboard above the door on its hinges, making it squeak. I banged as the clouds dropped their echoes like harbingers of the storm.

The same woman who'd brought Cécile and me our beers that night in October eventually opened the door. She didn't look like she was happy to see me. Didn't look like she was happy to see anybody.

"*Fermé*," she muttered. Then she seemed to recognize me and her eyes became small and piglike. The door promptly closed to a mere crack.

And me, I made it clear in polite French that I only needed a minute of her time. Could I please make a call, it was an emergency, I would pay her for it.

"I don't give a damn about your emergency!" she lashed out at me.

All I needed was the password. Just the password and ten minutes to sit on her porch.

"Get out of here! Go back to that accursed evil you brought into our midst!"

Did she take American Express?

Suddenly she turned all sly and said in an almost childlike, bullying intonation, "It doesn't matter anymore anyway. After tonight it will all be over and done . . . with *him*."

My heart nose-dived.

I wanted to ask what she meant, but just then a cry came from the clouds, loud enough to be ruled out as just an echo. I could have *sworn* that out of the corner of my eye I saw something tumble down from the sky. Real close. Above the rooftops across the street. The barwoman's eyes were suddenly like saucers and mortified, and during the one sec that my attention flagged, she slammed the door—*wham!*—right in my face. Angry sound of bolt rammed into socket.

I pounded the wood with my fists and shouted, "*Joyeux Morose, Morticia!*"

As therapy it didn't count for much, but you hadda start somewhere.

Admit it, you were losing this battle. Even if you found yourself some Wi-Fi, it wasn't like Julia could actually *do* anything from all the way in New York.

Anyway, my hands were doing the jitterbug again. The urge to call Julia suddenly displaced by a deeper need—a fix only Nick could supply me with.

It doesn't matter anymore anyway. After tonight it will all be over and done . . . with him.

What had that village witch meant by that?

On the way back, I heard the alpenhorns again, and across the fields above the village I saw a whole congregation of men and women lumbering along. Ethnic attire, hand-whittled walking sticks, and more of that stereotypical mountain shit. I wondered whether maybe they'd performed some kind of ritual on the edge of the forest to suck up to the Morose. A peace offering.

The slaughter of an innocent lamb or whatever.

When I looked closer, I saw that the man in the habit, holding a staff up front, was the same priest-slash-churchguy who'd come to our door weeks back.

When I looked closer, I saw that some of the people in the procession were crying.

What came to mind was a funeral cortege.

Yet there was no coffin. No urn.

I decided it was none of my business and went on.

At least the gridlock on the thoroughfare had dissipated. The road to the south, where it climbed toward the reservoir, had been closed since the last snowfall, and according to Nick it would stay closed all winter. I was just crossing the desolated tourist parking to reach the dirt road toward Hill House when I heard a car coming uphill at high speed.

Without signaling, it swerved onto the parking lot, burning tracks into the blacktop.

It was a Peugeot in obsidian black.

I knew this car.

You think, *She's gonna brake*, you think, *She sees me all right*, but brake she *didn't*.

Catching sight of me only as she barely missed me, and even then, it took her forty yards, smokin' wheels, and a helluva *whump* to come to a standstill.

Running, I covered the distance. The door swung open and Cécile literally stumbled out.

"Sam?"

"Cécile! Christ, what happened to your arm?"

I should only have asked what happened, *period*, because Cécile Métrailler, my *très ooh-la-la* Nurse Cécile, she'd been fully taken to pieces. Her left arm was in a sling, her fingers sticking out of a cast. She still had hips to hold up her pants and enough tits to fill her shirt, but there were at least twenty pounds missing from the rest. Even the rouge under her cheekbones couldn't mask the fact that, in three weeks, she'd aged ten years.

Despite all of this, she still managed to crank something up that was meant to resemble a grin. "Oh, that. That was a stupid accident." The grin broadened somewhat. "I broke my wrist. I fell off the stepladder when I was changing a lightbulb."

That statement unveiled the seasoned pro liar she truly was, but this wasn't the time for questioning. "What are you doing here? Shit, you look like a walking concealer stick."

"They said on TV a massive snow front was nearing the mountains, this year's first major storm. I remembered what my mamie had told us and I decided to come. I . . . I didn't want you to go through it alone tonight. You know, not with what's going on with Nick and everything."

That moved me. Despite my surprise, despite my suspicions, I got a lump in my throat. I put my arms around Cécile, careful not to crush the arm in the cast.

"I'm so happy to see you again."

"Me too, Sam. You're not doing too good, huh?"

"Nope."

Damn, now my bottom lip was starting to tremble, so I held on to her just a little bit longer. I've also been known to conceal things, and what's wrong with that? Besides, it was good to hold someone close. Someone who didn't give you visions of infinity and send you to the moon and back.

"My god, you can feel it everywhere. It's making me feel queasy all over. Has it been like this for long?"

"Since this morning."

"That's what I figured. And it looks like we're not the only ones to feel it."

I gazed at her and Cécile nodded upward.

The sky was darkened by flocks of birds. Way up high, they were heading north. They were coming from the mountains, thousands at a time. There was something ominous about their unanimity, something your brain either could not or would not process.

Where were they going? And would we ever get to see that place?

Cécile cringed against a sudden gust and said, "Come on." She avoided my glance and said, "Let's get in the car."

We did, but as we bounced over that bumpy road, I looked at her trembling hand on the wheel and realized I hadn't been able to decipher her expression.

6

"*Nom de Dieu*," Cécile whispered.

It hit us the minute we walked in. It was like walking into a poisonous cloud. As soon as we entered the hallway and the intensifying wind had slammed the massive door shut behind us, we sensed there was a greater danger lurking inside. The sensation was similar to when the Maudit would take over Nick, only it had gotten worse again. One lighted match and you'd transform Hill House into a smoldering crater. A crater housing three sets of charred, unidentifiable dental remains.

Nick, he'd stopped pacing. He was now standing still in front of the big window, face tilted upward, his eyes, reflected in the glass, large and staring and blind—blind at least to the things we could see.

Emanating vibes that made the hairs stand up on the backs of our necks.

"We need to drug him," Cécile said, obsessively scritch-scratching her hair.

Her pupils ping-ponging in their sockets: "Before it starts to get worse and that glass door isn't enough to keep him in here anymore." Tense fingers probing her open mouth: "He looks like he's hypnotized . . ."

I said, "Last time I drugged him I used oxazepam, and that worked fine." I started laughing, couldn't help it. *Last time I drugged him.* Find me a therapist who'd consider that a fruitful foundation for a relationship.

"Nick?" I called. "Nick, I've got Cécile with me. She's come here to help us."

In my head: *You and me, Sam. We don't need anybody else.*

No reaction.

The only sound his breathing, rumbling deep in his chest.

Cécile in the doorway, twenty pounds lighter and six shades paler than the last time she'd walked in there. You could hear her catch her breath.

"Nick?"

In the glass, the reflection of his eyes distorted, too hollow, too dark.

The reflection of his ruined face, grotesquely askew.

And Cécile, you could hear her whisper, "*Jésus Marie Joseph.*"

"Nick. Yoo-hoo." Walked up to him, touched his shoulder. Waved my hand up and down between his eyes and the window. "Cécile would like to examine you."

And Cécile: "*Tu con . . .*"

I looked around and shrugged. I kept trying, but nothing. It was like Nick wasn't there. As if I was looking at an empty shell. It was creepy. His gaze fixed on things only he could see. Except when one of those echoes erupted. One of those auditory illusions of cries in the sky. Then something alive in his eyes seemed to chase it. As if he'd heard it call his name.

A temptation luring him into the unknown.

The large window shook on its hinges. The wind had free rein of it and seemed to be incessantly prodding it, testing it, searching for weak spots. To get inside. Become bait for anything that wished to trail behind it.

A new thought made my blood run cold: *What if Nick decides to break out? You can lock the doors, but the chalet is no fortress.*

No other way—dope him up.

Cécile and I, we stumbled down the stairs together. To the downstairs bathroom, just in case he was listening in anyway. I took a strip of oxas from Nick's leather toilet bag on the sink. Said that he usually siestaed a coupla hours every day since his accident. That he usually imbibed gallons of water. Usually—but who knows if today was "usually."

"*What's his regular dose?*"

"*Two. I think. Three on bad days. Why are we whispering?*"

"*Don't know. Feels better. Okay. Give him six.*"

"*Witchy woman! We need to neutralize him, not knock him off.*"

Cécile rolled her eyes. "*Believe me, even if you take a whole pack of Seresta, you still wake up tomorrow morning. Okay, woozy, severe stomachaches, but you wake up. There are few prescription drugs available that are enough for a fatal intoxication by themselves. With good reason."*

"Okay, six it is. Will that be enough to take him through the night?"

"Um . . . I'm not sure. I don't know what kind of effect it has on—bon Dieu de merde! It follows you even here! It's driving me crazy; can't you hear it?"

Whether she meant the wailing of the wind or the subliminal message hidden in the wailing of the wind I didn't know, but the last thing I needed was a Cécile with her hands pressed to her ears, indulging in a nervous breakdown.

"Cécile," I said out loud, "get your act together." Popping six pills out of the strip and onto a dish, and there she was, snatching one off and swallowing it dry. I gazed at her. She gazed back, looking at me like *What?*

I said, "All right, if it makes you feel better."

I pressed another one out and crushed the six pills into powder with the bottom of a glass. Poured the powder into the glass, topped it with H_2O, sloshed it around. Result: troubled water. Result: not exactly how any self-respecting Putin poodle would slip you your daily dose of polonium.

"I'ma add some grape juice to it. Maybe he'll think it's Mountain Dew or something."

Upstairs, I did as I said I would and then put the glass on the end table next to the couch. When Nick turned around, it'd be the first thing he'd see.

"Now what?" Cécile asked, when I was back in the kitchen.

"Now we wait."

7

Just before two, we heard footsteps shuffling down the stairs. *Scuff-whump, scuff-whump.* Downstairs, in the direction of the bedroom. Up to this point we'd been keeping ourselves busy making coffee and conversation. My mix an epic fail of coffee grounds/Tabasco/shot of cognac. I called it the Intestinal Hemorrhage. The convo not much better—it all felt so forced. I had the impression Cécile was keeping back all kinds of stuff. If only I knew what it was.

And the whole time, that static energy crackling on your skin. Sometimes, out of the blue, it would make your hair literally stand up.

Now, hearing Nick go down the stairs, Cécile and I looked at each other. Waited for what seemed like an eternity, not moving, barely breathing. Then I couldn't take it anymore. I slunk toward the door. Silently pushed the handle down.

The living room was still.

The glass was empty. Our bait had worked.

I motioned to Cécile, gave her a nervous double thumbs-up. I walked through to the hall to listen in the stairwell for what was happening downstairs. Nada.

No sounds coming from the bathroom, no backwards-spoken incantations, no playlist Nick would occasionally put on to help him fall asleep. Total zip.

"What do you think?" Cécile whispered right behind me, me jumping out of my skin. "Oops, sorry."

"Jesus fucking Christ. I *hate* fake jump scares."

"Give him another fifteen minutes to fall deeper in sleep."

So we waited. Silently listening to the wind. Outside, the snowy slopes curving toward the reservoir at the end of the valley were now indistinguishable, the leaden sky an increasingly heavy, dense mass that had already choked the highest ridges.

After a quarter of an hour we snuck down the stairs.

Nick was lying in bed in the same clothes he had on that morning. Gray sweatpants and white T-shirt. His customary crib wear.

My boyfriend, his chest rising and falling with the rumbling breathing of the mountain parasite, his face shining scar tissue and the illusion of a raw, exposed landscape, otherwise stunning.

"Nick," I said softly. "Nick, are you asleep?"

I ran my tongue over my lips, touched his shoulder. "Nick?"

He was cold.

When I touched him, I felt a distant dizziness, but not like before. It was more the *impression* of dizziness. As if my mind had registered it but my body didn't feel it.

"Okay, he's out," I said to Cécile. "Let's go. Impulse control."

I drew the dusty curtains. Walked to the bathroom, shook Nick's whole depressing supply of cellophaned bandage rolls into the sink, a grab bag of shiny marshmallows. Back in the master bedroom, I tore a pack open with my teeth. Cécile, in the twilight of the doorway, was holding on to the post as if she was afraid she'd be blown away.

"Come. I need you here."

"What are you going to do?"

"What does it look like?" I hissed. "I'm gonna hold his head away from the pillow so you can wrap it like a baguette in cling wrap."

Cécile, showing no signs of going anywhere, she said, "I'm not touching him. You can't ask me to do that."

"*Nurse*. He's *sleeping*. He won't bite ya."

"Please. Don't make me, Sam. I really don't want to."

"But what's the matter?"

Cécile gripped her bottom lip and started to tug and twist it. Blood shot out, filled her lips and dripped down her chin.

"What the hell? Stop that!"

Her eyes strained, welled up with tears of pain.

I leaped forward and grabbed her by her shoulders. Cécile let go, crying, covering her face, the sling arm across her heaving bosom. For the second time that day I took her in my arms, this time looking over my own shoulder, eyes bulging, making sure Nick wasn't suddenly sitting up or coming at us or something. Lay on some *Psycho* shower strings and you get a pretty good sense of how I felt.

"Did *he* make you do that?" I stammered. "Cécile, did *Nick* make you do that?"

And she's just shaking her head, cuz she couldn't utter a single word. She tapped my arm, tried to tell me to give her a minute. Cupping her nose and mouth, trying to regulate her breathing. Giving me the time to run to the bathroom to get her a wad of paper.

Nick was sleeping through it all.

It hadn't been Nick, Cécile said, dabbing her lip, as dark blood blossomed on the paper tissue. It was her. She'd felt a panic attack coming on. This had been her last-minute tactic to smack herself back to the yin and yang. Cécile's version of the ultimate reality check.

I asked if self-mutilation was really the solution to her problems.

"You don't get it," she said. "You don't get it at all. I'm shattered, Sam, and that's because of him. You've been living with him all these weeks, but you have no idea what he's doing, do you?" She laughed and cried at the same time, hoarse, high-pitched, as if she'd only just understood it herself for the first time. "You really don't see it."

"See what, Cécile?" Not getting an answer, I said, "Let me get this straight, you hurt yourself to *prevent* yourself from getting a panic attack? So what happens if you *do* get a panic attack?"

Adding, she didn't really fall off a stepladder, did she?

Her face seemed to clear up a bit. Looked like a flush of embarrassment was flooding her cheeks. "Look at me," she said, smearing running concealer all over her face. "I came here to help you and now I'm the one who's a wet rag. I'm so sorry, Sam."

I thought, *You know absolutely nothing about her. You let a stranger into the cabin. At the end of the world. With the Storm of the Century a-brewing.*

Yep, and based on what, in fact? A shared desire to cure Nick?

Not that I was presuming to be Freud or whatever, but you didn't need psychoanalysis to figure out that self-mutilation wasn't exactly a sign of mental stability.

That familiar, sickly sizzling in my guts again. What was she actually *doing* here?

Cécile showed a faint smile and said, "Really, I'm so sorry. This has all been too much. And I *obviously* haven't been coping well with it. I've been having nightmares for weeks. Anxiety attacks. It was a defense mechanism to . . . you know . . ."

"Oh, I know all about defense mechanisms, girl," I said, "but that pulling and twisting, you gotta stop doing that. Your lips are way too fabulous for that."

She sob-smiled. "I considered therapy. But what do I say to a psychologist?" Nodding at Nick, nodding at what was going on outside, she said, "I have to face my fears. That's why I decided to come. As long as we haven't solved this, I can't let it go. So let's start with what you said. Let's wrap his face in bandages."

"Give me a break. When this is over, we all need therapy. Are you sure you're okay, Cécile?"

Another smile as she retreated into the bathroom to throw the bloodied tissue away. "Really, I already feel better."

Didn't buy it. She was being evasive. Hadn't given me her full story, either. But what could I do? Nick was the bigger of my concerns.

So we went up to the bed. I put my hands around Nick's head, lifting it off the pillow. In sleep, it was way heavier than I would have thought possible. Nick's hair was sticky and sweaty. That aside, it was like lifting a frozen leg of ham out of a freezer.

With the fingers of her good hand, Cécile stuffed the gauze behind his neck. Big eyes scintillating in the duskiness. Reached over the pillow, between my arms. Missed what she was aiming for.

Nick's hand slid off his stomach and fell onto the mattress.

Cécile and I froze.

Nick's breathing remained calm. Rumbling. But his hand . . . What it dropped onto the white sheet, what it had apparently been grasping all along, was a pointy piece of rock.

Nick's relic. His fetish. The Maudit's summit.

What came to mind was the centurion's spearhead, the one that pierced the side of Jesus Christ. The same spearhead that was said to have been in the possession of several bloodthirsty Roman emperors. Later, stolen by Persian armies. Later still, by the Nazis. A relic like that, it's just a thing. We decide to imbue it with significance, but all the same, it left behind a trail of blood.

If you knew anything about voodoo, if you knew anything about magical artifacts, you knew that simply throwing them away was no more than postponing the inevitable. That's why I carefully lowered Nick's head, took the rock off the mattress, and put it away inside the nightstand.

We'll worry about that later.

Cécile and I exchanged looks. "Come on, let's do it."

So I lifted his head from the pillow again and she started to swaddle, a tad clumsily with only a hand and a half, but it went pretty well until, halfway, Nick's mouth already covered, the muscles behind his face suddenly tightened and he said, "Did you forget to strap it?"

Cécile moaned and her hands jerked. I stood paralyzed, with Nick's head in my hands. The only sounds the wind bashing against the chalet and my heart thumping in places I didn't know was possible.

Nick's eyes remained shut. What he'd said was in English, not Dutch. Not his mother tongue. Mumbled, muffled, but still comprehensible, he muttered, "Jesus."

And me: "Shh. Go to sleep."

I felt his shoulders flexing as if he shrugged, and he said, "Oh well, it's gone. Nothing you can do about it now. Focus, man, we've still got a long way to go."

That was it. Whatever delusional dialogue he was hallucinating on, it was over now. He sank back into sleep. Cécile rushed forward and wrapped the last bands around his face. Clipped the fastener in place. I carefully lowered his head onto the pillow. Glad it was out of my hands.

My mummy, motionless on his tomb.

His nose sticking out of the gauze like an island.

It didn't feel right.

What it needed was a black, half-moon arc. What it needed was crossed edges for cupid cheeks. Didn't have a Sharpie, but there was a ballpoint in Nick's pencil case.

"Why are you doing that?" Cécile asked.

"For good luck."

"A smiley mouth. That's fucking creepy."

I examined the results. "Yeah, okay. You're right . . ."

"Wait, I have something else." Cécile was gone before I could say anything, into the hall, up the stairs. Me alone with Dr. Jekyll. Sleeping. *Smileying.* Thinking, *This way you'll always know it's me and never mistake me for someone else. When I smile, you don't have to be scared of me, okay?*

Cécile came back with two bright orange rubber earplugs. "I always have these with me, to help me sleep in a strange bed," she said. "But I doubt if there'll be much sleeping tonight anyway . . ."

Quick thinking. I squeezed them flat and gently eased them into Nick's ears. Call it overkill, but I took his wireless Beats from his nightstand, switched them on, and carefully lowered the leather cushions onto his ears.

"Noise cancellation," I said.

Cécile nodded. "Do you think it's a good idea to close the shutters?"

I nodded. As she opened the terrace door and I shivered from the cold wind that swept into the bedroom, I jumped at the chance. I bowed over Nick, slithered my hand into his sweatpants pocket, and found his phone. I mean, me and no iPhone—can't believe I'd survived this long. The screen lit up, everything around me suddenly darker cuz Cécile had unhooked the panels and shut them. 2:26. LOUISE GREVERS, 3 MISSED CALLS. MOM AND DAD HOME, 5 MISSED CALLS. All right already; keep your hats on. But, sorry, my turn now. I pried out the SIM holder with a safety pin, chucked Nick's card out, took mine out my pants pocket and inserted it. Doubled focus to keep my fingers from trembling. Swipe—passcode—unlock—waiting.

"Sam, come here a minute," I heard coming from outside.

"Wait, give me a sec."

Swisscom. 4G. A second later: *ploink*, JULIA AVERY, 36 MISSED CALLS. Swipe, and I called her back. My call skipping mountains and oceans in nanoseconds, bouncing off satellites, straight to voicemail.

"Sam," in the doorway.

And I shout, "What!" Opened WhatsApp. Entered my details—*Come the fuck on*—verified my number—*How long does this have to take?*

And Cécile said, "I think I see someone. Someone's going up the mountain."

8

"In Japan," I said, peering through binoculars, "in times of famine, they took the oldest members of the family to mountaintops or faraway forests and left them there to die." Focusing between rushing gray-white patches, I said, "The Inuit would leave them behind on the ice."

There. Hundreds of yards up, right on the boundary where the storm clouds swallowed up the snow-covered slopes above the village.

"In America they call it 'granny dumping' and it generally happens in nursing homes." Adjusting the view from blurred to sharp, I said, "Did you know that the numbers spike in the week before Christmas? That's when American families start to get hungry and don't feel like going on weekend visits anymore."

And Cécile said, "You talk too much."

"I always do that when I'm nervous." I lowered the binoculars. "That's the funnel that leads up to the Maudit, isn't it?"

The chalet stood on a steeply declining stretch of ground and the master bedroom downstairs bordered on the lower terrace, which looked out on the slope in the west. Cécile, as she'd gone out to close the shutters, had shivered from the phantom electricity in her neck and turned around. Stared up. Something had moved, she said. In the funnel. Against all that whiteness. Barely distinguishable. She first thought it was chamois. An ibex maybe. Then she realized it was a person. A dot, plodding upward in the snow.

November, avalanche risk level 4, storm coming—this was *so* not climbing season.

Meanwhile, on WhatsApp, a gazillion messages from Julia. I read only the last one, which said,

I really hope nothing has happened to you bro

and I texted back,

I'm OK, CALL ME.

One fucking gray tick, that's all I got.

So the two of us with the binoculars from the drawer in the hall, bringing that figure up close.

"It's a woman," Cécile pondered. The wind biting our cheeks, the curtains billowing out of the house.

Peering toward the slope, I said, "Lemme have a look."

Once you located the spot, once you synchronized reality with the prism image, you couldn't *not* see it anymore. The stooped figure, progressing with slow, weary steps, zigzagging a trail through what looked like knee-deep snow. You thought you saw a walking stick. You thought you saw a flapping cloak. You couldn't say for sure, but there was something about the posture, about the grim perseverance against the elements, that made you convinced you were looking at an elderly woman. She seemed to crouch against a gust of powder snow. Then she went on. As if she were under some spell.

"What's she *doing* over there?" I mumbled. "She'll never make it back down before the storm."

And Cécile stating the obvious: "I don't think down is where she's headed, Sam."

Oh, fuck. The procession I'd witnessed this morning above the village. The alpenhorns. The crying folk.

Christ almighty.

I told Cécile about it, and that's how we got here.

"In Japan," I said, "they call it *ubasute*, which means 'abandonment of the elderly.'" I noticed that my fingers were starting to shake. "We can't just leave that poor woman to her fate, right?" Cécile yanked the binoculars out of my hands. "She'll freeze to death up there or die of exhaustion. If it's true, she climbed up at least 2,000 feet."

As if she were under some spell.

"What do you want to do, go after her?"

"Can't we call that helicopter pal of yours? That . . . whatsisname?"

"They'll never come, Sam. Don't you get it?"

"But we have to do *something*."

"Fine, so call 1414. That's the Rega's emergency number. But I'll bet you anything they won't fly out." She licked her lips and said, "Waitaminute, I lost her . . ."

Nick's phone still in my hand, I tapped the number and put the phone on speaker. Up there, you didn't need binoculars to see that the funnel-shaped incline where we'd seen that dot move before was now hidden from view. The storm had swallowed her up.

Ten points for dramatic timing, but at that exact moment, the first snowflakes started to fall from the sky.

"*Rega, wie cha ich dia helfen?*" a woman's voice asked in Schwyzerdütsch—a language *not* in my repertoire, for a change. Switching to French, I said that there was an elderly woman in the mountains who needed help.

"What is your location?"

"In Grimentz. She—"

"One moment, please. I will put you through to the OCVS in Valais."

Cécile blinked the snow away and stared into the storm. Rubbing herself and her cast arm warm, the only thing you could catch a glimpse of on the slope was gray rock quickly taking on that legendary "hazy shade of winter." Cécile herself going that good ol' "whiter shade of pale."

"Opération des secours Valaisanne, s'il vous plaît?" A man's voice this time. The same spiel about a woman in trouble above Grimentz. We'd seen her struggling through the snow, hundreds of yards up from the village, all alone, and the storm was coming.

"Above Grimentz, you say?"

"Yes. We're afraid she's lost, because she's in the clouds and the weather is getting worse by the minute."

"Are you able to indicate the exact location of where you saw her?"

Cécile leaned toward the phone and said, "On the southwest side of the village, there's a stream that flows through a steep funnel, which is called the Torrent de Maudit. This funnel extends all the way to the Vallée Maudit." She looked at me. "We saw her there."

"Did you say Vallée Maudit?" Even with the speaker's tinny sound, you could hear something about his voice had changed.

"Yes," Cécile said. "But not too high. I think at around 7 or 8,000 feet."

"And what is your location?"

"Grimentz."

Silence. So we'd seen her from the valley? Yes. And did we know her? No. Silence again. Above us, the wind was whistling through the frame of the roof.

"Can they send a helicopter?" Cécile asked.

"Well, I'm afraid we can't just do that, you see. We don't fly out in this weather. Too dangerous." Hesitation. "Are you absolutely certain you saw it right? It sounds like it was quite a way away from you . . ."

Flabbergasted, I said, "We have binoculars . . ."

"Maybe you saw a chamois or something."

"A chamois with a rococo walking stick?"

Cécile snatched the phone away from me and said, "Listen to me, pal. I'm a doctor. You are losing valuable time. You *must* send a chopper, or I'll guarantee you this woman will die up there."

Defensive spluttering. He'd see what he could do. Asked if we could be reached at this number and said they'd call us back. Hung up.

I looked at Cécile. "Do you think they'll send a chopper?"

"'Course they won't. I just wanted to know if he knew. And he did. It's exactly what Benjamin said. They don't fly out to the Maudit."

After the call, we went back inside. Closed the shutters in front of Nick's bedroom windows. Nick in pitch-dark, his earplugs and his headphones and his bandages—maybe it was the storm, but suddenly it didn't feel like enough of a safety net. Maybe it was the fact that there was someone out there, lost and wandering in that godforsaken wilderness, but all of a sudden my face felt heavy and it was like all the chalet's darkest corners were moving around.

Twenty minutes later they called back. Us upstairs, the first snow sticking to the windows. Everything was all right, the operator said. There was a hut up there on one of those pastures, and they'd contacted them. Apparently the woman had been headed there and was inside by now, safe and sound and warming herself by the fire.

"No need to worry, *monsieur et madame*," he said, "but thank you for your vigilance. It's good deeds like this that save lives."

No way was there a hut up there.

Nothing in Nick's manuscript, nothing in Nick's stories, had indicated there was a hut up there. Nothing that you knew about that ghost mountain made it even remotely *likely* there was a hut up there.

Beyond Grimentz, the mountains were still.

"All right, thank you for calling back," I said. "One last question. The valley here is full of screaming. Should I want to send someone up as a sacrifice, do I direct the offering to the Catholic God or preferably to a more primitive deity like Huitzilopochtli?"

He hung up.

"Sorry, but you Switzers have no sense of humor." Slipping the phone back into my pocket, I said, "Come on. We're going to pay someone a visit."

Cécile jolted up and said, "What? Who?"

"I know someone in the village who's also an outsider. And anyway, she's been shirking her duties for about three weeks now, so she owes us an explanation."

"No, Sam! We can't go out now, you know what my mamie said about the Morose . . ."

"But aren't *you* curious?" I asked. "Don't you wanna know what that ceremony was all about? That old lady doing her Via Dolorosa?"

Cécile looked at me like she was again balancing on the verge of a meltdown. I squeezed her shoulder and said, "The last one to trek into that valley was Nick, remember?" Flashing my best Sam Avery smile, I said, "This is our only chance to find out anything. And the Morose, it hasn't started yet. Your mamie said it would sound like the valley is 'bewailing the death of the world.' The only thing I've heard crying up to now is a little bit of wind."

Total BS, but it seemed to ease her anyway and she sighed. "Of course I'm curious too. Sorry, I'm just out of my wits. Yes, I predicted they wouldn't fly out, but if they really did send that woman out into the storm, then it's a ritual of life and death. That freaks me out." Her eyes dark, she said, "How do you do it?"

How did I do what?

"Your act. Your jokes. Your always being hyper, always on the ball."

I laughed. "Sweetheart," I said, "*sugarplum*," I said, "sleeping downstairs is the person I love more than anyone in the whole wide world, and that mountain inside him is sucking up his soul. You think I'm not scared? I'm scared as fuck. Yeah, I'm scared of what's out there, I'm scared of what's about to happen tonight, but what scares me the most is that soon nothing will be left of him. And I still have to tell him the most important things of our relationship."

And that was the truth. Cold, honest, bulletproof.

"My act," I said, "is all I got."

Cécile gently squeezed my hand. "Thank you. That makes me feel much better."

9

According to the leather-bound instruction folder, Maria Zufferey-Silva de Souza lived in an elegant chalet in the upper part of the village. Even the ten yards between it and where you parked your Focus seemed too far to walk. Even the few steps descending from the street to the front door seemed a bridge too far, in the building storm.

Ten yards, and from the chimney, you saw wisps of smoke being immediately swallowed up by the white of the snow. You saw the valley through a haze of maybe a hundred swirling shapes that rendered the landscape unrecognizable and made your senses go haywire. A mere ten yards, but the sounds you heard coming out of the mountains could make you go insane. Each blitz by the wind more vengeful than the last. Every bellowing roar an octave higher. It prickled your scalp. It made you look up with constant certainty that there was someone right behind you, someone or something, a hovering, open mouth.

We rang the bell and waited. Just when you thought no one was coming, the door opened and a hot, yellow glow spread over the gray and white of the outside world. Maria wearing a purple fleece cardigan, she eyed us, startled. "My god, what are you doing out?"

"Madame Zufferey-Silva de Souza." I smiled, spreading my arms. Don't lecture me on South European mothers. Don't ask, but a sense of decorum makes all the difference in the world. "Storm chasing, of course. This is Cécile Métrailler, a friend of mine. We actually wanted to ask for your help."

Maria's gaze drifted briefly to Cécile but quickly shifted back to me. "If it's about the cleaning, I'm sorry I didn't come. I have arthritis, and when it gets colder my hands start acting up." From inside the house, voices came blaring from the radio. "I'll tell Mr. and Mrs.—"

"It's not about the cleaning, Maria. I know you stopped coming because you're afraid of Nick. Honestly, with the Morose coming, we're also starting to feel a bit afraid."

She went pale. "So you know about that."

"Well, it wasn't in any of the Office du Tourisme's flyers, but yes. This morning there was this whole hoo-ha ceremony with alpenhorns and whatnot, and just now, right before it started snowing, we saw a woman walk into the mountains. All the way up there." Swinging my arm in a dramatic gesture, I said, "Precisely where Nick climbed the mountain last summer."

Maria covered her mouth with her hands. "So it's true. He was there . . ."

"You can say that again. That's why we want to know what you can tell us about—"

A shrill, maniacal wailing came down from the snow, so close that all three of us ducked. So close that it was *real*, that it penetrated into the fabric of our reality and left a screaming blot in it.

Maria, she practically dragged us into the hall. Slammed the door shut, bolted it. "Come inside quickly. You have to know . . ."

"Right, and that creepy screaming from the clouds." Shaking the snow out of my hair, I said, "Why don't you tell us about that too."

Echoes, Maria said, after she'd poured us some strong herbal mountain infusion. When the Morose heralded the oncoming of winter, you could hear them tumbling down on this side of the Gougra. The night was full of them. Lost wanderers who couldn't be saved but didn't die either.

She'd thought about us, that morning. To warn us. Give us instructions to get us through the night. Us, strangers in Grimentz, immigrants, like she had also once been. But that husband of hers, Monsieur Pascal Zufferey, he'd forbidden her to have anything to do with us. Pascal, at this hour in the village hotel, setting up a night of festivities for initiates. Playing folk songs on his Schwyzerörgeli. Villagers bombarding you with a wall of artificial sound as they guzzled themselves senseless on Cardinal draft. If you've ever been to a Swiss *Bierstube* during a *Ländlerfest*, you'd know why Maria would rather spend the whole scream-filled night binge-watching Netflix.

"I'm totally hooked on Scandinavian crime," she said.

That, and fado.

And all of it through her headphones, of course. Ten to one they had noise cancellation.

Sipping lavender tea in Maria's kitchen, all those closed shutters made you feel you were inside a coffin. On the dresser a birdcage; inside it the motionless shadow of an alpine chough staring at us. That bird staring and Maria saying that the valley above Grimentz had been a place of power from the get-go. That even in the Stone Age, the old Helvetians would bring their enemies up there. Their enemies and, when they finally got the picture, their elderly.

These elderlies, 'course they died up there.

And you can bet your ass one of them birds would be there in no time flat to make room for your soul to toodle-oo by snacking on your eyes. *Whoosh*, and your last breath, it doesn't come from your frostbitten lips but from your empty eye sockets.

None of that was unique to this place, Maria said. This was just your standard mountain phenomenon. What this place got in the way of exclusivity was that, at that point, the souls had all been possessed by the Maudit.

At that point, the souls had been upgraded to immortality.

Those old-world Helvetians, their druids weren't all that cuckoo. They'd known that in the spiritual evolution of man, there was a breakup. A postmortem polarization. Good and bad. Everything in you that had been good reincarnated in one of those birds. All you had to do was clear your life away on that mountain's altar and you would rise up like a phoenix.

Free of sin. No luggage. And for good.

"What you saw this morning," Maria said, "was a farewell ceremony."

People always found ways to turn nature to their own advantage. To milk a miracle.

When the oldest villagers had the feeling they'd just about seen all there was to see, they chose to dress warmly and go for a stroll. One last pilgrimage. The ballad to a fulfilled life, in order for them to return as a patron saint. Not everyone, of course. It took a certain amount of self-sacrifice to give up your spot in paradise for a spot on your children's gable front or mantelpiece. But each year, you always had a few.

"This morning, two have gone up," Maria said. "The patriarch of the Gosselin family, who is eighty-seven years old but still mobile, and Muriel Solioz, the mother of a woman I clean for. An absolute darling, ninety-three just last week, and totally senile."

"And you just . . . dumped them in the woods?" Cécile asked. "As in actually left them behind?" She made no effort to disguise her disgust. "I don't know what's more incredible, that you sacrifice your elderly or that you actually think they can reach that valley at their age. That's a climb of more than 5,000 feet, in the worst possible conditions."

"Let me tell you, that's not even half of it," Maria said. "Old Mrs. Solioz hasn't been able to get out of bed without assistance for three years. I can personally vouch for that. But when Madame Ducourtil came into her room two days ago, she was on her feet at the window, looking up. Madame was calling out her mother's name, and when she looked back she said, 'It's time to go.' Then we knew that the Morose was upon us." Maria, absentmindedly flipping her phone in her hands, seemed to look past us. "Well, and because of the birds, of course. They sense it too."

You had to look at it like a ship waiting in port until the winds were favorable to sail out. The Morose, venturing into it was perilous . . . except if you *wanted* to go up.

If you *wanted* it to hypnotize you.

"Michel Gosselin was the first to leave, this morning," Maria said. "After that, they pushed Mrs. Solioz in her wheelchair to the edge of the woods. I heard that she stood up, hugged her family, and walked away. It was beautiful."

"How do you know all about it?" Cécile asked.

"The neighborhood app," Maria said. She turned her phone screen toward Cécile and said, "News travels fast here."

Sometime in the next few days, a chough would come and tap on the Ducourtils' window. A *Pyrrhocorax graculus*. This bird, possessed with all the good in Mother Solioz, would bring prosperity to the family for the rest of their lives.

According to the superstition, that is.

And the bad?

That was left behind, up there.

It would resonate against the mountains like an echo.

"What you'll hear screaming tonight," Maria said, "is all the misery of everyone who ever lost or gave their lives up there."

You could see them, Maria said, the screaming dead. You could see them falling. Out of the corner of your eye. The embodiments of human error. Crushed souls. Without hope, without love. All that remained of a person after their humanity had been slammed out of them. You could see them, but most of all, you could hear them. On restless nights, when storms raged in the mountains and conditions were the same as on the day they died, you could hear their dying screams even here in the village, in the clouds, against the slopes, in the valley.

Echoes, people called them here. Possessed by the Maudit, they dwelled in the valley, eternally drawn to the mountain. Sometimes they would come down and show themselves in places they held dear. A particular spot in the valley. Their childhood homes. But most of the time they would stay up there. Screaming their sins out at the gates of hell.

"During the Morose," Maria said, "it gets worse. Then the wind has a way of blowing through the notch of the valley that makes it carry all those sounds." Drinking steaming tea, Maria said, "Believe me. You've never heard anything like it."

No matter how awful it got, if you listened to it long enough, it enchanted you. You got the irresistible urge to join them—their voices a siren song from the mountains.

"They say the dead want to embrace you," Maria said. "That they want to warm themselves with your life. Because they're so cold. So very cold."

That was like a bullet in the head. Augustin's phone call. Back in Amsterdam. In the middle of the night. That trembling, whispering voice: *Kalt. Kalt. Kalt.* The static on the line, like the wind on the glacier.

What Maria had told us, it was something out of a horror story. But in the coffin of Maria's kitchen, with the rhythmic rattling of the heating and the radio blaring Schweizer spiel and the sporadic, almost imperceptible shuddering of the house in the storm, any horror story could be true.

I hadda clear my throat to get some sound going. Pointed to the motionless shadow in the birdcage and said, "May I ask you who that is?"

"That," said Maria, "is Catherine Zufferey, Pascal's mother." She sniffed, then added, "She's a real bitch."

In English.

As if she was scared the li'l pecker would understand her, otherwise.

"Can I look at her?"

"Do as you please."

It was just a bird. No white, cataract eyes. No clotted blood on the beak indicating that she was dead already. None of that stuff, but still your heart was thumping in your throat. Even if you bought all that karmic shit and accepted that only what's virtuous lived on in these birds, you still got goose bumps looking at one.

Unnatural, I thought. There was something unnatural about the way it quietly sat there, staring at us. Something almost sacral.

Except that I got the feeling it was ogling our eyes like a seagull would ogle a pile of oysters.

"How do you know it's her?" I asked.

"Oh, you know," Maria said. "Dead or alive, a mother-in-law always has her ways of showing she doesn't like you."

I turned to her. "Have you ever seen her echo?"

The way she tightened her lips into a pale stripe, you would have thought she was through talking. But she spoke anyway. "Once."

That's all she would say, no matter how much I insisted.

We really had to leave now, she said. The storm could break loose any minute, and she didn't want to be responsible if we were still out on the street. But before we even had our coats on, Maria grasped me tight, and now there was heartfelt fear in her eyes.

"Please, take him away from here." Those eyes big and round and sparkling gray, she implored, "That friend of yours. I don't know how much longer he'll be safe here. Take him to the valley and stay away."

"I'm sorry," I said, "but what exactly do you mean by that?"

"He's been up there. No one who goes up there ever comes back. He brought the Maudit into our midst, and ever since, the whole community has been disrupted. *Nature* has been disrupted. And it's all concentrated around your house, or wherever your friend has been seen."

I could still hear Maria, but my eyes were staring into the dim light in the hall.

All those sounds you could constantly hear on the edge of your auditory range.

All those motions you could constantly see just beyond the corners of your eyes.

Constantly around you, the dead. Always. Everywhere. You couldn't see them, but you could *feel* them. Like walking through a spider's web in an autumn forest.

Julia's screaming on FaceTime: *Who is that woman? Who is that woman in the corner behind you?*

Maria's hands, pale and cold, closed around mine. "I'm telling you this because I'm also an outsider. Even after twenty-three years they don't see you as one of their own. I know what people here think about foreigners. When people are scared, they react viscerally. But their fear is real." Maria, she shook my hands firmly. "Some people in the WhatsApp group are calling for action. There's currently a stalemate. But I don't know how long sentiments will keep up. If something were to happen . . ."

I said I'd take her advice to heart. "Thank you for not, uh . . . reacting viscerally."

Maria laughed, but there was something sad about her eyes. "*Querido,*" she said, "*eu sou Portuguesa.*"

10

Outside, it was dusky all over. Dusky and snowy. The world outside of Maria's chalet a colorless cold. What used to be the Focus was now a four-door igloo by the sidewalk. I was shocked by the amount of snow that had built up in such a short time.

As soon as Maria had shut the door behind us, the storm had me on my knees. My arm hooked around the steep rock walkway's balustrade, the other around Cécile's shoulders, gusts of snow smacked me in the face and took my breath away. Snow and dark and Cécile and me, our skin, our eyes, the details of the world around us an indistinguishable blur. The roaring of the wind and, up there, unmistakable, echoes. I plopped down behind the wheel, pulled the door shut. Cécile did the same on her side, all of it now shut out.

The windows started to fog up almost immediately. I fired up the engine, turned the fans on hot and high. Let the windshield wipers *swish, swish, swish* two semicircles in the snow. With nothing else out there in the dark, I turned on the brights, but that turned visibility to subzero, so I switched back to heads.

When I turned onto the road with crunching rubber, I actually wanted to ask Cécile what she thought about the whole story, but one sideways glance and it was clear that we were beyond headspace for a debriefing. I couldn't blame her. After all of this, my own Manipura needed some management, too.

I reached forward and wiped a peephole on the windshield with my sleeve.

"Please drive carefully," Cécile said. "Especially in the turns. You can steer all you like in this weather, but the car can still slide straight on into a snowbank. Or off a cliff."

The byway was diametrically opposed to how you'd like a byway to be. Unpaved. A quarter inch wider than the Focus. Beyond the last chalets, it plowed through a fallow slope, probably used as a piste in winter. To your right, safe and rising steeply. To your left, just as steep, but down. If you went into a skid here, the barbed wire wouldn't be enough to keep you from a backyard visit to an empty vacation chalet a hundred yards below.

We crawled up, snowflake by snowflake.

About a third of a mile beyond the village, the leaning pylon of a cableway loomed up. The cables were swaying drunkenly in the wind. Or maybe it was an optical illusion. Everything was moving, layer upon layer of swirling snow that swallowed up even the last remaining light. Behind it, the woods, nothing more than a massive, dark downward-sloping streak.

Can't tell you why, but I stopped the car.

"What are you doing?" Cécile asked.

It was like something weird had blown into the atmosphere. A held-breath feeling of danger that kept me from driving on. I looked out the side window. Suddenly, my skin started to crawl. Started to tingle, as if invisible fingertips were sliding softly over it. All at once, the isolated intimacy of the car too oppressive, and I opened the door. Snow lashed my face.

Behind me Cécile, alarmed, "Hey, what are you doing?"

Can't tell you why, but in some funny way it cheered me up to set foot into the snow.

For a brief moment the storm seemed to subside. I watched my breath freezing up into little clouds. Listened, fascinated, to the tempting darkness.

From the far faraway, it was coming nigh.

It had found us.

It started with a scream. Then a second. And a third. And a fourth. Till a whole chorus of lamentation was unleashed upon us from everywhere at once. Saying it made the hairs on my neck stand up wouldn't be a cliché but a total cliché soufflé, but sho'nuff that's what happened. It penetrated every pore on my skin. Every fiber in my body. There was a dissonance to it that made every axon in my nervous system go haywire. It was the kind of wailing that would make wolves cower away with their tails between their legs. So much pain, so much suffering, so much hatred, and so much hollowness: only the dead could cry like that.

It was the screaming of hundreds. Of thousands.

The Morose.

Cécile, she reached over her cast arm, dragged me back into the car and slammed the door shut. "Step on it," she said.

I gaped at her in astonishment. Sluggish and with a feeble smile, as if I'd just come out of sedation, I said, "Listen to them—the children of the night. What music they make!"

And *whap*—pimp slap. Me bouncing off the car door, as far from Cécile as I could get, shouting, "Dude, what'd you do that for?"

"Just to make sure." She pressed the auto door lock button. Pressed the radio button, Muse blaring at us through the speakers. Shouted, "Now step on it!"

She turned the volume all the way up.

So I slammed my foot down. Rear wheels whizzing round, slipping, spewing fountains of snow. Then the tires got a grip and we shot forward.

We fled through the dark with a horde of banshees on our tails.

The screaming gnawed its way into you, despite the engine's roaring. Despite Muse, our artificial defensive perimeter. It gnawed your mind away. Stubbed it out. The screaming dead. The wailing dead.

If these were the outer frequencies, I shuddered to think what it would be like up there.

Cécile screamed, "Look out!"

My left wheel ricochets off a bump and shoots to the left. I take my foot off the gas, grip the wheel tight till I feel the Focus is back on course, then put my foot back on the pedal, too fast and too deep. Us in a skid again and Cécile yelling. Cécile, gripping the door handle and shouting, "Oh my god, look at that! *Look at that!*"

I couldn't see anything, or maybe I *did* see something right then, something I didn't *want* to see, so I only saw flying snow, only the road back in view and my own breath—that's how cold it was inside the Focus.

Mouth on strike, I cannonballed us down the mountain and somehow managed to get the car onto the road to Hill House without trading in our souls.

"When we get inside," I shouted, so she could hear what I was saying, "when we get in, the first thing we do is turn on the stereo and the TV." I shouted, "Then we shutter ourselves in." Shouted, "You do the kitchen and upstairs, the attic. I'll do downstairs. We'll do the living room and terrace doors together. And keep shouting!" The Focus bumping over the bridge, I shouted, "I want to hear you, okay?"

Okay. She nodded. Good.

Hill House loomed up out of the snow like a nightmare.

I parked right in front of the porch steps. Kept the motor running. Let Muse blast away.

"Okay," I shouted. "I count to three, then we run."

I thought, *Cut engine. Open door. Run.*

Thought, *Engine. Door. Run.*

Cécile, she called, "What do we do against the sound?"

"Cover your ears and sing."

"What?"

"Sing!"

"Sing what?"

"What difference does it make? 'Bohemian Rhapsody' for all I care. If you sing, you listen to your own voice and not to what's out there screaming!"

I counted down, three, two, one, and we were off.

And fuck.

Fuck fuck fuck!

The first leak in my watertight plan: the moment I turned the car key, Muse fell silent and the night's wailing flared up and I needed my hands for, like, everything.

I started to sing, a loud and agitated "*Yalalalala!*" Seriously. That was the extent of my originality. It wasn't even melodic.

'Course Cécile was way gone by now.

After wiggling out of my seatbelt, after wiggling myself out of the car, all the sounds started to intermingle. My song, my *yalalalala*, the wailing chorus of echoes, Cécile's surprisingly euphonic "*I see a little silhouetto of a man*"—a wall of sound igniting a chain reaction that made you forget everything else. Not even that different from the way the Maudit took possession of Nick. The slamming of the car door. The roaring of the wind. Sound that bewitched you.

Cécile's superb soprano, "*Thunderbolt and lightning, very, very frightening me!*"

Our head, the host. We, the possessed.

That's how we made it to the front door. That's how we made it in. And that's how we somehow managed to carry out our plan. To shut out the sound. To insulate the chalet by drowning it out with might and main.

The TV on SF1, continuous news voices. The stereo pumping some French pop song. Volume all the way up.

Running blindly from room to room, it was like the vibrating air in the chalet was supercharged. All the lights on to dispel the darkness from every corner. Listening everywhere for traces of screaming. Anywhere you'd open a window in order to close its shutters, anywhere it would blow in with the wind. Everywhere, *wham*, the exorcism.

Oh yeah, and Nick.

Ten out of ten on the freaky fucked-up scale: when I went into the pitch-black bedroom, he was sitting *straight up* in bed. Eyes shut. Beats still on his ears, but his head tilted, like he was listening.

On the bandages, that smiley mouth.

I licked my lips and said, "Nick?"

Nothing. I could just push him back gently and he stayed asleep as if nothing had happened. But he *had* been sitting straight upright. I hadn't imagined that.

Cécile and me, we bumped into each other in the living room, and after everything there had been shut tight too, we stared at each other. Listened.

For dying screams *dans la marge de la marge*. In the extreme outer frequencies. Nothing. Right?

Nothing.

And exhale.

11

Right, so we're now jumping four hours into the future so I can tell you about a loud bang. Spoiler alert: that evening at nine, that bang would announce the end of my life as I knew it. And I wonder, could I have foreseen anything in the hours in between? Caught a glimpse of that black aura as a precursor of how unavoidably we were headed for disaster?

At six I was in the kitchen Antonio Carluccio-ing a veggie lasagna all'uovo. Tomatoes/zucchini/goat cheese. Cécile at the kitchen table, hair in a towel turban cuz her modus operandi for processing the preceding events was to seclude herself and take a long, hot bath. Face like the "Before" photo in a Prozac ad. Looking back now, that coulda been a hint. But what could I have done? Her face had looked like the "Before" photo in a Prozac ad *all day*.

We ate at seven. Ramses under the couch in the living room, flattened in the corner, eyes big and scared, and no matter how much I here-kitty-kittied him, no matter how much I tried sucking up to him with Sheba Fresh & Fine, he absolutely refused to come out. *Bzzz*—hello-o!—hint, hint. Think I got it? Nope. Simply thought he was hiding from those dying screams coming from the mountains.

At eight we were sitting by the hearth, the fire burning. Cécile and me alone and afraid in a house full of shadows and too many dark spaces where you constantly thought you saw something flash by out of the corner of your eye. By this point it was almost funny. I found a radio station that played nonstop yodel music. Cécile told the story of a Tyrolean who'd showed off his yodeling skills under a cliff and got buried under sixty tons of limestone, drilled off by the vibrations. With everything that was happening around you, the claustrophobia of the lockdown and the shuddering of the roof, you just hadda laugh. If you didn't laugh, you'd join in the screaming with the chorus of echoes.

And then it was nine.

Then we heard the bang and the laughing was over.

12

I whispered, "What do we do now?"

Cécile stared past me, down the stairs, and with hollow eyes and trembling lips whispered, "Go look."

I put one foot on the top stair. Forced the other one a step lower. Stood still, undecidedly.

Whispered, "I'm too scared."

The problem was the sound we'd heard. That bang. *First* the bang, massive and dull. A sound you could interpret in any number of ways. A bowling ball falling onto a carpet. An avalanche shaken loose high up the slopes above the chalet. A body rolling off a bed.

Then a couple of thundering bursts, vivid and sharp, and there was no misunderstanding this. A fist banging against the shutters downstairs. Against the closed panel doors in front of the room where Nick was sleeping. Or *had been* sleeping.

The problem was, you didn't know whether someone was trying to get *in* or get out.

"If that's Nick, then he's already opened the terrace doors." Cécile, her breath halting gasps of escaped air, said, "It couldn't be anyone else besides Nick, could it?"

More bangs. Hard. Loud. Compelling.

In the ensuing silence, the yodel music had lost all its treacly jolliness. It now sounded only screechy. Eerie. In the hall, much further from the source, the lederhosen trio's harmonies were disintegrating into an uncanny dissonance. It made you flinch. It made you shiver. Till you realized the cacophony was entering the chalet through the ether, not through the speakers.

Only then did it register that here in the hall you could hear the groaning of the roof. The storm's infectious wailing.

Once you'd heard it, you couldn't unhear it. Then it started to imprint its message into your brain, so deep that you couldn't reach.

Downstairs, nothing. Only the dark.

I had to be quick. There were no other options. I licked my lips and whispered, "Okay, let's go look."

So I go down the stairs, as quietly and as quickly as I can. Downstairs, the hall was empty. The door to the bedroom shut. At the top of the stairs, Cécile, she hadn't budged. I gestured to her to join me, mimed *Come on*, but she just stood there, staring down. Chin slightly up. Lips parted.

My concern for Nick overpowered my fear, so I walked on down the hall. Down here our auditory eclipse wavered even more. Here, the yodeling and the Morose morphed into an utterly off-key ensemble, a depraved, perverse sound, which made you aware of sounds *beyond* sounds, sounds not suitable for human consumption.

I listened at the door. Nothing. A bulging nothing. An enormous nothing.

I opened the door.

A wet, icy cold wave hit me in the face.

The room was as good as dark, but in the light coming from upstairs, I saw Nick standing in front of the closed shutters. Without his Beats.

The bandages hung in loops around his neck.

I was riveted to the ground. The cold in my face might have been just an illusion of the glacier wind, an echo of the storm in a hidden valley—but what was melting on my shoulders and cheekbones was powder snow, and that was real. Real.

Suddenly you knew you were being watched.

I spun around. No one in the hall. Only shadows.

And me in a rush back to the stairs. Expecting Cécile to be staring downstairs, but she was gone. The hall upstairs was also empty.

"Cécile!" I hissed. Looking over my shoulder, then up again, louder this time. "*Cécile!*"

Only the yodeling. The screaming of the dead.

My legs, I had no control over them anymore. They brought me back to the bedroom. Back into the darkness. Beyond the darkness, the screaming got louder.

Nick was gone.

Where he'd just been standing, there now were only the shutters. I rubbed my eyes. Big, dancing spots of nothing. Suddenly my heartbeat a rumbling drumroll. My breath, AWOL. I couldn't think straight anymore. Me, reduced to sheer reactive action.

The darkness came at me.

The doorpost beat an almost imperceptible rhythm under my fingertips. The wood trembling from the screams coming through the walls. Hypnotizing me.

Each step brought you deeper into the bedroom. With each step, you saw more dark space devoid of Nick.

The problem was you didn't know whether you had to protect Nick from the Morose or yourself from Nick, or all of us from some invisible thing.

One step deeper.

I called out, "Nick?"

No answer.

The bathroom. That was the only possibility. That, or under the bed.

The door to the bathroom stood open.

Inside, it was dark.

And in that dark, there were shapes.

I stared at them, waiting for my eyes to adjust. Expecting to see Nick's shape standing there.

The bathroom was *full* of Nick's shapes.

Human shapes, motionless, side by side. At least eight. Or a dozen.

There were people in the bathroom.

I blinked my eyes and the people, they were now *closer*, the two in front were standing in the doorway, and after that—a hole in my memory. A blinding flash, as if my brain had short-circuited. What I do remember is that I Usain Bolted through the hall, that I stumbled up the stairs, that I grazed the skin off my shin against a step, that I reached the upstairs hall.

Light, light, welcome light. Light to bask in. Music to bask in. It drowned out everything else here, and that was good, cuz suddenly electricity was flowing through my brain stem again, all those cells suddenly glowing with regained life, and I thought, *Those people downstairs. The people in the bathroom. What the fuck was that?*

And where's Nick?

And where the fuck is Cécile?

Into the living room. No Cécile. Only the fire, crackling softly. Considered taking a log out with the tongs and dropping it onto the carpet so we'd be free of this business *tout de suite*.

Cécile. I hadda find her.

Christ, the people in the bathroom. Those people. Those people!

All the outside doors were shut. Cécile's shoes, still in the hall, drying next to mine. No one had run away. The kitchen. Empty. Ran to the bathroom on the ground floor. Empty. The toilet, dark and empty.

Upstairs. 'Course, her own room. After her bath, she'd put all her stuff up in the attic. The stairwell narrow, a heavy wooden ladder leading up. Steep. Dark. But there was a light on upstairs. Sound of a continuous weather report blaring out of the small, old-fashioned TV set. More auditory eclipse.

And me up the ladder.

In the attic's vestibule only the dim, phantom shape of the drying rack. The ironing board. The light shone from behind the wall of the sleeping area. Boards cracked when you shifted your weight on them.

Cécile's name had almost passed my lips, but the sound died even before it had been born. There she was, panting, sniffing, sucking in too much air with each breath. Busy filling a syringe out of an ampoule. Her cast hand trembling so fiercely that the colorless liquid in the ampoule was sloshing around and she had to triple-try piercing the needle into it. On the bed, spread out on a towel, next to her wide-open Anna Field weekend bag, a second needle and a second ampoule and an opened pack.

And I'm no medicine man, but I sure as hell knew this wasn't an insulin injection. No cortisone shot.

She wasn't prepping this for herself.

I said, "Cécile?"

That was enough to make her jump with a yelp. She turned around, pulled the needle out of the ampoule, liquid spattering everywhere.

"Sam! I . . ."

"What are you doing?"

Her eyes wide. Her look one big neon confession. Suddenly, you understood it all. The whole charade. The whole reason for her being here. Cécile hadn't come to Grimentz to help Nick and me out of a fix . . . but to help *herself*.

And granted, what I next did, I did without thinking. I just wanted to overpower her. Yank the syringe out of her hands. I strode toward her, and

Cécile saw me coming. Too late, I saw that she was feeling around inside her sling, that she'd taken something out of it. When I grabbed her right wrist and pulled it away, she pressed her cast hand and its small surprise against my midriff.

And *bzzzzzzzzzzzzzt*—

And I went down.

And I screamed.

And the pain!

There was no blackout. No sense of time passing. No discontinuity. Only the most abominable pain ever. My muscles cramped up. For a second or so my heart seemed to stop. The attic's beams drifted toward me. Maybe the whole thing lasted just five seconds, but if that's true, they were the longest five seconds of my life. With Cécile bowing over me, a sensation like actual lightning was bolting right through my body. I literally saw stars, stars and comets in a kaleidoscope of colors.

Then it was over. Cécile, her voice, I heard her say, "Stay down." The voice somewhere far above me, she said, "I don't want to have to do it again, but I swear, if you get up you're going to go down again."

Get up? Who said anything about getting up? The only thing I wanted to do was moan, roll over the floor, spew out my whole repertoire of creative expletives.

Granted, not one of my finest moments.

When I finally opened my eyes, I saw that Cécile's face was plastered over with a sickening sheen. She was holding a stun gun in her hand. She'd Tasered me.

And I'd peed myself.

More than anything else, that totally pissed me off.

"*Cécile . . . Bitch!*" Tears in my eyes, my T-shirt soaked with sweat. "*What the fuck!*"

"It would have been better for you not to know," Cécile said, behind the needle and the ampoule. Sticking the former into the latter, she said, "If he could simply have died of an overdose."

And me lying there, my muscles burning as if I'd deadlifted the shit out of them.

"You can't see it, huh?" Cécile said. Drawing in the liquid, she said, "No you can't see it. There's a huge Sam-shaped blind spot in the way you look at the world." Said, "The boyfriend is blind, because the boyfriend is out of range."

And I yelled, "Blind to what?"

"He's a parasite, Sam!" Squirting air bubbles out of the needle, eyes possessed, she said, "Once he's touched you, once he's *cursed* you, he gets into your head and never leaves. He makes you *fall*."

And I said, "Fall?"

On TV, some guy in front of a map full of tightly packed lines, saying the storm had brought almost the entire Alps to a standstill. That much snow, he said, was unusual. And so early in the season.

Through the stairwell, through the cracks in the floor, the stereo yodeling its heart out. Deeper still into the chalet, where Nick should be, what you heard coming from there was nothing.

And Cécile said, "Oh, you have no idea." She laid the filled syringe on the towel and picked up the empty one. Took the second ampoule and said, "Did you really think I cut myself as a *defense mechanism*? That I bruise myself to prevent a *panic attack*?"

She let out a high-pitched, thin, scornful laugh and I thought, *She's gone totally nuts. She is* complètement coucou.

I tried to struggle up, but in two steps she was on me, brandishing the stun gun, and said, "Lie down! I meant what I said!"

And me twitching, me in the fetal position, arms raised to shield my body. "*Okay, okay! Go away! Don't! Get that fucking thing away from me!*"

If you've ever had the pleasure of being tasered, then you know why, the second time around, suspects always surrender to the cops.

"You really don't get it, huh?" she said. Back to her lethal cocktail, she said, "The only reason I hurt myself is because that's how I can prevent him from making me fall."

And me: "Cécile, what's in that needle?"

"Dr. Genet wrote in his suicide note that he had to know if it would ever stop. If the falling would ever stop." Her voice rising to a shriek, "*I heard him hit the ground, Sam! I heard him hit the ground! I won't let that happen to me!*"

And me: "*Oh god, what is in that needle?*"

And the guy on TV, producing all these snowfall charts from since the birth of Methuselah.

And downstairs, greatest yodel hits.

And Cécile, *squirt*, she said, "That's how he murdered Dr. Genet. That's how he murdered all those people in Amsterdam."

What the fuck was she talking about?

"Are you so blind?" She said, "Those people in the AMC, Sam! Your boyfriend is a mass murderer!"

My ears rattled. "Cécile, where did you . . . How the hell did he . . . Do you even hear what you're saying?" I stammered, "Nick would never . . ."

Me, so flabbergasted that I could only speak in mosaic.

Cécile took both syringes in her right hand and said, "It's regrettable, and it's unjust." With the stun gun in her left, "I know that Nick didn't choose to be like this. But there's no other way out now." Step, step, on the cracking floorboards, the black widow, she circled around me and said, "Just one more person has to die. One more death to prevent worse from happening."

And at that moment a dark rumbling sound rolled up through the stairwell, literally rocking the chalet to its foundations.

Nick.

The music stopped.

Cécile's eyes were bulging. Her whole body shivering. Quiet, halfway between the stairwell and me. Downstairs, the wind was wailing. Outside, the Morose was screaming.

And I shouted, "*Nick! Nick, look out! She's got a—*"

Bzzzzzzzzzzzzzt.

And it was like I'd been kicked by a mule into an electric fence.

And as I was rolling on the floor, as I was moaning with pain, Cécile started descending the stairwell.

13

Your boyfriend is a mass murderer.

Something awful was going on downstairs, but all I could think was, *Those people in the AMC, Sam.*

Are you so blind?

Once he's touched you, once he's cursed *you, he gets into your head and never leaves. He makes you* fall.

That's how he murdered all those people in Amsterdam.

Cécile's words, they seemed to have been branded into my brain by my all too recent electroconvulsive therapy session. And yet they were blown away by a roaring coming from downstairs, so inhuman that I'll have to get back to you on whether it boiled or froze my blood. Again, a thundering crash. Breaking glass, the buzz of fuses blowing. A shrill cry. The *bzzzzzzzzzzzzzt* of the stun gun. Quick footsteps.

Then, nothing.

What came up was a stiffening wind, so cold it made you shiver into a stupor.

What came up was the screaming of the Morose.

The echoes. *They had gotten in.*

Oh Jesus, what had Nick done? What had *Cécile* done?

Moaning, I got up. Almost fell over again straightaway. My whole body cramp city. It was like someone was wringing the juice out of all my muscles simultaneously.

I stumbled to the stairwell. Lowered my feet into it, leaning on the edges. Searching for the steps. The cold wrapping itself around them.

Down there, down in the hallway, lay legs.

I screamed, "Nick!"

The wind wailed. Gusts of snow sped through the hall. *The outside door was open.*

I almost fell down the stairs, reached the landing.

Nick was lying on one elbow, jerking all over, his face red and wet with sweat, and completely distressed, he cried, "Sam! Sam, help me! Help me, please!"

Nick. It was him, all the way. Not the Maudit.

And I didn't dare go to him.

It had been so awful he said, so cold he said, the pressure behind his face had gotten so bad he thought he'd never wake up again. And I just stood there under the stairwell, looking down at him. Raised my head to the polar wind billowing inside through the cave-black hole of the door to extinguish the heat rising up behind it. My yearning, my dependence, my addiction gone in a flash of the eye. Me, totally cold turkeyed by what I suddenly thought him capable of.

Asked if he was okay. If he was wounded. Asked where Cécile was, and Nick, he raised his hands to his scars and said, "Cécile?" His gaze fixed on the wet blotch on my jeans, he said, "What happened?" His face one twitch, one cramp, he said, "My whole body hurts."

I told him he'd been Tasered. That she must have literally Tasered the Maudit out of his head—for now. It's true, I said, Cécile was here and she wanted to kill him. One syringe was broken in a puddle on the tiles, the other had landed on the doormat and was still full of juice.

Whatever had happened, her plan had failed.

Nick, he looked past me, and I saw him go white. His knees knocking, his voice choked, he said, "What's going on out there?"

Yanked out of my apathy, I limped through that hall like I was stumbling through a wind tunnel toward a walk-in freezer. My breath clouding in the cold air, I wanted to reach outside to pull the front door shut, but I halted. Outside was hell. I have no other word for it. The wind a living, evil power that was tugging on my sweat-soaked shirt and sending uncontrollable shivers through my body. Ice crystals flew out of the dark and lashed my face, sparkling in the glow of the chalet's light. Massive volumes of snow had rendered the landscape unrecognizable. A choir of tormented voices was shrieking their lungs out from within the storm. They bewailed the death of the world. They screamed with the full pathos of human life.

The echoes were falling from the sky, and vaguely I noticed that it was already fogging up my brain, but what you were looking at was the footprints in the snow. A drunken trail swerving down the stairs to the right. Not to the Peugeot. Not to the village. But around the chalet, in the direction of Castle Rock. Moiry. The reservoir.

I roared, "*Cécile!*"

My voice didn't stand a chance as the night forced itself on me from all sides, dying scream by dying scream.

I shut the door and stumbled back into the hall. Cécile's sneakers, they were gone. In this weather, their thin leather would protect her feet from freezing for no more than ten minutes.

Nick in the meantime had lugged himself to his feet. He'd pulled a scarf off the coatrack and wrapped it around his face. "Is that the Morose?" he asked. "Is that what her grandmother told you about?"

Yes.

"Did Cécile go outside?"

Er, yes.

"If we don't go after her, she'll die out there."

And I said, "Did you hear me? She wanted to *kill* you."

Nick's face turned distant. "Can you really blame her?"

I looked at him.

Thinking, *And you will also find out what it's like to fall. To fall . . . and to fall . . . and to fall . . . and to fall.*

The boyfriend is blind, because the boyfriend is out of range.

I walked past him, and damned if I didn't go faint, so close to him. Damned if I didn't go all dizzy. Then I reached the living room and turned the radio back on. Said it had to stay on till this whole shitstorm had died down. Said this is your auditory eclipse. Nick, he seemed to somehow understand and didn't ask questions.

My lips trembling, I said, "You're right." Slowly, making a calculated consideration, I said, "We can't just leave Cécile to her fate. It's not her fault."

"Exactly! We should—"

"Not *we*," I said. "I'm going alone. I don't want you outside as long as the Morose is going on. If you go out there and that mountain zaps you away, I'll be nowhere."

"But . . . I don't want you to go out into the storm all alone, Sam. With all that's going on. What if her traces are snowed over? I don't want you to get lost."

Honestly, I couldn't *wait* to get lost.

I said, "Listen." Forcing my quavering voice not to break, I said, "I haven't lost much time yet. I'll put on your headphones. I'm stronger than Cécile and I can still catch up with her. But if I don't go now, she's going to become her own ghost story, and with what's luring you up the mountain out there, it's *totally* not a good place for you right now."

Nick's eyes dimmed and the worry I read in them was sincere. But he nodded slowly. "Okay, I understand. To be honest, I'm not so sure I'd get far anyway. My body has never felt this tired."

"Oh, right. That's on us. We drugged you."

He faltered for just a second.

I got ready to go as fast as I could. There, in the hall, reduced to a thousand thoughts you tried to block out of your head with all your might. Sweatpants, scarf, heavy coat, crisscrossed fleece gloves from the owner couple's drawer. Nick to the rescue with his La Sportiva mountain boots in one hand and his Beats in the other. The La Sportivas at least two sizes too big, but at least they'd keep out the snow.

"I have your iPhone," I said, launching its Spotify. "Don't ask; long story." Nick's account, first thing to attack your ears: fucking Spandau Ballet.

I clicked randomly on something else and said, "Stay inside." Walking to the front door, I said, "Don't follow me. Even if I don't come back right away. Go searching for me only once the storm is over. Promise me, Nick."

Nick, miserable, shoulders drooping, looked down and said, "I promise."

I turned to the door and started to put on the headphones, but Nick said, "Sam?"

I looked around.

"Please don't go. This is crazy. Stay here with me."

I shook my head slowly. Opened the door and didn't shrink back from the fierce wind.

"But Sam?"

"What?"

"Be careful out there."

I didn't say anything, lowered the Beats cushions over my ears and went outside.

14

The moment when I stepped off the porch, walked up to the edge of the darkness, and sank to my knees in an absolute wasteland of snowbanks, with Nick's '80s playlist in my headphones, felt like the greatest liberation of my life. The first steps you took through the haze of blizzarding snowflakes, the bashing, lashing, thrashing of the wind immediately yanking your hood off and Bonnie Tyler rasping "Total Eclipse of the Heart" at full volume, it was—in a word—sensational. Maybe it was because, following Cécile's trail through the icy landscape of my sudden doubts—who am I to miss a metaphor when I see one—the field of possibilities was now wide open. Insecurity is also power. Doubts give you the opportunity to refashion the fundament under your life. Whatever it was, the second I felt the storm biting into my cheeks I was alive and kicking.

Cécile's traces weren't simply the delicate footprints of her sneakers. The snow's depth and the way you had to drag your feet through it made them look like a yeti had walked there. Already filling up with snow, they were only vaguely distinguishable. Hunched forward, I followed them around the corner. Dark, shifting forms loomed up in the swirling drift, then disappeared again. Gradually your eyes adjusted and, left and right, you could now make out the steep mountain slopes and larches, practically buried under the snow. The trail zigzagged past Castle Rock to the edge of the woods and disappeared into the wilderness.

"*Cécile!*" I shouted. "*Cécile, come back!*"

You *had* to yank Bonnie Tyler off your ears in order to listen, but the only thing that cried back was the Morose. The echoes sounded so close that they burned into you like acid, eating into your cognitive abilities and hollowing out your rational thinking.

Just as I was about to rebury my ears under the leather cushions, I saw something flash, out of the corner of my eye. I froze. Waited. Stared dead ahead.

There it was again. A falling flash. A falling scream. Swallowed by the snow.

Again. And again. *It was all over the place.*

And real close. Just behind the first snowbanks, but if you looked at them, they disappeared before your very eyes.

What you'll hear screaming tonight, Maria had said, *is all the misery of everyone who ever lost or gave their lives up there.*

Staring into the dark, I tried convincing myself that they'd only come to warm themselves with my life. According to Maria, they only wanted to embrace you. Because they were so cold. So terribly *kalt . . . kalt . . . kalt . . .*

The people in the bathroom, I thought. *That was them. They were in the chalet. The bathroom was full of them.*

This was the kind of old-fashioned horror story I woulda dug when I was a kid. Nine years old, begging my grandpa to make his stories even creepier and bloodier, knowing it was more than just the wolves and the shrieking of the wind howling out there. This was your payoff. The story you'd been waiting for since you were a boy. If you knew how these stories went, you'd accept that Maria's echoes really were the lost souls of people drawn to the mountain where they had died. Then you'd accept that, if the wind carried their sad, flickering consciousness out of that valley and into the village, it was reasonable to assume that they could sense the Maudit in Nick.

That's why they wanted to warm themselves *with our chalet.*

And me, I knew how these stories went. If you accepted that echoes were what remained after you'd reincarnated all the *good* out of a corpse, then you knew that it wouldn't end with them just *warming* themselves.

Staring into the dark, frozen in Cécile's yeti trail, I thought, *Run away. Go back. You've got your credit card. You've got your life. If need be, wade through the snow all the way down to where the roads are clear and hitchhike to the nearest airport.*

And yet, when I started to move, my feet didn't turn around but only led me deeper into the night. Because, sometimes, you knew there was a layer buried underneath that story.

A good horror story didn't end with death but with something worse.

I followed Cécile's trail into the wilderness, using the pale light of Nick's phone. There, with Billy Idol's "White Wedding" in my ears and finally enough distance between me and the chalet to let the thoughts in, I heard her uttering the worst possible option: *Your boyfriend is a mass murderer.* Cécile's voice, shrill like the wind itself: *The boyfriend is blind, because the boyfriend is out of range.*

Once the seed had been planted, you couldn't think about anything else.

Had I been blind?

Was Cécile right?

The thought hadn't even crossed my mind that Nick could have had anything to do with what happened that night at the AMC. Truth is, with everything that happened since, I'd almost forgotten about the whole thing. When some big government gun had squashed down the rumor of biological terrorism after a coupla days, even the talk shows had dropped the subject. Thirty dead due to some seizure-inducing hospital bacteria outbreak scored less than a desert jihadi with a PhD in virology. What stuck the most in *my* mind was Nick emailing that he'd been placed in quarantine in the ICU cuz they wanted to test him for suspicious symptoms. But that had just been protocol.

They hadn't suspected any *involvement*.

If there'd been even the slightest suspicion that Nick had been patient zero, he would never have been sent home a week later with a bunch of flowers and a Get Well Soon card.

Right. Except that his doctors wouldn't go looking for involvement in the realm of the supernatural.

With Pat Benatar's "Love Is a Battlefield" in my ears, I felt my lips drying up in the freezing cold. Could what Cécile had claimed be true? Was it possible that Nick was responsible for thirty deaths?

Plowing through the snow, each time I shouted Cécile's name, each time I briefly took the headphones off my ears in order to listen, I heard the echoes falling closer. Sometimes I *saw* them in my peripheral vision, standing between the trees and staring at me with hollow, gaping eyes. And each time I looked away and advanced deeper into the wilderness.

The echoes didn't scare me anymore.

What *did* scare me were the words Nick had typed on his iPad, the morning I woke up wearing orthodontic headgear made of steel wire. Diana Ross's "Upside Down" in my ears and Nick's words still fresh in my mind: *I didn't mean to hurt you. But that person on the other side of the window did. And I couldn't stop him. . . . If it can let me do things like that, if it can let me do such terrible things, where does this end?*

Truth is, I'd never really believed that.

What was driving him was a force of nature, not a rational consciousness. Forces of nature have no will.

Whatever cruel things Nick had done, they had originated from *within him*.

Nick. My Nick. My perfect smile, emerald-eye boyfriend, who'd once slammed me against the UvA gym's lockers and put his tongue in my mouth and then asked shyly if I wanted to go out to dinner with him. A mass murderer.

Your boyfriend is a mass murderer.

No.

I was letting myself get carried away. Fact is, in the early days of his rehabilitation he hadn't even been physically capable of getting to his own hospital room's crapper. Tethered by transparent tubes to the rattling IV and tripping on joy juice, he'd been in no condition to go on a killing spree throughout the AMC.

Plus, it was *Nick* we're talking about here, dammit. I *knew* Nick.

But did I?

You bet your ass I did. So shut up.

He never got violent.

Nobody died.

And what about Dr. Genet? The doc that power-dived off the roof to find out if the falling would ever stop?

But Nick had been in a coma. Dr. Genet's suicide was said to have happened more than a month after the operation. And who was your Deep Throat? Exactly—Cécile Métrailler. I never checked out her story. If she'd been crazy from the get-go, she coulda added this chapter to her tale too.

But *why* would she do something like that? Nurse Cécile, maybe she flipped out in the end, but before, she'd been on our side. I'd *liked* her. What had driven her to go to the mountains on the most dangerous night of the year, to try to mainline Nick with a lethal cocktail?

Necessity.

Once again, I felt my guts twist. Suddenly Cécile's voice again, real close: *Once he's touched you, once he's* cursed *you, he gets into your head and never leaves.* Cécile's voice, itself a curse: *He makes you* fall.

I started out of my reverie and stopped. Tore off my Beats. The storm was raging, but the echoes now sounded further away. Or was I being fooled? Looking around, I could see nothing, no trace of where I came from. No valley, no mountains. Nothing but the desolate night tide on the densely wooded slope. Nothing but the frozen air that made your throat sizzle. Only now did I realize how exhausted I was, how much energy it had cost me to plod through the deep snow. The storm was lashing me and making my hands numb. My thoughts liquid.

Cécile's trail was gone.

I looked around. It just wasn't there.

"*Cécile!*" I shouted again, but without conviction. The night had swallowed her up. Whether the trail had been snowed over or I'd lost it, it was the same outcome. She was gone. And, at the same time, I realized with my hollowed-out mind that the reason I was out here was never to find Cécile. This was my own escape. Getting lost gave me power. Control.

The opposite of what Cécile had meant by "falling."

Queen's "Another One Bites the Dust." I de-snowmanned myself and went on. Lionel Richie's "All Night Long," George Michael's "Faith," the cold and the ongoing tumult of the storm bashed time into liquidity. Michael Jackson and Kim Wilde and Paul Simon, the storm and my reason for being here meant nothing anymore, the music meant nothing anymore, it was but a mix of sounds spinning in and out of my awareness. The dude who kept tugging on the strings of my hood with numb hands, I didn't recognize him. The rime of his frozen breath on my scarf wasn't mine. I must have been wandering onward like this for hours. The batteries of both the Beats and Nick's iPhone had given up the ghost sometime during the night, but all I can remember is the hypnotizing wind. Maybe the Morose had died down, or I had strayed too far from the valley's mouth to still hear its echoes. All I knew was power, the power of moving forward. You would have literally needed a wall to hold me back.

It came. I literally bumped into it.

I noticed it only at the last moment. A lee in the storm. The wind lessening a bit. Then it loomed up out of the dark, right in front of me. High beyond measure. Wide beyond measure. A gray, concrete colossus. If I'd kicked it and was standing at the pearly gates, God's idea of paradise was pretty Stalinist.

This was where my quest ended. Here, I would either die or be reborn. I took off my frozen fleece gloves. The palms of my hands red and waxy, I laid them on the concrete. Felt it vibrating. A deep, dark vibration, whizzing through my whole body, as if deep within this wall a gigantic, demonic generator were chugging.

I imagined that the vibrations were the mountains' breathing.

After a while, I pressed my cheek against the wall too, so it could fully absorb me.

15

Run-of-the-mill moment, nothing special, the next morning. You wake up, or something of the sort. You don't recognize the moment itself as such. Only that you suddenly realize that you're staring at a still, snowy mountainscape. You have a vague perception of the life of the atmospheric tides in the sky above you. Endless ebbs and floods on the horizon of the universe. But when you're awake, there's daylight. The night has segued into day unnoticed. The storm has died down.

The dimensions are boundless. The still sky, boundless. The mountains, enormous. The wall you're sitting against, which you recognize as the Moiry dam, immense. You're in a land of giants.

In all their silent splendor, you finally see the beauty of the mountains.

It takes a long time before you feel able to set out on the long descent. Before you've hit and rubbed enough sensation back into your limbs to make the blood flow and make it possible for you to get up. You don't feel any pain. Or your lips, for that matter. Or your ears. Your nose. Only a general, heavy-as-hell fatigue. Your head is strangely empty.

It stays that way as you progress through that strange, quiet valley. The sky is a smooth white and holding its breath. Sometimes the mountains shake off occasional avalanches, but they don't touch you.

Only once you've almost returned to the civilized world, once you've rounded the valley's curve and under the wooded slope you see the chalet and the road of polished ice that winds toward the village, do you see that someone in the distance is coming toward you. At first you think it's Nick, then you see the delicate posture and think Cécile. The figure runs through the snow, stumbles from time to time, then falls to its knees.

Only at the last moment do you see that it isn't Cécile. She's approaching you, crying.

And I say, "Julia?"

And I fall into her arms.

THE GREAT GOD PAN

PASSAGES FROM NICK GREVERS'S DIGITAL DIARY

I knew I had looked into the eyes of a lost soul, Austin, the man's outward form remained, but all hell was within it.

—Arthur Machen

1

November????

Almost over now. Can feel it. *See* it, literally. There's a mist before my eyes. A pale, half-transparent haze, a cataract in my mind. Everything disappears behind it. I'm fading away into a big and blind nothing!

And nothing I can do about it. Desperately and very literally clinging on to the world. On the edge of my bed, on the desk or even the laptop I'm writing on. But the sounds of the house are getting duller, and in my head I hear the wailing of the wind in the mountains louder and louder. Unbearably oppressive. The disorientation is suffocating. The stiff embrace of the nothing, the impending white of absolute infinity, and the tangible presence of the Maudit just behind my face bring on a horrific, intolerable fear.

I don't want to live like this, but . . .

Nine days.

Nine days till my surgery.

I can't bear it that long!!! No choice, but the pressure behind my face has never been this bad. Can't resist it much longer. Feel like I'm being pushed out of my

2

(later)

Myself again. Soaking with sweat. Took an oxa and am a bit more lucid now. A bit.

Cécile is gone. She walked into the night and disappeared, which means she's dead. A rescue helicopter just flew overhead, but it went in the direction of the reservoir, not to the Maudit's valley, and it disappeared almost immediately. Seems more for appearance's sake than they're actually starting a search. So they can tell the family they flew out. Two Police Cantonale cops came by earlier and asked Sam some questions. They too left within ten minutes, and took Cécile's possessions with them. A little while later, a truck came and hauled her Peugeot away, and that was that. The same cover-up as with Augustin. They *know* people disappear here from time to time. It's a calculated loss.

Only I can't just accept that loss. Because I'm responsible.

Sam says Cécile was here to kill me. He said she had run from the hospital last August when she was changing my dressings and that one of the last things she apparently told him was that, since then, she's been *falling.* Did that ring any bells with me? Well, no. Sam looked at me for a long time. His gaze unsettled me. Don't know if he still believes me. And I *swear* I know nothing about it—cross my heart and hope to die—but how long can I keep telling myself that? If the Maudit did something to her, then it has done so using *my* head. My mind. The longer I think about it, the more I'm convinced that's what I saw in Sam's eyes when he was studying me.

Sam isn't doing well. But Julia flew over from New York! Thank God. Our guardian angel. And so unexpected. Could turn out for the best, because maybe she can convince Sam to go back with her. Don't want him here if something bad happens. If what I *think* is going to happen really happens. Sam must not be exposed to any danger.

Cécile. Dead. I hope with all my heart that she's found peace. *But what did she mean by falling???*

Did I

Oh hel peveruthings gone whitr can hardlu see hte kehboard

3

(even later)

Woke up by the creek. No bandages. Pressure receded but mist before my eyes still there. Shivering with cold, I crawled on hands and knees through the snow to the bank and looked at my distorted reflection. The rushing water changed my face into something more monstrous than it already is. Screamed at it. Cursed it for all the ugly in the world.

Something strange happened. I squeezed my eyes shut to get rid of the haze and when I opened them again, I didn't see my own reflection staring back at me on the creek's surface but the horned head of an ibex. In a reflex, I raised my hand and felt my face, and in the water I saw my mirror hand touch the grotesquely shattered snout. It was dangling on a stringy strip of skin from a dark, bloody hole. *And I recognized her.* I looked at her and, unmoving, she looked back at me with her honey-colored goat eyes.

Maybe I'd always known that she'd come back. Everything you're responsible for comes back to you eventually.

Come to me, the ibex doe said in my reflection. *Surrender yourself to me.*

She spoke clearly and understandably, even though her mutilated snout didn't move. I heard her words in the center of my head, in the exact place where the Maudit was hiding. In the exact place where, all those years ago, the Punta Rossa started to speak to me in order to lure me into the wilderness.

It was me.

"What do you want?" I stammered, though I knew exactly what she wanted.

I felt the urge to scramble away from the creek but was paralyzed. Couldn't pull my gaze away from the ibex's glassy, dreamy eyes.

It is your nature, the creature in my head said, and I heard the hunger in her voice. *Embrace it. Then everything will be all right.*

Although I still hadn't moved, I saw her reflection growing. Coming closer. As if she wanted to swallow me up. Her wrinkled horns expanded on the water's billowing surface. Groaning, with a voice I could hardly recognize, I groped around me. Grabbed a rock. Flung it blindly at her. I spattered the reflection, breaking it apart.

It became quiet.

When I looked again, it was simply my own reflection again in the creek. Over the opposite bank, pine branches hung heavily laden with snow. All was quiet, but I still perceived a faint animal scent in the wind, and I had a sneaking feeling that glassy, honey-colored eyes were spying on me from the woods. I spun round and quickly walked home.

This is not my nature. The Maudit is not my nature. I could have embraced it but I overcame it. That means I still have a chance, right?

And fate has *got* to be on my side, because as soon as I had gotten out of the shower and warmed myself up, my phone rang. The clinic in Montreux. A slot has opened because there was a last-minute cancellation. As if it were Providence! My scar correction was nine days from now, but now I can be treated the day after tomorrow. The day after tomorrow! And consultation tomorrow! That *has* to mean luck is on my side, right?!

There's something ugly inside me. And from the very beginning I've known that it's connected to that ugly, mutilated face. Go ahead and cut it out, then. Get rid of it. I'm taking a risk, possibly a very big risk, but after what I saw in the house behind Andenmatten's taxidermy shop, I know this is my only chance.

I'll take oxas. Immerse my face in ice water before the bandages come off. So it won't get out. Anything to suppress it. I'm not worried about the surgery itself, because I'll be out with anesthesia.

Two days should be doable.

Everything seems to be falling into place. The timing. Julia, who's here to distract Sam, so I can slip out unseen. Coincidence? Maybe, but can't I believe in fate just a little bit too?

4

November 9

Said good-bye to Sam last night. Most awful moment of my life, because it really *felt* like good-bye, a definitive good-bye, and I couldn't tell him anything!

Was about to tell him about the surgery but couldn't do it. Too big a risk. He'd want to stop me.

Oh, sweet Sam! Saying good-bye to my life, I can accept, but not to you. Never could I imagine you and me not growing old together. Sam Grevers and Nick Avery for now and forever. If only I had listened to you! If only I had never gone to the mountains!

Cried in my sleep. Just woke up. Lethargic. Sam wasn't beside me. Maudit is close, I can feel it. There's a haze covering the world, stretching out in all directions. I can hear the glacial wind crying on the edge of the horizon—and my horizon is getting smaller and smaller.

Went upstairs to look. Sam's gone and so is the Focus. When he comes back, I'll take it and go.

(later)

Where the hell is he??? Can't wait much longer

(even later)

Now or never. Julia is taking a walk to the village. Sam still away with the Focus, but Julia's rental is out front, and the key is on the coffee table. The coast is clear. I can make a clean escape

Can I even drive in my condition? Gonna have to

Bye Grimentz, bye Val d'Anniviers, bye Maudit

Please don't let this be my final note in this document!

Dear Sam, if I don't come back, know I love you. Now and forever.

AT THE MOUNTAINS OF MADNESS

NICK GREVERS'S MANUSCRIPT (PART 4)

It would be cumbrous to give a detailed, consecutive account of our wanderings inside that cavernous, aeon-dead honeycomb of primal masonry—that monstrous lair of elder secrets which now echoed for the first time, after uncounted epochs, to the tread of human feet.

—**H. P. Lovecraft**

I didn't know if I was ever going to revisit this document again but here I am. It's eleven p.m., and I'm in my hospital bed. The AMC is calm after all the commotion of the past few days. My MacBook's screen is bright, the lamp next to my bed is on, the curtains are drawn, the darkness has been shut out. Yet I still feel that power, roaming around up in that valley. It bulges over the edge of the col and, here in Amsterdam, my body goes cold, as if it's right outside my window. I hear the constant hiss in the background, like the whispering of falling snowflakes or the approaching drone of accumulating forces. I start when I hear footsteps in the hallway. I'm startled by a shadow. Since I woke up into this nightmare, I've been living with the unthinkable, and I need to come to terms with what happened. I know that's impossible. At moments like this, I deem the darkness capable of anything, as if it can lash out at me from that forgotten place up in the Alps, as if it can make me go mad only by me trusting these words to paper, as if it can even affect *you* just by your reading them.

Because we climbed the Maudit, Sam. Despite everything.

There's a hole in my memory, after my confrontation with Augustin on the moraine. The psychotherapist says that memory loss is normal after a traumatic experience like mine, but there's something else going on here. It's not simply like not remembering how you got home after a drunken night out. Something happened to me the moment Augustin's elbow hit my cheekbone and I smashed against the embankment. And what's most terrifying is that, after that, I seemed to have had no more control over my own will.

And that is the story in photos 8 to 16. Shapes. Jagged, screaming horizons, silhouetted black against the dark blue of the dying light. Crooked and chaotic. These are the only images I have of the Maudit, Sam, and they tell a story of madness. I don't remember taking them, but they're on my GoPro, and judging by the light, it must have been not long after the encounter on the moraine. The longer I look at them, the more they seem to confirm what I already know: something had taken power over us and sent us up that mountain.

* * *

I remember nothing of the night in the bivouac.

Nor of the start of the climb.

There are only flashes, like fragments from a delirium.

At one point, I'm ascending through a bitterly cold tunnel of gusts and darkness, my crampons crunching on a crust of frozen glacier snow. Somewhere, from a faraway place, my mind is vaguely alarmed that the only thing I can see in my Petzl headlamp's pencil beam is the rope, which is being pulled in by some invisible force in front of me. The numbing stream of ice particles lashing my cheeks is making me sleepy and causes my mind to drift off. I think I'm the last man on earth, but instead of filling me with dread, the thought consoles me.

At one point it's light, and now I understand why I couldn't see anything in the dark. We're surrounded by clouds. And I'm not alone at all. Augustin is there too, and I feel a brief but intense stab of envy when I see him clamber up against the blizzard and through the clouds as if he reigns over the weather. The idea amazes me more than it surprises me. When, a bit later, I follow in his footsteps through the steep snow couloir, I think, *How did he do that?*

At one point, something shoots past me from the whiteout under my feet. I almost lose my balance. I slam my ice axes deep into the wall and a frontal wave of spindrift washes over me. As I look down, gasping for breath, it seems like the chasm is coming to life. In a suffocating panic, I trudge on, clambering in the snow.

"Augustin!" I shout, but the wind cuts me off. The jerks on the rope are the only evidence that Augustin is still there, but I'm suddenly convinced that there's something horrifying tied to the other end, something I absolutely don't want to see.

There also are lucid moments. In these moments, I seem to be more myself, and the madness of the situation hits me.

This happens when we reach the east ridge. Through gaps in the cloud cover, I see massive, ice-clad bulwarks of rock looming up before me, alternated with knife-edged arêtes. Cornices of unstable snow dangerously overhanging the north face block our way. *Nicht empfehlenswert*—that's what the guidebook said: not recommended. That almost seems like a joke now. The wind assaults us from the invisible glacier below and howls through the notch we just reached.

This is not a normal summer storm. We're no match for it.

Still, Augustin has gone ahead. He impatiently tugs on the rope.

"Augustin, wait! What the hell are we doing?"

He turns around and spreads his arms. I need to brace myself in a niche in the rock to remain on my feet, but he's standing in the middle of the ridge, exposed, unyielding to the elements battering him. It's totally surreal, but that is how I remember it. *"Feel that power!"* he shouts, exhilarated. *"Feel the storm! Isn't it fantastic?"*

"Augustin, this is suicide!"

"Nah, we can do this! I've never felt this strong! Can't you feel it?"

He's right. Despite my fear, despite the storm, despite the fact that we may not be able to come down anymore in these conditions, I feel strong and want to continue to the summit. Whatever power is present here, it has got a hold on me too.

If you were to ask me to provide a route description for the Maudit, I wouldn't be able to. My fear was too paralyzing and my excitement too liberating to form a clear recollection. I wouldn't even venture to estimate the difficulty, because conditions on the mountain were bordering on epic. But it was the toughest climb I have ever done, and despite the influence of that strange, hypnotizing power surging through my body, at many times I remember thinking, *I'm going to die here.*

The most precarious moment I recall is when we traverse an overhanging and intimidating-looking rock pillar. Augustin has rounded it via perpendicular, ice-covered slabs and a twisting vein of blue ice on the north face. He now belays me up. Visibility is practically zero, but I'm still aware of the electrifying heights around me that seem to hollow out my stomach. Icicles hang from the rocks like a predator's fangs. I try not to think about how vulnerable I am, and I surrender to the wall in a dreamy concentration of axe hammerings and power surges in my legs.

Bereft of solid ground beneath my feet, adrenaline rushes through my veins as lactic acid rapidly wears out my muscles. My breath comes in gusts and my calves tremble from the exertion. I feel more confidence in the security offered by the rope than in my own abilities. When the blue vein dead-ends, I slam my axe right through the treacherously thin ice curtain, and the scent of cordite bursts out of the rock under it. The impact shoots to my elbow and makes me lose my balance. Just in time, I manage to regain it. I don't even have time to scream.

Increasingly panicked, I look up at what is waiting. The terrain forces me to search for delicate holds in slippery rock, into which I can hook my axe's spike. I feel the front spikes of my crampons move—carrying my full weight in 0.1 inch of ice. If I rest now, I will waste energy and fall. But I can't keep this up much longer. And Augustin has cleared this so easily! Didn't even put in a screw for extra security. If he had fallen, he would have disappeared at least thirty yards into the north face. Am I such a wimp?

Smash! one, *Smash!* two, *Smash!* three steps higher. The spikes of my crampon scrape over rock and I fall. I see wind, I see ice flashing past, I see my axes swaying on my wrist straps. Then Augustin has locked off the rope to arrest the fall and I'm left suspended in my harness. It's over before I realize it has begun.

No, it isn't. Because the next moment I'm pulled *up*. I scrabble up the slab with the spikes of my crampons, vainly try to get a grip, then break the icicles off with my axes before I get staked right into them. They drop into the abyss like shattered glass.

Augustin is lending me a hand. It doesn't take long before I'm past the outcrop and the incline eases out, allowing me to scramble over mixed terrain, up to his anchor. When Augustin sees my bewildered face, he bursts into whoops of laughter.

"Fuck, I was fit to drop," I pant. "Thanks, man."

[*Was I aware right then that it's literally impossible to pull a man's weight up on a rope? I don't know, Sam. Yet it happened.*

Because Augustin was in a hurry.]

The next moment I recall, I'm alone. I don't know where Augustin is. He's gone ahead, unroped, to look at how the route proceeds, but he hasn't come back. I don't care. Somewhere deep inside me, an alarming fear flares up, because I know he's gone beyond a state of confusion and his actions have now become dangerously reckless and irrational, but that feeling is dulled, doesn't seem to matter.

The Maudit is *my* mountain, not his.

I feel its charge: it flows from the rocks through my fingers, as if a battery is buried under the mountain's surface, crackling with static electricity. Never have I felt so strong, so resistant to the pounding machinery of time. It's an overwhelming sense of individuality, of my *own* power. The high-voltage kick juices me up, as if I'm on speed.

And just as every mountain stands alone, I refuse to allow anyone to share it with me.

Maybe it was only a matter of several hours that I moved on like this, but it seemed timeless to me. No before, no after, only an endless *pushing forward* induced by that raw, elementary soulification that has animated my body. I don't think about the rope buried in my backpack for a second, nor about the notorious reality of *one misstep and you're dead*. Could I have stopped if I had become aware of what I was doing? Heck, I don't want to stop. I don't feel the Maudit; I *am* the Maudit. The mountain is a geological E-bomb.

How close I came to my own death I don't know, but I think it was extremely touch and go. I'm scared to think what would have become of me if the possession, which was growing ever stronger during the climb, hadn't suddenly let go of me on the summit. Because that's what happened.

It felt like something alive, something almighty, something completely insane had caught sight of me for an instant . . . and then lost interest at the last minute.

* * *

[*I realized I was standing on the summit only when I had it in my hand. Literally. The Maudit's summit is a two-by-five-inch piece of gneiss—the same piece of gneiss I was holding in my hand a couple of days ago when I woke up in the middle of the night in the corner of the hospital room. You know I always keep them as trophies: the top rock, the handful of snow I scoop from the summit, melt into a little plastic screw cap bottle, and pour into a glass flask at home. I sticker them; I label them. They tell the stories of my personal triumphs.*

Once again, I ask myself how the summit ended up in my hand on the night of the disaster. I can't explain it. The rock had to have been in the inside pocket of my Gore-Tex coat the whole time, and my parents were supposed to have brought it home along with the rest of my stuff. So how did it get here, to the AMC?

It's a simple piece of rock, irrelevant to the mountain. That this of all rocks was forced to the surface in millions of years of rising continents is sheer coincidence.

Yet I believe that it was my salvation. Because it has symbolic value to me. All the mountains whose summits I added to my collection lost their magnetism, after I conquered them.

Maybe that's why picking up the Maudit's summit somehow took the sting out of it—because I was immediately back in myself.]

Around me is a barren world. The summit ridge is jagged, snow-covered, and so narrow that it would be impossible for two people to pass each other. There's no stoneman to prove anyone has ever been here before. The snowstorm bulges over the crest like a living creature and shrouds everything in a gray, horizontally shifting blur, but it's clear there's no place to go up anymore; from here on, it's only downhill.

I don't feel the liberation or the fulfillment I normally do when I reach a summit. Only a terrible, rudimentary awareness of where I am: in a claustrophobic realm where death is silently hunting me. After the intense charge of before, it now feels like I'm inside a waiting vacuum, an echoless hollow that is holding its breath.

Behind me, where my footprints lead back into a gaping abyss, I can see the ice field that splits the horned summit in two, shimmering between rips in the clouds. I remember that when we saw it last night, it was shining like a bloodred eye. Its dimensions are beyond comprehension. My god, did I traverse that thing all by myself? And am I actually standing on top of *this* mountain? The concept is so frightening that it staggers my mind.

What kind of power was it that drove you to come up here? And what the hell gave Augustin the power to hoist you up so easily, as if you were a sack of potatoes?

But I know the answer: it's the Maudit. The mountain is a living organism that has infected us like a virus.

I force the thought out of my head and with numb fingers put the Maudit's summit away in my inner pocket. I put the gloves back on and try to rub my hands warm. Christ, it's cold. Hunched against the lashing wind, I stumble to the westerly end of the summit ridge, looking for a possible way down. I've come to terms with the fact that I'll probably die here, but it doesn't seem appealing to me to just sit and wait, half crazed with loneliness, till the cold and the exhaustion take their toll. If it has to happen, then let it be in an attempt to go down.

Only right before I get there do I see that the hump on the rim isn't a boulder but Augustin. He's still here! And he's alive!

At the edge of my consciousness, a wave of piercing anger rises—*What gives him the right to have arrived here ahead of me?*—and all of a sudden, I am deeply alarmed. But it's only an echo. It disappears immediately. I lick my chapped lips and taste fear.

What if it isn't finished with me yet?

We have to get out of here. Right now.

I have to scream to be heard above the storm. "*Augustin . . . how are you doing?*"

His dull eyes don't react, and his mumblings are carried away by the wind.

I instantly see that it's all wrong. Nothing is left of Augustin's earlier rapture. He looks muddled and apathetic, like someone who just woke up and doesn't understand where he is.

Hypothermia, it flashes through me. I assess the situation in an instant: critical. He's a much faster climber than me. God knows how long he's been sitting here on the summit, exposed to a windchill that could stop a heartbeat. His face is waxen and withdrawn. Snow has accumulated on his collar and in his fluttering hair. If I can't speed up his sluggish circulation, he won't survive.

I stare past him into the void. Fifty to sixty yards below, at the foot of the summit bastion, the west ridge starts its steep decline into the clouds. It doesn't look inviting, but it's also not as menacing as the ice field on the east side. I switch to pragmatic mode.

This is a challenge I'm up to, a problem I can handle.

I turn to Augustin, pull the hood over his head, and tighten the cord. I shake him by the shoulders and shout the words into his face: *"Augustin, we have to go down, do you understand me?"*

"Yes," he mumbles. His voice is barely audible, but it's at least something.

"You've been sitting here too long. If you stay here any longer you'll freeze to death. You have to move your body, do you understand that, too?"

"Yes. Down." He nods absently and sticks his hands under his armpits, setting off a shudder.

"Stronger, dude," I say. I shake his arm up and down by the elbow.

Like an echo, he starts moving it by himself.

"I want to try going down the west ridge, okay? I think it's better than back over the ice field."

"Okay."

"Do you think you can rappel?"

"Okay."

I gaze at him indecisively. This isn't working. *"Know what? I'm going to lower you on the rope, a whole pitch. That should get you on the ridge. Then I'll join you in two rappels. But listen: you gotta make an anchor at the bottom and untie yourself from the rope, okay? So that it's free for me to rappel."*

He looks at me as if it's all Greek to him. This is impossible. So I just go ahead and start preparing the rappelling station, hoping the familiarity of the rope work will reawaken part of the old Augustin. I find a good, solid rock, sacrifice a Prusik cord, and coil the main rope. My hands start warming up, my fingers come back to life, and I enjoy the sense of retrieved control. Every small victory counts. Augustin is on his feet now and gaping past me at things only he can see. I click a carabiner to the loop on his harness and attach him to the rope. When I've got him locked, I take all his climbing gear. It feels safer to have it with me . . . in case something happens to him.

I tie a sling onto his harness and put the carabiner at the end of it into his hand. *"Okay, this is your belay for when you get down. Get off the rope and hang the sling on a rock. Then I'll come down. Capisce?"*

He nods and clicks the biner absentmindedly onto his gear loop. That's good—a simple, familiar routine that gives me some confidence. But it's still a leap of faith. My nightmare scenario is that he'll fall back into his reverie and forget to get off the rope. In which case I'll be stuck.

Suddenly Augustin gives me an unusually fierce look. "You want to get me out of here, don't you?"

It takes a while for it to sink in. *"What did you say?"*

"You want to go down."

"Yes. I'm going to lower you down, and when you're there, you're going to get off the rope so I can rappel. Like I just explained."

"I'm not going."

"What?"

"I'm staying here!"

Words can't knock you down, yet it happens, and if I hadn't secured myself to the anchor, I would have permanently disappeared into the south face. For a second, I have the dizzying and nauseating feeling that I'm actually falling and frantically flailing my arms, searching for a grip that isn't there. Then I understand it's an illusion. Rattled, I haul myself up with both hands, my crampons scraping the slippery rock.

When I feel able to speak again, I start, *"Augustin, we have to, otherwise we'll—"*

But my words die on my lips. Something passes over from Augustin to me. A biting, cold rush of air. And it's that moment when I know that it's not Augustin in front of me but the mountain itself.

A chasm of loneliness opens up before me. Frozen in time, I feel myself in the midst of it, still, immutable, an apathetic sense of *being*. Trapped in rock and ice for as long as the mountain will exist. It's awful. I understand that if I fight Augustin—fight the *Maudit*—this is what will happen.

And I don't doubt for a second that he can *make* it happen.

I do the only sensible thing I can think of: I smack him right in the face. His head flies sideways, snow spatters off his hood. Even the Maudit, which could snap me like a twig in an instant, is surprised. But I too am stronger than I should be. I vibrate with the power that is awakened by the struggle to survive in the face of death.

It achieves the desired effect. Augustin gazes at me in stupefaction, and the mountain is gone . . . for now, at least. Driven by fear, I shove him with all my might, causing him to fall onto the rope with his full weight. I lower him over the edge and shout to him, *"Remember your belay when you get down! Get off the rope!"*

* * *

During my endless minutes alone on the summit, lowering Augustin, my mind continuously balances on the edge of panic. The wind keeps knocking me more and more to the rim of the ledge, and I feel the invisible threat of this place building up all around me. If only Augustin will keep resisting the storm raging within; if only he will untie himself . . .

Finally, the weight is off the rope. I pay out some more, but it just becomes slack. Augustin has solid ground under his feet.

I wait.

I tug the rope.

It doesn't give.

I do it again. Nothing.

I wait longer, an eternity, my heart in my mouth.

When I tug on it again, it is loose and I'm able to take it in.

Not much later, I reach him, and so begins our long, exhausting descent of the Maudit.

As opposed to the way up, I remember it clearly. What I suspected earlier turns out to be true: the mountain has lost its hold on me. This means I'm now leading this expedition, instead of Augustin, and both our fates are in my hands. It provides a feeling of fulfillment, allows for a cool levelheadedness in which only the rational decisions I make in conquering the next challenge count. It's remarkably refreshing, and for the first time I feel hope.

Before we set off, I meticulously prepare our descent. Our only remaining provisions turn out to be a little water from a half-frozen bottle and a couple of power bars I find in the front pouch of Augustin's backpack. I eat and drink half of it and force Augustin to take his share. We'll need all the energy we can get. Augustin's reactions are still slow and drowsy, but a little color has crawled up his face, and for now, at least, it seems I can move him around. His Seiko says it's quarter past two, and I hope to reach the bivouac by nightfall. Not that we'll stop there—we're going to make sure we get the hell out of there, away from this valley's clutches. But we have more provisions in the bivi and can power up some strength.

Just before I let go of Augustin's arm, I see something that gives me such a shock that I almost seem to detach from my body. The Seiko's GPS says we are at 16,519 feet.

Nearly 800 feet higher than the summit of Mont Blanc, the highest mountain in the Alps.

There *are* no summits higher than 16,000 feet in Western Europe . . . and I shudder to think what this implies.

We climb down over invisible chasms, while I secure Augustin on a running belay. Oh Jesus, the drops that shimmer through the clouds. Those flanks. Whenever the terrain gets tricky, I lower Augustin and then climb down or rappel with extreme caution. The west flank turns out to be an endless labyrinth. The ridge's progression is barely distinguishable in the snowdrift, and I can only pray we won't go amiss or be in for any surprises.

The further we get from the summit, the creepier Augustin behaves.

He talks agitatedly in German to someone who isn't there.

Most of the time, he's incomprehensible, like someone talking in his sleep, but suddenly he gestures wildly and starts screaming. Is this Augustin trying to fight whatever has possessed him, or are these the demons inside? I don't know. As I hear his shout mingling with the howling wind to form an eerie duet, a chill goes down my spine.

At first, I believe that I still have a semblance of control over him, but at some point, his behavior becomes so unpredictable that I start fearing for my own safety. We aren't in a place where we can afford to make a single misstep, but Augustin slips several times or accidentally kicks free boulders that rumble down the south face and disappear. I keep a sharp eye on his every move and lock the rope as shortly and tautly as I dare, with an occasional loop around a jutting rock to create anchors. Time and again, I become aware of the mad roulette I'm letting Augustin play with my life. If he falls *here*, he'll drag me down with him.

And yet.

I don't dare to correct him or to urge him on anymore. Because as soon as he's reminded of my presence, he directs his wrath at *me*.

He doesn't want to leave the mountain.

The division is showing. Part of him meekly submits to being led down, and another part wants to stay, because that other *is* this place.

To that other, I am the culprit.

[*The looks he gives me, Sam. The vistas he opens before me. Of a completely desolate future, a precipice that cannot be put into words. It makes my blood curdle.*]

And it makes me lose my balance. At first, I think it's the pull of the abyss that keeps making me stumble, the void's hypnotizing magnetism, which can set your mind dangerously close to wanting to jump in, to simply diving forward, without having a free will that can resist it. But it's not that. It's *him*.

Each time Augustin looks at me, it feels as if I'm on a balance beam and someone is pushing my back.

By this time, I've stopped worrying about whether he's going to make a misstep that will seal our fate. I'm now convinced that he *intends* to hurt me. There's a pitch where I have no option but to turn my back to Augustin as I climb down a delicate slab, over which I'd just lowered him. He's waiting at the base, and I feel his gaze fixed on me. I feel him *staring*. I miss a grip with my foot, the spikes of my crampon scrape against the rock. I regain my hold. Grow dizzy. Any moment, I expect to feel hands on my shoulders that will throw me into the abyss, despite the fact that the rope between us will cause him to plummet as well.

The last steps. I'm within arm's reach. I flinch; my movements tense up. He *can* do it. I'm completely vulnerable.

He doesn't. But when I stumble past him and fix my eyes on the ridge, I'm convinced that it was *close*.

Despite everything, it doesn't occur to me to unrope and stop tending to Augustin. In his state, it would be tantamount to a death sentence. And I feel responsible. I was the one who saw the Maudit. It's my fault we're here.

Much lower, I suddenly realize there's something strange in the atmosphere. Without our noticing it, it has gotten darker, a freakish transformation of light that gives the grayness the color of slate. It couldn't be nightfall; it's too early for that. Or is it? Intently I study the sky, which is strangely attentive and calm, as if something is about to be born.

Then two things happen more or less at once: Augustin's hair stands on end on both sides of his helmet, as if someone had rubbed it with an invisible balloon . . . and my ice axes start to hum with static.

Never will I forget how the atmosphere starts rumbling: a deep, subterranean sound that seems to be coming from the mountain's core and causes the earth to tremor. The sense of vacuum is an illusion; the mountain's faces are speaking. Even Augustin is startled. To my bewilderment, I feel my skin start to tingle, a prickling that invades my body and travels down my spine, making the hairs on my neck stand up. The humming of the aluminum turns into an electrostatic crackling. I realize we're in the midst of a negatively charged thundercloud, which is causing an enormous positive charge to build up in the rocks around me.

With all the metal on our bodies, we are human lightning rods.

The wind rips a cloud fragment apart, clearing the view to the glacial basin to the right, about two hundred yards into the abyss. I suddenly see that after a last upheaval in the ridge, there's an easy descent to a saddle, from which a wide snow couloir gives access to the glacier.

"*Augustin, now!*" I shout.

I start driving him like cattle. We scramble, we stumble, we run on rocks, faster than we can think, faster than the wind. It's our only chance to make it off the ridge before the thunderstorm—

The world perishes. The snowstorm explodes in a forked branch of white fire. The sound crashes right through me, a pandemonium, as if the mountains are flinging house-sized boulders. It crushes my spirit and shatters my mind when tens of thousands of volts strike somewhere up the ridge. I believe I'm screaming, but if I hear it, it's only in my head. A blue, crackling flame shoots from the spike of the ice axe on Augustin's backpack. I even *feel* a shock, though I probably only imagined it.

Augustin starts to scream, and it takes a moment before I realize it's a pouring forth of ecstasy. Arms outstretched, he stands like an insane imitation of Dr. Frankenstein.

I shut him up by lashing him with the rope, and then we hurry on, because I feel the storm is building up to strike again. And it does, as soon as we stagger onto the saddle. I throw myself to the ground, flat against the snow. The thunder makes us forget that light exists. Augustin starts laughing hysterically.

"*Down!*" I scream, after I have recollected myself. I search feverishly for a way to reach the relative protection of the couloir. The first part is extremely steep—more than sixty degrees is my estimate—but after about ten yards, a lonely rock protrudes, from which I can possibly lower Augustin past the worst bit.

Traversing down to that hump of rock is the most treacherous thing I've ever done. The powder is so deep that I sink into it up to my hips, and I keep kicking it away in sugar avalanches. It's like I'm climbing something that doesn't exist. By now, Augustin is completely out of control. Leaving him behind on the saddle till I've set up an anchor would have been the only option under any other circumstances, but the chance that he'll be hit by lightning is too high, so I have no choice but to take him down with me. I laboriously dig my way down, facing the wall, my axes clawing into clouds of powder. I shout to Augustin to follow me closely.

The next thunderclap seems to light up the snow from *within*, and I try to literally separate myself from the wall. To my shock, Augustin is scrambling *uphill*. The snow shoots out from under his boots and he slips. He crashes into me, almost bowling me off the wall. Everything around me starts reeling. Luckily, the distance between us is too short for him to gain speed, otherwise that would have been the end of us both. I shorten the rope to less than a yard, so I can practically hug him down. He doesn't even realize that I am now supporting his feet as they search for a hold in the snow.

I don't think we'll make it. The whole time, I think we're going to fall.

But we do make it. Somehow, we make it to the hump. I throw a sling around it and, out of breath, hang in the anchor.

With the storm growing relentlessly stronger, thunder and lightning now follow each other in rapid succession. Without wasting words, I free the rope in order to lower Augustin. He disappears with rustling powder avalanches into the gray mass. Numbed, I let the rope slide through my hands. I watch it go through the hitch.

Over and over, sparks of lightning illuminate the narrow glacial canyon, a combe surrounded by the grimly etched cliffs of the facing mountains. The combe acts as a natural amplifier, causing the thunder to rumble with ferocious, evil animation. The storm doesn't feel any less threatening, now that we're off the ridge. The mountain has not let us go yet. This is an irrational certainty I can taste as clearly as the ozone in the air.

An eternity later, I have climbed down the whole stretch. When I reach Augustin, the incline is somewhat attenuated. We are now halfway down a steep slope of powder that leaves us no choice but to descend unanchored. But it's no more than 150 yards, and the closer we get to the *bergschrund*, the less steep the couloir becomes. And wonder of wonders, the quality of the snow has improved.

It's stickier here. A lucky break, for the first time. The path to the glacier may not be paved, but we should be able to cross the *schrund* within ten minutes.

I tie twelve yards between us, tie brake knots in the rope, coil it in loops in my hand, and keep Augustin locked at a constant five-foot distance. It is a mistake I will pay for dearly.

We're off. Augustin first, me following. Step by step, we come down. A hundred and twenty yards. A hundred. Eighty. The slope's inclination eases up to forty-five degrees and we can now step down facing the valley, our heels dug deeply into the snow. Augustin does what's expected of him, and I'm pleased with our sudden speed, without losing my guard for even a second . . . not realizing our fates have already been sealed.

I look at the glacier, search out a descent route. Augustin slows down for a moment, the rope slackens. I haven't noticed that a loop has slipped out of my hand.

An earsplitting thunderclap. When Augustin slips, it happens so fast I have no time to react. The rope's loops are yanked out of my hand and I stare as they disappear behind him, twisting in the air. I understand my mistake but refuse to believe it; I keep thinking I will arrest his fall. It is the voice of denial. Before the jolt comes, I have time to think, *So this is how it must end? The fall I'd always dreaded.*

Was it a rash decision induced by the threat of the storm and the Maudit? Was it the deceptive proximity of the glacier with its hidden crevasses that had brought me to tie us in as one should on a glacier but never, *ever* in steep snow? Or did I merely fall prey to the age-old law that stipulates that climbers lose so much concentration on their way down that they end up making the fatal mistakes they always thought they never would?

A massive blow on my midriff yanks me off the wall. I fly forward, momentarily weightless, carried by the wind, too fast to breathe. Then the fall explodes in a wave of blinding white. My helmet protects my skull as I roll over my head, but my head snaps back and something cracks in my neck, spouting hot, numbing fluids through my muscle tissue. The fall flings me downward in dizzying somersaults, which causes my axes, one dangling from my wrist strap, the other on my harness's gear loop, to bite at me like grinding teeth. The second axe's spike digs deep into my thigh and I try to scream, but my mouth fills up with powder snow, which has the consistency of ice-cold feathers. There's something relieving about it, and I think, *At least I'm going to die with a mouth full of velvet.*

There's no stopping it. My momentum shoots me past Augustin, pulling the rope tight again so that I yank him from his downward slide into a silent, forward somersault. Before you know it, we're tumbling down in a tangle of rope, backpacks, and climbing gear. Something tears in my groin. The wind lashes my ears, the snow flashes by and I catch a glimpse of the glacier, now frighteningly close. For a blinding split second, I'm pierced by fear: *the bergschrund!* Then it's already behind us and we land with a smack on the snow cone spearheading the flat glacier.

It's a cruel prank the Maudit is playing. We slide sixty, seventy yards further and are starting to slow down. My thoughts are left behind, frozen somewhere into the wall we came down from, but I seem to intuit that we'll come to a stop, wounded, battered, but alive. Then the glacier splits open under Augustin and he sinks down a gaping black hole. The knots don't catch; the snow is too powdery. It all happens so quickly I can't do anything. I career toward the crevasse, on my back. Following a load of snow, I disappear into undulating darkness.

With my eyes squeezed tightly shut, I feel the acceleration. I don't dare look at my grave. I only perceive its awful darkness, its ice-cold breath. Then the tug on the rope, the pendular motion, the crash against solid walls.

Everything goes quiet.

* * *

I swivel slowly.

I haven't lost consciousness, not for a moment, but I'm completely confused. I don't understand what happened or how my surroundings could have changed so quickly from the mountain flank's open expanse to this enclosed tomb. On both sides rise solid blue, unforgiving walls of cracked ice. The weight of my backpack has pulled me backwards and I'm dangling upside down, entangled in a jumble of coiled rope. Spinning, I work my way out of the loops, let the excessive rope slide away from me, and pull myself up by my lifeline, until I'm sitting right side up in my harness.

The silence is terrifying. The gloom crawls up on me from the crevasse. I look up, following the rope, and see that it's hanging from a bridge of brittle ice connecting two opposing walls, about ten yards above me. Thank goodness it didn't snap. The glacier's architecture doesn't conform to any esthetic conventions, but it is formed by millions of tons of ice that violently tear themselves loose and scrape against each other. The crevasse is a labyrinth of cracked ledges, unstable bridges, and balconies formed by frozen, conglomerated snow. Far above me, I see the hole in the roof we came through. It is by sheer coincidence that my fall followed a free trajectory and I didn't get my spine shattered on jagged ice sculptures.

The thunder rolls over the glacier. I hear its muffled echoes vibrate softly against the crevasse's walls. The toll has been paid. The mountain lets out a satisfied rumble.

Augustin. Where is Augustin?

With a shock, I realize how precarious my situation is. The only thing holding me aloft is the counterweight of Augustin's body, which must be lying on the snow bridge. Is he dead? Or just unconscious? I observe impassively that it won't alter my fate. Any moment, my weight can pull him off the edge, or the fragile ice that holds him there can break. Rigid with fear, I quit twisting and turning. Under my dangling feet, the excess rope disappears into a subterranean darkness. It completely swallows up my attention. It is so dark down there that I can't even see the end of the rope.

"Augustin!"

I hear sheer panic in my voice. Only the echo comes back, then dies away against the ice.

Suddenly a high-pitched, dismal whistling resonates. A gust of wind that seems to be coming from deeper down the cavern. It finds me and slowly starts to sway me. Oh Jesus, stop swinging! I *have* to do something. The harness is blocking the blood flow to my legs and they're starting to numb. If I do nothing, I will lose my strength and die here, mad with fear, when the ice bridge collapses and we plunge into the gaping gorge

(*where the death birds are waiting*)

or, in the unlikely event that doesn't happen, dangling and miserable, of thirst and hypothermia.

With utmost care, I try to stretch as far as I can, but the walls are beyond my axe's reach. My only hope is to go up on the rope, while my movements continuously tug on Augustin's deadweight.

Indecisively, shivering helplessly, I almost allow the panic to overcome me. If that happens, I'm done for. I force myself to subdue my fears. It's just like on the summit: I can't do anything about how we got here, but I *can* concentrate on the next step.

I take off my gloves and click them onto my harness. I carry two Prusik cords on me, and after carefully fishing them out, I start winding them around the rope. The Prusik knot is a fantastic mechanism that, when taut, locks on to the rope but when slack can move freely. Positioning two of them on top of each other on the rope gives you a belay and a leg loop, which then allows you to inch up the rope by alternatingly shifting your weight from one to the other. I slide my belay knot as far up as possible, then test it by hanging on it. It locks tightly. I immediately start swinging around, but I can't do anything about that. The real test will come when I stand in my leg loop.

I use my left leg because the right one was wounded by the fall. I don't know how badly—there's a dull, throbbing pain in my thigh muscle. I'll worry about it later.

With extreme caution, gazing intently upward, expecting Augustin to fall on me any moment and plunge us into darkness, I stand in the loop. The swinging intensifies. I tense up, slip back five inches. It's only the Prusik knot. It locks, and I work my way up.

After repeating this maneuver three times, I suddenly shoot down two feet in a sickening air pocket. Silence. Then again, at least three.

From the darkness of the glacial cave comes an insane cackling that makes all the muscles in my body go weak at once. I feel hot dampness trickling down my thighs and realize I've lost control of my bladder. At first, I don't understand where the sound is coming from, because its echoes resonate off the ice walls all around me. Then I recognize Augustin's voice. But instead of feeling relief, I am beside myself with some sort of terrible primordial fear. He must be dead. Only the dead are capable of producing such distorted cackling—not animal, not human, but *almost* human.

"*Augustin!*" I scream. Abruptly he falls silent. I hear the rustle of clothes scraping against ice and drop another five inches. "*Augustin, don't move!*"

The rope scrapes over the edge, ice particles spatter in my face. Then the cackling again, hollow and hysterical.

With cramped upward jerks, I start prusiking madly up the rope. My body starts to swing, my stomach muscles are burning, I spin around like a pendulum gone wild. When I get to the first brake knot, which is impossible to untie on the tight rope, I have to untie both Prusiks and tie them again above the knot, which costs me time I'm afraid I don't have. Sobbing with exertion and despair, I inch higher and higher, while the loop of the rope hanging on my harness steadily grows. I have my eye on a blue ice ledge several yards under the bridge, which leads to the right, away from Augustin, away from the edge, upward to a balcony of piled-up snow and ice. To climb up to Augustin and to *see* what is waiting for me on the other side of that edge, whether it's dead or alive—and in case of the former, to see what terrible thing has possessed him—I can't do it.

When I reach the ledge, I take both ice axes and hook them behind it with a stifled groan. I pull myself in toward it with both arms, but I fear I will swing back as my belay on the rope is pulling me away from the wall. Dismayed, I let one of my axes dangle on the wrist strap and start jerking at the Prusik knot. It's stuck. I have to shift my balance off the wall in order to relieve the pressure on the knot. My cramped muscles are trembling, and I think I'm going to fall. Then the knot unlocks, and with a last burst of strength I'm able to lift myself onto the ledge. I suck air into my lungs, and with my weight finally off the rope, I try to calm the dizzying spin of my thoughts.

The ledge is the upper edge of a disengaged, upright ice slab. It's a foot wide, and there's a pitch-black, narrow crack between it and the wall. After carefully working myself up, I am able to find a precarious balance on the spikes under my shoes, my face pressed against the cold wall. Inch by inch I shuffle to the right, sliding the Prusik with me, not thinking about what would happen if I lost my balance and fell off the edge.

I reach the other side on quivering legs and hammer my axes into the balcony's jumble of snow and ice. Even before lifting myself onto it, I see black holes glimmering through. The platform is no more than an accumulation of fallen blocks of ice, frozen tight and filled with snow, hovering above an enormous depth. Still, it is my oasis, a safe haven compared to being anchored to Augustin's wobbly, dead-alive body. I twist an ice screw into the wall, and as soon as I've anchored myself to it with a sling, I collapse onto it, panting with exhaustion.

It has become darker.

I hadn't noticed it before, because I was too preoccupied with trying to extricate myself from my perilous position and because my eyes have become accustomed to the diffuse light. But it's darker now, the shadows are creeping upward, and, suddenly alarmed, I sit up. It couldn't be evening already, could it? By no means do I want to spend the night here.

I take out my iPhone and wait impatiently till I can enter the code. A shock of disbelief when I see it's 8:17 p.m. So it's true. Despite knowing better, I fervently hope it will find a carrier, and when it doesn't, I'm so disappointed that I burst into miserable tears. Safe? How could I think I was safe? I'm trapped, and it will get pitch-dark very soon. The glacier up there, the storm's constant rush—it's a different world, guarded by reticent, overhanging walls of ice, as distant as the sun and the moon.

I just can't accept the fact that I won't get out of this crevasse tonight. The prospect is terribly demoralizing, but no one will come and look for us. I could never climb out of this place in the dark

(*if you can at all . . .*)

and seeing as I have to fend for myself, I'll have to try my luck by daylight. I feel sorry for myself, feel damned, refuse to accept my fate. Not like this. Never in my life have I felt so estranged from myself, so alienated from life and so close to death.

I open WhatsApp. Your last message: "Love you. Be careful." You almost never say "Love you." I try not to read it as a prophetic farewell. *I remember typing it, the day before he died. Normally I wouldn't have said it, but it was on the spur of the moment, an emotional impulse. Now I'm glad I at least let him know . . .*

With a stab in my heart, I turn off the phone to save battery power. Even though the phone is useless and it's the circumstances that force me to turn it off, it feels like I'm severing my last link to home.

I have the impulse to scream, to call for help, but if I give in to it, I know I'll never be able to stop. It's completely pointless; the echoes will turn against me. I start to shiver. Now that I've stopped moving and the adrenaline's effect has worn off, the cold penetrates my bones like an assassin. With a sudden decisiveness I take my Petzl out of my backpack and stretch the band over my helmet. The bright beam reinvigorates me and I start searching my backpack, watching my breath disappear in tiny clouds. If only I'd brought my down jacket. Fortunately, I find my neck gaiter. I take off the helmet, pull it over my head, replace the helmet, and put on my gloves. There. At least I'll keep warm a bit longer.

I hear stumbling and feel two gentle tugs on the suspended rope.

"Augustin?"

The beam cuts through the dark, and wherever I shine it, shadows move, shapes that come out of the depths of the sparkling blue-and-silver walls where my headlamp can't reach, and that dance away from the edge of where I can see. I try to believe they're a play of the light, unwelcome and unnatural in this lifeless place, but I can't help thinking that some of them look like horribly deformed people.

Then I hear the cackling again.

And something cackles back.

The second and third echoes come from far and deep, and somehow far to the left, creating the illusion of an enormous expanse teeming with ghosts.

I suppress the impulse to call to him. Really, I should go and see how he's doing. That would be the morally just thing to do. I have no idea how badly wounded he is. If he fell on the ice with both legs out, his shinbones will have gone right through his knee joints, same as Joe Simpson's on the Siula Grande. But it could also be his back. In which case he's paralyzed and will probably die during the night. If I traverse the ledge and venture to climb up several yards of slippery, vertical ice, I can assess the situation. But what difference will it make? There's nothing I can do for him. The more time goes by, the more acceptable that idea seems.

Okay . . . but that's not the real reason. You're afraid of him. Admit it. Even now that you've had the time to observe the situation from a more detached point of view, you're convinced it's not Augustin who's cackling there.

Unwilling to admit to this thought, I tend to my leg. When I unzip the side of my pants, I see the wound looks worse than it actually is. The axe's spike has pierced my thigh and left an ugly, purple gash, but the cold has stanched the bleeding. I dress it with gauze and disinfectant from the first aid kit and wrap it a couple of times with a roller bandage, teeth clenched. By the time it's done I can barely see the hole in the roof anymore. Night has fallen on the glacier like a blanket.

After a while, Augustin's cackling turns into squealing.

I listen to it, beg it to stop. But it doesn't.

I suddenly notice that the slack rope suspended between us is still attached to my harness. In the unfortunate event that Augustin falls, the ice screw will probably not be able to withstand the impact. Relieved to have something to distract me, I turn my second and last screw into the ice, a short distance from the first. I clip the rope into it. Now I can untie myself from the rope. If Augustin falls now and the screw doesn't hold, at least I won't be dragged with him into the void.

The excessive rope is still dangling from the screw, into the abyss. I start hauling it in, hand over hand. I look into the gaping depth, where even my Petzl's beam can't penetrate the subterranean darkness, and a halo of ghostly light reflects back at me.

The shadows are crawling again. A chilly gust of wind comes up with the rope, a deadly kiss from the depths. I start pulling it in faster, overcome by a sudden, irrational fear that something is staring back at me from the abyss.

Augustin's screams have awakened something unnamable.

If it sees the dangling rope, it may come up with it.

The ice groans. Silence. With a dull thud, something breaks off in the distance. My face flinches, the hairs on my neck stand on end. Something ricochets off resonating walls, again and again, slowly dying away in the depths.

There's something there.

I stare wide-eyed, deeper into the crevasse. I suddenly get the feeling that the darkness will reveal more if I don't shine into it. I impulsively take off a glove with my teeth and switch off my headlamp with a bared finger.

In that one, inert second of total darkness, I feel the shadows coming at me from the crevasse, and I know with paralyzed certainty that they're *real*, not just the play of light on the ice. I very consciously hear a *click* in my head: the floodgates of madness are open. The outside of my face under the windbreaker is a frozen, plastic mask. Inside are hot, living streams of sheer mortal fear. I reach for the Petzl, but—

I can't turn it on.

I immediately let go of the rope. I hear it sway as it falls back into the abyss, and then the metallic yank as it jars to a sudden stop, suspended on the carabiner. Something is fluttering down there. With both hands, I tug on the headlamp, my fingers cramped like frozen steel. It's the panic that is causing them to tremble, making it impossible for me to find the button at first. Then the beam bores through the crevasse. Like a child, I flail around me to fend off the mirages, but of course they're only

(*death birds*)

mirages. There's nothing there in the dark that can—

Augustin is gone.

I stare toward where his ice bridge had been, but it's gone. Only emptiness and the rope disappearing into the distance, beyond the reach of my Petzl's pale light. No, far away, a reflection of ice, the shape of the bridge, *but it's at least 100 feet away.* Augustin's cackling sounds thin and dismal, the distant call of a fallen climber. And the crevasse's roof . . .

The walls rise up into infinity.

I slap myself in the face, pinch my cheeks, wildly shake my head.

Now the crevasse's walls look all topsy-turvy.

I'm going crazy.

I dig and scrabble with limp limbs as far away from the edge as my belay permits. My hands sink into the snow, I stagger upright, I look around me, my heart thumping in my chest. I grab the aluminum space blanket out of my backpack's pouch and snap it open, crawl under it, close it around my head and body, expecting something from out of the crevasse's depths to wash over me at any moment—and that *something*, I know, is the mountain's soul, the Maudit's soul, and if I turn and face it, it will make me go immediately insane. The last thing I feel will be its frozen breath, and the last thing I see will be its dark, hollow eye sockets, deep inside of which something will be glowing, eye sockets like holes, and I will fall into those holes for eternity.

Leaning against the ice, I sit hugging my knees, looking at the silvery sparkle of bright light on taut foil. Outside my cocoon, the crevasse's maniacal screaming and the shrieking of the death birds.

That night, I discover the true meaning of the abyss.

1

The stage was set. Brother and sister. Back in the mountains. Back in a cabin. Snowed in, a fire crackling in the fireplace. A ghost story between us. *Half* a ghost story—because no one ever, ever, ever told the whole story.

Somewhere, we took a wrong turn.

Somehow, we ended up back at square one.

After Louise Grevers's call, I walked back into the room and saw Julia looking at me. Julia and me in Hill House and the only thing missing was the gentle, cozy ticking of Grandma's knitting needles. The taste of Grandma's blueberry waffles on our tongues. Grandpa's oldster voice saying, *Once upon a time, long ago . . .*

And Julia looking at me, looking right through me with her blueberry-blue eyes, she says, "That wasn't good news, huh?" Her Tumi travel pack between her slippers and Ramses purring on her lap, she says, "Wanna talk about it?"

I say, "I dunno." Totally shaky, I really didn't know. Sank down onto the couch's armrest, missed the back of the couch when I made a grab for it to keep my balance.

"You still have to make a choice," Julia said. "What are you gonna do? This has gotten completely out of hand."

My li'l sis, my total stash of people who could still save me at this point—and I didn't have the guts to look her in the eye.

"A woman has gone missing," she said. "She's probably dead, and you lied about it to the police." Provocative, trying to get me to look at her, she said, "Or to me."

I hadn't lied to her, I protested.

"But you didn't tell me the whole truth, either. And that's okay," she added immediately. Julia, scratching Ramses behind the ears, the cat stretched all the way out in a posture that was a clear *fuck you* to me. "Sam, I'm your sister. I *know* you. More than anyone else, I daresay, no matter how close you and Nick are. And I know that if you deliberately didn't tell the police that Cécile had come here to harm Nick, you must have had good reason not to. And it wasn't to put yourself in the clear."

Julia and me in Hill House, a log snapping in the fireplace, and the only thing missing was me in a loincloth and the tongs in my hand. Dr. Jingles, Twig, and Porcupiny in attendance before me on the rug. My teddy bear, my cuddled-to-rags indefinable whatever, and my what-the-name-implies.

My version of humanity.

The only thing missing were the words *I, the mighty Prometheus, shall bring you fire!*

Julia, she traveled halfway around the globe to catch me from falling. And jeez Louise, had she cut it close! By the time I'd landed in her arms on the slope out back of the chalet, I'd practically been smashed to pieces.

"Sam!" she'd repeated over and over. "Oh my god, Sam, I'm so happy I found you!" Brailling my face top to bottom like she was trying to make sure it was really me and not a hologram or some supernatural impostor. My cryogenic cheeks under her bloodshot fingertips and me mumbling her name again and again, hardly able to believe *she* could be real.

Look, at that point I was out of ideas. My whole identity, based on the concept of Nick and me, had been blasted away in light of the previous night. Walking to the valley had been sheer survival instinct, but what the next step would be after getting there, who knew? *Hikikomori* sounded good. Total social isolation. Woe, the Japanese and their weltschmerz.

Julia, feeling up my face, she said, "I was so worried about you when our FaceTime call got cut off. The way Nick was coming at you. It was bad trouble. I could feel it all over."

Asked if I was okay. Where I was coming from, why she couldn't reach me. Where was Nick? Questions, questions, questions.

"That woman, Sam," she said. "The woman in the corner of the room. Who was that?"

And I said, "What woman?"

Julia, when evening had fallen on New York, she hadn't been able to shake it off anymore. She'd called Dad and the old man had said, "Go. If you're really convinced he's in danger, go over there and make sure he's safe."

"I was too late for the night flights to Europe," Julia said, "but there was a flight yesterday morning that could get me to Switzerland on the same day. From Boston through Heathrow, and even then the transfer was so tight that I'd probably miss it. But Dad booked me a business seat so I'd be first in line and said go for it." Wiping away her tears, Julia said, "I only just made the connecting flight. And even then only because the flight to Geneva had been delayed."

It was already past eleven when she arrived and finally got my text from yesterday afternoon—*I'm OK. CALL ME!*—but by then, I was out of reach again. Me, drifting and delirious and desperate; fuck Swisscom in a snowstorm. In Geneva, the Hertz guy was already closing up shop when Julia came stumbling in. This guy asked where she had to go, and when Julia said Grimentz he said, "No way in hell you'll get up there tonight." All the roads were closed cuz of the snow.

"I cried out of frustration and then he gave me a car anyway, because he said he'd never seen anyone who needed to get somewhere that urgently. But he insisted I'd be careful." Julia said, "I tried, Sam. I really tried. But they hadn't even begun to salt the roads in the mountains. Not even the highway. I had to give up and find a hotel. Seriously, I really tried, but I was so, so tired . . ."

And me, sentimental softie, me with a lump in my throat. "No big deal, sis!" Smiling and saying, "You're here. You made it. I'm so happy you came."

By morning, the road was plowed clear and, *vroom*, Julia up, up, and away. She'd fished the address out of our standard email about our stay in Switzerland. The shutters shut, it was sheer intuition that made her walk around the chalet when no one answered the door, not knowing what to do next. And then her answer came staggering out of the snow toward her.

I hugged her, duh. Smothered her with thank-yous.

"Thank Dad, Sam. Seriously. It's by his doing that I'm here. He picked me up at two in the morning from NYU and drove me to Logan."

"What? Dad took you . . ." Whoa, fuck. Now I had to turn my face to the wind to stanch the tears welling up in my eyes.

"He said, 'Bring him home, Julia.' And that's what I'm gonna do."

That was this morning.

After that, the logistics. The call to 1414 to report Cécile's disappearance. Warming up. The half-assed dialogue with the Police Cantonale—no mention of any murder plot or ghosts dropping from the skies, just a nurse who came to check on Nick and wandered off into oblivion. The cop who, just before splitting, had said, "Jeepers, the wind here can get pretty haunting at night, but don't you worry about that."

Maybe me withholding evidence was something he *should* have worried about a tiny bit . . . I'd pitched Cécile's hypos into the fireplace; the stun gun probably was still with her when she'd run into the night. Full disclosure: I'd also reset her iPhone and slipped my own SIM into it and "forgot" to give it to the cop with the rest of her stuff. A tad unethical perhaps, but she'd come here to murder Nick, and I needed an iPhone, so technically it was self-defense.

Julia and I watched as they towed Cécile's Peugeot away, and that's when Louise Grevers called.

2

"It's so nice to hear your voice," my mother-in-law's voice said, after I withdrew to the kitchen.

I knew it was gonna be bad news even before picking up. Not to put too fine a point on it, but after everything that's happened, you knew bad news had a good sense of timing.

Louise, she said, "I heard on the news about the snowfall in the Alps. So early in the season, they said it was causing a lot of trouble. But I can imagine that, for you, nice and cozy in your chalet, it must look like a fairy-tale landscape."

Sure does, said I. One of the grim ones, in which you froze to death in a bewitched forest. Didn't say that.

She asked if I was doing okay. Whether I'd managed to get my bearings in Switzerland and had been able to come to terms with everything we had to go through. Only after all of that did she ask about Nick. That's how she is, Louise Grevers. We all want a little voice in our head telling us we can do it. In my case, that voice was flesh and blood and drank algae shakes.

"Harald and I are worried," Louise said. Nick hadn't responded to any of their messages and calls for a while. "I have a feeling he's going through a difficult phase at the moment. Do you happen to know if that's true?"

What can I say, he's going through a deep depression. He still has a big mountain to climb. Nothing we couldn't work on, I said.

Me, the perfect son-in-law, honest to the core.

Okay, tiny asterisk: don't tell a mom that her son had probably done too much damage already. That maybe it was too late for his exorcism.

"Really," I said, "he'll be overjoyed to hear that you're thinking about him."

Nick, who I assumed was downstairs. Taking a rest. Or the Maudit was phasing him out again. Something like that—you couldn't be sure.

Homecoming had been totally awkward. He'd been lying on the couch, sleeping off his oxazepams, the radio still on WYDL. Hadn't even noticed I'd been gone all night. He fluttered open a woozy, beauty-sleep-filled eye, saw Julia, and said, "Julia?" More absently than usual. Julia's coming at least a big enough distraction to keep him from noticing my aloofness.

Or so I hoped.

I could deal with all the rest of this shit, but not with Nick.

Not without a definitive answer.

Louise's voice, on the other side of all those stories you didn't tell: "Okay, well, let him have his rest. Do you know if Nick is still planning to have his scar surgery?" He'd talked about it with Harald, she said. "It's scheduled for next week or the week after, I think, but we haven't heard anything about it for a while."

Looking out at the snowplowed road to the valley, I knew that, for Nick right now, surgery would be the number one all-time worst idea ever.

I said that he was still thinking about it.

"Well, we'll ask him about it later." Louise said, "Will you please tell him I called?"

Oh, and yes, she'd gone over to water the plants and pick up the mail. There was an urgent summons for Nick to file his quarterly tax statement. A letter to me from UvA . . . did I want her to open it for me?

And a funeral card. That was such a sad story.

Here we go.

Rosalie Timbergen, she said. A child that had lived a couple of doors down. Only three years old. Asked did we know the Timbergens well?

And I heard myself say, *Not well, no.* Heard myself say, *I would see her passing by on her tricycle from time to time.* Heard my heart thumping, *pa-WHUMP, pa-WHUMP, pa-WHUMP.*

Loes Timbergen's face in the doorway flashed before me, snarling, *He scared the living daylights out of her with that mask of his!* The sincerely fearful expression in the mother's eyes when she said, *She's all out of sorts, it's made her sick.*

"I bumped into Adelheid on the sidewalk," Louise said. 'Course. Our next-door neighbor, gossip queen of Amsterdam-Zuid. "She'd been to the funeral at Zorgvlied cemetery. It must have been awful. I could see she was still shaken when she told me about it. Still so young, poor child. And the parents, inconsolable . . ."

And my own words, before I had slammed the door in Loes's face: *It's not Nick's fault she's sick, got it?*

It's not Nick's fault.

It had looked like it was the flu, Adelheid said. Nausea, dizziness, throwing up. No painkillers had given her any relief. The family doctor hadn't been able to find any direct cause but wasn't too worried. Just a case of diminished resistance. There was a lot of it around, after all. Tucked in bed, freshly squeezed OJ, ginger tea, and Grandma's chicken soup. Then her lungs filled up and she drowned in her own bodily fluids.

"It was pulmonary edema," Louise said. "They were too late; the paramedics couldn't do anything for her anymore. If she'd been correctly diagnosed, maybe they could have helped her in time . . ."

With my vision starting to dim, I heard myself say, *It's not Nick's fault she's sick, got it?*

My vision narrowing into a tunnel, I heard Louise say, "According to Adelheid, the doctors were baffled."

Pulmonary edema.

I'd read about it only recently. Cuz pulmonary edema was what you died from when you had acute altitude sickness. Your lungs started leaking. In the end, your brain.

Which didn't cross the doctors' minds, because Amsterdam's elevation was exactly minus seven feet.

"Losing a child, I cannot bear to think what that would be like," Louise said. "In that regard, we should be grateful that we still have Nick, wouldn't you say?"

Yeah, I said.

So grateful.

3

So there we were. Julia and me, back in the mountains. Back in a cabin. As if we'd never fully descended the Panther Mile.

"What would you do," I said, "if you suspected the person you loved had done something terrible? Something really terrible." Thinking out loud as I spoke, I said, "Maybe he wasn't altogether himself when he did it—diminished capacity, let's say. Temporary insanity. And you also think that he won't do it again, cuz he has much better control over the impulses that made him do it. But still. It happened, and you have a strong suspicion that he's responsible. What would you do?"

Julia hesitated for about a quarter of a nanosecond. "First thing, I'd want to know for sure if it's really true. I would never want to risk falsely accusing anyone."

"So, gather evidence."

Yes.

"And then?"

"Then I'd confront him. If that's possible, at least. Ask why he did it. I'd wanna know. And after that, it depends on the circumstances. What exactly happened, is there a chance he'd do it again, who are the victims? But I'd still somehow let justice prevail. Especially if other people are involved." She looked at me. "And even if it's at my expense. Of my love for him."

I suddenly felt like crying. Julia picked up on it and took my hands in hers, causing Ramses to jump off her lap. Julia, suddenly real close, said, "Bro, whatever it is, you can deal with it. You're strong."

But I wasn't.

"Yes you are. And I should know." Julia, real close, "We went through hell together, remember? You rescued me from a burning house."

Was *that* how she remembered it?

Julia said, "You've always been my hero, Sam."

I pulled myself free. Pulled myself free and stood up. Me, a hero. Fuck off. If there's a chance he'd do it again? All of this was one big *again*. Nothing different, but the same story you told over and over again, about how you did something terrible when you were a kid and lived your life hoping that one day you'd get the chance to redeem yourself. To make amends.

Well, this *was* your chance, and you fucked it up. Dr. Genet. Cécile Métrailler. A *three-year-old fucking girl*. Not to mention all those people in the AMC. *I'd been right there and I hadn't seen it.*

I hadn't done a thing to prevent Nick from sending all those people to their deaths.

Me and my escapades. I'd woken up the monster in him. I'd *nurtured* the monster in him. Now I was watching the fire around me spread. Me, the father of the fire, and the only thing missing was Grandma screaming. Grandpa face-planting the snow like a smokin' human torch.

How life made you run in circles and turned you into an uber epic failure when it served you a second chance and you didn't take it.

I was no hero. I was the monster.

Julia bit her lip and said, "I brought you something."

She bent down, picked up her Tumi travel pack, and put it on her lap. Unzipped the main compartment.

I couldn't believe what she took out.

I was the kind of kid for whom a single stuffed animal just didn't cut it. If you were to pay a visit to my New York bedroom between the Huckleberry Wall winter and, say, puberty, you'd have seen that it was, um, stuffed with plush elephants. Plush monkeys. A plush *T. rex*. And all hand-me-downs. The pandas had eyes missing. My duckie was squashed flat. Ears were frayed. Furs worn out. Ma Avery once asked how come I only had these duds with torn seams and Pa Avery said, leave him be, he sticks up for the underdog, it shows character. Till one day he walked into my room and saw me beat a baby seal to a pulp with my Hasbro lightsaber. Saw me rip the stuffing out of my rhino plushie like a poacher on the Serengeti.

He's precocious, the shrink said. Can't argue with a diagnosis like that.

Seriously, all those sessions and I don't think the guy ever got a single smile out of me. Like I was gonna tell him anything. What was the point, if an asshole like that didn't understand that every kid had a favorite stuffed animal? That I'd set mine and the rest of my childhood accidentally on fire?

And my grandfather. I'd set him on fire, too.

Everyone gets stretch marks when they grow up, but there comes a point when you're stretched to the limit. Then you just snap.

And that's why it was completely, insanely impossible what Julia took out of her Tumi travel pack, here, fifteen years later.

Dr. Jingles.

"I always kept him," Julia said. Scratching herself behind the ear. And me, I got it now. No mystery at all. It was a teddy that *looked* like Dr. Jingles. He had the same plush golden retriever fur. The same friendly snout. The same shiny eyes. The bear Julia took from her bag, his entire hindquarters were all singed, like he'd sat his big fat ass on a barbecue. What you were looking at was a knockoff. A carbon copy. A clever fake. Why? Who knows, but the teddy that, cuz of me, got caught in a shower of smoldering ashes in Huckleberry Wall had disappeared in a raging inferno. Gone up in smoke. Cremated, together with the rest of humanity.

I took the bear from her and held it out in front of me.

The slightly skewed snout. The worn-out patches on his paws.

I remembered that the real Dr. Jingles had a tiny tear in the lining at the bottom of his back, through which you could see the gray stuffing. Julia's bear, I turned him around. There was a tiny tear in the lining at the bottom of his back, through which you could see the gray stuffing.

Just above the edge of the singed patch.

I pressed my nose against his chest, just like I always used to do when I was a kid, and inhaled deeply. What I smelled was myself. What I smelled: the sunlight through the tall windows when you woke up on Saturday mornings. What I smelled: the sirens and the din of Second Avenue. Sweet July and driving the Montauk Highway to the Hampton Bay Boys Camp. Mom, coming to kiss me good night. My jammies with the sailboats. Hadn't thought about any of that for eighteen years.

Burning pinewood. Shrieking monster birds circling above the snow-laden branches, searching for prey, while a big, smoking devil pulled us onward on a sleigh. A devil I'd summoned.

All the things I'd run away from, all those things I smelled.

It *was* Dr. Jingles.

I had to clear my throat before I could say, "Where'd you find him? I mean, what do you remember about that night?"

Everything was shaking. My fingers. My lips. Everything.

"The panic, mostly. You woke everyone up, and the house was full of smoke and Grandma was screaming and then there was panic. I vaguely recollect picking up Dr. Jingles in a flash while you were hauling me out of the house by my arm."

"I did that?" And then, more importantly, "But where? Where did you find him?"

"Oh, I don't know. I was six, remember. I just have the image of snatching him up on the way. From the bed, I suppose. What matters is—"

"That's not where he was."

"O . . . kay."

It dizzified me. If Julia had taken Dr. Jingles, it meant he didn't burn. Then the way I remembered it all these years was wrong. The way *I* remembered it is Grandpa screaming that we had to get out of the house. Julia and me dragged along by *his* hand, me looking over my shoulder to see whether there were still any traces that could unmask me as a pyromaniac. Traces of Dr. Jingles, Twig, and Porcupiny. What I remembered: the living room one red-hot, burning oven where nothing could survive.

Pull out one, and the whole house of cards comes tumbling down.

All. Those. Years.

Everything I'd believed in.

My whole trauma. My whole execution.

And Julia said, "Listen, Sam. There's nothing in the world that you can't do. You can end this today." Took a breath, reached out for my hand. "You *have* to get out of here. Get away from Nick for a while. Gather your wits. That'll help you see things more clearly. So you can do the right thing."

She held Dr. Jingles up and showed me his singes. "Sooner or later, we all get burned. We all make mistakes. But without you, all of us would have suffocated from the smoke, Sam. If you hadn't woken us up, we wouldn't be here right now."

Julia, she fixed me with her gaze and said, "You can be a hero again."

4

Google. LinkedIn. Instagram. Facebook. Eyes wide open, hunting through the right profiles, the right lists of friends, using the right search terms. That's how you gathered evidence. Julia's words in your head: *First thing, I'd want to know for sure if it's really true.* Your MacBook on your lap, your face glistening with sweat, and Julia's words: *I would never want to risk falsely accusing anyone.*

Three thirty in the afternoon. Julia out on the sofa, power napping her jet lag away. Dr. Jingles staring glassy-eyed into the fire. Dr. Jingles, who should have been millions of minuscule ash particles spread over the Catskills, and me, since I was reunited with my old teddy bear I couldn't get warm again. My lungs unable to suck in enough air.

Nick. How dangerous *was* Nick?

And I thought, *Time bombs.*

Julia said she hadn't felt anything when she'd hugged him this morning. No dizziness. No vertigo. Julia's skepticism about the supernatural was one thing, but if you asked Rosalie, you'd get a different story. In Rosalie's case, there'd been more going on than just vertigo. A lot more.

It had haunted Rosalie, just as it had haunted Cécile. And Dr. Genet. All three had been unfortunate enough to cross paths with Nick, after which they'd been walking around like ticking time bombs.

And now all three of them were dead.

Once he's touched you, once he's cursed *you, he gets into your head and never leaves.*

Time bombs.

How long before Nick's parents would explode? Harald and Louise? How long before Julia would?

And me.

And you will also find out what it's like to fall. To fall . . . and to fall . . . and to fall . . . and to fall.

All those people in the AMC. Did they fall too?

If Nick had placed time bombs in their heads, then they'd been really short-fused. A timer set for *right the fuck now.*

Thirty people. A complete demolition squad.

I *needed* evidence.

My only lead connected to Nick's time in the AMC was his shrink, Dr. Claire Stein. She was the one I needed. But the three sessions I participated in, they'd gone through Nick, and I didn't have her number.

What are you gonna do if it's true? If he really is a mass murderer?

Shut up. We haven't got that far yet.

So I log in to Nick's Gmail. Yep, I knew his password, and whoever's got a problem with that at this stage—see this finger?

Claire's last email was an out of office autoresponse from September 24. Ten days before we left for Switzerland. She had her cell number in her signature, but when I tried calling I got the "This number is no longer available" notification. That was weird. No voicemail. Simply disconnected.

I copied her address, then opened my own email and tapped,

Dear Dr. Stein. I would like to talk to you about Nick. It is *very* urgent.

I thought a bit, then added,

It may be a matter of life or death. Sam Avery.

Send.

Ping!

Out of office.

I waited. Looked for updates about what had happened that night. The August Fright Night. The official story was still that it was most probably the outbreak of a hospital germ that had caused seizures followed by heart failure. What germ? Unknown. One of those next-of-kin lawyers bitched on a primetime talk show about the vague information disclosure, which only served to fuel the conspiracy theories. On a late-night talk show, he said he was repping a family that wasn't allowed to see their mother after she'd died. Said the casket was closed and that officials refused to tell them why.

Every five minutes, I refreshed my email.

After the third time, my hands started to shake again. What did it mean that Claire's cell was no longer available?

I searched for her Instagram, but she didn't have one. Not even Facebook.

Frustrated and more or less numbed out, I scrolled through my own feed, getting burned on pics of abs and boobs and sports cars and luxury retreats. Scrolled through my notifications. My chat messages. Everything felt empty. Hollow. Outside, behind mountain slopes and clouds, the Maudit was staring at me right through the window. Downstairs, something terrible was dormant.

There was a message notification in my requests, from someone I wasn't connected with.

Emily Wan. A profile pic of an Asian-looking woman. Two messages. Both from yesterday, 10:34 a.m. The first was practically identical to the email I had sent to Claire:

Hello Sam. You don't know me, but I would like to get in touch with you about your partner Nick. It's urgent.

The second, that was the clincher. The second message said,

Like him, I'm one of the survivors of the August 18 AMC tragedy. I need to ask you something. I hope I'm not too late.

Holy fuck.

Emily Wan. I scrolled through her photos. There weren't that many. Good-looking, with a sophisticated flair to her bearing. Chinese, living in Amsterdam, two kids. Speaking gig at some expo center. "31st European Neurology Congress Madrid," the dais-wide text beamed onto the screen behind her lectern.

Heart thumping, I tapped out a reply:

And I've got about a million things to ask U. Call?

It didn't take long for her reply to come.

I'm so relieved that you wrote back! Sorry about the strange request. Yes, please!

And a number.

Bingo!

5

I called out on the porch, cuz I didn't want Nick to hear me, in case he woke up. I could still feel last night's cold deep in my bones.

A whole different kind of cold wrapped itself around my heart.

Emily Wan answered right away, as if she'd been waiting with her phone in hand. You could hear just a hint of that melodious Chinese intonation in her voice. What you also heard was nerves. No—scratch that. What you heard was a woman who was dead scared but trying to play it cool.

Said she was glad we could talk so soon. That I must have been weirded out by her message. It was awkward for her, too, she didn't really know how to say this, and oh heavens, she completely forgot to introduce herself: Emily Wan, how do you do, living in Amstelveen and a neurosurgeon at the AMC. Her credentials totally highbrow, but she rattled on as if she were staring wide-eyed into nothing. She was beating around the bush, afraid to broach the subject this call was all about.

So I said, "Let me guess. You were there that night in August, and now you're having flashbacks. Aftereffects. And you think Nick may somehow be responsible."

Long silence. When she spoke again, her voice was no more than a whisper. "So it's true?" Barely audible: "Please tell me what you know . . ."

Her fear seemed genuine, but still, I was on guard. What credentials did I even have on her? I didn't know this woman.

So I inquire, how did she even find us?

"Through . . . through a doctor friend of mine." Trying to control her voice again. "Someone who'd been treating your partner, Nick. And, God, yes, what you say is true. I was there when the disaster happened. Unintentionally, I got more personally involved than is good for me."

I asked what she meant by that.

"I had an emergency operation. The patient we were treating died during surgery. And not from the problem we were operating on him for."

I closed my eyes. Afraid that the answer would irrevocably lead me toward a truth I couldn't face, at least not just yet, because I was partly responsible for it, I asked, "What did your patient die of, Ms. Wan?"

And Emily said, "I can't tell you that. All the hospital employees who were working that night had to sign a nondisclosure agreement." A clearly intended pause—implying that she *wanted* to tell me. Just not over the phone.

She was afraid someone was listening in.

Paranoid? Sure *sounded* like it. But what did I know, at this point?

Emily said, "I can hear by the sound of your voice that you know more than you're telling me, am I right?"

And I said maybe I didn't know anything at all.

"Sam, I need your help." The desperation back in her voice, this time out in the open. "Because the other thing you said is also true. It's as if since that night . . . It's like I've never been alone anymore. Something is following me. It's attacking me. All the time. And . . ."

Could we maybe meet? Get together somewhere?

I said I wouldn't mind except that I was in Switzerland at the moment.

"In the mountains?" Her voice sounded sharper. "Is Nick there too?"

"What if he is?"

"What are you doing there?"

"The official story is trauma therapy." The valley's cold cleared the soup of my thoughts a bit and I said, "Just suppose, okay . . . ? Suppose I did know more about what's up with you. And suppose I'm prepared to tell you about it." I was thinking out loud. "What would you *then* tell me about that night in August?"

"Not on the phone, Sam. Please don't make me. I can't. I *won't*."

"What kind of aftereffects were you talking about?"

"Can't you come to Holland?"

Symptoms of altitude sickness?

"I'm afraid I don't have much time left . . ."

Dizziness? Vertigo?

"Please, Sam . . ."

The feeling that she was falling?

Again, a long silence. Only after a while did I realize it was because she was crying. That shocked me more than all that came before. Emily Wan, through her tears, said, "Oh, it's true—he's making me fall, Sam. And when I fall, I experience infinity. Then I'm afraid the falling will never stop."

6

"You gotta do *what?*" Julia asked. Staring at me in disbelief.

"I gotta go to Amsterdam. Tomorrow morning."

Five o' clock and almost dark.

And Julia said, "O . . . kay. Okay. That's good. Yeah, good. I said so this morning, you have to get out of here. Take a time-out. I'll have to rebook my ticket, but . . ."

"Actually, I was gonna ask you to stay here."

And my li'l sis, waitaminute, *wut?*

I looked away. Gazing into the fire. "I'm afraid to leave Nick alone. In his state." The subtext being that I was afraid of what he could bring about if he started to wander around. The subtext being that I was even more worried about his *own* safety. For what the townsfolk would do to him if they happened to cross paths with him. For what he would want to do to *himself* if he lost control.

Then a real black thought popped into my head. *So what? Maybe you should just let it happen. That'll solve all your problems.*

That made all my hairs stand on end.

It's still Nick we're talking about here, remembuh?

I said, "It's just for one night. I'll leave tomorrow morning, and if all goes well I'll be back the next evening."

"But . . . what is it you have to do there?"

"Gather evidence."

Julia looked at me inquisitively. I hate it when she does that, cuz she's just about the only person in the world who has the gift of being able to look right through me and read me like an instruction manual. She said, "Can I ask you something?" And without waiting for an answer: "You said that Cécile had come here to harm Nick. But *she's* the one who's missing. Sound familiar?"

What did she mean?

"Augustin, dummy."

Right. My baby sister, trust her to find a pattern I hadn't even seen yet.

She asked, "Does Nick have anything to do with Cécile's disappearance?"

"As a certain wise woman once said, 'I would never want to risk falsely accusing anyone.'"

"So last night, nothing . . ."

"He didn't kill her, if that's what you're getting at. And you know I'd never leave you alone with him if I thought you'd be in danger."

Sounded good, but was it true?

The music had stopped *before* Cécile had snuck downstairs with her stun gun.

And the front door had been wide open. A red carpet for anything out there that would have wanted to sneak inside.

Okay, it could have been Cécile who did that. Point was, I didn't know what had gone on downstairs after she electroshocked the Maudit out of him. Didn't change the fact that I was positive it was safe to leave Julia alone with Nick, even if the Maudit took him over. I'd done it myself for weeks. The key issue was that all the bad things—*if* they happened at all—had happened *in the beginning.* Even if you wanted to believe that Nick was indirectly responsible for Cécile's death, then the time bomb would have been planted when she peeked under his wrappings, in the first days after the fatal expedition. Nick could control it a lot better now.

Theoretically.

Bullshit, I thought. *If you think he has any control over it, you're burying your head in the sand. It's getting worse; you know that. And this time it's your sister's life on the line. What if something goes wrong now? Do you really want to be responsible for that, too?*

But the Maudit had never harmed anyone Nick loved. That was a fact.

Before my common sense could stir up more doubts, I opened my mouth. "Listen," is what I heard come out. As if I was trying to convince myself by saying it out loud, I said, "You really don't have to be afraid of Nick."

"Oh, but I'm not. I'm worried about *you*. It's destroying you, Sam. You spent the whole night in a snowstorm. And now you wanna drop everything and—How far is it, anyway?"

A thousand klicks. Six hundred miles. Ten hours, with a bit of luck. Once you're out of the mountains, it's basically a straight shot on the German autobahn.

"That's what I mean. You wanna drop everything and drive all the way over there by yourself. And then back again the next day."

I took Dr. Jingles from the couch and held him up to her. "I *have* to do this. Seriously. I know you're thinking I'm letting Nick's trauma fantasies influence me, but let me do this and I promise I'll explain everything."

"Try me."

I sighed. "Okay. One of the last things Cécile said was that Nick was haunting her. That he'd gotten into her head. The mountain. The Maudit. Said he made her fall, whatever that means. She was really scared of him, Julia. So scared she felt she had no other choice but to kill him."

"That's a lot."

"You see? You think it's all a load of bull crap."

"I don't think it's bull crap that *you* think it's true. I also think you've been under a lot of pressure lately."

"What if I told you you *did* see someone on the webcam?" I said, "The woman in the corner you asked about."

"I really thought I did see someone. But I may have been mistaken. It all happened so fast. And I was afraid that Nick would hurt you." She smiled, but there wasn't a hint of mockery about it. "Or are you trying to tell me that besides that spooky mountain there are also a bunch of ghosts roaming around in the valley?"

Not ghosts, I thought. *Echoes*.

This was exactly the reason I hadn't told Julia about the Morose. Maybe you've figured out by this point that I have a tendency to avoid tricky conversations if they aren't absolutely, incontrovertibly necessary. And this one wasn't. The forecast for the coming days was stable weather. Thaw, even. That strengthened my confidence it would be safe for her to stay.

"Thing is, there's someone in Amsterdam who claims the exact same thing. Someone who has also come into contact with Nick. A neurosurgeon, of all people." I said, "If there's anyone who knows about brain trouble, she's it. This woman is my last hope."

That wasn't the full story, but—fuck it, period that sentence.

"So go," Julia said. "Go ahead and I'll keep an eye on Nick."

"Seriously?" I bear-hugged her. "You're my hero, I mean it . . ."

"Yeah, yeah, yeah, okay. I'm only doing it because I think it'll do you good to go away for a while. And if this doesn't get you anywhere, we do it my way. Promise? Then we take Nick to Holland, make sure he gets the help he needs, and you'll come home with me for a while."

"Promise."

But that wasn't gonna happen. The truth was simple: after I had my talk with Emily Wan, the road forked in two. Go left and there'd be no reason to assume Nick was responsible for the catastrophe in the AMC. If that was the case, I was willing to accept that Rosalie's death, Cécile's disappearance, and Dr. Genet's suicide—if it really did happen and wasn't a figment of Cécile's imagination—were all coincidences. Then maybe Nick still had a problem with the Maudit, but he wasn't the monster my imagination had blown him up to be. That was still possible.

Go right, though, and there was blood on *my* hands, too.

And whichever way it turned out, I had ten hours of solo time in a car to mull over my next steps.

Julia pushed me gently away and looked at me. "You guys are going to all ends to avoid each other, huh?"

What was she talking about?

"Nick hasn't shown his face all afternoon and you haven't so much as looked at him today." Julia's blueberry-blue eyes looking right into me, "And now you've got this guilty look on your face."

I held Dr. Jingles in front of my face, shook his noggin and rumbled with my best bear voice, "Bear don't like busybodies."

But her last comment had hit a nerve all right, and my evening started with a big rock in my stomach. A big rock and a premonition of impending doom I just couldn't shake.

What I did was focus on the practical. Texted Emily I was coming—my plan was to hit the road tomorrow at seven, so, including the pit stops, I could be in Amsterdam by six p.m. and—*ping!* Emily's text already in: Thank you. And a home address.

What I stuffed into my backpack was just the essentials. Passport, laptop, card. Started pumping volts into Nick's Beats. Anything to keep busy. Distracted. Halt my train of thought, cuz it was rocketing straight toward the double tunnel entrance into the darkness of my conscience.

I'm avoiding him, but he's avoiding me too. Triggered by what Julia had said, it came to me in a flash.

He's up to something.

File it, floodgates: check. No room for this. Had my hands full with myself.

If only I'd paid more attention to it.

When I went downstairs late in the evening, he was in bed. When he saw me, Nick immediately stretched out his arms, and it looked like he was calling to me from behind the bandages, even with no sound coming from his lips.

I saw something was wrong right away. Something about his eyes. A white, milky haze came and went over his pupils, came and went. Not the white of a cataract, but the white of a glacier, the white of a snowstorm. And each time it happened, a wave of dizziness flowed through me.

I sat beside him and took him in my arms.

"Shush, boy," I soothed him, enduring my dizziness. "I'm with you. It's all right. It's over, it's okay, you're in control. Look, Nick, you're in control."

And he was. The storm in his eyes died down. I don't know how long I held him, but Nick didn't utter a word.

He was dropping off, but just before he fell asleep his eyes opened one more time and clung on to me, full of fear and loneliness. "Don't go away, Sam," he pleaded. "Please don't go away. Don't leave me alone . . ."

It gave me a shock. A heat behind my cheeks.

Even though his words could be about anything, even though he most probably meant here and now, I couldn't hear anything in them but a prophecy.

A warning.

And I couldn't comply.

I kept holding him for a long, long time, while Nick's breathing slowed down, me fully unaware of the many things that were simultaneously going down with the tragic precision of fate. Nick's life quieted in my arms to languidly flowing liquids in a timeless perseverance, and me fully unaware of the tragedy unfolding in Amsterdam at the very same time. But in this particular, untouched moment, all the things I suspected his involvement in didn't matter, because only Nick and I existed, and I loved him as I had loved him ever since that improbable, one-in-a-zillion chance occurrence when our paths had crossed.

7

Outside the Focus, it wasn't just one long road. Outside the Focus, it was *all* the roads. All the hairpin turns and tunnels and gas stations and overpasses. All the place names and license plates and flashing taillights that brought you home. Inside a car, you brought your own universe, but outside everything always changed.

It was a strange sensation to drive out of the winter and back into fall. Below the snow line, the Rhône valley was a palette of browns. After a while, it was like the snow had never existed. In your rearview mirror, in a few switchbacks, you could still see the distant, white sawteeth of the highest peaks, but one flick of the wrist and the mirror stopped hassling me. I felt strangely upbeat. Beats covering my ears, this time my own playlist, and not in life support mode but in the knowledge that I was taking action. Singing along with "Tongue Tied," singing along with "Get Out," drumming on the wheel, and when you reached the highway by Sion you swung to the left lane and put your foot to the floor.

Next to me, riding shotgun, seatbelt on: Dr. Jingles.

Outside the Focus, the E62 and the E27 and the E25. Outside the Focus, the roads curving through ever-changing mountains, ever the same. Outside the Focus, the only diff was they got lower and lower. Less threatening.

The first gridlock was between Bern and Basel. Rain. The northbound lane, a miles-long chain of red taillights. The southbound lane, a miles-long string of white headlights. Drivers were silhouettes behind swishing wipers. The GPS showed red dots all the way to the German border. Seriously, you'd think fate would be on my side for a change.

Outside the Focus, the world crawled by you stop-and-go, till *x* klicks before Basel you cut off the highway into a sardined *Raststätte*. Filled 'er up. Took a leak in a putrid pissoir.

Scored a Red Bull.

WhatsApped Julia to ask if everything was all right over there and she texted back,

Everything A-OK, drive carefully, bro!

Then Emily, that my ETA had now shifted to eight, barring more delays. A single gray check. Followed it up with a regular SMS.

Reached the border at eleven thirty. *Heil, Deutschland,* land of unlimited speed limits. Pretty much horizontal horizons. The weather and the jams had cleared up and I gunned it, cruise control set to a smooth 100 mph.

Two hours later, just past Karlsruhe, the jitters set in.

Maybe Emily was at work. Maybe her phone was off.

From the phone mount, that single gray check kept staring back at me.

I called her but it went straight to voicemail. Called Julia. Had she seen Nick? Yes, he'd come upstairs in the morning. They'd eaten breakfast together.

"Oh, really?" I asked, "How's he doing?" Asked, "What did you say?"

"That you had to search something out. About this thing you guys are working on—that I didn't know the ins and outs. That you'll call to let him know when you'll be back." She said, "He seemed to accept it."

There was something strange about her voice.

"Anything else?"

"We didn't talk about it. About what's going on."

"Really?"

She didn't want to make him feel uncomfortable. About Cécile. About his face. So no.

Maybe I was chasing ghosts.

Outside the Focus, the A6 and the A5 and the A67, and inside your own universe Julia spent the next half hour telling you about NYU and Mom and Dad and about her Tinder dates with Abercrombie-clad frat boys. Outside the Focus, Germany and overcast skies, and inside your own universe you did everything to kill time. To reinstate normalcy.

Nothing felt normal. Everything felt wrong.

"Are you sure nothing happened?" I suddenly asked, and Julia, she said no, nothing happened.

We said good-bye and I drove on.

Stretched my legs. More Red Bull. Yawned. Before Frankfurt was a ton of roadwork, so you could only do fifty. We did thirty-five. Stopped. I called Emily a couple more times and checked my email just to be sure. Then we were moving again. I gobbled up a whole bag of wine gums. A pack of M&M's.

"It doesn't mean shit," I said out loud, but the sound of my voice in the empty car made me shiver.

What if she changed her mind?

Something was wrong. I could feel it all over.

Dr. Jingles stared glassy-eyed at the glove compartment. We'd been inseparable when I was a boy, but his presence, which was effectively impossible, didn't do anything to ease my mind. There was a lot we had to talk out, Bear and me.

Outside the Focus, the Ruhr. It got dark and the weather got worse. By then I was really tired. Outside the Focus, big trucks slugging ahead in endless rain. Even before Köln we were gridlocked into a standstill, and the voice in my subconscious had swollen to an ominous and downright menacing chorus. It reminded me of the Morose's wailing.

My phone rang, startling me. Julia. I put on the Beats and swiped her on.

"Sis!"

"Hey. Where are you?"

"Near Köln. Cologne. Ugh, this road really sucks, sis. Jammed as far as the eye can see. Like, the whole fucking drive."

"How long do you still have to go?"

"Three and a half hours. If nothing new happens, that is." I held on to the wheel with both hands and said, "Everything okay, sis? You sound . . . not okay."

"I'm not."

"What's wrong?"

Silence on the other end of the line.

I said, "Hey, what's up?" Then I heard a sob. Julia was crying. "Hey! Li'l sis, what—"

"I'm so sorry, Sam . . ."

"What is it?"

"Nick is gone."

"*Say what?*"

Since this morning, she said. "I didn't tell you because I didn't want to worry you. And there wasn't any *reason* to be worried, I thought he'd come back any minute. But it's gotten dark now and he hasn't come back yet and now I *am* worried . . ."

"Well, he's wandered off before when the Maudit takes over, but if they see him in the village . . ."

"It's not that, Sam. He took the car. He took my rental, when I went out to that little grocery store."

And me, yup, tongue-tied. Nick, he hadn't touched the car in *weeks*.

The look in his eyes last night. His despair. He had something up his sleeve. It had been written all over his face.

Don't go away, Sam, he'd said. *Please don't go away. Don't leave me all alone . . .*

He'd been up to something and wanted me to see through it. To prevent it from happening . . . because he'd been afraid.

But of what?

Fear tearing through my body. Thin and sharp like shards of glass. I squeezed my eyes shut, and when I opened them again it was just in time to avoid rear-ending a Volvo V90. Focus, you doofus!

I cursed. "Did he say anything? Something that might tell you where he was headed?"

"No," she said. She sniffed. "But there's something else, Sam."

"What?" I wasn't sure I wanted to hear it.

"It got ahold of me too. That thing you've been talking about for so long, it's gotten me too." She said, "He looked so *tall* this morning, Sam. I couldn't help it. I told myself not to act like an idiot, but I was afraid of him. And . . ." A gasp for breath. "And I got dizzy."

"Did he have his bandages on?"

And Julia said, "Yes. But that's exactly what was so wrong. The shape of his face underneath them, it was all wrong."

The V90 in front of me suddenly braked and I honked. Spit expletives.

I said, "Listen." Said, "Keep an eye out for him, okay? If he comes back, let me know right away. But be careful. If he's himself, there's nothing to worry about. But if you notice even the slightest oddity about him, just avoid him. Leave him be, but lock the doors, keep the keys with you, and stay away from him."

"I'm so sorry, Sam." Her voice still soft in my Beats, her voice trapped in a chalet four hundred miles south, she said, "I feel so guilty."

"This is not your fault, Julia."

I said I'd call back and hung up. Called Nick. The phone rang. Kept ringing. Went to voicemail.

"*Fuck!*" I shouted, and slammed the wheel with my fist. The Focus swerved.

Called three more times and then I had the brain wave. Fierce and hard, like steel biting into my bones. A claw hammer smashing into my skull. *Was Nick contemplating suicide?* Was that why he'd begged me not to leave him alone? Had he thrown in the towel because, let's face it, after all those weeks in Switzerland, we hadn't gotten an iota closer to anything resembling a solution?

But why did he need the car, then?

I texted,

Nick, please call, worried sick here!!!

Two gray checks. Received, not viewed. So his phone was on. I called again. In my mind's eye, a phone was ringing in the wreck of a rental hanging in a larch, in a narrow ravine halfway up the Val d'Anniviers. Nick with his head on the steering wheel, bleeding out of all of its holes.

There are holes in the ice. They look just like eyes.

I was driving myself crazy. Nick would never—

The water inside freezes and thaws, freezes and thaws.

Stop it! Nick would never, ever commit suicide without saying good-bye to me. Right?

But I couldn't shake it off, and by the time the traffic started moving again and I'd had my last pit stop, even my playlist couldn't distract me anymore. It came at me from everywhere. The powerlessness was unbearable. I had a strong urge to turn around. Go back. But what was the point? I was too far away.

I had to wait till I heard something from him.

Outside the Focus, the rain was hammering the windshield. Outside the Focus, the restless evening. Outside the Focus, the Dutch border.

It was after eight. On the bright blue signs over the A12: AMSTERDAM 117. Kilometers, that is.

I was almost there.

8

I was planning to drive to the address I got from Emily Wan right away. It was in Amstelveen, less than a mile and a half from our house in Amsterdam-Zuid. For three years of my life I'd lived here, and yet I felt absolutely nothing when I drove into the city. My sense of belonging, my home, my anchor here was Nick, but Nick belonged to the mountains now. The only thing I found here now was a vague feeling of discomfort. You couldn't ascribe it to my fourteen-hour motor marathon. To the fact that Nick was missing. Uh-uh. The discomfort came from my growing feeling that everything was about to derail even more than it already had.

Something ugly was waiting here.

And although I didn't want to see it, I had no choice.

Emily Wan lived in one of those typical Dutch row houses in one of those typical Dutch upscale neighborhoods. I parked the car on the street. In the streaming rain, I saw a light burning behind the drawn curtains. That was good. It was something. Rain streaming down my neck and the sign next to the doorbell reading EMILY WAN—JULIAN AND NAOMI.

I rang the bell.

Almost rang it a second time, almost backed down the walkway, but a second too late, cuz then the door opened. What I saw played a disturbing game with my expectations. The woman in the doorway, she *looked* like Emily Wan's Insta pics, but at the same time, you were looking at someone altogether different. This was Emily Wan if she'd led an altogether different life with an altogether different career on an altogether different continent.

Let me guess: it was Emily's sister.

Let me guess: here from Beijing or Shanghai or Chengdu.

Let me guess . . . I think I knew then what was coming.

"How can I help you?" the woman asked, hesitant and with a heavy Chinese accent. A pale girl, about five years old, slipped past her legs and looked up at me. Her right eye was swollen almost all the way shut.

Let me guess: Naomi.

"I . . . I'm here for Ms. Emily Wan," I bumbled.

"I'm sorry, she can't speak to you now."

The door swung shut. I instinctively shot out my hand and blocked it. "But I have an appointment with her."

The pale kid reappeared in the narrow doorway, PJs and whatnot, and like any other kid would have said "My mommy is a policewoman," she said, "My mommy is dead."

All the blood flushed from my face. The woman babbled at Naomi in Chinese and I, ever the linguist, couldn't even tell if she was snapping at her or comforting her.

The door opened a coupla inches more, and now, in the light of the outdoor bulb, I could see how tired the woman looked. "Excuse me for being so impolite, but it's been a very long day for all of us." She said, "My name is Sue. I'm Emily's sister."

But was she *dead*?

"I'm sorry. She died last night."

"But that's impossible . . . I spoke with her last night!" Not your consequential masterpiece; it just slipped out as an expression of my shock. "We had an appointment to meet today."

"Sorry, may I ask who you are?"

"I'm Sam Avery," I said. "I'm . . ." Yeah, who was I, actually?

But she was already like, *Ahh*, as if my name rings all sorts of bells, and she goes, "Wait a minute please." And withdraws back into the house.

So there I am, standing there, rainwater on my lips. Totally stunned. That little girl Naomi in her jammies and her puffy eye looking up at me.

And Naomi said, "My mommy is dead."

What do you say to a five-year-old who's just lost her mother?

My clever contribution, "Aw shucks, man."

Naomi stretched her pajamas tight with both hands and said, "I have teddy bears on my PJs."

I said, "If *I'd* been wearing PJs, I could have warned them in time and the house wouldn't have burned down."

Sometimes people are just in shock.

There was a sound, and Naomi looked around and skipped back into the hall. Sue reappeared, an A4-size envelope in her hand. She came outside, under the leaking awning, and pulled the door to. Held the envelope against her body to keep it from getting wet, but even then you could read the two words written on it in neat and steady handwriting: *Sam Avery*.

"I'm afraid I can't invite you in, because of the children. May I ask you what your relationship was to my sister?"

We were friends, I lied. I was supposed to meet her today about . . . about a number of things. Work-related things. What happened?

Sue let out a shaky sigh. "Emily took her own life last night. I'm telling you because she apparently knew you well enough to leave you this envelope." She handed it to me and said, "It's inexplicable. We knew she suffered from depression, but we didn't see this coming." Still she added, almost offhandedly, "She had delusions."

Sue had arrived from China the previous day and, after seeing what Emily had done to her little girl, warned Child Protective Services. She'd been granted temporary care of the children as Emily was taken to PES. There, she'd apparently managed to convince the social workers that she'd calmed down. That it was safe to let her go.

And all of that, yesterday evening. Must have happened right after she texted me her address.

Still it didn't tally with the rational manner in which she'd gone about it. Wan's suicide seemed a calculated act, committed by someone who'd considered all the possibilities, crossed them off one by one till she saw no other way out. She'd left a neat stack of papers on the dining table. Her will. Her deed to the house. Passwords, cards with codes. The works. Plus an envelope for her children. An envelope for Sue. For me. Emily Wan had been an organized woman, she'd even paid all her due bills. As if she were going on vacation.

"After that," said Sue, "she went up to the hospital roof and jumped off."

9

Back in the Focus, I ripped the envelope open. It contained a pile of printouts. A paper clip on the top left corner. The top sheet wasn't clipped; a letter. The halo of the streetlamp created moving patterns of rain over the text. My wet fingers wrinkled the paper.

'Course, I asked myself later what would have happened if I hadn't read Emily's letter. If I'd given in to my first impulse: Turn it into confetti. Drive off. Go to the North Cape or something.

But, duh. Like not reading it was an option.

So I flicked on the overhead light and read it.

Dear Sam,

It is a shame that we were not able to meet each other. On the telephone, you sounded like a nice young man. I am sure this whole business must affect you deeply, because you are so closely involved. Maybe you are even more scared than I am now and that says a lot. I would therefore like to express my admiration and respect for your strength.

A few things have happened tonight that made it clear I cannot go on living. Not only have I hurt my children—which is unforgivable—but I realize now that what's happening to me will also happen to them, if I don't end my life right now. I have been carrying a virus ever since that terrible night on August 18 and my children must absolutely not be infected by it.

There are no words to describe the infinity. It is too dark.

Therefore, I have no choice. I'm terribly sorry that it has to end like this. I had hoped that I would have more time. Possibly then we could have joined forces to fight it. Although I seriously doubt it. What your friend brought down from the mountains cannot be explained by scientific hypothesis. That is what scares me so much and makes me take a somber view of what is in store for you. From my own professional experience, I know that if we cannot explain something, we often cannot cure it either.

I hope I am wrong. It is too late for me, but maybe not for you. I am leaving you my notes. I hope that my insights can be of use to you.

I beg you from the bottom of my heart: end it, Sam. Whatever it is, you have to make it stop. Whatever it takes. Before there are more innocent victims.

I will die in the hope that you, if you survive, will help my children understand one day that I haven't lost my mind.

万段 *Emily Wan*

Rain was hitting the windshield. The wind was blowing wet leaves over the street with the roar of an invisible force that seemed to have come from the mountains themselves. It had found me, even here, even here.

And you will also find out what it's like to fall. To fall . . . and to fall . . . and to fall . . . and to fall.

Emily had fallen too.

Small, fragile Sam.

I leafed through the bundle of notes. Couldn't resist reading the first lines. When I got to the second paragraph, I moaned, flung the sheets of paper onto the shotgun seat, and pinched my eyelids.

I was shaking. Shivering. From the cold. Because I was soaked. With misery. I was empty. Tired, exhausted, but mostly empty, empty, empty.

I sat like that for a long time, not knowing what to do next. Then I slowly drove home.

The house was quiet. Dead.

I took the covers off our bed and cocooned myself in them. I sat on the couch and started to read.

IN A GLASS DARKLY

EMILY WAN'S DOCUMENT

I remember everything about it—with an effort. I see it all, as divers see what is going on above them, through a medium, dense, rippling, but transparent.

—Sheridan Le Fanu

October 16

It started again this morning. I don't want to work myself up, but I have to take a realistic view of my situation. I am certain now that it was a targeted attack. Sue has forbidden me to call it that, but she hasn't experienced it. Everyone who *has* either doesn't talk about it or is dead. That's how things stand now.

It happened during the condolence service for Dr. Claire Stein, a colleague from the PMU whom I half knew from our Pilates group class at the gym. Her death affected me deeply, because I *know* it was not an accident. It may have looked like an accident—her car shot off the overpass on the ring road with such high speed that the impact crushed her body even before it was flooded with the Amsterdam–Rhine Canal's black water. But I've made inquiries and the coroner found an extremely high concentration of Rohypnol in her blood. No psychologist takes seventeen capsules of Rohypnol, then gets behind the wheel without intending the toxicology report to function as a suicide note. The recently widowed Victor Rijneveld knows it too. It was written all over his face. The sudden death of a loved one always leaves deep furrows—mirrors don't lie, after all—but a violent death such as murder or suicide is so unmistakably, fundamentally harsh on the relatives. Rijneveld barely seemed present when he accepted the condolences. Lost in shock and incomprehension, he kept groping at the empty space beside him with his pale hand, as if he were trying to confirm the absence of his wife. It was all so very sad.

But there's another reason for why Dr. Stein's death has had such an impact on me. I suspect that it is in some way I do not yet fully understand, connected to what is going on with me! And she is the one who sowed the seeds of that suspicion, when she came up to me after Pilates, only four days before she died.

I'll write it all down—but first today.

It hit me when I left the funeral procession and joined the coffee table. I felt it coming, that was the worst part. As if it had kept an eye on me during the ceremony, waiting for the right moment to strike.

It all came back: the acute goose bumps, the air pressing too heavily in my lungs, that sense of increased electricity, as if the nerves running through my spinal cord were literally dilating. In neurology we call it an aura: some epileptics can feel the onset of an attack by a strange taste in the mouth or by certain hallucinations. This was *my* aura, but there was something else.

The sudden certainty that there was someone there, someone I couldn't see. Right behind me.

I instinctively turned around but saw only the bleak faces of the attendees. Men in suits and women in black jackets or dresses, hospital employees, loved ones, Dr. Stein's friends. I felt the gazes of those who were nearest to me. And then I understood: *They felt it too.* As if I was surrounded by a cloud of poison gas. They sensed it, couldn't place it, and dismissed it as the charged atmosphere of mourning. But when I excused myself and wriggled out of the line, people moved away from me and dispersed, as if I were emanating some sort of negative force.

Because it was following me. I could feel it.

I pushed through the crowd toward the washrooms and got there just in time. The door had barely closed before it happened. My brain switched off the film of my perception and started to absorb reality in photo flashes, the kind that stick in your mind and allow you, even in a state of total panic, to assess situations with extreme clarity. In those flashes I saw myself reflected in the mirrors above the sinks. And I won't beat around the bush: there was someone there, leaning over me. It is my professional duty to say that it must have been a figment of my imagination, the brain fooling itself into seeing human shapes in shadows that scare the living daylights out of us. But I can't believe that any longer.

I could see it, right behind me.

And it didn't have a face. Just like the shadow in the hospital.

Next, I heard an aural sound: the alarm blaring in the AMC's west wing. Hurried footsteps in the corridor. Panicked voices. The quickened beeping of the electrocardiograph of the patient whose calvarium we had just opened. My pager beeping too. And finally, that deep, subterranean rumbling of something big coming closer.

It was awful. I can't even write about it—I don't want to experience it all over again. Maybe later, when I can take a more detached perspective.

When I finally emerged from the washrooms, the back of my left hand was purple and swollen. I must have hit it against the sink. Bruised, I presume, hopefully not broken. There was also a graze on my right arm, but I could cover that with my sleeve. With my left hand hidden in my right, I stumbled straight to the doors—not in a million years was I going to stay here and attend the interment—and avoided the gazes of most of the attendees, but at least ten of them must have seen my tousled hair and my sweat-soaked, disheveled clothes.

On the drive home, I did what I hadn't done during the funeral: I cried. When I hit the overpass where Dr. Stein had driven to her death, the ring road seemed to drop away before my very eyes, and I screamed. I really screamed. There comes a point when it overwhelms you, and then it all just comes falling out.

Oh, it's back! I really thought it was over. That it was some kind of post-traumatic cocktail, a reaction to the August 18 tragedy, a delayed stage of mourning. No sugar rim, no umbrella. But now I know I was wrong.

Dr. Stein is *dead*, and I keep thinking about what she hinted at during our conversation.

About Edgar.

(later)

Julian and Naomi are in bed, and I had an argument with Sue. I don't blame her for not believing everything I told her just like that. No one in their right mind would. I'm not saying that Sue thinks I'm lying, but she does think I'm imagining things. I know all too well that I have lost all semblance of reasonability by anthropomorphizing what she calls my "delusions." She and her well-intended advice! On WeChat, all the way from Beijing, with no idea what's going on with me. At some point you just explode!

And okay, I'll be honest. I've had four glasses of wine, and that's three more than is good for me. The wine makes it easier to accept that I'm thinking of things that are not only diametrically opposed to the principles of neuropsychology but to everything that can be scientifically substantiated. But it didn't do my temper any good!

In any case, I shall write down my suspicions about what Dr. Claire Stein told me before I change my mind.

Nine days ago today, she walked up to me after our Pilates class. I heard later that she was already on sick leave and had referred all her patients to other doctors, and I'm quite certain that her sole reason for coming to the gym that morning was to talk to me. As I was on my way to the main building, she stopped me and said, trying to sound as offhand as possible, "Say, I understand you were there that night, on the eighteenth."

"That's right," I answered, immediately on my guard. So many journalists are still circling the AMC like moths around a streetlamp—some of whom have, in all their subtlety, dubbed the tragedy the "August Fright Night."

Yet it was obvious to me right away that Claire Stein had different motives. She was clearly ill at ease, and she was wearing a thick sweater and a scarf, despite it being a pleasant early autumn day. That struck me as strange right off the bat.

"I wanted to discuss something with you. It's a rather strange story. And it's maybe related to what happened that night."

"Oh? Maybe it's better to take it to Inspection, then."

But Dr. Stein said she wanted to talk to someone who had actually been there, and despite everything, she had my interest. We all share our sense of curiosity, don't we? Sometimes too much.

"But I'm not sure if I can give you the information you're looking for, Claire. You're probably aware that we're not allowed to talk to the media or anyone. We all had to sign an NDA."

Dr. Stein said that she had absolutely no intention of getting me in trouble, and then she came to the point. She told me she was treating a patient who'd been facially disfigured last summer in a violent assault while mountaineering in the Swiss Alps. One of those young outdoor types, she called him Edgar for convenience's sake. She said his climbing partner was most probably the culprit. Besides his slow recuperation, Edgar suffers from severe psychological trauma as a result of the incident, but at least he survived. His climbing partner was never found. I asked the obvious question of whether she believed Edgar had something to do with his disappearance.

"I can't rule it out," Claire said. "Edgar claims that his partner had fallen into a crevasse during the incident. The Swiss police, however, say it was an accident and don't mention violence at all in their report. It's all very unusual. But that's not what this is about. Edgar claims that he is possessed by the mountain where it all happened."

Paranoia is not uncommon among patients suffering from severe trauma. When the brain's metabolism is disrupted, its functions undergo a quick transformation, which can lead to the illusion that the loss of control is caused by an external presence. Part of me knows that my own hallucinations are illusions too, but there are obscure areas in the human psyche in which illusions can sometimes seep through reality like a caustic acid. I know of a case in which a Dutch patient with severe schizophrenia suddenly started speaking fluent Swedish (which, according to his family, he had never done), in an old woman's voice. In older days, he would undoubtedly have been assumed to be possessed by the devil. Nowadays, we know that mental disorders are capable of stretching the spectrum of what we consider to be normal human behavior practically without limit. That idea is actually much more haunting. Because we, in fact, still understand so little about it.

Claire was silent for a moment, then said, "Two weeks ago, I had a clash with Edgar. He was so ashamed of how he looked that, even after his recovery, he would still wrap his face up with bandages. I tried to get him to confront his mutilation and asked him to remove them. But I didn't do it for his sake, Emily. I did it for mine. I was afraid of him. There was something entirely wrong with him. I don't have any other way of describing it. And when he did . . ." She shivered all over. "Something happened. And, since then, something has changed."

"What was it, Claire?"

"He showed me something. Something I wish I hadn't seen." Her hand trembling, she took off her sunglasses. Only now did I see how bad she looked. "And since, I've been having seizures," she said.

"What kind of seizures?"

"I'm suffering from what I call, for want of a better term, psychosomatic hypothermia."

I asked her what she meant by that. Claire continued but expressed herself in increasingly vague terms. It's a common phenomenon that psychologists can sometimes get caught up in their patients' warped realities and she wanted to avoid giving that impression at all costs. Without much success, I have to say.

"I'm cold all the time," she said, "no matter how warm I dress. First I thought it was a late case of summer flu, but that's not it. I had a couple of seizures during which I just couldn't stop shaking. Yesterday it was so bad my husband took my temperature. It was 93.4° F."

"I don't think that's psychosomatic. Have you seen your GP?"

"Yes. She thinks it's an underactive thyroid gland and prescribed hormones. But she's wrong, Emily. I'm afraid that . . . I'm afraid that I have a slow-working variant of whatever it is that killed the victims of August 18."

Now I couldn't conceal my amazement. "But what makes you think that? I'm sure you know that—"

She grabbed my wrist, and I'd be lying if I said I wasn't startled by how cold her hand felt. I saw blue veins running beneath her skin and her fingers were so white, they looked like there was no blood circulation at all.

"You were there that night," she said. "You must know more. Isn't it true that a number of the people who died had symptoms of hypothermia?"

That story was exposed by *de Volkskrant*: at least fourteen of the thirty-two victims were said to have succumbed to hypothermia. Naturally, it was a big issue, so the AMC was forced to confirm it. The cause is still a mystery (making it a breeding ground for conspiracy theories—the most ridiculous of which claims that liquid nitrogen had been spread through the hospital's air filtration system). They now call it an "unknown medical anomaly," which makes neither the hospital nor the general public happy. The bizarre thing that happened with *my* patient, the boy we were operating on, most certainly *wasn't* hypothermia (or epilepsy, as was written on his death certificate), but at least fourteen others, as they say, "froze to death" that night.

I didn't tell Claire that, because I didn't want to fan the fire of what was obviously a false notion. Instead, I asked what gave her the idea there was a connection.

"Edgar was there too. He was a patient in the AMC and was recovering from his injuries."

At first, I was under the impression that Dr. Stein thought her patient had been infected by what had happened that night and that he, in turn, infected her, but I was wrong.

She thought he had *caused* it.

She took my hand again, with both hands now, and said, "During the last seizure I had a hallucination, Emily. The same hallucination that Edgar showed me when he took off his bandages in my office. I found myself in an ice cave. And I wasn't alone. The whole time it felt like there was someone right next to me, but I was so overcome by the cold that I couldn't find out who it was. The cold had descended into me, all the way into my bones. I just knew it was someone *bad*."

I carefully withdrew my hand, because I started to feel uncomfortable. "The crevasse, the cold—it must surely be obvious to you too where these associations come from, Claire. It's your patient's story. And you said it yourself. You were hallucinating. Have you considered undergoing more neurological tests? A CT scan maybe, to rule out a few possibilities?"

But she shook her head. "Don't you have any symptoms since that night?"

I hesitated only very briefly before I said no. Claire looked at me inquisitively, but I had collected myself again, and my reply was adamant. And I *had* no symptoms. Not the kind Dr. Stein was talking about.

I advised her to make an appointment with Neurology and gave her my card, in case she felt the need to talk again. But Claire was visibly disappointed, and after that, she never contacted me again.

If only she had!

If only *I* had acted on it. The truth is that I almost did, three days later. The day before she died. I was about to walk to PMU and track her down. And yet I listened to the voice of reason, which was telling me I was chasing ghosts.

What haunted me was the last thing Dr. Stein had said before we said good-bye. That she was experiencing her hallucinations as if they were lasting forever and never stopped.

"That was the worst," she said. "When I woke up from my own screaming and realized that my husband was soothing me, I was convinced I hadn't seen him in years."

Four days later, she drove into the Amsterdam–Rhine Canal.

The same forensic pathologist who told me about the high concentration of Rohypnol in her blood let it slip that when they hauled her out of the canal, she had been practically naked. She had taken off her cardigan and blouse and was in the process of removing her trousers and panties when the car plunged off the overpass. He thought it was a sexual thing, but I don't believe that. "Paradoxical undressing" is a phenomenon when just before victims of hypothermia lose consciousness, their subcutaneous veins suddenly dilate, causing a sensation of intense heat. Sometimes, people who get lost in the snow and have severe hypothermia will tear off all their clothes. Because they are so very hot as they are freezing to death.

Am I chasing ghosts?

I lied to Claire when I denied having any symptoms, since the tragedy of August 18. The first couple of weeks, I did suffer from posttraumatic flashbacks. But by the time Claire had spoken with me, I was convinced that I was rid of it. Yes, you could call the similarities with Dr. Stein's description of her experiencing infinity remarkable, but I wasn't prepared to indulge in such fallacies. I didn't want to put myself on a slippery slope.

But I was wrong. It hasn't gone away. Thinking back on the past few weeks, I can see now it was always there, dormant in the background. This morning, in the funeral home, it came back in full force. A seizure, just like that night in the AMC.

I also have a hallucination. Not that I freeze, but that I'm falling. It happens again and again. And it never ends.

Infinity is just a word, a concept without significance. But once you have experienced it, its meaning is abhorrent.

This has nothing to do with psychology. I've been carrying something inside me since that night in August. Something that has been eating into me like a parasite. Is it the same thing that has sent Claire Stein to her death? If so, what am I supposed to do?

Imagine I have a seizure with the children around. Or during an operation! I can't control it. The best I can do is isolate myself when I feel it coming on—*if* I feel it coming on. But what if a day comes when that is impossible?

I can't stop thinking about what Claire said about her patient.

The young man with his face covered in bandages.

The shadow I saw leaning over me in the mirror this morning had no face.

Tomorrow, I will apologize to Sue, because I have been unreasonable. Maybe Huib wouldn't have known what to do, but he would have at least taken me into his arms, and today that would have made a difference.

God, I miss him so much!

October 20

It's getting worse. Had two major attacks. Yesterday afternoon. At home, thank God. I gave myself a prescription for muscle relaxants and Rohypnol, which seem to be helping somewhat (hmm, it comes to me now that Dr. Stein also took Rohypnol). I talked about it with Sue, but I have to be careful what I do and do not say.

I talked to a colleague from Reconstructive Surgery, using a fabricated story about a young athlete whose face got mutilated. I said that I had been told that they had treated a mountaineer with similar injuries and that I wanted to get in touch with him, in order to observe the long-term effects of his disfigurement on his functioning. Most hospitals have a culture of sticking together. In other words, special favors, pulling strings, is not uncommon. The doctor remembered the patient and offered to get in touch with him about my request. I don't expect it to lead to much, but more importantly: he had let his name slip.

Edgar's real name is Nick Grevers.

October 31

Keeping this short, because I have to pick up the kids from school. No more attacks, twelve days now, and I have to keep pinching myself to make sure I'm not dreaming!

I decided to leave it be. Yesterday Sue and I had a long talk on the phone, and I asked her to do the same. I have been obsessed with my delusions for a while, but I'm seeing things more clearly now.

Talking about obsession. If Nick Grevers found out how much information I have managed to gather about him, he'd accuse me of being a stalker! I know he writes for Lonely Planet. Amusing, crisp pieces. I know he has a boyfriend from New York, whose name is Sam Avery. I will be honest—I completely sifted through both their Instagram profiles. They're both your typical fun and good-looking kind of guys. What sticks most in my mind is a selfie they took last year at a Shania Twain concert in London. Arms around each other's shoulders, beer in hand, Nick with a hat on, which Shania has apparently thrown into the audience. It's such a happy photo. It's tragic that the accident has put an end to all of that so drastically.

There is something ominous about the last post on Grevers's profile. It shows him and his climbing partner with big smiles hiding behind their mirrored sunglasses on a high, glaciated summit in the Alps. He tagged it *#livingthelife*. Nothing after that. A couple of days later his climbing partner was dead, Grevers was mutilated, and that was the end of his online happiness. His boyfriend hasn't posted anything since August either.

It almost feels like I know them, and that means I have let myself become too personally attached. It's none of my business. I have to pick up the pieces of my own life. Whatever mystery has sent Claire Stein to her death, it's a mystery of the human psyche. Of human madness.

Worrying myself silly appears to be a habit that is hard to kick, but sometimes you need to flip the switch and start *living*, right?

Gee, forgot the time. I have to run!

November 1

I could *cry*!!! Oh, goddamn stupid asshole *motherfucker*! It's back and it was much worse than before. The kids are finally asleep, but I keep crying. Afraid I can't deal with this any longer.

"Falling" not once in their reports. Modern medicine is too pragmatic. No one had *seen* them fall, after all, but that is exactly what happened. They fell and they fell and they fell till they crashed to the ground.

November 2

Back to my notes. Put the phone on quiet because Sue won't stop calling and I don't have the energy to defend myself. She wouldn't understand. I only just understood it myself! Poor Dr. Stein. It snapped her mind in the end and I believe the same has happened to me.

If it weren't for the kids, I think I would have already ended my life by now. They keep me going. It's for their sakes I need to be strong. Just like Julian was at the critical moment. Oh, the way he took care of his little sister! Huib would have been so proud.

They were there. It was my worst nightmare, and it came true. We were having dinner when it happened. I didn't even have time to get ready or brace myself. It hit me with such force that I must have fallen backwards in my chair and hit the floor. By then I was already out. The only thing I remember was my head was suddenly full of noise, and all the shadows in the room were plunging into me. Then I began to fall. But the children . . .

It must have been awful for them to see their mother like that. Apparently, I had a glass of red wine in my hand when it happened, because I came to surrounded by glass splinters, and the back of my right hand was all gashed because it had been thrashing about in it. Julian and Naomi were cowering in the corner, but even though he was crying himself, Julian had his arms around his sister and was comforting her. Later, he said that he had been so scared that it hadn't even occurred to him to call 112. But the worst came when I dragged myself toward them, moaning and bleeding, and they *shrank back* from me. Naomi screamed, "Why did you hurt me, Mommy? Why did you hurt me?"

It's true. Julian told me. She had run up to me and I had knocked her to the ground, not once but twice, before Julian was able to pull her away from me. It's awful! Her cheekbone is black and blue, and there's an enormous bruise on her arm.

Huib and I never hit the children. Never. She must have been terrified!

Naomi gazed at my hand and said, "Mommy, you're bleeding," and if that was the case, if Mommy had hurt herself too, then it must have been an accident, then Mommy hadn't hurt her on purpose. She let me hug her—thank God. I put ice on her cheek and bandaged my hand. I had to use tweezers to remove the glass from my skin. And Julian was so sweet and helpful! Sometimes he seems so grown up, with that worried expression of his. Then I really see Huib behind that small, young face.

Damn it, I'm crying again.

In any case, it took a long time before Naomi had calmed down, but I let her choose a big Disney Band-Aid, and she liked that. It covers the wound on her face, but I'm afraid that her teacher will ask about it on Monday. When I tucked her in, I said, "You can tell Miss Marian that Mommy is sick and that you fell, but don't tell her Mommy's hand hit you by accident, okay? She doesn't need to know that. That'll be our little secret."

I'm so ashamed!

I hope she won't say anything. But there is nothing I can do about it.

Okay, so I said I was sick. Naomi accepted that, but Julian is more inquisitive and asked what I have. I said that the doctor doesn't know yet and that I sometimes have an attack, but that it always goes away in a jiffy, even though it may look very scary. I told him that he was a wonderful big brother and that if it were ever to happen again, he should take his sister to the bedroom and wait there till it was over.

Later, when he was in bed, he said something terrible. He said there had been someone next to me.

I asked him what he meant, but he couldn't tell me much more other than that he thought he had seen a man in the room when I was screaming and swinging my arms. But he hadn't seen who it was, because the man didn't have a face.

Don't tell me I still have to be rational now! Or that there is some natural explanation for all of this.

Julian said something else. That it had looked like I was floating.

He fell asleep and I collapsed.

Oh, will I ever be able to explain to anyone what it's like? What I feel when I'm falling?

Let me at least try. Maybe by writing it down I can at least create some sort of order. Maybe that way, I will find a way out of this misery. A clue I didn't see before.

As I am writing this, I am looking out over the city through the attic window. Hidden under a nightly glow beyond the houses across the street is Amsterdam-Zuidoost: the ArenA, the Ziggo Dome, the Amsterdamse Poort retail park. Farther south is the AMC. That's where it all started, so that's where I will start.

My patient's name on the night of August 18 was Tim van Laerhoven and he was only fifteen years old. After a trip through South America in late July, he started getting headaches, fever, and dizziness. A series of tests at the outpatient department and General Internal Medicine later, he was sent home with a provisional diagnosis of a chronic infection and a prescription for cotrimoxazole. His fever went down, but Tim remained listless and complained, his father told me during the intake, of a "pressure" behind his temples. "I didn't give it much thought, I get the occasional migraine too." The senior Van Laerhoven shrugged (the anesthetist said he was the slap-a-Band-Aid-on-it kind of type, even if his son were to be dismembered). On the evening of August 17, he found the boy in the bathroom, unconscious, convulsing, eyes half-open, and now he *did* give it some thought. An ambulance rushed Tim to the AMC, where a CT scan showed an enormous abscess under the cerebral membrane with acute symptoms of impingement. That's how Tim van Laerhoven came to be my emergency call that night.

Stella, a young nurse in Neurosurgery, was the first to see it, and I will never forget her choked scream.

"*Jesus, he's moving . . . That's impossible—the sedation!*"

"Stella, behave yourself," Stefan snapped at her from behind his surgical mask (Stefan is Stefan Rudnicki, assistant surgeon). I think he didn't say it in reaction to *what* she said—in his eyes, that must have been an impossibility—but to *how* she said it, because OR protocol stipulates that under no circumstances should one raise their voice, so as to not disrupt the operating surgeon's concentration. (For the same reason, the OR is practically soundproof, and that's why we had no idea what was going on in the corridors right then—what was going on in the *whole building*. It was just after three a.m.)

We had sawed open a flap in Tim's skull and opened the meninx. It's very possible to treat a cerebral abscess if you operate on it in time, and we did, but only just. The moment it started to go wrong, I had been focusing on the neuronavigation monitor and was on the other side of the tent of sheets we had put up around his head. Therefore I didn't see what Stella had seen. But I heard it all right, because the beeping from his electrocardiograph started to suddenly increase. "Fast heart rate," the anesthetist announced. "Heart rate 96, guys."

"96?" I asked, looking up from the monitor. "Where's that coming from?"

"Cerebral functions stable, blood pressure a bit high, heart rate now 104."

"Sufentanil and vecuronium, and stat," I said. There was no way he could be waking up from his sedation, but you'd better be on the safe side. "And what do you mean, 'he's moving,' Stella?"

"*Look, his arms!*"

Irritated, Stefan looked around the tent, and he gasped, "Jesus Christ."

I looked, and then I saw it too. The boy's arms—both arms—had risen off the operating table's blue sheets and were hovering five inches above them. "Vecuronium, *now!*" I said. "Stefan, check for hemorrhaging and leakage. Hold his arms, Stella. His head is in the clamp, but if he gets a seizure it can come loose."

"How can he get a seizure if—"

"No hemorrhaging or leakage," Stefan said. The anesthetist had given him the sedatives, but to no effect. The electrocardiograph monitor was going wild. His heart rate had gone up to 130 and was still rising.

I think Stella screamed when the boy's body started to rise. He wasn't floating, not like in those cheap horror flicks about people who are possessed. His hips came off the operating table and his body formed a supple bow, and it reminded me of a circus trapeze artist who gets hoisted into the air by his hips. Stella let go of him and shrunk back, bumping against the microscope, and now his arms were floating too. His shoulders and heels never came off the table, and although with some muscular strain one might imitate the posture his body had assumed, the boy's limbs were completely relaxed. I could *feel* it when I tried to push him down, and that made it seem so unnatural. There were no cramps, no spasms, no epileptic seizure, nothing of the sort. Tim van Laerhoven's sleeping body was behaving as if it were floating on air . . . or falling through the sky.

I think all four of us were too dumbfounded to do anything but stare at our patient. Stefan was the first to have the presence of mind to react. "Strap him down before he falls to the ground."

"What with?"

"*What difference does it make, damn it!*"

Under the tent around his forehead, Tim's eyes opened. We all saw it. The boy was under general anesthetic, we had sawed open his skull, but all the same, his eyes opened. Only there weren't any eyes, just bulging white. And he was smiling. That smile was the creepiest thing I have ever seen in my life. It was a blissful smile, the smile of a boy riding a roller coaster and enjoying the butterflies in his stomach.

Then his body literally snapped in two.

The sound it made was like a hefty bundle of dry branches breaking all at once. But there was also a *wet* sound, a *splash*. The boy died in front of our very eyes. He smashed to his death. He came down on the operating table with a thundering crash and literally bounced back up before landing again, this time for good. The plugs on his chest were pulled loose and the electrocardiograph immediately let out a shrill, continuous beep. The tent around his head collapsed, the instruments table fell over, and all the instruments crashed to the floor. And Tim . . .

All the bones in his body were broken. If I remember correctly, the autopsy report said that only three of his vertebrae and a metatarsal were spared. Everything else was simply pulverized. But his skin—human skin can withstand enormous forces without tearing. What was lying there before us in that blue hospital gown was a shapeless bag of skin, within which complete destruction had taken place. In death, people shrink. The violence of his death had colored the thing that was once Tim a deep purple and shrunk him with a shock, without spitting out its contents. That's what the wet sound was.

Except for the skull. That looked like a lead weight had fallen on it. Skulls are full of holes, and this one had one extra sawed into it. Stefan got it all over him and screeched like a little girl.

I screamed too. The anesthetist cowered in a corner of the OR and looked like he was going to faint any second. Stella ran from the room crying and left the door wide open. That's when we heard the siren wailing out in the corridor.

So this is what the media described as the "strange fractures" found in the bones of at least sixteen victims that night. This, too, was subject of the wildest theories, as is always the case with great mysteries that remain unsolved. Convulsions brought on by epilepsy. An aggressive infection. Arsenic poisoning. Nerve gas. Convulsions can cause bones to break, but not like this. Not *anything* like this.

Well, we declared him dead; that's all we could do for him. Once I'd freed myself from that sterile OR center and was standing in the corridor, only then did it start to filter through that something much bigger was going on in the hospital. I was too rattled to react. My hands refused to stop trembling, and all I could see before me was that boy's smile. It didn't fully register, but I heard the wailing of the alarm, the screaming, the running feet, and the constantly repeated, ominous message over the intercom: ". . . *not yet contained. I repeat, not yet contained. Patients and staff are requested to remain in place unless otherwise instructed by qualified personnel. It is strictly forbidden to leave the hospital premises. First aid personnel to Unit 2A right away, I repeat . . .*" But the hallway in front of the OR center was eerily deserted. I rushed into the first ladies' room I could find.

And that's where it happened. I felt it immediately when the automatic lights came on and I smelled chlorine and disinfectants. The atmosphere in here was charged, seemed to crackle with energy. I saw it with more than my eyes; it was deep within my brain, because this time—I know that now—*I* was the possessed. The walls expanded and spun around me. For a second, I thought I was going to faint, because I mistook the rising of the wind for dizziness in my vestibular system. I was already bracing myself. Then I noticed the cold mass of air that was menacingly pushing forward, pregnant with—and this is true—large snowflakes. The mirrors fogged up in a frozen bouquet of ice flowers. High above the suspended ceiling I saw electromagnetic sparks, as if the bitterly cold air was charged, and the black flashes of birds tumbling and diving in a rapid, spiraling descent. A storm was coming. I steadied myself on the sinks and stumbled back into the corridor.

There was someone there.

At the end of the hallway. There was a deep void. An immense darkness.

I saw a shadow between drifts of snow that were now rushing through the hall in front of the OR center, a shadow without a face. Where it came from I do not know, but I knew one thing more certain than anything else: that shadow had caused all of this.

Then I started to fall.

I fell with sickening speed through merciless winds. I barely knew what was happening to me. Suddenly the ground under my feet had disappeared. I flailed my arms, looking for something to hold on to, while gravity took possession of me. The cold and the wind slammed the air out of my lungs, tensed up my heart and caused my scream to die away above me. My intestines protested against the velocity of my fall. I know that skydivers can relax their bodies while free-falling, but I couldn't. My fall was uncontrolled, a disorderly and dizzying descent through a degenerate darkness, and the feeling it produced in me was a degree of intolerable horror.

And it wouldn't stop.

The only thing you can think about when you're falling from a great height is the ground, which you will hit any second now, and the only impulse is to brace yourself against the impact that will crush the life out of you. But it didn't come. I kept on falling. The extension of death was not a source of solace; it did nothing to remove my piercing fear of it, nor did it relieve the suffocating pressure on my lungs. On the contrary. The storm through which

I was falling prolonged my demise into hopeless, endless agony. Awaiting me down there lay infinity.

Weeks and years went by, and I fell.

The manifestation of infinity is beyond our comprehension and that is, I daresay, the salvation of our sanity. But I've seen it. I was offered such a perspective—and one look at the place our pathetic, individual lives occupy within it, instantly made me want to hit the ground.

But slowly an even more suffocating, more alarming fear dawned on me: *that this was not going to happen.*

I realized that I was awake only after staring for a long time at my hand. It was lying flat on the linoleum floor of the hallway. My cheek too. Something painful in my body was throbbing (I would later find out I had a rib contusion and bruises all over my arms). Minutes went by before I understood where I was. The siren and the intercom had fallen still. I had no idea how long I had been unconscious.

I tried calling for help but discovered I had no voice. The fall had ripped it out of me. So I knew that it had really happened. Nevertheless, here I was, and the storm had blown over.

But that was the biggest illusion of all, I now know. Because the storm had never really died down. Twice, I have made the mistake of thinking I was free of it, but it keeps coming back worse every time.

It follows me day and night.

Every time it attacks me, this is how it happens.

I fall through the pitch-black void and experience infinity. Hell is repetition, they say, but being trapped in infinity over and over again is the everlasting destruction of the soul.

Where will this end? But I am afraid I know the answer.

I am looking at Instagram photos again. I know the faceless shadow I saw in the corridor in front of the OR center was Nick Grevers. It's the same shadow that was chasing Dr. Claire Stein in her attacks. The same shadow that Julian saw leaning over me last night.

Was it what some would call an astral projection? A sort of out-of-body manifestation or, what's it called again—a doppelganger?

As I scroll through his pictures, I can only speculate as to what kind of unnatural quirk of fate has made him capable of impregnating his traumatic experience in the mountains into his victims and penetrating their reality. The falling. The freezing.

Why did he kill all those people and let Claire and me live?

Maybe he has no control over it.

I can't go to the police.

I almost sent his boyfriend a message. If there is anyone experiencing Nick's affliction, it's got to be him. But I am too scared. And what would I say?

Oh, if only I knew what to do!

November 8

The Child Protective Services! How could she *do* that????!!! This is beyond betrayal!

Just when there was a glimmer of hope. Just when there was light on the horizon. I was supposed to meet Sam Avery tomorrow.

But I know what I have to do now. This morning I found Naomi in bed, feverish and shivering from cold. She said that last night a man had sat on the edge of her bed. He had the face of a mummy, but the bandages had hung loose, "all in loops."

I carry something poisonous in me, and I will keep carrying it for the rest of my life. I will infect others with it. I am the gateway, and I have to shut it now, for the sake of the children. Only then can I be certain that they will be safe.

I'm so terribly sorry, Huib. Please catch me when I fall!

AT THE MOUNTAINS OF MADNESS

NICK GREVERS'S MANUSCRIPT (PART 5)

I have said that Danforth refused to tell me what final horror made him scream out so insanely—a horror which, I feel sadly sure, is mainly responsible for his present breakdown.

—H. P. Lovecraft

The cold makes waking up a protracted, disoriented dream. My mind crawls slowly over the edge of my consciousness, seems to topple back, then gets ahold of it. When I extricate myself from the space blanket's semidarkness, I see dull patterns of light gleaming on the ice. My Petzl's batteries are dead, but I can see through the hole in the roof that the sky is clear and colored by the dawn's first light.

Apathetic and shaking uncontrollably, I stare at the blue-gray cave, the ice screws, the suspended rope, and try to push away the echoes of a traumatic night. Sometime during the night, Augustin's screaming stopped, and the unforgiving silence is sucking up all the energy. I need to pee, feel the clotted blood flow sluggishly through my stiff muscles, can't think straight. Symptoms of hypothermia, I know. The crevasse provided shelter and my backpack under my body and the space blanket some extra insulation, but the clothes I'm wearing were not made for a night in a freezer. I'm lucky to have woken up; the cold could have just as easily embraced me with the eternal sleep of the crevasse.

I force myself on my feet, furiously stamp ice grit off the balcony, slap my thighs and lower legs with both hands, then my chest and arms crosswise. I put all of last night's anger and fears into it and when, fifteen minutes later, I'm done, I feel stronger, both physically and mentally. The worst of the cold is gone from my bones, my blood has started flowing again. I see the cave now as nothing more than what it is: a hollow cavity in a tens-of-thousands-of-years-old mass of seemingly unmoving ice.

I gaze upward at the walls and a plan slowly starts to take shape. The hole we fell through is clearly out of the question, but the crevasse extends to the left, where it opens up again. The walls there are rougher and closer to each other. A broken ice tower stretches up into a funnel of frozen snow that leads all the way to the hole. If I can reach Augustin's plateau, maybe I can avoid having to climb up along the slippery, overhanging walls.

Augustin. Is he still alive?

I'll find out soon enough. If he's alive, I can start plotting on a rescue operation. If not, I'll at least need his ice screws.

I unscrew mine from the wall and stuff my things into my backpack. After making a belay on the rope—same technique as the day before—I start pepping myself up. My gaze is constantly fixed on the way out: the ledge, the wall, the bridge. Then the traverse, the tower, the funnel. Obsessively, I repeat these words out loud like a mantra. All of a sudden, the crevasse is no longer a crypt but a series of complex obstacles that can be tackled one by one. The hole is all that matters; that's where I need to go.

Three times I climb a few steps up from the balcony, try to accustom myself to a coordinated rhythm, the perfect balance between power and elegance, which my crampons and axes will soon need on the ice wall. As soon as I get the hang of it, I set off. I know I need to take advantage of this rush of self-confidence before the uncertainty sets in.

I cautiously traverse the ledge, sliding the Prusik knot forward on the taut rope. For the first bit, I must rely on Augustin's body as my anchor, should I fall. I hung on it yesterday, after all, so theoretically, it should hold.

Better not fall.

When I reach the other side, I can see much further down, thanks to the daylight, but the shadows are erratic and there is still no bottom in sight. Nevertheless, the abyss is now less threatening. I focus on the ice wall that rises above me. Only four yards of slippery ice, then I can slam my ice axes into the bridge. I slide the Prusik as high as I can reach, feel the reassuring weight of the axes in my hands, and take a deep breath. It's now or never.

My calves are screaming, splinters of ice tinkle down like glass, and my stomach clenches, but I still manage to somehow climb up and hoist myself onto the plateau with a triumphant scream.

Holy shit, I'm so proud of what I've achieved, I could cry. Reeling from the exertion, my head throbbing, I scramble to my feet and pull in the loops of rope. Then I look to see where I am.

Augustin is lying on his side, pressed against the raised edge, and I see the grooves in the ice where the rope has cut into it. His weight has only just anchored him, by the looks of it. Augustin's legs are at an unnatural angle under his body. Broken, after all. Worse, he is showing no signs of life. His complexion is oily and bleak, and there's dried, frosted blood stuck under his helmet. Despite his eyes being shut, his features are frozen in an expression of bewilderment.

I recall last night's hoarse screams and shiver involuntarily. By daylight, the memory seems distant, but I can hardly blame myself for believing he was possessed or dead, when he screamed like that.

I gently shake his shoulder, take off my gloves and put my fingers to his lips to feel if he's breathing. Nothing. I want to know for sure and reach under the lined collar of his Gore-Tex coat for his neck.

Augustin rolls over and his hand grips my leg like a spider.

"Jesus Christ!" My scream echoes shrilly against the ice walls. I leap backwards, flail my arms, and almost fall off the bridge.

Augustin opens his eyes, but there aren't any. Because the death birds ate them up last night. Where his eyes should have been, two big, black holes are staring at me.

"I'm so cold, Nick," he whispers. White clouds of breath rise from his lips. "So cold . . ."

It isn't real, I think, but sheer, stone-cold panic grabs hold of me and I throw myself back against the crevasse wall. *Not real, it's making you see things. Like yesterday when Augustin's Seiko said our altitude was over 16,000 feet—not real. It's trying to unhinge you now that it has lost its hold on you.*

I squeeze my eyes shut, shake my head, cover my face with my hands. When I look again, I see spots.

The holes where his eyes should have been are staring into me as he lies there, utterly motionless. There aren't even any eyelids. Only those two deep, dead tunnels, in which the vacant, riveted stare looks like it's been torn away from some distant place—a horrifying, *charged* place.

"Help me, Nick." His whispering is almost inaudible. "I'm so, so cold . . ."

"Jesus Christ, Augustin, you're still alive!"

But is he? If his eyes have been picked out and his soul has escaped, is what remains of him really alive?

Augustin lifts his arm, and his stiff fingers reach helplessly for me. No way am I coming any closer. No way am I going to touch him. Still, I notice that my feet are making their way toward him. I *have* to get real and convince myself it's an illusion that it's really Augustin and that he needs my help.

"Hey, man . . . how are you feeling?"

No answer. I come closer.

That hand, reaching out for me. Those holes for eyes.

I need all my willpower to hoist him up by his shoulders. I don't dare look into that bewitched face. Any moment, I expect something awful to happen. But Augustin doesn't budge. His body has gotten precariously cold. Making sure his thighs don't turn the wrong way, I tug him into a sitting position against the perpendicular edge. The relief I feel when I let go of him is immense.

Augustin turns his face up to me. I get the feeling that he's trying to tell me something but isn't able to, as if last night's trauma not only robbed him of his soul but also of his ability to speak. Something is glimmering in the holes where his eyes should be, like mist on distant arctic plains. His mouth forms inaudible words that reveal a bleak emptiness.

"Listen," I say, in an attempt to appear as matter-of-fact as possible. It's a childish thought, but if I don't let on that I see it, maybe it won't see me either. It feels like my only chance. "I'm going to have a shot at climbing out of this place, okay? When I top out, I'll get you out of here too. I have enough gear for a *Flaschenzug*, so I'll haul you up. It's going to be all right. The sun is shining out there. Can you see it? You only need to hold on a little longer. When I get you out, we'll call for a helicopter."

I realize it's all very iffy—*if* I manage to climb up, *if* I'm at all able to haul Augustin up, *if* my iPhone finds a carrier—but it's all I got.

If it's still Augustin.

I reach for his gear loop to take his ice screws and Prusiks and get all queasy when I see that the black holes are following my hand intently.

My heart thumping, I turn my back to him.

I quickly start twisting an ice screw into the wall. With four screws, I can more or less belay myself during my kamikaze climb on the traverse and the tower. I estimate the roof to be about fifteen yards up. If I go in four-yard pitches from screw to screw, the most I could fall is eight yards. If I manage to top out on the glacier and make an anchor there, I'll have to rappel all the way back down to free the rope and climb up all over again, but better safe than sorry.

Before the ice screw is halfway in, my hand seizes up.

It is completely light now, and the sunlight is glaring through the opening in the dome. It entrances me, and I immediately forget about Augustin. The light possesses an intensity so sublime that, after last night's cold threat, it endows the ice vault with the appearance of a cathedral, with sparkling walls of snow crystals. It's so beautiful! All the tribulations melt away in that light, make way for the essence of what I'm really here for: the longing for the immutability that only mountains possess, a longing that, in all its vulnerability, I can find only in this landscape. When I gaze up from the ice bridge at that sacred light, it overwhelms not only my soul; it hijacks my every movement.

And without giving the rope or the screw a second thought, without even seeming to have any control over it, I start climbing the ice wall head-on.

[*Honestly, Sam, I have no idea how I got out of that crevasse. I don't know why I abandoned the safe plan of traversing to the left, or how I succeeded in free soloing fifteen yards of rock-solid, overhanging ice and in dragging myself through those crumbling crusts and powder snow avalanches over the cornice and onto the glacier. There are people who are capable of those kinds of feats, but there are also people who can run the hundred-meter dash in less than ten seconds, and I'm sure not one of them. I don't remember anything besides climbing in a trance of power and topping out onto the glacier in bright sunlight, and that I was no longer afraid of whatever was haunting Augustin, and that was that.*

I keep thinking about Augustin pulling me up during the ascent over the ice-covered slabs on the north face. Truth is, I don't really believe in the kind of superhuman strength, powered by adrenaline, which they say enables you to do things in extreme circumstances that you normally couldn't. Not to this extent, anyway. There are simple laws of nature that limit human ability.

And that raises the question: Did the Maudit *really let me go?*

Sometimes I think I'm about to wake up only to discover that I'm still trapped in the crevasse.

That I'll still be hearing Augustin's screaming all around me when the death birds release his soul.

And then, Sam? What then?

Maybe it will be a relief, because the alternative is worse: that I'm no longer in the crevasse but the crevasse is in me.]

My recollections solidify again from the moment that, invigorated by the warm sun on my back, I'm digging into a deep layer of powder snow, in the lee of the mountain faces that enclose the upper glacial combe. Finally, I hit solid snow, into which I can bury my ice axe as an anchor. I tamp the snow. It feels hopelessly unstable, so unstable that I untie myself from the rope, preferring to expose myself to the dangers of possible hidden crevasses than to take the risk of plummeting into the void with Augustin, should the anchor go. But it's the best I can do. The *Flaschenzug* is Mountaineering 101; you just hope that you will never actually have to put it into practice: a pulley made of Prusik knots and carabiners on the main rope, which divides the weight you have to pull out by three.

"*Here we go, Augustin!*" I shout.

I hang on the rope with my full weight, one hand around the unlocked Prusik knot. I have no idea whether Augustin has heard me. As soon as he's hoisted up, he'll have to support himself so as to not put any weight on his broken legs. Nothing I can do about it; he'll have to bite the bullet.

How heavy is he—140, 150 pounds? Soon it will all be on the anchor. The sling is cutting deep into the snow. For a second, I think the buried axe is moving in the snow, and I look intently at the anchor. Nothing. I return to my hoisting.

When I'm halfway, the axe *does* move, at least five inches. No doubt about it now.

My heart racing, I run back to the anchor and tamp the snow as carefully as possible, afraid that the impacts will actually disturb the delicate balance. I look at it indecisively. It will have to do. Back to hoisting, as fast as I can.

Finally, a sound: a spatter in the snow on the edge of the crevasse.

I crawl to it on hands and knees, aware of the cornice's instability.

The rope is cut in too deep.

Augustin is hanging under its edge, sweeping the powder snow away with his axes. He doesn't look up at me, and I can't see his face under his helmet.

"Wait, man, let me help you."

I scramble back, hoist him up another half yard.

The anchor moves. Oh Jesus!

As fast as I can, I crawl back to the edge. I have to be quick now, have to get his weight off the axe.

Augustin is suddenly very close and has struck off a big piece of the cornice. I prepare to lie prone in the snow and reach my hand out to him . . . but then he looks up.

And then.

And then.

* * *

Sometime later, I wake up. I don't recall the moment itself. I only know that I become aware that my eyes are open, and I'm looking into blazing, blinding sunlight, and a gust of snowdrift is blowing into my eyes like sand.

I have no idea where I am. I'm lying prone, my face flat in the snow, my limbs motionless beside me. I feel an irregular, icy texture under my body but can't place it. All I know is the cold.

Only later do I realize how seriously low my body temperature had dropped, inferred from the fact that so much time goes by before it occurs to me that I could actually get up and do something about the situation. But even then, it takes a long time before I actually manage to shake off my apathy. Eventually, the thought of Augustin forces me up. Augustin and the Maudit. Did I hoist him out of the crevasse? I have no idea what happened after the anchor started slipping.

I hear a zipper-like sound as I pull my left cheek off the snow, so gruesome that I expect to have torn off half of my face.

Oh, Jesus, the snow is full of blood.

It isn't fresh blood; it has seeped in too deep for that. *But there's so much of it.*

I raise my right hand to my face but don't feel anything. Both my face and my fingers are numb, except for a dull thumping in my right cheek, intense, like a throbbing toothache. My palate feels so dry and swollen that my tongue can't recognize my own mouth anymore.

Nausea and panic sweep over me. It takes all my willpower to not let it hamper me. God, what has happened to me? A gust of wind blows on my face and I wait for my head to clear.

Eventually it does.

When I stand up, I'm astonished to discover that I am now much lower on the glacier. Behind me, my trail loops from the upper glacial combe, across overlapping, snowy slopes, to here, where I had eventually collapsed and passed out. In the north, where the ice, riddled with scree and talus, bulges downward, I see the lake, a perfect circle, and behind it the moraines where our bivouac is. The valley lies anchored in the sun, and despite my severe hypothermia, I realize that it isn't cold anymore. You can tell by how wet the snow has become. Holes are forming where it is caving in and melting, revealing the scree below. That's my salvation. If last night's storm had persevered, I probably never would have woken up. There is no more wind now in the atmosphere's upper layers, yet there's something strange brooding in the air, as if the impression the wind had pressed into it hasn't been wiped away yet.

It's all I can do to not give in to the urge to lie down again. I swing my arms around, ignore the shivering, and rub myself, trying to get warm so I will remain conscious. I roll my head on my neck. Gradually, I start getting warmer and feel my lethargy ebb away . . . but with mental clarity also comes the pain.

My face. There's something wrong with my face.

Something happened. Something serious. What it is, I don't know. I don't dare touch my face. Don't dare feel it.

Why does my tongue feel so thick?

I drift toward the valley on frozen feet. The crust of snow is thin, the ice under it bare. The glacier has renounced its dangers. I stick my frozen hands under my

Gore-Tex coat and in my armpits. The burning pain that takes over my fingers as the blood flows back into them pushes all my thoughts out of my head and I have to scream. Even the pain in my face pales into insignificance compared with the fire in my fingers. When the pain recedes, I try wriggling them and bury them deep into my sleeves. My gloves are gone. I must have removed them near the crevasse when I was hoisting Augustin out

(*Where is Augustin, by the way?*)

and left them behind after

(*after what? What happened?*)

I lost my backpack too.

As I walk down the glacier, I suddenly feel like I'm being watched. Augustin? Or . . .

I begin to hurry, insofar as my condition permits, because no matter how I try rationalizing my situation, I can't shake the feeling.

I'm worried about my feet. When I try moving my toes, they refuse. They feel like spongy lumps of dead meat. I've lost all feeling in them

(*like in my face, oh God, what is the matter with my face?*)

and I can only hope that it will come back.

I try not to think about it but to concentrate on the descent. Then I realize what causes the feeling of being watched. Behind me, to the right, the Maudit's enormous north face rises. I feel its massive presence towering over me. All at once I'm split inside with a burning, devilish dilemma: I want to turn around and look, understanding full well that a single glance will destroy my only possible chance of escape. As if, just by my looking at it, the mountain will regain its hold on me and strike mercilessly. So I focus on the way ahead and don't look back. I *don't* look back.

The pressure on my face increases, makes me dizzy.

I don't look back.

A hundred yards down, the urge is so strong that I look *halfway* back.

I'm now on the glacier's bare, boulder-riddled tongue, which is twisted and broken

(*just like mine*)

and sinks into the moraine in a labyrinth of cracks and half-frozen pools of muddy water. Behind me, steep snow slopes rise up to the Maudit's forbidding north face

(*but we're not going to look at it, we're not going to look at it*)

pummeled by avalanches of powder snow from up high. Powerless, I gaze at this shadowy landscape. It looks like a timeless, lifeless place, untouched by the centuries. But appearances can be deceiving. Here, I can feel that power more than ever, the soul of the rocks and of the ice. I can feel it mocking me. And we thought we stood a chance against it? It's a preposterous idea.

I reach the edge of the glacier. The moraine curves toward the lake, and I start following it.

My face.

It is screaming without any sound passing my lips.

My lips, hanging open flaccidly, or so it seems.

Sensation starts to flow back into them, and now my face screams for real.

It doesn't take long before I see the surface of the water, dark and smooth. It looks cold, an immeasurably deep, round hole, right at the foot of the Maudit. Involuntarily, it makes me think about what happened to Augustin's eyes. Those eyes, ripped out by the death birds. I feel that power in the lake as well. It hangs in the silence, holds its breath, and whispers a wordless welcome.

I stagger closer to the bank. Drop to my hands and knees. I need to know what happened to my face.

I see dripping ice residue on the boulders, I see muddy snow, I see the reflection of something incredible bowing over me.

Could you have looked away?

Could you have simply *not* looked?

I see it as soon as I put my hands into ice-cold water. I think I imagined it—I *must* have imagined it. I slowly turn away and shut my eyes, as if by doing so, I could undo it. Then I turn back and lean over the water.

I see it again, and this time for real—my face, horridly mutilated. I see the truth, which my mind had until now refused to accept, had suppressed, had put away in a dark, fragile place, but which now, in the face of the mountain, is irrevocably dragged out into the light.

Because earlier, as I stare into Augustin's eyes on the edge of the crevasse—eyes that aren't eyes at all but holes in ice—he starts to bellow so wildly that the blood in my veins immediately curdles and my sanity shatters. It is such a devastating, inhuman roar that I wonder whether I hear it with my ears or if the sound is only in my head. And I know it's not Augustin who is bringing it forth. It's the roar of an avalanche, the screeching of a crevasse. In a flash, I see the horned mountain before me at the end of the valley, its gloomy shape tall and dark and hideously steep. It isn't Augustin who's bellowing out of the gaping crevasse. What I hear is the maniacal, raging voice of the mountain.

I see the swing of his axe in slow motion, I can even hear the air move. I must have instinctively drawn my neck in and jerked my head back, my mouth falling open in a wordless scream. Otherwise he would have slashed the ice axe right through my throat. Now the spike pierces my left cheek, grazes my tongue, and comes out on the other side. For a second we are frozen, stuck in a moment of stupefaction. I taste ice-cold metal in my mouth. I hear nothing. The shock must have temporarily deafened me. Augustin wrenches the axe, renews his grip, and pulls me forward by my cheeks.

Then the anchor shoots out of the snow and the rope swishes. With an all-destructive yank, the axe tears out of my cheeks. Augustin falls into the abyss, the axe flying after him, and as I fall into the snow I think I am dead.

And now, now as I stare at my face in the glacial lake's water, a swollen and bloody mask is sneering back at me with torn-open cheeks through which you can see lower-jaw teeth all the way to the back. The bottom half of my face has all the colors it isn't supposed to have, and the torn edges are pitch-black.

The bed of snow and ice has done a perfect job of freezing the dead flesh.

Behind that monstrous face, *my own face*, rises the horned Maudit's distorted reflection, its impenetrable north face the mountain's hidden visage.

I start to scream.

THE MODERN PROMETHEUS

NOTES BY SAM AVERY

How slowly the time passes here, encompassed as I am by frost and snow!

—Mary Wollstonecraft Shelley

1

Outside the Focus, everything looked exactly the same as the day before, only in reverse. Flashing red taillights southbound and bright white headlights northbound. Cologne, Frankfurt, Mannheim, a movie that was rewinding itself into a déjà vu. Windshield wipers swishing away miles of Germany to the east.

Inside, the same pink bubblegum flavor of Red Bull in my mouth. The only thing keeping my foot on the pedal in my present condition the caffeine kick, the reverse psychology effects of sugar and taurine. The rest of my body—one big, banging NO. My elbow against the window. My head leaning left in my outstretched hand like a bowling ball. Heavy as a bowling ball. My fingers rubbing scuffs into my temples, my swollen tongue tightening my throat.

The cause of all this was that number: thirty-two. Flashing on in your head like a brain cramp.

Nick's body count in the AMC.

Like a young wolf in a meadow full of sheep. A beast that had killed for fun. Playfully testing out its newly discovered powers.

Nick's body count, thirty-two and counting. Dr. Genet, Claire Stein, little Rosalie, Cécile, Emily Wan. That made it thirty-seven. Thirty-seven I *knew* about. A body count of thirty-seven demoted even Charles Manson and Jeffrey Dahmer to amateurs.

Thirty-seven and counting, if Emily Wan's little girl, Naomi, had also been infected.

I am leaving you my notes, Emily had written. *I hope that my insights can be of use to you.*

Oh, they were, all right. More than I bargained for.

You finally knew what Cécile meant by "falling." What Dr. Genet meant in his suicide note. You finally knew what kind of horror was hiding on the dark, unknowable flip side of your hubby's face.

The description of that kid in the OR. How all his bones broke when Nick had made him crash to the ground.

And Emily: *End it, Sam.* Emily: *Whatever it takes. Before there are more innocent victims.*

You finally knew how royally everything was fucked.

What I thought about now was how I had held Nick in my arms. That milky haze in his eyes appearing and disappearing like clouds of mist rushing by. How it had dizzified me and how Nick had only calmed down cuz *I* had managed to calm him down. Why hadn't *I* fallen like everyone else, as I was standing on the rim of the abyss and had looked right in?

You finally had your answer to that, too.

Even in the abyss, I'd still seen Nick. *My* Nick.

And that's why he was my responsibility. I was the one who had to do something about it.

But what? And where was he now?

Suicide was no longer my prime concern at this point, cuz the check marks on my WhatsApp messages had turned blue. So he'd read them—at 8:23 this morning, to be exact. So Nick had been enough himself—the Maudit too busy, what do I know, eroding or something—to check his WhatsApp. What's more, Nick had been somewhere with network coverage. Wi-Fi. A charging station. My fears that, in a coupla weeks, we'd find his remains in the mountains, eyes picked out by birds and lips drawn back from big, dead teeth while Nick had settled for an astral existence in his Maker's lap, turned out to be unfounded. But according to Julia, he didn't come home to the chalet either, so where the hell was he? And what did he have up his sleeve?

Something, that's for sure.

No matter what I texted, he didn't text back. No matter how often I called, he didn't pick up. After a while his phone was off again. And me, lips tight. The scuffs in my temples deeper and deeper.

Julia—breaking character—had been a nervous wreck since this morning. I'd told her the whole story, crawling ahead from one highway job site to the next—give me one more BAUSTELLE sign and I'll plow my car straight through it. But all we had today was time. Time and unlimited data. Julia couldn't clarify why she'd had such a foreboding feeling of unease. It was indeterminable, a meandering shadow, and of course my story didn't make her feel any better, so each time I had her on the line, every hour I obsessive-compulsively called her back, she said *Please hurry up, bro. Please come quickly . . .* and consequently, my fear flared up, cuz she really might be in actual trouble, should Nick unexpectedly come back. In hindsight, in hindsight—so I kicked that pedal a coupla inches deeper.

Aaand . . . brakes. Even before Mannheim the rain was gushing down. The autobahn jammed tight. Drumming on the wheel, right leg restless-legging out of control over the accelerator, and then it was one thirty and the phone rang.

A +41 number. Switzerland.

And I thought, *You don't wanna hear this.*

Nope, I sure as hell didn't, but this was my poisoned cup. I had to drink it up.

So I answered. "*Bonjour?*"

In French, the dude on the other end says, "Good afternoon, this is Dr. Alain Rambert from the Clinique Esthétique Le Châtelard in Montreux." Through the Beats, his voice trembling with trepidation, he says, "Am I speaking with Sam Avery?"

What you need to know is that Alain Rambert is an alias I just vamped up, cuz I honestly have no idea what the guy's real name was. Cuz right then, with a two-second delay, the meaning of *Clinique Esthétique* had hit me—its *true* meaning, with all its implications—and that shut off everything that had come before. I felt my heart freeze in my chest. Felt my eyeballs drying up and saw white in the rearview mirror, a whole lot of white, bloodshot white. Suddenly I got it. I got everything. Oh no. No no no no no. Nick had made the biggest mistake of his life.

In the distance, I heard myself say, "Do I get a complimentary tooth bleaching if I say yes?"

"Er, no sir. I'm calling with a grave message. Are you acquainted with a Nick Grevers?"

"Yeah, I'm his partner." *In crime*, I thought.

"Ah, I'm glad I got hold of you. Monsieur Grevers provided your number as the family contact person. You are probably aware that he had a scar revision appointment at the clinic today?"

"Of course," I said, and in my thoughts I followed the whole trail of Nick's bandages, hand over hand, into the darkness. Loop by loop I unwound it, and who you came across in the dark was Cécile, who had changed them before she ran screaming from the CHUV. Who you came across in the dark was Dr. Genet, who had operated beneath them before and, less than a month later, his brain in ruins, had put an end to his life. Loop by loop you followed it deeper into the darkness, and then you saw yourself, peeking through them before those black birds flew out from under them. There was little Naomi, who had seen them hanging off the shadow on the edge of her bed, "all in loops." Faster and faster, and after you'd unwound all the strips you saw, in the center of the darkness, Nick, trembling and apathetic, coming to himself again in a corner of his hospital room—Nick, who saw them dangling from his face, stinking of wound cream, while all around him a terrible tragedy was unfolding.

It came out when he took off his bandages. For months, he had let the pressure build up. *Cut* him in his face? You might as well release the Kraken.

"Of course," I repeated. My voice distant, as if from a thick mist: "I just thought it wasn't till two weeks from now?"

Enough time to talk him out of the whole unholy idea.

"That was supposed to be the case"—the surgeon just as distant—"but we had a cancellation. Monsieur Avery . . . I don't know how to tell you this."

"Is Nick all right?"

"I can't say. There is no easy way to explain this, so I'll just lay it out as it is: Monsieur Grevers walked out in the middle of the operation."

And I said, "Walked out." Thinking, *I can work with that.* Then, *Oh, Jesus, what's the damage?* See here: the flexibility of the human brain. See also: total shock. Take your pick.

"But wasn't he under sedation?"

"Yes, he was, and that's what's so strange." What came to mind was Emily's patient. The kid whose body rose up as if he were flying. *He'd* been under sedation. "Considering the size of his scars, we put him under general anesthesia. He was on a ventilator, and both his heart rate and the EEG showed he was unconscious. We had just started the procedure when things started to go wrong."

What exactly? Nick had woken up, *that's* what had gone wrong. The anesthetist rushed to assist, of course, but Nick shoved him aside, and then it all happened very fast. Nick's eyes opened like a sleepwalker's, seemingly blind and rather lugubrious, the doc said. And without a word, he'd torn out the IV and intubation and walked away. Bleeding like a pig from the incision in his scar.

"Really," the surgeon stammered, "we tried to overpower him, but he couldn't be stopped. We were so dumbfounded that he had already left the clinic before we properly realized what had happened. And now he is, um . . . missing."

Imagine: Nick in a blood-splattered OR gown, his face hanging open, staggering through the streets of Montreux like Frankenstein's monster. Picture it: frenzied crowds running for cover. None of the above. Turned out not a single report had been made. That was the strangest thing of all. The Police Cantonale had issued a missing person alert—imagine the details of *that* description—but Nick, he seemed to have disappeared off the face of the earth.

"It is of utmost importance that he returns to the clinic as immediately as possible," the surgeon said. "I hope he has bound up the incision, but the risk of infection is high, and the longer the wound stays open, the more difficult it will be for us to perform the correction with at least somewhat acceptable results." Adding, "But that is regardless of the fact that we are completely baffled about—"

"Did anything happen when you started cutting him?"

"I don't understand what you—"

"Something strange? Did you have a vision?"

Silence on the other end.

"Did you feel cold? Did you have the feeling you were falling? That an abyss had opened up under your feet?"

On the other end of the line, you could just *hear* the guy going white.

I said I had to know everything. Lives could be at stake.

After a long, shaky silence, he said, "I will be forthcoming if you give me your word you won't talk to the media. Or I might as well wrap up my clinic. I know we don't look good, and it *appears* as if we made an error administering the anesthesia. But here's the thing: I was the one monitoring it. I'd stake my reputation on it that no errors were made."

And I said I believed him.

The second he put the scalpel to Nick's face, the surgeon said, he'd gotten a dizzy spell. "I was about to warn my assistant, but it happened so fast." He said, "I saw spots before my eyes and was suddenly overcome by a very unpleasant sensation. And a smell. The sweet, sickly smell of decomposition. It brought back a memory."

When he was eight or so, his parents had taken him on a picnic in the mountains. He'd walked up the stream, and on the bank, what had permanently traumatized his tender, innocent soul, were the partially decayed remains of an ibex, steaming in the sun and teeming with maggots. The stench of rot had caused him to barf up all his potato salad. It was that same stench the surgeon had now smelled.

"I looked up, thinking I'd see the OR, but instead of that I saw the mountain at the end of the valley, towering above me. Only it wasn't the same mountain I remembered. This mountain was horned, like the devil. And it was *wrong*, you see? I don't know how to put it in other words. What I saw was emanating something very wrong. And it wasn't just a memory. It was so crystal clear that it seemed as if I were really there. I saw the crisp light, I heard the stream, but most of all, I smelled the stench. The sweet stench of decay."

He wasn't the only one who'd seen something. His anesthetist had run from the clinic right after Nick did and wasn't answering his phone. His assistant had stayed behind but flat-out refused to talk about what had happened. At this very moment she was still sitting there, staring at her lunch, white as a sheet.

And I figured, at least no one died. No one had been snapped in two yet.

The surgeon's voice broke in a sob. "That smell, the rot, I can't get rid of it." Shivering, he said, "I can still smell it now."

Goddamn.

Almost said, *It'll smell a lot stronger before you die.*

"Please." Practically begging now, "We'll find Monsieur Grevers, I'm sure of it, but in the meantime, please tell me what you know. Because you do know more, don't you? I can tell by your reaction."

I said I had my suspicions. Said that in due time I'd tell him everything, but right now the first thing I hadda do was to call the police. Call his family. The guy had no idea that I was blowing him off.

"One more thing," he said.

What?

"When we put your friend under sedation, he was scared. Real scared. Just before he went under he started to panic, and his eyes opened wide, like he'd suddenly had an epiphany. He grabbed hold of the anesthetist and cried out, 'Cut out my eyes. Don't cut my face. Cut out my eyes.' Then he slipped into unconsciousness. Now, it's not uncommon for people to say strange things in that moment of intoxication, but in light of what happened . . . does that have any significance to you?"

"None at all," I said, and hung up.

2

After that, chaos. My right foot switching from gas to brakes to brakes to gas. Dodging jammed cars, cursing, honking when some German in a mega BMW didn't let you squeeze through. My finger floating over Julia's name in my recent calls list when the phone rings again. No Caller ID.

And I said, "*Bonjour?*"

The Police Cantonale. Yes, I had been informed. No, I didn't know his address in Switzerland. Didn't he provide the clinic with it? Oh, okay, I said, somewhere on Lake Geneva in any case. No, me, I was in Denmark.

Hoping, *begging* that some jerk there wouldn't run my name through the system and stumble on a questioning from two days back concerning the disappearance of one Cécile Métrailler in Grimentz. Nick's name not linked to the case—*those* cops had been way too busy covering up their own mystery to pay attention to some recuperating patient on the ground floor. At this moment in time, there was no suspicion of a crime and I was simply the concerned relative, but if some jerk were to link A to B, then not only would he see right through my lies, it would be DEFCON 1. Any dick worth his salt wouldn't believe in chance when faced with *two* linked, exceptionally strange cases.

The Police Cantonale were worried about Nick's well-being. I was worried about the well-being of the Police Cantonale if they found him.

Oui, it was a bizarre story, and *oui*, I'd let them know as soon as I heard anything from him, and would they *s'il vous plaît* do the same. *Merci* fucking *bien*.

Oh fuck. Oh fuck oh fuck oh fuck oh fuck. I called Julia. "Julia, you need to get out of there. Now."

And Julia: "Excuse me?"

"Take a bus or hitchhike to the valley and check into a hotel. Nick is on the loose and I'm really scared that it's for good this time." I give her a play-by-play of the preceding events. Julia freaking out, Julia suitcasing all her stuff even before I'd reached the end of my story. Shit almighty, someone who actually *did* what you asked them to. Praise the Lord. I said, "I don't know what he's going to do or whether he'll come to Hill House, but if he does, I want you out of there. He's dangerous."

And Julia said, "I don't know if I'll be able to go down, Sam. It's snowing, I don't know how long the roads will stay open."

My stomach sank. "That wasn't the forecast, was it?"

"All I know is what I see outside."

"Okay, then at least go to the village. There's a hotel there, too."

Julia wavered. "I . . . I'm scared, bro. I was trying to call you the whole time, but your line was busy." She said, "There were people here."

People?

"From the village. A whole bunch. They were looking for Nick. For 'the man with the bandaged face.' And they didn't look like they had friendly intentions. They were pretty aggressive, frankly. I was afraid they were going to hurt me."

Christ. So Maria and her neighborhood app were right. The shit had hit the fan. But what had made them come there specifically *now*? Was it possible Nick had—No, there hadn't been enough time for him to get there. Not yet.

"What did you say?"

"That both of you had left and I was looking after the house."

"Hero."

"But they didn't leave, Sam. They hung around the chalet for a really long time. And they weren't being sneaky about it, either. I think they were trying to make sure you were really gone. They only left when they knew for sure."

I said she did the right thing. That she had to hurry now. And be careful, please. What else could I say to put her mind at rest? Between Julia and me were three hundred miles of blacktop. With my luck, it would be Xmas before I got there.

Idiot. I should never have left her all alone. Now I was powerless.

Fear in my bones, fierce as the wind whizzing through the Focus's spoilers. By then we weren't even crawling anymore; we'd literally come to a standstill. Entombed by chrome and rubber. You couldn't shake the feeling that you were being held back by something. That you were being manipulated, while something terrible was about to unfold in Switzerland, or was already unfolding. Something you couldn't prevent. The sky in the south looked as if it were night. The rain had turned to sleet. Thirty-five F, your display said. And we weren't even *anywhere near* the mountains.

Outside the Focus, a face with hollow eyes was staring at me through the side window. Holy crap—I'm not the first fuckwit in history who jumps at his own reflection, but the trickling streams of thawing snow distorted it, dehumanized it, turned it inside out.

There was nothing out there, outside the Focus. Nothing evil roaming around. Just some phantom with holes for eyes, a phantom with an inside-out face. Every person had a flip side, a darkness that made us capable of committing the most heinous crimes. It's just that most of us were lucky enough never to come across a detonator that would set it off. Was it sheer bad luck that Nick did? So how many close calls did we have in our day-to-day lives without our even realizing it? How close were we all to the edge of the abyss?

That question chilled me to the bone.

An hour and a half later. Twenty miles further. Julia again. She'd tried to walk to the village but was chased away. Like a stray dog. None of the hotels had wanted to rent her a room. As if she were cursed.

The weather in the mountains was rapidly deteriorating and La Poste stopped its runs to the valley. Walking in these conditions was not an option. Conclusion: my sis was stranded. Compelled to wait it out in the chalet. My only consolation: if it was getting difficult for Julia to go down, it would be just as difficult for Nick to go up.

Except that a mountain was controlling the weather.

A mountain was the *source* of the weather. Creating its own microclimate.

Which was the *last* thing you wanted to think about.

The Police Cantonale called back, too. By then it was late in the afternoon and on the radio they were talking of a weather alert, of a severe front unexpectedly advancing over Central Europe toward the Alps, of snowfall records that would most probably be shattered in the course of the night. By then they were talking of truckers who would have to spend the night on the shoulder, a travel warning that advised against any driving unless absolutely necessary; but tell that to all the people stuck in gridlocks, crawling behind South German salt trucks.

This Police Cantonale rep, she assumed that Nick must have found a place to stay somewhere. With the weather this bad, he wasn't going to be wandering the streets. As long as they didn't know where he was, there was nothing they could do.

It got dark. Julia was alone in Grimentz. I was stuck in traffic ahead of Basel. Nick had disappeared without a trace, and in the mountains even the echoes were quiet, waiting for what was about to come.

3

You wouldn't believe this: one a.m. and still not up there. My brain way past the stage where Red Bulls could do it any good—what I'd kill for was a Long Island iced tea. A Cuba libre. A hundred milligrams of Ritalin.

You wouldn't believe this: so I'm driving behind the flashing orange lights of a snowplow. Zigging and zagging at a snail's pace from hairpin to hairpin, sprays of road salt biting into the profile of my summer tires, higher and higher into the Val d'Anniviers. Or that's what I hoped, cuz the only things I could make out in my fog lights were the snowbanks the V-shaped plow shoved onto the side of the road and the spiraling ice crystals. It'd taken my full array of special persuasion powers to even get the guy to go up, but five minutes into the blizzard in my role as father-to-be and a cockamamie tale about junior's fontanels already being compressed, as we speak, by his mother's puffing cervix, and I was wide-awake. Past Bern, I'd almost nodded off into the guardrail, but now my eyes agreed to stay open. Way beyond exhaustion. What took its place was unease. The fear that I was too late—too late to ward off an invisible doom. Bullshit, but true all the same.

The mountains outside the Focus, I couldn't see them, but I felt their presence, more threatening than ever. Their crooked summits, groping like fingers. Their dark caves full of blind eyes, peering into the night. Their cold, dead breath. Sometimes they seemed to hypnotize me, and then I feared I'd lose sight of the orange flashing lights, that I'd be stranded here, alone on the frozen mountain road, alone with whatever horror was lurking out there in the snow.

And *smack!* Slap in the face, cut the crap. Press the pedal down carefully, make sure you don't slip.

Waiting at the end of this gauntlet was Hill House, and with it, the unavoidable was coming closer: What was I to do if I had to face Nick? His being up there defied all logic; the last update I got, when Julia hit the sack around eleven, was that there'd still been no sign of him. And yet . . . And yet . . .

Sixteen hours alone with my thoughts and not a single strategy popped up. Not a single epiphany richer.

One twenty. Peering through the snow-free half-moons cleared by the windshield wipers, and suddenly the light from my phone comes on. Groping through all the shit on the shotgun seat: my open backpack, my half-eaten McFilth, Dr. Jingles—my iPhone. My Beats. Peering at the road, I tried pulling them over my ears with a single hand. The screen lit up; two missed calls. Just in time to answer the third one and pick up the Bluetooth signal.

"Julia!"

And Julia said, "Why didn't you pick up?"

"Sorry, it's a hairy situation here on the road. Hadda link it to my Beats first. Any news?"

"I . . . no." Her voice sounded strangely hollow. Maybe she'd just woken up, or maybe she hadn't been able to sleep at all. "Where are you?"

"On my way. You okay, sis? You sound weird."

Short silence, then a sigh. "Yes." She said, "It's just, this storm is driving me crazy. How long will it take you to get here?"

"Um, beats me. Get this: I'm driving behind a snowplow! Only way to go up tonight." So I tell her that after Bern the jams had *finally* broken up. That the roads had emptied out but that it only made conditions worse. I tell her about the weather alert, about the avalanche alarm in the mountains. Talking to Julia was good. The sound of my voice made me feel a little less alone with the orange lights flashing in my retinas and the strange, filtered wailing of the midnight storm through the noise cancellation. And, okay, a little less scared. At some point, the only reason I was rattling on was to listen to my own voice.

". . . cuz I slid sideways across the road all the way to the shoulder before I got it under control. After that it got a bit better cuz they're spreading salt, but they can salt till the cows come home, it's not gonna do any good. Totally awesome, all the gear these Switzers bring out to keep their roads clear. They're a zillion times more equipped than us, but hey, they're Switzers, man . . ."

On the other end of the line, a clattering. A phone dropping from somebody's fingers. And I said, "Hello?" Said, "Hello? Hello? Are you there?" Said, "Julia?"

"Yeah, I'm here."

"Oh, okay. Wonder woman. Anyway, it was weird driving past Montreux cuz Nick was there today and, who knows, maybe he still is . . ." I listened. The silence on the other end was oppressive. "Hello?"

No breathing. Just soft static. As if the storm itself was breathing on the line. You read stuff like that in old books, but was that even still possible with wireless satellite networks?

Not the storm. The breath of the Maudit.

And I said, "Julia? Julia!"

"Sorry, I . . . I dropped you. Keep talking, I'm here."

I heard a floorboard creak through my Beats. Julia was in the attic.

"I dunno, the connection keeps breaking up, I think." I listened—seemed okay now. "Anyway, so when I finally got to the valley, what I was afraid of actually happened: the road to Grimentz was closed." All the way from the highway, I told her. And then the whole story about me bamboozling the snowplow guy. The snowplow that just happened to drive by while I was taking out my frustrations on the upholstery of Nick's Focus. The roadworks dude with his reflective vest, he mounted snow chains on my front wheels—that's how I could get moving, even if it was slow. And meanwhile, this sign looms up on the abyss side of the road, its snow growth shaven off by the razor-sharp wind: VISSOIE 3 GRIMENTZ 11 ZINAL 15.

That dude, he said he could get me to Grimentz, but not via the direct route, which twisted all the way down to the valley floor and climbed back up on the fault side of the Navisence. Too dangerous. We were following the main road and turned off just before Zinal. That way was longer but lay in the lee of the forest and was less steep. I said I don't care how you get me there, as long as I get there in time to chop off someone's umbilical cord.

"Seriously, it's hellacious. I think the road behind us snowed up again right away. Some of the time I can't even see the plow's taillights through the windshield and I'm only ten yards behind him. I was really lucky. He wasn't supposed to go any further than Vissoie tonight, but—You still there, Jules?"

And Julia said, "Did you get to the valley yet?" As if it only just dawned on her.

And me, "Yeah. That's what I've been trying to tell you."

"Please get here quickly,"

"I'm doing the best I can, sis, but I can't go faster than the snowplow. Eight or nine miles to go, I think. Half an hour, forty minutes tops."

Something in her voice stilled me. In the end, a voice in your headphones only gives you a false sense of security. In reality, there was an endless tunnel of whirling snow shapes between us. My eyes stared into that tunnel till they started tearing, shooting left to right in their sockets to catch any sight of danger. To see what it was out there that was hunting you. The deeper you penetrated the mountains as a human being, the more you became a handicapped animal stalked by something with drooling jaws.

I shuddered, pushed the thought out of my head, couldn't do it. "I tried calling Nick," I said softly. Licked my lips, which felt like parchment. "His phone is still off." Said, "I'm scared, Jules."

And all of a sudden, like an epiphany, I realized that the danger wasn't here, on this mountain road, but to the south, in Hill House.

This was way bad. And I was too late.

I whispered, "*Julia . . .*"

And Julia shivering, hyperventilating: "W-wh-what?"

"Julia, what's going on? Are you crying?"

"No, I'm . . ."

"You *are* crying! Sis, what is it?" Two hands clawing at the wheel, cold sweat in my neck. "Did anything happen?"

"Please come, oh god . . ."

"I'm coming!" My voice caught now. "I'm on my way, you know that, but I can't go any faster! What happened?"

And Julia said, "There are people here."

"What?"

"There are people here."

"Whaddya mean, 'people'?"

"In my bedroom."

"Whaddya mean there are people? From the village? The people from the village who came earlier?"

"No, not them."

Julia's voice, a choked peep. What she just said sank in only now.

In my bedroom.

A piercing shriek, a loud *thud*. You didn't hear it with your ears but with your heart and soul. The floodgates that finally opened, the realization that fell into place in my brain. The shadows I'd seen at the peak of the Morose, thronging the bathroom. The echoes. Oh Jesus.

Maria's voice, itself now an echo: *They say the dead want to embrace you. That they want to warm themselves with your life. Because they're so cold. So very cold.*

"There are people here . . ." Julia peeped again. "The whole room is full of people and they're staring at me. Oh god, Sam, they're getting closer! Oh Jesus. They keep getting closer. Help me. Please come right away. There's a woman and she's staring at me, she's standing next to my bed and she keeps staring at me . . ."

I felt all the color draining away, not only from my face but from the world. "Julia! Oh god, do they have eyes? *Do these people have eyes?*"

And Julia started to scream. My baby sister. My Julia. Screaming.

"*Julia, get the hell outta there!*"

Julia screamed my name, and her screaming pierced into my ears like a dagger. Only once before had I heard her scream like this—when the smoke alarm in Huckleberry Wall had started wailing, fifteen years prior, and back then I'd been there for her, back then I could save her, but this time I was here, this time I was too late. *This time I was too late.*

"*Get out of there, now! Julia! Julia! Oh god, Julia, run, go downstairs, get away from them, go now now now!*"

Too late, you realized that there was silence. The line dead. So I call back—straight to voicemail. One more time. Twice. Three times. *Come on, come on, come on*, maybe we were calling each other at the same time, *okay, Julia,* you *call* . . . But the seconds ticked by and Julia didn't call.

Her phone dead. Gone. Destroyed.

There are people here . . .

Oh fuck, if it were the echoes if they were *in the house* if they were *active* then their behavior had changed then they could feel the Maudit and *that meant that Nick was there too, Nick was there, only it wasn't Nick anymore, it was the Maudit, his becoming had been completed.*

And me honking, swerving, tailgating, *splash* and a fan of road salt splattered my windshield. Taillights finally flashing, the plow stopped. I flung the car door open, jumped out of the Focus, fucking *freezing*, the wind and *zip* immediate face-plant, eating snow, I gasped for breath and was running again before I'd even properly gotten up.

"*Mon gars, relax,*" the guy screamed out of the plow, me hanging on his door. "*What's the matter?*"

"*Faster! We need to go faster! It's started! Please step on it!*"

"*I'm going as fast as I can!*" He looked at me and shouted, "*For someone about to become a happy father, you look pretty rattled. Is everything all right?*"

"*Step on it!*" I yelled, already on my way to the Focus.

Crawling those last five miles to Grimentz, excruciatingly slow behind the snowplow—they were the darkest moments of my life. My panic was complete. My very own sister. Julia Avery, Manhattan's finest. If anything were to happen to her, her blood would be on my hands. I'd been blinded by Nick, still was, by what I didn't believe he could be capable of. And in the meantime, reality had caught up with me. From, like, everywhere. How could I have been so fucking stupid?

Zoom out: a scream in a car, a whirling snowstorm, a frozen valley, an electrically charged blanket of clouds, and a trillion cold, dead stars in a universe where none of the above had even the slightest significance.

4

Thirty minutes later, I flew into Hill House for the last time in my life. The house or me—one of us was going to kick the bucket. And don't pretend like you're sorry about it. I was a total failure who didn't deserve anyone's pity, and these types of mountain cabins, let's face it, they're just a pile of kindling waiting to be set ablaze.

Story of my life.

Every path to your destiny goes in circles.

Every path to hell leads up some mountain.

Fast-forward to the dude in the snowplow who wished you lotsa baby luck. Did I want him to hang on for a while, just in case? No, it had already gone down, a doctor from Grimentz had come by and bye, I was now going inside to take the little critter into my arms. Fast-forward to the orange flashing lights I saw disappearing in the direction of the valley as me and my blurred vision ran the last coupla yards to the chalet. Fast-forward to snow-covered mountain slopes coming at you from all sides and mocking you with whispering voices: *Julia, Julia*, whispering in the wind, *We have Julia*, me screaming "*Julia!*" and those whispering voices, *Julia, the mountains got Julia . . .*

No rental in the vicinity of the chalet, but that made no diff to the adrenaline shock waves surging through your constricted veins. Nick was *here*, the mountains were *here*—but where was Julia?

The front door was open a crack. In the snow a trail, almost wiped clean by the wind, so clean you couldn't tell whether it led to or from the chalet. Julia would never have left the front door open. She'd closed the shutters and Fort Knoxed the entire house before going to sleep. Felt safer, she'd said. But there were things here bolts weren't going to keep out

(*there are people here . . .*)

things that left no tracks in the snow

(*the whole room is full of people . . .*)

but lured you into the night with their dead cries.

Fast-forward to the porch, to me screaming "*Julia!*" To the hallway: darkness.

The cold from the mountains had descended on the house.

Fast-forward to me screaming, "*Julia!*" Screaming, "*Julia, where are you!*"

The door swung shut behind me. And holy—Total darkness. No, not total after all. A vague light coming down the stairwell. Screaming Julia's name, up the steep staircase in one, two, three leaps.

What you *didn't* see in the attic: people. What you *didn't* see: Julia. I yanked the covers off the bed. Julia's iPhone, dead. A wet spot on the mattress. Fear sweat. Peed bed. Me desperate, not knowing what to do, me screaming, "*Julia!*" Screaming, "*Julia!*"

Even though there weren't any people anymore in Hill House's attic, *something* had remained. It is said that bad things leave an imprint in the fabric of reality. That strong emotions from the past have echoes that resonate in the here and now. Same thing here. Whatever had happened after the line went dead, it had cut the house open like a poached hare's belly. Through that gash, through that gaping wound, the crushed souls of the Maudit were peering out over their shoulders, and you could still hear their dying screams trembling in the air's molecules.

Cuz they would have screamed in the end. Oh yeah. They had screamed when they were warming themselves with Julia's life, and that could only mean that Julia had gone out, into the storm.

To become one of them.

The trail in the snow, that was *Julia*. Not Nick. Julia, she'd left the door to the house open cuz she'd fallen prey to the Sirens' call. My li'l sister, she'd followed in Cécile's tracks. *Into the mountains.*

After all my efforts, after all my good intentions, I was still too late.

Story of my fucking life.

Whimpering, I stormed down the stairs, hoping against hope that Julia would still be down there; whimpering through the hallway, with both hands I wrenched open the living room door and—

It wasn't dizziness that got ahold of me there. Wasn't dizziness that caused the seething darkness to suddenly come to life, my surroundings to float, and the whole concept of a floor to fall away from under my feet.

Categorizing something like that under "dizziness" would be like calling Mount St. Helens a corporate barbecue.

One look into that room and all the panic, all the emotions about Julia, gone like a shot. One look and the *room* was gone. Where the interior and the large windows used to be, a vista unfolded before me that was beyond comprehension. What I saw there, any attempt to describe it would fall short of its actual magnitude. The panorama defined a curve through space and time, punched holes into dimensions, and triggered an avalanche of the nerves, an overload of electromagnetic pulses. My mind, my soul, had two choices: die or look.

And I said, "Nick?"

There he was. There was Nick. Always and everywhere. Nick was the Maudit. Rising sky-high into the macroverse and carrying me up with him. A jagged peak, sharply outlined against the night sky. Black ridges etched by a ghostly silver light that seemed to be falling directly out of the stratosphere. Snowy ledges carved by the wind into sharp edges of shiny steel. Like this, he reigned over his landscape, straight through the eons, and laid me down on his summit. Shackled and naked. Stripped not of my clothes but of all my life's burdens. This was more than making love; this was a transcendental fusion. Nick and me. A pairing of souls.

Sure, if I'd heard myself talk like this a coupla months ago, I woulda thought, *Dude, go flex your macramé club or something*, but for a split second I knew what it was like to be him—and be part of the geomorphological processes that life had blown into him. That split second, it stretched out over a life span of millions of years. Bound to his summit, alone but not alone in pure *being*, that's where I felt the mountains' heartbeat. That's where I saw it all. Everything that, because of one spark, one chain reaction of lies, I'd spent my whole life hating.

Forests.

Brooks.

Glaciers.

Mountains.

The scars of a silent, scorched landscape.

And as I was looking at it, the wheel of the universe turned above my head and I understood what infinity was. One glimpse had robbed Cécile, Dr. Genet, and Emily Wan of their sanity and had sent them to their deaths.

And I thought, fuck it.

Because all of a sudden I got it. How I could give meaning to a fucked-up life.

Cécile Métrailler, a gazillion years ago in Hôtel du Barrage: *That place mutilated him, Sam. . . . It's a* bad *place. And don't get me wrong, but I'm not sure Nick was supposed to come back from it.*

Sooner or later, all roads led back into the mountains.

Nick had come back to the chalet only cuz there was still a bit of the human left in him. Within that primal force that had grown inside him, I'd still seen Nick. *Because I loved him.* That had been my trump card. That's why I hadn't fallen. Hadn't frozen like all the others. I had looked into the abyss and had still seen Nick.

But the abyss had looked back . . . and Nick had seen *me* too.

I was the umbilical cord that still connected Nick to the valley.

Nick had come back to the chalet because he wanted to take me out on a date.

My future: everything I'd seen in my vision. How you gave meaning to your life: the ultimate lovemaking on the mountain's summit. Chained till the end of time. Your ultimate bondage fantasy.

Hail Prometheus, not the narcissist but the sacrifice.

Here was my penance. My self-sacrifice.

If this was how I could lure the monster Nick had become out of the world, if this was how I could avenge his victims and prevent more slaughter, what did I have to lose? I'd gambled Julia away, I'd gambled away my own sister, and it's not like I was dying to face Pa or Ma Avery. Not exactly something I was thinking of adding to my CV.

It took only a single moment to fuck up the rest of your life. It took only a single moment for redemption.

And there, in the middle of time, in the middle of my vision, in the middle of Hill House, Nick's face finally loomed up in front of me. Nick's perfect face, that flawless face, it was shocking, it was brilliant, it was abundantly beautiful. The snow crystals adorning the vaulted and cleft tissue of his deformity radiated, sparkled, phosphoresced when he smiled at me, and the cuts in his cheeks split open. His teeth, glistening white all the way to the back. His eyes glittering like heated diamonds. They expressed both an infinite tenderness and an incredible detachment, like the corona around the sun or an orographic cloud covering distant peaks.

And Nick said, *Hiya.*

And I said, *Hiya.*

Omigod. We were back in first date territory.

So here we are, he said shyly.

This was all so Romeo and Romeo.

Where exactly? In the chalet?

To a certain extent, yes. He pulled the collar of his Gore-Tex coat down and scratched behind his hairline, a gesture that, despite everything, was so incredibly Nick. *Things didn't exactly go as planned, huh? Not like we thought they would.*

Nothing ever goes as planned. Remember the first time we met? When you were making a show of doing your bench presses in the UvA gym, hoping I'd look your way?

Of course I remember. How could I forget?

I thought within a few weeks you'd probably have a girlfriend. That's how provincial you seemed to me then.

But you looked anyway.

Yeah, I said. *I looked anyway.*

A shadow passed over his face, like something sad suddenly remembered after years of silence. *I'm sorry,* he said. *About everything. I had no control over it.*

Doesn't matter. You did all that stuff because you're emotionally deranged.

Wow. Look who's talking.

Oh, come on. I may not be completely balanced, but next to you I'm Mike Pence's marriage.

He tilted his head.

And I said, *Aww,* looking out into the distance. Maybe I coulda said more. Maybe I *shoulda* said more. Maybe I should have said there was a possibility we could pretend that all those things never actually happened. That everything could simply go back to being as it was before Nick had gone into the mountains. My stomach clenched in an almost painful longing for that possibility, but I was afraid, so terribly afraid that if I were to utter those words, they'd turn out to be lies. You can't unopen Pandora's box.

Instead, I said, *Hey, if I go with you, can we take Ramses? I'd hate for him to be left behind all alone and not knowing where we are.*

Of course, Nick smiled. *You just have to envision his travel carrier and he's coming with us!*

So I did, and the next thing, Nick was holding up the cat, his one forepaw still wrapped and tied in white bandages. Maybe the concept of *Sturm und Drang* didn't do full justice to Ramses's expression, but it sure came close.

Hey, smiley face, Nick said and he scratched the cat's tummy. *Feel like going on vacation with us one more time?*

Ramses looked at him, and somewhere, lava turned into glaciers. Nick eased him into his travel carrier and closed the flap. Then he stood up and showed all his teeth. *So, you ready to go?*

And I said, *Yeah. Let's.*

And that's when some maniac bashed his axe through the shutters and smashed the chalet's large window into smithereens.

5

So this was how it all turned out. A cold snowdrift whirling inside through the hole. An infernal orange shine. The roaring of a crowd, and not the dead this time. Only Maria's neighborhood app, IRL. Democracy in its rawest form.

The axe was pried out of the hole and smashed into it again. Splinters flying everywhere. The hole got bigger.

Instantly jerked out of my vision, I tumbled right into the here and now. What I saw was Nick, a floating silhouette, he swirled around in a single motion toward the opening, and I swear, from somewhere deep in the earth came a profound rumbling, causing the furniture to tremble and the collection of génépy bottles on the wall to tinkle.

What I saw was an angry mob in the snow outside the chalet, waving bamboo garden torches. Pieces of wood with nails hammered into them. Seriously: pitchforks.

Everyone knows how these kinds of scenes end. No ritual, no exorcism, just an old-fashioned lynching.

How it all turned out. Go figure. I was too late even for my own redemption.

A Jägermeister bottle came sailing through the hole, trailing a tail of fire. But you could bet your ass there wasn't any Jägermeister in it, cuz when it belly flopped onto the ground—which of course it did on the exact same spot in front of the fireplace where, fifteen years earlier, I'd scattered burning coals over humanity—it exploded in an inferno that instantly set the sofas ablaze. Set the curtains on fire. The moment you realized you could kiss your deposit good-bye was the moment when Nick's clothes caught fire.

Let's face it, with me here, this was an accident waiting to happen.

And I shouted, "Nick!"

Don't tell me anything about how fast fire can spread. What they didn't tell you on Airbnb: your tasteful suede sofas, your south-facing million-dollar mountain view, and the ghoul gamboling about in your living room, they were all category I combustibles. Arms flailing, Nick swirled around again while the flames consumed more and more of his clothes. Consumed more and more of the chalet.

Through all of this echoed the wailing of lost human souls, like a chorus of wild hounds—or maybe it was just the smoke alarm. And I figured they were uncorking more than a single bottle of Jägermeister. In no time, the inferno in the chalet had become so fierce and so hot you couldn't even look at it. My skin started to glimmer, the hairs in my nose started to singe. In a split second of utter despair, I stared at Nick, but his scream, it wasn't so much human as it was the rumbling of thunder. It wasn't so much pain as it was the raging of wrath.

And I knew something terrible was about to happen.

And I ran.

The power of fire is that you can't stop it. You have no control over it. Your only control is your own position in its vortex—if you're lucky. As I ran, part of me must have already known how this was going to end, because at that moment I had only one goal in mind. Leaping over licking fingers of fire, bouncing down the stairs in one, two, three leaps, I screamed, "*Julia!*" Screamed, "*Grandpa! Grandma!*" Tears suddenly streaming down my cheeks, I screamed, "*Julia, wake up! Wake up!*" Screamed, "*We gotta get out!*"

In the bedroom. The bed. The nightstand.

I found what I was looking for.

A subtle, almost imperceptible power shift took place in the universe, high above the highest summits of the Alps.

Then something shattered through the bedroom's terrace door and I was struck to the ground by a heavy object. In my head a flash of light, an explosion. It was less a KO and more that suddenly everything was moving in extreme slow motion, swallowing the earsplitting buzzing in my brain and leaving room for only one single, solitary thought: *My face! They bashed in my face!*

Oh, Jesus, I couldn't focus. Everything was fuzzy. Everything was swimming around me in pungent, suffocating smoke. Julia, I had to warn Julia. Shouted, "*Julia!*" But I still saw leather boots walking into my vision, snow between the shoelaces. I still saw wet jeans. They grabbed me by the legs and dragged me outside. And me kicking, me screaming, me clutching, but all I got ahold of was a handful of blankets from the bed, which I pulled behind me like a bridal train. Then over the threshold and sliding through frigid snow.

What looked like a long braid of dark maiden's hair hanging out of a castle tower window was in fact a trail of blood from my split eyebrow. What looked like an inferno against a backdrop of angry mountains was in fact an inferno against a backdrop of angry mountains.

And still, despite all that, from the corners of my eyes I saw the flashes of falling echoes coming down over the chalet.

Faint and weak, I heard their dying screams.

Then they grabbed me by the collar and hauled me to my feet. My head spinning on my neck like there were ball bearings inside. Rough hands were holding me upright in the middle of the circle of torch-bearing townsfolk. Of raised clubs and pitchforks. I looked around, blood leaking into my left eye, I looked around and saw them all. I saw the orange glow on their haggard faces. Over the roar of the fire, over the roar of the storm, I could almost hear the chattering of their teeth. The village folk, they were hella scared, of course. Here they were, triggered by ancestors who had kamikaze'd themselves against the bars of their birdcages. Living barometers that shot over the max cuz they'd sensed the coming of the Maudit.

Here, in the sloping terrace behind our burning house, in the lee of Castle Rock, they were chanting some slur. A chorus. An incantation.

In the midst of the mob, I saw that dude with the white jabot. That churchguy with his congregation. One of those bozos next to him was holding a whopper of a birdcage, inside it a screeching black chough, inflamed by the fire or by the clamor of the crowd. At the bottom of the cage was a neck-wide hole.

You didn't need to explain what the cage was for.

Only now did my grogginess ebb away enough for me to hear that what they were chanting was supposed to be English. That and the fact that they were Switzers, and their accent contained more holes than Emmental cheese.

They were chanting, "*Come out! Surrender! Come out! Surrender! Come out! Surrender! Come out!*"

Oh, Christ. I was the bait.

They were all going to get themselves killed.

The guy holding me, I tried to jab him in the stomach with my elbow, and I shouted, "*Run!*" Shouted, "*Run while you can! Before it's too late!*"

Switched to French, shouted, "*You don't get it! You don't stand a chance! Run! Run for your lives!*"

A coupla those morons stopped chanting and looked around hesitantly, waiting to see what the others would do. Most of them carried on. Fists raised at the fire. Right then, a part of Hill House's front wall collapsed and a swirl of flames and sparks rose up into the night sky. Ashes and soot whirled through my lungs with every breath.

And I hollered, "*Fly, you fools!*" Me, totally Gandalf.

The figure that stepped out of the conflagration, nonchalantly stepping onto Hill House's balcony, that wasn't Nick. His Gore-Tex coat burned away to the seams, his hair incinerated, his fuming face a shredded Frankenstein's monster mask that *resembled* Nick's face but wasn't: soot and blood and charred flesh and two gaping, bewildered eyes.

The villagers, they saw the devil and crossed themselves.

I saw the Hermit from my grandpa's story.

In the midst of my trauma soup, someone here was having his own déjà vu.

But instead of falling headfirst off the balcony, face-planting in the snow, and melting right through it with a sizzle, Nick opened the hole of his mouth and let out such an annihilating sound that I thought I'd instantly gone deaf. That sound, you couldn't even put it in terms of volume or frequency. It was so heavy and sonorous that you could only hear it in your skull. In a flash, I saw the horned mountain at the end of the valley. In a flash, we all saw it.

The townsfolk dispersed like cattle. Torches died, pitchforks left dentate impressions. Me, suddenly no longer under arrest, I fell with my bare hands onto the snow. The thundering carved its way into the world, suddenly reduced to earthly proportions: it came rolling out of the clouds like Wodan's fucking Tesla. I couldn't help turning around and looking to see where it was coming from.

Back in the valley, Grimentz's lights went out. The hotels and the empty ski chalets on the slope—where they had once been, I now saw billowing clouds of snow, rising, bulging into the night's darkness like a volcano's pyroclastic flow. Trees were swept away. Grimentz was buried. The air rumbled, borne by the avalanche.

To this, you cannot react. Cannot act. A scene like this—all you can do is stare.

And the village people, whaddya think, screaming, of course. Screaming for those left behind in the village. Screaming for their ancestors. Houses could be dug up. People could be saved, but birdcages on housefronts would be pulverized.

And then you thought that was it—but nuh-uh. What came down from the balcony, smoldering and charred like a steak on a barbecue, it wasn't through with its destruction. What looked out on the fleeing, screaming crowd like a tsunami on its coastline was impassive in the face of the terror it induced. Only the guy in the jabot, he hadn't budged. His eyes wide and round behind his fire-reflecting glasses, he raised both hands and called out in clear English, "*Stop! Let us help you!*"

Then he started floating, of course.

Nothing ever changed. A fire would always consume any house you ever lived in. Nick's terror spree would always keep spreading, like a deadly virus infecting the entire world. The way my life was unfolding, nothing ever got resolved.

The dude in the jabot, his arms were flapping in a vain search for something to hold on to, like a fledgling learning to fly. He looked down in shock, down at Nick, who was now standing in front of him in the snow. His feet swung upward behind him till he was floating facedown above the ground, on a meditative bird's-eye tour of the snow. His habit fluttering in the wind, all he managed to let out was a squeaky "*Mon Dieu . . .*"

Then they all started to float. All the fleeing villagers. One minute they were scrambling through the snow, the next they were scrambling through the air. You could see the panic in their eyes. You could see that, in their perception, they'd already started falling.

And I thought about that kid in the AMC. Thought about how he crashed to his death in front of Emily Wan's eyes, his skeleton pulverized.

And I screamed, "*Stop!*"

Absently, as if tugged out of his thoughts, Nick turned what was left of his face to me. And I confess, I staggered—but I convinced myself that what I was looking at was only the destruction of necrotic tissue. Only the oxidation of cooked fat and muscle, which, with a certain degree of effort, you could scrape off the underlying bones. Like the charred rims off a leg of ham.

Everyone has scars. With a certain degree of effort you could look right through them, and then you simply saw Nick.

I said, *Let those people go, Nick. They're none of our concern. Put them down.*

I said, *You and me, we have a mountain to climb.*

And Nick, he smiled at me with that boyish longing.

Everywhere around the burning house, bodies plopped softly onto the snow. The people of Grimentz looked around in a daze, as if they'd just woken up from a dream.

Hill House was burning down, but the sky above the chalet was at rest, and the only thing echoing now was the silence.

The Maudit had flown, and I was flying along.

6

Don't wanna sound psychedelic or anything, but I have no idea how we got up there. Every human body reaches a point when it just gives you the finger. Enough is enough, it says. Sleep comes and takes over your body like a mountain takes over your mind.

At such a pivotal moment—that's what I call submission.

The human condition: in situations when all control is snatched from our hands, we capitulate. It's in our DNA. Anyone who gets on a plane accepts his fate, whether it's Captain Sully behind the stick or not. If Tolkien sent you eagles cuz you're in a dead-end situation, it's your cue to shut up and say thanks for the ride.

Ethon or your Uber driver, for some reason we always have complete trust in whoever's behind the wheel.

Nick and me, who knows, maybe we actually really flew. Trekking into the mountains through Nick's mindscape, ideally you pictured it as a purely spiritual affair. You didn't want something like that to be too material. But it wasn't a one-hundred-percent out-of-body trip, either, cuz sure enough, our bodies ended up in that bewitched valley. After all, we needed them for the transition. In order to set our souls free, something still had to be spooned out.

The way *I* pictured it was that, as I was catching those Zs, I was being pulled uphill on a sleigh, right through a tunnel of snow and ice. The constant crunching of ice crystals under the runners. Around my shoulders a wool blanket, keeping me warm against the stinging wind. Between my legs a thermos of Swiss herbal tea with a dash of something that smelled like *Pflaumenschnaps*. Every time I dozed off, I would fall over onto Ramses's travel carrier, from which two gleaming eyes were giving the darkness the silent treatment.

The travel carrier—Nick had said that all I hadda do was think about it and I'd make it real. And that's why I can't say how real this all was. The sled, the blanket, even that friendly ol' thermos, maybe I'd thought them into existence and could just as easily think them out again, like when you flick a switch and kill the flames of a gas fireplace, instantly reducing it to a pile of phony stone logs in a hotel lobby.

And admit it, it wasn't such a leap to imagine that the weight of the blanket was actually your grandma's arms embracing you. That it was her sobbing that you heard, not the luring call of the echoes in the wind. If you created your own reality, then it wasn't such a leap to think that the big, dark shape pulling you ahead, hunched in intense physical exertion, wasn't Nick, wasn't Grandpa, but was the Hermit. The mythical, faceless figure you had feared your entire life, his skull and shoulders still smoking because he'd stepped right out of the flames. All these things were as real as the cold. Yes, it had been extremely cold that night, Auntie Bernstein had said. When you got older, once the cold had settled into your bones, she'd said, it never really went away anymore.

Louetta Molignon had also said something about that particular night fifteen years ago in the Catskills. Cécile's mamie, according to her, there most definitely had been birds. Really big ones, with long beaks, looking for prey.

And yes, they were there. Every time your consciousness drifted over the line between sleeping and waking, you could catch glimpses of them. Death birds. The carrion consumers of the mountains. They circled high above the slopes, never too far from the sled, like vultures above a dying animal in the desert. Sometimes they would chatter or loop and roll, but they never attacked. Not yet.

I think it was then that I realized where I really was.

We once started on a descent here, but it had never come to an end.

What I'd see if I were to follow the Panther Mile all the way back up to the top had always filled me with utter terror. Now, that fear had faded into a vague, throbbing unease. I felt it pulling, felt it waiting for me up there at the end of the valley. The charred hole where Huckleberry Wall once stood. A possessed mountain. It stared, with holes for eyes, in which it was freezing and thawing. Holes like scars in a face, breathing out the eternal cycle of time.

Thus we climbed on and left the valley behind us. Mountain passes slipping into stone under a thick layer of snow. Alternately floating through real and unreal things and being rooted in the steep funnel that was the doorway to the Maudit. My ticket to redemption was one-way only, but I accepted that.

That's to say, until everything tilted forward so far that you could no longer hold on.

If gravity took hold, we would all fall.

7

It's difficult for me to write about what happened next. To tell the ending to my story.

It's not the ending I'd wished for. If you're rooting for me even just a little bit, you'd hope for something melodramatic, our own Thelma and Louise, but that was not to be. Such an ending, an ending of enduring love, of love beyond death, it would have given us both more consolation, because deep inside, you wanted something like that to be true. But here we are, on the last leg of a journey we started a long time ago, and if I start bullshitting now, everything up to this point will no longer have any meaning.

What I'm giving to you is the inevitable ending. The naked ending. As true as you and me. They say there's no point getting mad about the inevitable, but sometimes it crushes you with such incredible force that you just can't help it, right?

Nick and me, we reached the col at the dawn of a new day. Again, beats me how exactly we got there, but I do remember that I swung out of sleep mode and into the waking world and thought, *We got there. This is Nick's sanctuary.*

In front of me lay only this floating landscape of deep, subdued colors that was living up to its hyped-up reputation. The storm had died down in the course of the night. Layered, dispersing shreds of cloud were still trembling in the air, fading into vague puffs of breath from the mouths of the highest summits. The valley before us, I recognized it from the description in Nick's manuscript, except that everything wasn't gray but purple. Everything was violet. Magenta. Azure and turquoise. It was ice sparkling in an alpenglow you'd call corny on Instagram, cuz there was no way it could be real. But it was, here. The anticipation of sunlight before there was sunlight, reflected on ice crystals in a charged atmosphere as polished as a Cartier diamond.

And at the center of this arena I finally saw, for the first time, the Maudit.

You knew it was the Maudit the minute you saw it. Even I knew it. I had to lean my head all the way back and still had to look even higher in order to absorb its full magnitude. The Maudit, it loomed up out of the mist on the glacier like the iceberg that doomed the *Titanic* must have loomed up out of the mist—grand, sudden, unavoidable.

This was, as they say, a mountain.

Even I could get why Nick had fallen for it. He was right. There was mystery concealed here. Something timeless and dreamlike that was calling to you. In the devastating beauty of this mountain, in both its all-encompassing wilderness and its peace, I saw precisely the part of Nick I had totally fallen for from the get-go. The part that had been so far away from me. Whispering, it floated over to me and seduced me with the promise of absent things, and following it up in the sky seemed as tempting as being lifted up by a dream . . .

Just so we're clear, that was the hypothermia talking.

When the cold penetrates deeper into your body, you get woozy. Lethargic and distracted. You yawn, you stretch your jaw, you relax. Freezing to death is number 1 on Tripadvisor's Top 10 Best Transports to the Hereafter. Because it's so peaceful. Everything seems agreeable as you glide closer and closer toward your hibernatory coma. Everything feels nice. Everything feels good. Then your heart stops.

By definition, I wasn't worried about it.

The rustling of my coat's seam sounded strangely subdued in the silence. Turns out I was wearing Nick's spare Gore-Tex. What a surprise. I'd even thought this ultimate fashion faux pas into existence for the sake of pragmatic comfort. All sounds here were strangely subdued. Nick was right about that, too. For a place the folks down there called the Valley of Echoes, it was suspiciously devoid of echoes.

A dark shadow sailed over me. In the sky, a rather ominous but strangely melodious call. A few yards away, one of those black birds touched down in the snow. It hopped a coupla curious steps my way. Looked at me with cool, lidless eyes. A look without even a trace of depth, just hunger. The penetrating smell of organ meat. Thymus or something. Liver.

"*Shoo!*" I called out, and absently threw a handful of snow at the critter. It flew up and disappeared.

When I looked up I saw Nick.

This was your cue for a gasp. This was your cue to hold your breath.

The sudden transition to light was hard to take in. The colors suddenly became more intense. They took the deep blue hollows out of the mountain. Took the dark purple shadows from the north face. The steep crests anchoring the summit, they'd captured the first rays of sunlight and burst into yellow and orange and pink glitter. Nick stood exactly between me and his temple and it was like you were looking into a mirror inside a mirror. Because Nick was glittering with the same sparkling colors. His body, you could tell by how hunched it was that the fire and the ascent had gravely weakened it, but what I was looking at was something loftier, an amalgamation. For a moment, I thought it was a reflection or a mirage, but the colors were really flowing out of him and swirling into the air, where they entered into their courtship display with the Maudit's aura.

He'd come home. His becoming, his *unification*, was complete.

A warm hand of blazing sunlight stretched out toward me and I took hold of it.

There was a slight tug of the soul when I was pulled out of my body. Then I sailed away, a gliding bird high above an anchored mountainscape. Around me, a whole flock. Their wings spread. Their feet clenched. We rode the invisible waves of the thermal, soaring higher and higher. It shoulda felt awesome to be part of that flock. The refinery process of the human soul, completed.

But it wasn't awesome.

It felt like I was suffocating.

Something huge was weighing on me, something lonely and heavy that wanted to take me back to the col where our bodies had been left behind, and it took all I had to keep it from pulling me all the way down.

Somehow I must have managed to resist it, because when I slid back into consciousness I finally found myself in the place where life had been leading me, in large circles, ever since that night in the Catskills fifteen years ago. And I'd been here before. In terror-filled dreams. In nightmares about monstrous birds and ripping beaks, from which, as a boy, I would wake up screaming. Later, in fantasies you didn't tell anyone about. And in the vision I'd shared with Nick.

My penance.

My redemption.

Me, the altar *and* the sacrifice.

Hail Prometheus. I was even wearing the loincloth to complete the outfit.

I was chained to the mountain's summit. There was no cold anymore, no fatigue. Only the pink and orange light of dawn on the endless horizon. Shackled, not in iron chains like my childhood hero, but with a bundle of energy that blew life into my echo. An echo, was that what I was going to be up here? Deprived of all the good—not that it was much or anything. Nick would come every night, my nemesis, my paramour. We would make love, and he would eat up more and more of my emotions and feelings, till nothing would be left besides an echo of what I had once been. Something that resonated against the valley's distant stone.

We'd be together forever.

Somewhere down there in the valley, it wouldn't take too long before my body would stop breathing. It wouldn't take too long before one of those death birds would come and rip its eyes out. A bird like that, it didn't care whether its snack was still breathing.

Talk about birds and snacks.

The sound of mighty wings. I looked up and there he was. Nick. The way Nick was meant to be. The Maudit had done to him what the Greeks did when they sculpted their gods in marble. Your best Insta filter, your cuteness overload. Picture all of that and you're warm. Abs: check. Pecs: check. Eagle wings: check. Nick's face was back to how it used to be, before this mountain had destroyed it. He was smiling at me. His mouth formed inaudible words but I still knew what he was saying: *My Sam.*

And oh, that instant. Oh, Nick. Oh, Nick, sweet Nick, my Nick.

If only I could have returned your smile.

If only I could have answered your words.

Supernovas of dizzying, dark deepness opened up in my stomach. I suddenly understood what it must have been like for Cécile and all the others to fall.

Because.

Because this wasn't my redemption.

Back to the sled. Back up the Panther Mile. That epic descent, that epic climb. If you imagined that the night of Huckleberry Wall and the night of the Maudit were essentially the same, that Grandma really was sitting behind you on the sled, then it could only be fulfilled if another someone were there too.

At some point I'd dozed myself awake and seen that Julia was there too.

Like the old folks who took their last journey during the Morose, so Julia had embarked on her journey to the valley. The echoes had gotten hold of her. Bewitched by their luring call, she'd plodded up through the snow. If some geriatric crone from Grimentz could get the job done, so could Julia.

Sometime during the night we must have caught up with her. Sometime during the night I must have thought her onto the sled.

Julia was alive.

That meant that the spell could be broken.

The image of you waiting down there on the col till you turned into bird feed, the image of empty, bloody eye sockets in a mummified, semi-decomposed corpse that would maybe one day, in thousands of years, be exhibited in a museum as the new Ötzi—if it were me we were talking about, that was one thing. But if Julia was lying there *too*, and those black birds were hop-, skip-, and jumping her way, then there was no more time for me to lose.

I felt inside my loincloth and wasn't surprised to find what I was looking for. What I had fished out of Nick's nightstand in my epiphany, while Hill House was burning to ashes around me.

It was a sharp piece of rock.

Nick's talisman. The Maudit's summit. The souvenir he'd brought back down from the mountain.

The conquering or destruction of trophies has always been the decisive factor in overtaking someone's power. Let's face it: if your name was Sam and Mount Doom was on the horizon, then you were predestined to fling some magical artifact into an abyss.

Only at the last moment did Nick see what I was doing. The chain that shackled me, the Prometheus chain, was the umbilical cord that bound me to Nick.

Using the rock, I cut it.

The ravine of tormented shock that opened in his eyes was infinitely deep. When I let go of the rock, I watched it disappear into its depths. A tiny red dot that fell and fell and fell and would be forever out of reach.

Then I turned around, looked down from the summit's ridge, and jumped.

E P I L O G U E

THE EXORCIST

NOTES BY SAM AVERY

From the cab stepped a tall old man. Black raincoat and hat and a battered valise. He paid the driver, then turned and stood motionless, staring at the house. The cab pulled away and rounded the corner of Thirty-Sixth Street. Kinderman quickly pulled out to follow. As he turned the corner, he noticed that the tall old man hadn't moved but was standing under the streetlight glow, in mist, like a melancholy traveler frozen in time.

—William Peter Blatty

Okay, maybe the last thing was a bit of a gamble, a pretty wacky gamble maybe, but it paid off. And it was a calculated gamble. No one ever pioneered by playing it safe.

Pioneering didn't mean you fell back into your body with a *smack*. You didn't plop down into the snow on your back the way it would happen in the movies. No shock, no gasping for breath. I simply became aware of the weight of my body and the cold that was eating it away. The flapping of my Gore-Tex coat's collar.

And a vague aroma of liver.

What I saw when I opened my eyes was one of those choughs, head tilted, beak yellow. Looking at me the way a Frenchman looks at a plate of escargots. Alarm clock from hell—see that and you're wide-awake in no time flat. You forget about the cold, too.

Screaming and flailing my arms, I jerked upright. The bird flew up. *All* the birds flew up. The whole flock that had gathered around me. Me *and* Julia.

Julia, she was lying not far from me in the snow, next to the sled. All around us, raked footprints. Shivering from the cold and moaning from the pain in my limbs, I plowed my way to my sister and fell to my knees. Eyes: check. Pulse: check. Breathing: check.

Julia: check.

But where was Nick?

I looked around and no one saw that I was being stared at by a gaping void. No one felt that I was engulfed by an unbearable sense of loneliness. The dawn's light show was over and the last of the vivid colors had disappeared off the summit. The light had shifted; the Maudit was trembling far away in the hazy sky. I wanted to touch it. I needed to be consoled by the illusion that it would be close, but it was just drifting there, far off in the distance, out of reach above the mist on the glacier, which had now climbed further up its flanks.

The scene was unfathomable. It swelled up in my chest and overwhelmed me. Crushed me. Exposed an ugly, deep wound. I felt that I was sinking and could only think, *No. Please no. Please, I don't want this.* Could only think, *I can't deal with this. I don't want to be alone. Not without Nick.*

I collapsed onto the snow, pulled Julia against me, and wrapped the blanket that had saved our lives fifteen years ago on the Panther Mile around us. I started to rub her warm. Blow her warm. Julia's hair fluttered over her forehead in the calm breeze coming down from the glacier. I tried to think a hoodie into existence but couldn't. We had to make do with what we had.

We sat like that on the col, who knows for how long, till I felt a wrinkle in time. Till I heard Julia say, with a shaky voice, "Oh my god." Julia, she stammered, "Sam, it's so beautiful here . . ."

And me rub, rub, rubbing. I couldn't stop, know what I mean? I couldn't stop. Whatever resided here in the silence, I had to cling to it. Had to keep it close, before it would slip away from me forever. You had to put up your mask, cuz you were terribly afraid of the idea that the world could see your weakness, despite your attempts at faking confidence. Sam Avery, always in control. Maybe there's a heart in there somewhere, but all we get to see is granite.

It didn't work, and I started to cry.

Startled, Julia turned around, but I couldn't see her anymore. I hid my face in the inside of my elbow and felt only hot tears.

"Hey, bro . . ." She wriggled up against me and squeezed our bodies till she was the one hugging me instead of the other way around. "Is Nick up there now?"

I could only nod. That's what it had all come down to. Nick was up there now. I was down here.

I cried aloud and Julia tried to console me.

"Sam," she hushed, "bro," she hushed, "he *belongs* here, can't you see that? Nick came home here, he *is* this place. You gotta know that, right? Just look! Look at the mountains and try *not* seeing Nick in them. That's impossible!"

I looked, and all these things were true, and that's why I cried. I couldn't stop anymore. I had no restraint. I had lost my anchor.

"I really tried," I said between sobs, searching for the right words to say the things I wanted to say. "If there'd been another way to exorcise him, to make him stop doing all those things . . ."

Julia wiped the tears off my eyes with her thumbs and looked into me the way only Julia could. Hands on my shoulder, she said, "I know." Said, "There was no other way."

"It was too strong, Julia. The thing inside him. How can you fight against something as big as . . . as—"

"You fought it. And you never stopped loving him. That's why you were able to set him free."

"I want him to come back so much, Julia . . ."

"Sam."

"I just want . . ."

"Bro . . ."

"I love him so much! He's done such terrible things, but really, that wasn't him. It wasn't really him who did it, Julia. He was sweet, he really was—"

"Sam." Stern. Her fingers squeezing my Gore-Tex shoulders. Flat on my cheeks, pinching, shaking, like she was squeezing out an orange. "Listen, all of that is true. It hurts a lot and it's going to hurt a lot more. *That's why I came here.* You once took care of me, and now I'm going to take care of you, you understand?" She rocked my face up and down with her hands, nodding my head for me, which made me laugh through my tears. "But now you have to say good-bye to this place, because we still have a very long way down ahead of us, and I don't think you'll ever be coming back here."

New tears came; I couldn't hold them back. Julia took the thermos and screwed the top off. Poured steaming tea into the lid and let me drink. No, uh-uh, another sip. The thermos had kept the concoction nice and warm, and whatever kind of sugar coating was in there made my throat burn.

"Whoa, someone sure has spiced up that tea, huh?" my sister said, when she'd taken a sip herself. Not that she could care. Julia's got the liver of a sperm whale.

When I was feeling a bit better, I said, "I started the fire in Huckleberry Wall."

"I know," Julia said.

My eyes hot and wet and searing, I looked at her in shock. Took a while, but eventually I came up with, "Since when?"

"I've always known. And now you told me, so it doesn't have to be a thing for you anymore."

I was stunned. "But . . . how?"

"It added up." She said, "It wasn't that hard to see. With all you had to carry with you through all those years. I don't think Mom and Dad ever knew, but I'm your sister, huh? I can see right through you. Here, wait."

She walked to the sled and came back with Ramses's travel carrier. Of course! The cat! I totally forgot to check on him. But when she opened the flap, it wasn't Ramses she took out but Dr. Jingles.

I didn't get it *at all* anymore.

Julia handed me my old teddy bear with his singed little ass, his snout just a wee bit askew, the bald patches on his forepaws. Just like a coupla days ago, I pressed my nose into his fur and sniffed the aromas of my childhood.

I asked, "But where's Ramses then?"

"He's probably waiting for you down in the valley," she smiled. "I'm sure he's going to be really happy to see you."

Julia, she told me that a coupla weeks before she flew to Switzerland, she'd suddenly felt the urge to go for a drive. An upstream drive along the Hudson, into the hills.

She parked Dad's open Corvette Grand Sport more or less on the same spot I'd parked it two months before. At the bottom of the Panther Mile, along the yard of the last house there.

The Last House on the Left.

The Cabin in the Woods.

"I went for a walk with an old acquaintance of ours," Julia said.

And I said, "Get out."

That old acquaintance, it was Abigail Bernstein, of course. "She said you'd also been around. A couple of weeks before, she couldn't remember exactly when."

I said, "You know Auntie Bernstein died years ago?"

"Yeah," Julia said. "I know."

The silence hovered between us. "You didn't keep Dr. Jingles all those years, did you? I knew there was something weird . . ."

She shook her head slowly. "Auntie Bernstein gave him to me. She said she'd found him where Huckleberry Wall used to be but that you weren't ready to go all the way up yet. She said I should give him to you. That there was a chance you'd be needing him sometime soon."

Julia stared to the south, up into the valley. I tried to figure out exactly what I was feeling, but it was all too much. Too painful.

"Did you go all the way up?"

"Yep."

I wasn't sure I wanted to know, but I asked anyway, "What did you see up there? At the top of Panther Mile?"

"There were no more signs of the fire. I recognized the big maple tree Grandpa had hung the swing on—you know, the one with the old tire. And the slope we always sledded down in winter. But you know what's weird? Behind the house, there's that mountaintop we always thought looked like an eagle . . . remember that?"

Of course I did.

"I didn't see it anymore," Julia said. "It was just a mountain."

We got ready to go down. Even though I felt I was able now, I noticed that my gaze was drawn to the Maudit again. Only the summit was visible now in the slowly shifting mist, the mountain floating in its breathless silence. The sight of it filled me with an intense, chilling pain when I thought about the prospect of the days, the months, and the years that lay ahead of me. The pain would always be there. The missing would always be there. Every time I smelled his scent in a piece of clothing, every time I saw his picture and thought about him, it would come back.

I felt like I was going to cry again and quickly looked the other way, tried to let the cold of the wind numb the feeling. That pain, I wasn't ready for it yet. It was too much. Time erodes even the highest, sharpest mountain peaks down to rolling horizons. But the mountains had a prospect of millions of years. I only had my life.

And there was something else.

A good horror story didn't end with death. It resonated with the echo of something worse. Something buried underneath, a layer worse than all the others.

That layer was the pernicious fear of the stilled life that would fester up here forever. Maybe, if you listened carefully, you would hear its cries from down in the valley. What if it decided to come after me? It would dwell here, lonely and frozen. A pained face floating in silence, unseen but constantly peering over the horizon. *Nick's* face. The nights would be too cold. Too dark and too long.

And yet there was hope, I decided, when I'd cast a final glance over my shoulder and the rising mist had covered the mountain. Maybe I'd stay in Switzerland a while longer. Buy a birdcage somewhere in the valley. Look at the horizon. Maybe, out of the mountains, a bird would come.

When you had hope, you had faith. Then you could imagine him landing on your shoulder. Maybe he'd peck you once in a while, but I'd gladly carry the scars, because they'd be mine.

With Julia on one arm and Dr. Jingles in the other, we descended down the slope toward the valley.

This is how mountains are born.

You take two tectonic plates and twirl them into one. They twist, they crack, they raise each other up and release explosions of energy that manifest as quakes and eruptions. But they push each other higher up than ever before, higher than they could have reached on their own, even in their wildest dreams.

Their snow and their rock, their hearts and their bones—they never come undone.

May 24, 2015, 's-Hertogenbosch–November 11, 2018, Mook

ACKNOWLEDGMENTS

Echo is my sixth novel, but it was the hardest to write.

The previous five I wrote in relative anonymity, and for a relatively small Dutch audience. Then *HEX* was published, the rights were sold to I-don't-know-how-many countries, and people whom I've admired my entire life talked up the book. What followed were more readers than I could have ever dreamt of, promotional tours on four continents, and, of course, a major writer's block. I hadn't been prepared for the pitfalls of success.

I am a mountaineer who, like Nick, collects the summit as a keepsake. But as soon as I'm back down in the valley, it's just a piece of rock that has lost its magic. My eyes dwell up to even higher, more challenging peaks in the distance. The urge to always aim higher is something I've felt my entire life. That's why writing the book after *HEX* felt like such an impossible task.

When climbers face a difficult or lonely route, they turn to the help of mountain guides. My mountain guides in this particular matter were Herman Koch and George R. R. Martin. Their personal stories and indispensable advice helped me to find my voice again, and for that, I am eternally grateful.

Their advice, of course, was no magic. It was simple: write the best book you have in you *and have fun while you're at it*. That's what I tried to do. I've had fun, and I hope you love the story and its characters as much as I do.

My agents, Sally Harding in Vancouver, Ron Eckel in Toronto, and Marianne Schönbach from Amsterdam, form the best and most professional team I could wish for. Their warmth and wisdom are invaluable to me. Sally, the unbridled energy and understanding you showed in working on *Echo* are awe-inspiring, and my gratitude reaches beyond horizons.

Several people opened their homes for me and offered fantastic writing retreats. Claartje and Frans Hinnen in the Swiss Alps, whose chalet was covered in snow as I was writing about the Morose. Annelie Hendriks in Thailand, whose ceiling lizards tried to strike up a conversation each time I got stuck. Adelheid den Hollander in the Netherlands, whose garden toads I had to help cross the road each night. And my grandpa and grandma's house in the Dutch woods. That house stood empty by then, but still I played boogie on the old piano every day, so my grandpa could tap along from out of the walls. I owe them all a lot.

Translating is a challenging and important job, and finding the right voice for Sam was even more challenging. We found it in Moshe Gilula. Moshe, your language rocks and swirls. Your creative solutions for tough linguistical problems are fabulous. It was a true pleasure to edit a translation that was so brilliantly good to begin with. Thank you—I foresee a long road ahead for us.

Good people read this book and made it better. Diana Sno, my Dutch editor, has the extraordinary talent to expose within one sentence why a scene works the way it does and what to change to make it stronger. Miriam Weinberg at Tor Nightfire and Oliver Johnson at Hodder & Stoughton read the English manuscript, gave valuable insights, suggested nuanced structural changes, and turned this book into an improved version of what it was. Ann VanderMeer worked tirelessly on getting the required permissions. I'd like to thank them all, along with all the great people on Team US and Team UK who turned this book into the beauty you're holding in your hands. Special thanks go out to Hajnalka Bata, my Dutch publisher, who completely and unselfishly helped me through the long nights of editing in a language that's not my native tongue.

Shout-out to the many friends I made around the world during the journey *HEX* has taken me on. Raquel and Bruna in Brazil. Lena in Ukraine. Emily in China. Iwona in Poland. Mike, Ann and Jeff, and Megan in the US. Also, shout-out to my international publishers, who have so expertly guided my work to readers in their respective territories, and who have so patiently waited for *Echo*. Joe Veltre and Gary Dauberman, thank you for your respective expertise and vision in bringing my work to the screen—it's a helluva ride.

In July 2017, Pieter Grosfeld died. Aside from being my longtime friend and climbing buddy, Pieter was a beautiful and loving person. Not long before he died, I read the first one hundred pages of *Echo* to him. High up in the Swiss mountains, as we were spending the night in a bivouac, where we'd always tell each other our stories. I wish he were still there, so I could read him the rest. If anyone ever could sense the life in mountains, it was Pieter. I miss him every day. I dedicate this book to him.

David Samwel stood by me all those years, and that makes me the lucky one. Each and every day you amaze me again, David, and that's the most precious gift people can give to each other. This book isn't only about the mountains, it is also about love, and therefore I dedicate it to you as well.

Lastly, I want to thank you, my reader, wherever in the world you are. The bond between author and reader has always fascinated me. Without the reader's imagination, an author's words are dead in the dark. Only when you open their book do you make them come alive. It's like a spell. And you spread that magic because you talk about the book, post about it, or give it away to someone. Your involvement has been invaluable for me these past few years, and I owe you all a thousand thank-yous. I can't wait to meet many of you when I'm on the road again, and in the meantime, I'd love to hear if you enjoyed this book. You can let me know through Instagram, Facebook, Twitter, or my website. I read all your messages and try my best to answer as many as I can.

I promise: the wait for the next book is going to be much, much shorter. I conquered that mountain already. It's called *Oracle*, and by the time you're reading this, the translation will already be done and waiting to go to the presses.